Dawn of the Mad

Brandon J. Huckabay

This book is a work of fiction. Names, characters, places and incidents either are products of the author's imagination or are used fictitiously. Any resemblance to actual events or locations or persons living or dead, is purely coincidental.

Astigbooks
Humble, Texas 77396 and Caloocan City, Philippines 1405
www.astigbooks.com

This book can be ordered on the internet at www.amazon.com

ISBN-13: 978-0615840949
ISBN-10: 0615840949

Cover art by Duncan Long
Author Photo by George Gaylor
Formatting by Polgarus Studio

ACKNOWLEDGMENTS

There were many people who helped along the way either by reading rough drafts, offering suggestions, or helping with editing. Anyway, you know who you are and I thank you.

I would like to thank my wife Rose who has taught me a lot about life and not giving up on my dreams.

PART ONE

CHAPTER 1

Corporal Joachim Scotts sat uncomfortably in the bottom of the muddy trench. The visor on his helmet was raised, letting the raindrops splash on his youthful, albeit bearded, face. He hadn't the time or the inclination to shave because of the rapid pace of the campaign. His body armor kept pinching him as he shifted position in the cramped confines of the trench, trying in vain to get comfortable.

The sudden escalation of the war had prevented, or at least delayed him from fulfilling his dream of becoming a fighter pilot. Halfway through the pilot's course, he had been yanked out and drafted into the assault infantry, subjected to being soaked to the bone, on the remains of this god-forsaken planet. He clutched his battle rifle and wondered what day would be his last.

"An offensive is coming." Sergeant Matthias's weary voice trailed through the thick fog that had settled on the forward trench. He absent mindedly began drumming his fingers on the hilt of a large knife protruding from his belt.

"How do you know that, Sarge?" Scotts asked. "We haven't been given an attack order." Scotts bit off a piece of bread as he leaned back against a muddy trench wall. With his mouth partially full of dry, pasty bread, he continued, "or have we? I hope not."

"No attack orders yet, but there are signs to look for when you've been out in this hell as long as I have." As Matthias spoke, he stood up abruptly and slogged his way down the muddy trench. Scott's got up dutifully and followed close behind. When Matthias reached a wooden ladder, he tugged on several of the rungs to test their strength. Satisfied that the ladder would hold his weight, Matthias climbed, pausing just below the lip of the trench. Snipers posed a constant risk. Matthias peered through his binoculars over the battle-scarred trench line, scanning the desolation of no- man's-land. The thick fog enveloping the enemy trenches would prevent any sniper activity for now. An eerie quiet had settled in over the still, breezeless air, creating an almost supernatural feel, as if the men were fighting between worlds, in limbo. Sporadically, enemy soldiers could be heard talking in hushed voices, their voices drifting across the no-man's-land. Through his binoculars Matthias saw numerous fires and smoldering remains of destroyed equipment from the last push on his thermal scan.

"You see anything?" asked Scotts.

"The engineers are digging our lines closer to the city. I imagine there will be a push soon."

As he manually adjusted the light spectrum on his binoculars, the ghostly outline of the smoldering cityscape emerged faintly in his viewfinder, like a spirit emerging from its grave. Satisfied with his quick scan, Matthias climbed back down the ladder into the welcoming confines of his trench.

Assault Sergeant Roger Matthias was old by trooper standards, reflecting his ability to survive. He brushed his graying hair off his face, one that marked him as a serious, but calculating individual. His powerful frame contrasted sharply with that of his tall, thin protégé, Corporal Scotts, who was still fidgeting beside him. The kid was a near genius but could still joke and make him smile, in even the direst situation.

To Matthias's left and right, dozens of weary troopers sat in stagnant water with their backs against the trench wall. Mud coated everything. Matthias's uniform was no exception, caked with both mud and dried blood. Some of the blood was his, but most of it was not, and all of it resulted from the last push. The left breast pocket of his tunic sported a gold cross bearing a silver eagle with diamond claws, the infantry's highest award for bravery. He tried his best to keep this decoration mud-free.

Most of the troopers now slept, taking advantage of the rare calm. The last push had proved horrendous for both sides. They had agreed to a temporary cease-fire to clear the dead, re-arm, and prepare for the next onslaught. The battle had been sickening cycle of death that seemed like it would never end. Of the troopers who were awake, some were writing messages to loved ones back home, holding on to hope that they would survive to return home. Others simply stared at nothing, too desensitized to care anymore. Many of them had accepted that death was inevitable; with the only real question being when would it come.

The trench showed signs of recent combat. Blood-soaked bandages littered the muddy ground, and spatters of blood decorated the earthen wall itself. Many of those who did not make it back to their lines were simply left to die; stretcher bearers could bring back only so many and some had fallen in areas too dangerous for the recovery crews to reach. The wounded men who were trapped in no-man's-land faced death, sooner or later, without medical aid, food, or water.

"You smell that?" Matthias asked Scotts.

"No," Scotts replied absentmindedly, not really trying to pick up the scent. "I can't smell anything but the stench of the dead." He longed for sleep, but sleep came and went whenever it pleased, not when he wanted it.

Matthias cocked his head back and inhaled deeply. "There. See? It's hot chow in the rear. They always give us a hot meal before a big push."

Scotts craned his own neck back and inhaled deeply to humor the sergeant. "Yes, I do smell it now," he replied, somewhat surprised. Stale bread and cold mystery soup was the norm, except for what the sergeant said —a push usually meant a hot meal. His stomach suddenly rumbled, as if on cue, and he quickly remembered how hungry he actually was.

"Not the most ideal conditions for an offensive, but there must be one coming if the field kitchens are moved up," Matthias noted.

"Sergeant?"

"What?" Matthias replied, slightly irritated. He fumbled around in his pack for probably the most valuable piece of equipment he had—his mess tin. It was nowhere to be found.

"The colonel has never let us down before, has he?" Scotts asked. "You'd know better than I do. I mean, you've been fighting a lot longer than I have."

Matthias closed the flap on his pack and sat down inside the trench, avoiding a puddle of brackish water, and put his hand on Scott's shoulder. "I would follow the colonel anywhere," he said, as he released a deep breath. "He is the only reason why we have not yet lost this war."

His comments appeared to do little to soothe the apprehension in the young corporal's face, so he added, "Stay by my side. I'll keep you alive the best I can."

Scotts managed a weak smile and changed the subject. "I never realized I would be fighting out here. I had high hopes of becoming a star liner captain once the war ended."

Matthias's buttocks began to get numb, and he shifted his weight, trying to get comfortable in the cramped trench. "Well, as I always say, this hell is my home. It's been too long since I have seen a green blade of grass, or a bird for that matter. I'm not sure I would know what I would do if the war ended tomorrow." Matthias pushed his soft cap over his eyes and continued. "Perhaps I'm already dead. Go find yourself some chow, kid." He closed his eyes and almost immediately drifted off into a deep sleep.

I wish I could do that. Sleep seemed to be almost as elusive as the end of the war.

Scotts fished around inside his pack for his grey, woolen blanket. Finding it, he drew it up around his neck. To his dismay, it was wet. There wasn't a dry part on his body. He was soaked, but he couldn't remember the last time he had actually bathed. He had become accustomed to that, and to battle conditions in general. His first couple of combat actions had resulted in his bowels releasing involuntarily, but fortunately he had gotten past that.

About four months ago, an influx of conscripts and draftees from various service branches had arrived to help hold the line. Scotts had arrived with two dozen other confused and terrified souls straight from the main recruit depot, each of them loaded down with the bare necessities to fight: food, ammunition, weapons, and armor.

The conscripts had gone through recruit training, but no classroom or textbook could teach the grim realities of combat. The best teachers were those who had learned from their own experience the skills of adaptation and survival, but most of them were too valuable in the field to be brought back as instructors. It was customary to be assigned to an old hand at the front and Scotts felt himself fortunate that he had been assigned to Sergeant Matthias. Soon, if he survived, he would be considered one of the old hands.

Scotts began to wonder about the impending attack, and if it would actually take place, like the sergeant had predicted. The fog had remained in place for almost a week now. The regiment had tried a big push two days ago, attempting to utilize the fog to its own advantage in hiding its movement, but the effort failed dismally. The enemy counterattacked, with both sides suffering casualties and leaving many to die in no-man's-land.

Visibility was less than a few feet, not enough to be able to aim and shoot someone. Scotts inhaled deeply once more, taking in the faint and distant aroma of the field kitchen.

Slowly, so as not to wake anybody, Scotts made his way down the overcrowded trench to the rear area. After several minutes of walking, he reached a large bunker dug underground. A field kitchen was indeed set up inside. The rear wall of the bunker featured a faded standard of a fanged wolf, with the word "Dreadwolves" painted in red script underneath. He grabbed his mess tin from his pack and held it out for the portly mess trooper. Without him even asking, his tin was filled to the top, almost overflowing. This was a double portion. To Scott's delight, he detected what appeared to be chunks of meat in the thick, soupy mixture. The double portion provided a good clue that Matthias was right. With a big smile on his face, he walked out of the bunker and began to drink the gray, chunky porridge greedily, not even bothering to use his spoon. A strong, firm voice behind him interrupted his meal.

"I wouldn't eat so fast, Trooper. It may be some time before full rations are brought up again."

Scotts turned around and nearly dropped his mess tin as he came face to face with his regimental commander, Colonel Chuikova. The colonel, fully armored, removed his black helmet, cradling it in his left arm. Scotts came to attention but refrained from saluting because of their close proximity to the front. Saluting was forbidden as it would make officers tempting targets for enemy snipers. The colonel nodded and said in an almost fatherly voice, "Relax, corporal. Eat your chow."

Scotts resumed drinking his gray sludge, although he made sure he went a little slower. Although he had been surprised by the colonel, he knew the colonel frequented the front lines, something unheard of among senior officers. As the war progressed, most of them were content to hide deep in underground bunkers, giving each other medals and making unrealistic demands on under strength units. The fact that most senior level staff officers were out of touch with conditions at the front had a profound impact on morale; yet orders were carried out without question. Scotts had never before seen the colonel in person. What he knew of the colonel he had learned from other troopers, particularly from Matthias. He had heard that the colonel had repeatedly turned down promotions, just so he could be with his men at the front.

The colonel stepped in front of Scotts and looked around him at his troopers. The ones who were awake nodded toward the colonel and whispered to each other. Scotts noticed that the colonel's kinetic power armor was caked in mud. Very few officers owned kinetic armor suits; it was ancient technology, passed down from generation to generation, and had been bestowed upon only the most adept warriors. Most sets were family heirlooms. The frayed cloak indicating his rank of commander that trailed behind him should have been a radiant purple, but it too was covered in mud. His battle sword rested in its magnetic sheath on his back, ready to be whisked out in an instant. The colonel enjoyed no luxuries that his men did not have, and it was this for which they loved and revered him. They would die for him, and this the colonel knew all too well.

"Can I ask you something, sir?" Scotts felt incredibly nervous asking the colonel a question, but he had heard the man was approachable. Besides, he had heard from others and found from experience that you couldn't get an answer out of the lieutenants. Most of them didn't last beyond a week of their deployment anyway.

"Within reason," the colonel replied, somewhat amused.

Scotts cleared his throat. "Is there going to be another push soon?"

The colonel stopped, a thin smile broke across his weary face. "That's quite a question, trooper. You will know soon enough. Whose platoon are you in trooper?" He eyed Scotts more closely, and a brief hint of recognition flashed in his eye. He made it a point to try to keep tabs on his more experienced troopers. Experience came with surviving, and those who survived usually made good sergeants, something he always needed.

"Sergeant Matthias' platoon." Scotts replied.

"I thought so. He told me you are quite resourceful. Stay by his side. He will get you through." The colonel nodded and headed down the trench, sidestepping sleeping troopers and acknowledging those who were awake. Scotts suddenly felt as if he was infused with some sort of supernatural energy. Suddenly, he was not content to just wait for his time to take an enemy round and die. He wanted to live, to fight, and to serve his colonel as best he could. A wide grin broke across his grimy, mud-caked face as he ran back to his position in the trench line with renewed vitality.

Explosions tore up the muddy ground in front of the trench line, showering the expectant troopers with mud and debris. Occasional napalm rounds detonated in a random manner, briefly scorching the earth and the rare small bits of vegetation that remained before being extinguished quickly by the rain. The fog still had not lifted, and to make matters worse, the steady rainfall was filling some of the shell craters with enough water to drown a trooper who wasn't careful. Both warring sides had dropped numerous mines and other obstacles, making traversing no-man's-land a matter more of luck than of anything else.

Low and constant thunder rumbled, following orange and yellow streaks of lightning across the pale sky. Although it was late morning, the twin suns were nowhere to be seen, obscured by the thick cloud cover. The artillery barrage had been going on for a short while, and because of the recent shortage of artillery shells, no one expected it would last for very long. In reality, all that these preliminary barrages did was alert the enemy to an impending attack and prompt retaliation with their own barrage. Assault Sergeant Matthias yelled at the top of his lungs at the gathered troopers, who listened as best they could amid the deafening explosions of shells in front of their trench line.

"The artillery is cutting a path ahead for us through the wire! Follow me into the breach! Once we are through to the other side, we will re-form and concentrate our attack!" Matthias inserted several shells into his slug thrower, racked the action and press checked his pistol, pushing the slide slightly to the rear to ensure a round was in the breach. Up and down the trench, bolts could be heard slapping rounds into chambers, and a crescendo of whining noises indicated rifles being powered up.

The troopers were as ready as they could be. They nervously rechecked and reloaded ammunition magazines and fixed their bayonets. Scotts grasped his rifle tightly. He suddenly lost count of how many times he had gone over the top as he prayed that this one wouldn't be his last. He felt the urge to urinate and didn't resist the temptation, staining the front of his overalls.

Almost as quickly as it had begun, the outgoing artillery bombardment stopped. The enemy's retaliatory barrage continued for only a few moments longer. The enemy also seemed to be having ammunition shortages also, as their barrages never lasted very long either. A momentary silence ensued, broken only by the cries of the dying and the wounded drifting over from the other side, revealing that some of the shells had hit their targets. The troopers' ears rang, as they almost always did after such exchanges. Their helmets weren't built to block out the noise of an artillery barrage.

A whistle blown somewhere down the trench signaled the start of the ground assault. A series of rapid whistles followed, and the near silence was broken.

"Over the top!" Matthias yelled as loudly as he could. He heaved himself over the trench wall first, blowing his whistle in short, rapid blasts. His troopers began screaming "Urrah! Urrah!" at the top of their lungs as they unhesitatingly followed their seemingly immortal sergeant into the abyss.

Scotts yelled as loudly as he could and plunged into the awaiting chaos of no-man's–land. He aimed and fired, guided by targets that flashed quickly, with their estimated ranges, on the integrated targeting display (ITD) inside his helmet face shield. Ghostly outlines of enemy troopers began to appear at the lip of their trench as the opposition desperately tried to stave off the attack. The ITD gave Scotts the ability to penetrate the fog and engage the enemy at close range. Working in conjunction with his weapon sight, his helmet ITD provided far more targets than he could engage, but he tried his best, going through magazine after magazine, his rifle emitting the telltale green energy waves as rounds exited its muzzle.

Enemy artillery and mortar shells began again in earnest, exploding all around in angry retaliation, throwing up the already scarred terrain. Hidden mines, blue plasma bolts and machine gun fire dealt death in the most excruciating way to the advancing troopers. Limbs and broken bodies flew around like rocks in a shaken tin can. Somehow, Scotts got through to the edge of the enemy's trench. As he peered down into the trench through his activated night vision, his eyes briefly met those of a terrified enemy trooper who was firing wildly into Scott's comrades. Scotts quickly fired an aimed burst point blank, releasing a stream of death that vaporized the soldier's head into a fine red mist. The headless body fell backward into the water on the trench floor, already stained red from the new battle.

Scotts hopped down into the trench, among dozens of fresh corpses, and fired again and again, killing indiscriminately. Taking prisoners was not an option; there wasn't enough to feed them. Ahead of Scotts in the trench, Matthias engaged in spewing forth his own version of hell to the enemy. His slug thrower left a trail of broken and contorted bodies behind him as he cleared out a machine gun bunker and set off down the trench looking for more targets. The blood of his enemies covered him from head to foot. Scotts watched with awe as he observed Matthias run out of ammunition and switch seamlessly to firing his pistol and slicing with his battle knife. Unlike most troopers, Matthias and many of the old-hands considered rifles to unwieldy in the trenches and preferred close combat weapons, such as pistols and slug throwers. Matthias truly fought like a man possessed. The sergeant, caked in blood-soaked mud, seemed almost to blend in to the earth, much like the bodies lying around him. The rain and the mud worked in tandem to take the dead away from the battle and into the earth. Many of the fresh corpses sank into water-filled shell craters, and others were trampled underfoot. The sight of Matthias's gold cross, impossibly still bright and shiny on his tunic, gave Scotts an intense, supernatural feeling, as if Matthias wasn't even human.

"Watch your head, trooper!" Matthias yelled in Scott's direction, breaking his trance.

Scotts ducked just as a knife sailed over his head, to strike an enemy trooper right between the eyes, splitting his skull and exposing his brain. Matthias smiled grimly and resumed his path of destruction through the trench. Scotts wondered if it was a smile of satisfaction or one of sad regret.

Scotts took a deep breath and brought his battle rifle to his shoulder, focusing on his ITD for more targets. He had only one thought now: to survive and live to see tomorrow. He suddenly longed to see his family farm again, and to play with his younger brother and sister in the fields. He charged toward Matthias and the rising pile of fresh corpses, firing at any of the enemy foolish enough to cross his path. Behind him, dozens of other troopers joined in the trench clearing, thankful that they weren't the first ones in, and overwhelmed that the burden of their imminent death they carried with them into each attack was briefly lifted.

Eventually, the trench in Matthias' sector was cleared. Up and down the line intense fighting continued, the outcome of the offensive could still go either way. Firing began to subside in the immediate vicinity. Matthias sat down beside three headless bodies and removed his soft cap, wiping the sweat from his bow. He quickly reloaded his weapons and cleaned their actions of mud and debris with an old, water-soaked handkerchief. He checked the three corpses for any food or water rations. Finding none, he let out a deep sigh. Scotts trudged through the muck and sat down beside Matthias. Neither trooper spoke a word as the fighting continued further ahead and behind the trench line. Matthias wiped fresh blood and brain matter off of his blade and took a sip from his canteen. He held his canteen out to Scotts. Scotts removed his tactical battle helmet and took a swig. He felt the rotgut burn his throat, but he did not flinch. He handed the canteen back to Matthias.

His eyes readjusted to the foggy gloom. More troopers were hitting the forward trench now, surging forward. Armored tanks began to creep through cleared paths in the mine fields. Scotts inserted a fresh magazine and power cell into his rifle. Hearing the rifle emit a low whine of acceptance, he rose to his feet. After putting his helmet back on, he offered his gloved hand to Matthias, who accepted the help with a grunt. Once on his feet, Matthias smoothed his shoulder-length grey hair back and replaced the soft cap back on his head.

"I'm getting too old for this," he said with a chuckle, securing his canteen on the back of his belt. Nodding to Scotts, he heaved himself over the back lip of the trench, knife and pistol in hand, with his slug thrower slung over his back. Both men followed the steady stream of troopers pouring into the enemy's rear area, accompanied by the sound of gunfire.

CHAPTER 2

"Marshal Von Jesonik will receive you now, Colonel." The small, balding man said as he bowed graciously. His immaculate white robes, trimmed in an intricate gold pattern, fluttered around his ankles as he lead the visitor, his sandaled feet silent on the polished white floor.

Colonel Chuikova and Sergeant Matthias had needed almost a full day to fully clean the colonel's kinetic armor of all the mud and grime caked on it. They couldn't do much about the numerous nicks and scratches resulting from long days of constant battle, but eventually they had the armor polished back to its former glory. The colonel was always in motion, rarely at a desk, whether it was visiting his troopers on the front lines or berating his junior officers for lack of aggression in the rear. Complementing the colonel's powerful, broad-shouldered physique was his 50-inch electrostatic battle sword, secured on his back. A thin layer of dull purple plasma encased the 39-inch blade and rippled across the surface. The sword was secured magnetically to the colonel's armor, eliminating the need for a scabbard.

Marshal Von Jesonik's summons had arrived quite unexpectedly, forcing the colonel to relinquish command of his regiment at a critical juncture of the campaign. His beloved Dreadwolves had just penetrated the outer defenses of the capital city, Elohim Prime, with limited support from division or even the expeditionary force. Although the city lacked tactical importance, taking such a symbolic city could demoralize the enemy and quite possibly free up resources for operations on other sectors.

Two massive oak doors opened inward to reveal the inner sanctum of the marshal. He held the title of Chief Adjutant of the Assault Infantry High Command to the supreme chancellor. He was the assault infantry's representative in the High Command, along with others who represented the other military branches, most of whom had attained the rank of marshal as well. The colonel's cleaned and freshly repaired purple cloak trailed behind him as he passed through the doors, leaving Sergeant Matthias outside. The colonel immediately noticed a gigantic banner hanging from the vaulted ceiling, depicting an eagle grasping a sword stained with crimson blood in its talons, the colonel's weary mind was still on high alert as his eyes scanned his surroundings. He took note of the many rare items of luxury that decorated the office of the marshal. Ornate and artful tapestries hung along the oak-paneled walls, including a stoic painting of the supreme chancellor, who had been Hellenheim's leader for more than thirty years. The colonel stared a moment at the painting before shifting his gaze at the large panoramic window that overlooked the vast industrial and military infrastructure of Luriana, Hellenheim's center of government and military establishment. Multicolored clouds of factory by-products belched from overworked chimneys, further defiling the decaying atmosphere. Neither a green blade of grass nor a tree could be observed for as far as the eye could see.

Standing in front of the window, introspectively admiring this colorless landscape, was the Star Marshal, Carolus Von Jesonik. An intimidating figure standing nearly seven feet tall, he towered over most men, an attribute he used to his advantage when dealing with nonmilitary bureaucrat types. His close political connection to the supreme chancellor was no coincidence. Marshal Von Jesonik had made it known that he should be considered the rightful successor to the chancellorship when the time came. He turned to welcome his guest. The colonel stopped, assumed a rigid position of attention, and brought his right arm up stiffly, giving the traditional military salute.

"Thank you, Ernst," the marshal said to his aide in an evenly toned, authoritative voice. "That will be all." Ernst bowed graciously, exited through the double doors, and closed them behind him.

Von Jesonik walked around his desk to the front of it, coming face to face with the colonel. He returned the colonel's salute casually. Although the colonel held distaste for many senior officers, he held the marshal in high regard. The marshal's service record spoke for itself, and he was a capable leader, even if he was commanding the 1st Assault Expeditionary Force from the home planet. He knew, however, that the position of marshal is as much a political appointment as military, and he did not envy the marshal's position on Hellenheim. Politicians had no business running a war, and the supreme chancellor had tried on many occasions to influence campaigns how he saw fit.

"Please, Johann, relax," the marshal said to the colonel. "We speak as friends today, not as officers. You have endured so much for so long; I—as well as the remaining district governors and, of course, the supreme chancellor—are forever in your debt."

Colonel Chuikova nodded, placed his mirror-polished black helmet on the massive desk, and sat down. He quickly removed the thought from his brain and noticed a box of cigars resting invitingly on the marshal's desk. He couldn't remember the last time he had actually savored one. His troopers were lucky if they got a hot meal once a week—unless, of course, an attack was planned for which they would need their strength.

Von Jesonik followed Colonel Chuikova's gaze and imagined he could read his thoughts. He smiled and gestured at the open humidor. "Go ahead, take one." He raised his gaze to match the colonel's, attempting to catch the slightest hint of emotion emanating from the man's steel-gray eyes. Seeing nothing, he reached for a decanter and poured two drinks of the dark brown liquid.

"Thank you," the colonel said. He leaned forward and selected a cigar, holding it to his nose, savoring the intoxicating tobacco aroma. He placed the cigar in a pocket inside his cloak. He accepted the drink and drained it in one gulp.

"I must ask why you have summoned me away from the front. My regiment is so close to taking Elohim." There was disdain in his voice, almost as if his regiment had been defeated. "I hope you did not summon me here personally to discuss our lack of ammunition, replacements, and support from divisional command."

Von Jesonik turned around and walked back behind his desk. He gazed out of the window, seemingly ignoring his guest. Chuikova reached back into the humidor and selected another cigar, this time rolling it between his thumb and forefinger. His short, spiked gray hair and the lines on his face marked evidence that the war had not aged him kindly. He appeared not to have slept in days. Von Jesonik sat down behind his desk.

"Johann, I am fully aware of your tactical situation. Your actions on Elohim Prime are legendary, to say the least. Your regiment does the work of an entire corps—perhaps an expeditionary force." He produced a lighter and promptly lit a cigar. He offered the lighter to Chuikova, who accepted it. "The war has been hard on us all. You are correct that I have not brought you here to discuss strategy or the evolving front."

Von Jesonik tilted his head back and blew a puff of gray smoke toward the ceiling. The rosy aroma hung in the air momentarily, before fading away. He continued, "You are here because you are being relieved of your command, effective immediately."

Chuikova rose immediately to his feet and slammed his gloved fist down on the desk. "How can this be? This is heresy! My men will be wiped off the face of that god-forsaken planet!" he bellowed.

"Calm down, Colonel! Do not forget where you are!" Von Jesonik retorted sharply. Chuikova sat back in his chair, his face an angry red.

"With respect, my apologies," Chuikova muttered under his breath, barely audible. He thought about lunging across the desk and grabbing the marshal by his throat. Instead he sat back into the chair, lit his cigar, and attempted to relax.

"This is not punishment, but rather a reward. The front has not been kind to you. Frankly, we are running out of experienced commanders. You are different, Johann, in that you lead from the front. Most commanders prefer to hide underground and commit what amounts to mass murder in sending their boys over the top. I cannot influence battle plans any longer. My position is more political now than ever before. The supreme chancellor plans operations and alters campaigns, and often even I cannot change his mind. He is surrounded by those who crave power, even as our empire is slowly dying. But I digress." Von Jesonik took another long pull off of his cigar, blowing the grey smoke up towards the ceiling. "You have an immaculate record. You are cunning, daring, and reckless. You inspire your troopers, and your mere presence can swing the odds in your favor. You give them one thing they so often lose sight of."

Chuikova looked at Von Jesonik, still unable to hide the disgust and disbelief in his eyes. "And what would that be, marshal?"

"That would be hope. Hope in victory and faith in their world."

"Your words are flattering, but I cannot see how being relieved of my command is a reward." He almost spat the words out. Von Jesonik's glare reminded him that he should not push too far. Chuikova's voice calmed. "I apologize." He paused and poured another drink. After throwing it back, he relaxed. The two shots of liquor now worked quickly in unison, calming his nerves to a more appropriate level. Surprise at the effects of the liquor overtook him briefly, as he realized that his tolerance had diminished greatly since he had been on the front, devoid of spirits.

"You brought me up like a son when I was field commissioned as a lieutenant," Chuikova noted. "I trust you, but I do not see how replacing me at such a critical time as this could be of any benefit. If we take Elohim Prime, we have control of that entire sector."

"Your concern is noted." Von Jesonik rose out of his chair and turned back again to the window overlooking the massive industry below, his gloved hands now clasped behind his back. The last rays of the setting sun somehow found a break in the polluted clouds that lasted long enough to send shards of orange light bouncing off the dozens of shiny medals hanging on his dark emerald tunic. "What is below us will be gone in a few short years if we lose this war, perhaps even sooner," he said quietly. "We only have four allied planets left in an empire that at one time stretched for three star systems. If the 1st is destroyed on Elohim Prime, our only recourse would be to sue for peace. The Auger-Lords have foreseen this in their visions."

"I have never believed that group of outcast wizards," Chuikova related to Von Jesonik's back. "They have never done anything for our people except predict what is already known," he continued, unable to mask the contempt in his voice.

Von Jesonik ignored the response. He next spoke in a soft, fatherly tone. "The supreme chancellor himself has planned a special mission based on intelligence we have received from our state security agents, as well as guidance gifted to us from the Auger-Lords. He has entrusted me to select a competent and capable leader. The mission is bold and daring, which is why I chose you. The enemy is developing a new weapon, and we must have it or destroy it. The chancellor demands success, and you are the only one that I feel can achieve what the chancellor wants. You see now that this is much bigger than Elohim Prime. If you succeed, Johann, you will be an immortal hero in the eyes of the people. What we need in these turbulent times are heroes. This righteous conflict will soon come to an end, and we will herald a new age of peace and prosperity!" Spittle spewed from Von Jesonik's mouth as his voice reached a crescendo.

Chuikova stared at the floor, seemingly lost in thought when Von Jesonik ended his oratory. Von Jesonik turned toward his desk and activated a keypad. A holographic image appeared, showing a large complex with many rooms and passages, formed in the side of a rocky plateau surrounded by a strange looking forest. "Our intelligence agents as well as stealth satellites obtained these plans, as well as technical information detailing the experiments within this desert planet located in the outer fringes of known space."

"I don't follow. The outer fringes? That is hostile territory. Pirates and mercenaries rule that sector. I am used to leading armies on fields of battle, not special operations," Chuikova interjected as he watched the images rotate above the desk. He put his half-smoked cigar into a gold ashtray on the marshal's desk. He knew fringe space was dangerous. Once the war between planets broke out, refugees were the first to begin the exodus out of the star system. Soon, pirates, mercenaries, deserters, and many others sought the relative safety of fringe space. Governmental presence did not reach that far out. If the enemy had an outpost in fringe space, there could be no telling what they were up to.

Von Jesonik nodded his head. "Your concern is duly noted. We lost many agents in acquiring this information. I know you are a military man, Johann, and politics never interested you much. The supreme chancellor has distrust among his ranks, as do I. These are turbulent times, and I dare say it, but our government is destroying itself from within. Many would like the supreme chancellor removed from power, yet others that say it is only his iron will that is keeping this empire together."

Empire. Chuikova had started his military career on Karn and was a junior commander on Celbrius. Those planets were long since destroyed, their cities shattered and enshrouded in lethal clouds of radiation. If there were any survivors, society would be reduced to medieval by now, or worse, and those survivors would be forgotten by their own brothers.

Von Jesonik continued, oblivious of Chuikova's wandering mind. "I know I can trust you, Johann. This project is enshrouded with the utmost secrecy. Only the supreme chancellor, I, our Auger-Lord brethren, and now you know of its existence. The experiments within this complex are rumored to concern a new weapon that could turn the tide of the war in the enemy's favor. That is why I am giving you this mission. Your assault force will comprise three platoons that are already garrisoned here. They know they were selected for a special mission, but they don't know what it is.

Captain Cruwell is assigned as your executive officer. He is a very accomplished officer who will serve you well."

"I take it you have a way to get us into fringe space undetected? It won't be much of a mission if we are detected by their fleet. They have spies everywhere."

"Not to worry. Star Admiral Raus will take you to your drop point in his flagship. You will use a modified drop pod that that will enable you to return home if Raus is destroyed by hostile forces. The Auger-Lords have divulged this ancient technology. Even they fear our destruction."

"You speak too much of the Lords! Why do they hoard the technology of their ancestors? They could have given us a technical advantage decades ago!" Chuikova continued. "I sometimes wonder if they are prolonging this conflict intentionally. Their ability to foresee certain events must show them something."

In a hushed voice, Von Jesonik replied, "I suggest you don't try to figure out their ancient ways. The Auger-Lords and their seers are guardians of power we cannot conceive, and they must maintain the balance of power. We have co-existed with them in harmony for thousands of years. To take sides against them would unfairly upset the natural course and have disastrous effects on the future."

"Very well." Chuikova knew it was futile to argue, and he was a man of his word and a man of honor. Questioning the motives of the Auger-Lords and Auger-Seers was dangerous. Their reign reached back beyond memory; they had always been the custodians of unimagined power and energy.

Most of the populace on Hellenheim caught only brief glimpses of the highly secretive sect of reclusive priests who called themselves Auger-Lords. Schools taught children about an ancient race that had been in their galaxy for hundreds of thousands of years, perhaps longer. These lords were able to harness tremendous amounts of energy by mining remnants of collapsed neutron stars. The neutron pulsar energy powered everything they possessed, including ships of massive size that could travel to the furthest reaches of space.

With all of this power, however, came unpredictability. As it is told, one star mining crew unknowingly entered into the gravitational pull of a supermassive black hole while conducting mining operations in an uncharted solar system. Trying to escape the gravitation pull, the crew fired its pulse drive, which emitted a brief, intense electromagnetic charge from within the ship's pulse drive core. The crew did not foresee that the electromagnetic charge would penetrate the black hole's event horizon, along with all matter and light in the surrounding area. The ship was pulled through, toward the black hole's singularity, still emitting its electromagnetic beacon toward its home planet. The forces of the singularity stretched and compressed the ship beyond its design tolerances, and combined with the already salvaged pulsars in the cargo hold, destroyed the ship. Instead of adding to the mass of the black hole, the release of energy transversed the ship's electromagnetic beam to its point of destination, effectively destroying the Auger civilization.

This history is documented in ancient texts and scrolls maintained in the chapel sanctuaries on Hellenheim. The Auger-Lords are direct descendants of whose who survived that disaster. They continue to influence political as well as military leaders when it suits them. The people of Hellenheim know little about them, only what the Auger-Lords permit to be taught. The Auger-Lords emphasize that their relationship with the human populace is symbiotic, formed when the first humans arrived from another galaxy.

The Auger-Lords permitted certain technologies to be utilized for expansion of the human civilization and conquest of planets. The Auger-Lords were few in number, and through their relationship with humans, they had found the perfect means to extend their own reach. Throughout the millennia they lay in virtual entombment beneath the surface of their shattered world. Their bodies decayed, yet their minds evolved, with the remnants of their technology keeping them alive.

Certain segments of the human populace were selected to become Auger-Seers. The Auger-Seers were tasked with integrating within society more openly, acting as eyes and ears for their masters. Few dared challenge this symbiotic relationship; the consequences were dire. Chuikova knew that further argument was futile and dangerous.

"I knew I could count on you, Johann." Von Jesonik reached out and clasped Chuikova's hand in both of his. "My adjutant will give you the technical readouts of the complex and all mission parameters. You will train your strike element to your liking, and you will rendezvous with Admiral Raus. Captain Cruwell will assemble your men in Star Port Number One with the drop pod.

"There are men on the front who I would like by my side, strong soldiers who—"

"I am sorry, but there is no time. I cannot permit that." Von Jesonik interjected. "I am sorry if I didn't make that clear. There must be utmost secrecy. You will train Captain Cruwell's strike force here on Hellenheim. You have your orders, and you are dismissed. I have other obligations to attend to."

"Of course, please forgive me." Chuikova retrieved his helmet from the desk and saluted smartly. Von Jesonik came to attention and returned the salute. Chuikova retrieved his half-smoked cigar from the ashtray and exited Von Jesonik's office. Ernst appeared as if out of thin air and quickly closed the double oaken doors behind him.

Sergeant Matthias rose to his feet, from a sofa situated against a massive circular concrete column. He quickly dropped the red bulbous fruit he was savoring and quickened his pace to catch up with the colonel.

"That was fast. What happened?" Both of their footsteps resonated loudly on the white marble floor. Ministry Administrators, their heads buried in their data pads scurried out of their way.

"We will not be going back to the front, Sergeant." Chuikova's matter-of-fact tone told the sergeant that the colonel was seriously upset. He had always called him by his surname, Matthias. His commander hadn't called him by his rank in quite some time, except in front of the troopers. Matthias had been at the colonel's side through the duration of the Elohim Prime campaign.

"We're not going back to the front?" Matthias had a hard time believing the statement, but he was not entirely displeased. *A little R and R with the ladies would be nice.*

The colonel stopped abruptly and looked Matthias directly in the eye. "I don't like the idea either. A lot of the men are going to die needlessly back in that hell hole. He resumed walking toward the turbo shafts that led to the ground floor of the Ministry of War building.

The colonel related his plans to Matthias as they walked. "We have been tasked with a new mission to recover a weapon the enemy has developed that may turn the tide of this war in our favor." His voice was firm, and he spoke matter-of-factly. "Meet me at 0500 tomorrow in the main hangar bay. You have your orders."

"Yes, of course," Matthias replied slightly dejected. "I guess I am not getting laid tonight. Damn." Matthias started to leave when Chuikova stopped him.

"Matthias?"

The sergeant stopped and turned around. "Sir?"

The colonel reached into his breast pocket, produced a cigar and held it out toward Matthias. With his other hand, he produced the lighter he had liberated from Von Jesonik's office. Matthias didn't need any further invitation. A big smile broke out across his scarred face as he grabbed the cigar and accepted a light. After a couple of puffs, the cigar was lit. Nodding appreciatively, Matthias walked away, down a hallway, leaving the colonel to himself. After a solitary moment, the colonel replaced the lighter in his pocket, entered the turbo lift, and contemplated how he was going to lead this strike force of unknowns. More important, he wondered about this weapon that was supposed to turn the tide of the war. He faced the nightfall as the turbo lift rapidly descended the monolithic building, 200 stories tall.

CHAPTER 3

"Attention!" As Colonel Chuikova's order echoed throughout the massive hangar, all the troopers snapped to the position of attention, their rifles clutched with both hands in front of their armored bodies. Three platoons were assembled inside an active hangar filled with spacecraft of all shapes and sizes, including a two-story-tall ovoid drop pod. When called to attention, technicians had been loading crates into the pod.

"The troopers are ready for inspection, colonel," said Captain Cruwell, who faced Colonel Chuikova and saluted. The colonel quickly returned the salute. The colonel began to pace down the first rank of the three platoons, Sergeant Matthias trailing him, chewing on the remains of his cigar.

"I'll make this short and sweet," the colonel said, "because I have some heavy drinking to attend to." A few of the troopers stifled laughs. "My name is Colonel Johann Chuikova. I am here to fight and to win this war. If you do not share that goal, step out of formation now and you will be reassigned to the front." Seeing no one move, he continued. "All I ask is that you fight and give me all you have. You shouldn't expect anything less from me." The colonel stopped in front of the middle platoon and nodded at Sergeant Matthias. He spoke in a low voice to his veteran sergeant and asked, "What do you think?"

Sergeant Matthias removed the chewed stogie from his mouth. "They are right out of basic, although they have received commando training. I think they are a good core. We have good snipers and heavy weapons operators, and our equipment is the newest available." The colonel nodded in response to the sergeant's assertions.

New equipment was hard to come by nowadays, and its availability indicated that this mission was high priority. The troopers were issued a synthetic body skin that worked well against both heat and cold, as well allowing the skin to breathe. Troopers wore olive drab utility overalls over this second skin. Veteran troopers found out quickly that the body skin suit wore out quickly since it was meant to be changed and cleaned periodically, which was difficult to accomplish in battle conditions. It was not designed for extreme environments or for long-term uninterrupted use. Within a few weeks, troopers wore their utility overalls with nothing underneath. The body armor was designed well, with ballistic form-fitting plates protecting the legs and arms and a highly functional hardened ballistic vest encapsulated the torso. The most important component of the armor system was the jet-black helmet. Besides offering moderate ballistic protection, the slightly bulky helmet provided night vision, thermal imaging, and a targeting system integrated with the primary weapon sight. Although the troopers' ballistic armor was sufficient protection against standard slug and projectile ammunition, it could not stop a projectile fired using magnetic cell technology due to the incredible speed at which they were launched from the rifle. Troopers were lucky to get fed a hot meal once a day, however medics and doctors were generous in their distribution of "brain-pills", amphetamines designed to keep troopers awake and alert for days on end.

The troopers were, however, allotted sufficient quantities of ammunition for whatever weapon system they carried. The Electro-Magnetic Battle Rifle, or EMR, was standard issue to basic troopers. The EMR, in its basic configuration, was referred to as a generation one and had few weapon attachments, only a bayonet and an advanced optics system that could detect heat which worked in conjunction with the trooper's helmet. The EMR was built into a bullpup configuration, with the magazine and power cell located to the rear, behind the trigger mechanism. The bullpup design permitted a compact weapon design, with no sacrifice of barrel length, so that accuracy was not compromised.

In addition to ammunition magazines, troopers carried extra power cells for their rifles. The ammunition was of a simple, caseless design composed of a metal projectile available only through the teaching and discoveries of the Auger-Lords. The power cells produced an intense electromagnetic field that launched the EMR's ammunition, which could travel great distances.

After a round exited the barrel, a telltale green energy wave followed it to its target, giving the impression of a laser or pulse energy weapon.

The EMR had some drawbacks, such as overheating and power drains from defective cells. For these reasons, troopers often carried traditional projectile assault rifles and pump action slug throwers in reserve.

Sergeant Matthias continued his appraisal of the new recruits for the colonel. "Corporal Scott's and a few of the other troopers are versed in the operation of our analysis equipment. In short, this is definitely not your average recruit platoon. The troopers are highly trained, with most receiving simulated combat drops as well." Colonel Chuikova nodded in understanding. These troopers may be well trained but they were also fresh. He could, however mold them to his needs more easily than if they were a veteran outfit from another command, used to procedures and command different from his.

"Captain," The colonel said the single word briskly. "Put them at ease," the colonel instructed. "Tell them we will begin training in the morning. If there is something they need to do, they should do it now. I want to see you in my quarters in one hour, captain. I suspect you would like to know what kind of mission you will be undertaking."

The colonel turned and walked away, Sergeant Matthias trailing behind, chewing on his stogie. Captain Cruwell executed an about-face and surveyed his eager and enthusiastic troopers.

"At ease!" Cruwell addressed his men in a booming voice. "Fall out and assemble here at 0600 tomorrow to begin training." Several of the troops cheered at hearing this, and the room swelled with the bellowing of a synchronized "Urrah!"

Captain Cruwell made his way down the main hallway of the officers' quarters, a long, featureless tunnel of metal. Most of these quarters were empty due to personnel being on deployment somewhere. He reached the colonel's room and activated the call button.

"Come in."

The metal door slid open silently. Captain Cruwell entered the colonel's sparsely decorated quarters. The room was barren save for the rudimentary effects: a bed, two chairs, and a data access terminal. Behind a closed door was a shower and toilet. The colonel wore a black sleeveless shirt with the image of the eagle and sword on the left side of his chest, the symbol of the United Consortium of Planets (or what was left of them). Hellenheim had been the central seat of government over several planets in the system. Now most of those planets were broken, with the few that remained putting up resistance. The last UCP Governor's conference before the outbreak of interplanetary war seemed to narrow on a rewriting of the social contract. With Auger-Lords now interjecting themselves as creators and de-facto rulers of anything and everything they could reach with their probing minds, open protest amongst the planets was quick. Also, the rise of Hellenheim's supreme chancellor from out of nowhere was the breaking point. Unwilling to surrender anything further for a central government that seemed corrupt and unjust, the United Consortium of Planets quickly flamed into an all out war.

The colonel sat in front of the data terminal, rapidly scanning the screen, the symbols scrolling both vertically and horizontally across the screen. Captain Cruwell noticed the distinctive fanged dreadwolf tattooed on the colonel's right shoulder, with the inscription "Eternal—Death Never Dies" below it.

"Please sit down, captain." The colonel quaffed the small amount of murky rust-colored alcohol remaining in his glass. "Can I get you something to drink?"

"No thank you, sir, I do not indulge in spirits," Captain Cruwell replied. He shifted from one foot to the other. The colonel waved his hand at the second chair. The captain sat down and put his helmet on the table.

The colonel poured two drinks and handed one to the captain. "I do not trust any officer who cannot handle a drink. Please, humor me."

Captain Cruwell looked at the glass and took a small sip. The liquid burned as it went down his throat, forcing him to cough.

"Thanks," the captain said.

The colonel managed a weak laugh. "If you are to be my executive officer, I'd like to know your name."

"Captain Cruwell, sir. Sebastian Cruwell," he replied weakly.

"Sebastian, this is your first combat drop, is it not?" The colonel took a heavy pull from his glass. Setting the glass back down, he absentmindedly ran his finger inside the rim.

"Yes sir," the captain replied, his voice tinged with nervousness. "Although I have undergone simulator drops."

“I thought so. I hope it will not be your last. We will be shipping out in five days. Since you are my XO, I will brief you on the mission as best I can.”

“Yes sir.”

The colonel began to type on the data terminals keyboard. He reached up to a small camera looking device perched on the top of the monitor and adjusted it gently. Satisfied, the colonel pushed a single key on the keyboard and a large holographic image projected itself in the middle of the room, detailing a vast complex.

“This readout is of a research facility deep into fringe space. Enemy concentrations are unknown. We are to strike and recover a weapon the enemy is developing. The supreme chancellor himself drew up the plans for the mission.” The colonel paused to take a drink. “Upon landing, the first element will be led by Sergeant Matthias. He will lead a veteran squad that accompanied me from the front and will assist in training the new troopers in the short time we have here. Matthias’s element will exploit the breach in the blast doors and make entrance inside.” The colonel indicated the doors on the map. The colonel activated another holographic image detailing three more levels of the complex. “Once Level One is secure, you will bring up the second platoon and breach Level Two. Level Two is the main genetics research wing where our objective is supposed to be.” The colonel pointed to a room on the image. “It is critical that you succeed as quickly as possible.”

“What exactly are we after?” Cruwell interjected.

“I do not know, exactly. All I know is that it is a weapon of some sort. The intelligence stops there. Many previous missions have sought so-called ‘secret weapons.’ They all either failed to reach their targets or turned up nothing.” The colonel sighed heavily, “I suspect concentrated resistance there. Captain, make sure you achieve your objective.”

The colonel brought up one more image of Level Three of the complex. The image contained only one large room, with a tunnel that branched off from it, but the image was cut off. “This level is incomplete. I believe it to be a storage facility or a hangar.”

“Is three platoons too much if we are to achieve surprise and remain undetected?” Cruwell asked.

“We are going in with around 40 troopers, the same ones you inspected at formation earlier. These platoons are smaller than usual, but we must be ready if we are opposed by a security force.”

"Is there any intelligence of the resistance to be expected?" Cruwell took another small sip of his drink and this time tolerated it, albeit not much better.

"Stealth satellite imagery has detected very little surface activity on the desert planet, a few small primitive settlements, not much else. However, this plateau the facility is on throws the scanners off the charts. This forest surrounding the facility is teeming with life."

"What do you mean?" Cruwell asked, slightly confused.

"The latest intelligence reports say that this is mainly a genetic research laboratory. Detailed surface scans show strange and aggressive wildlife and plant life all over the place." The colonel walked back over to the data terminal and pushed a single key on the keyboard, shutting off the map image. He set his empty glass on the table and picked up a manila envelope, the words "Top Secret - Eyes Only" were stamped in large red letters across the top.

"I received these photographs earlier today." The colonel pulled out a series of hi-resolution photographs and spread them on the table. The photographs showed strange multi-colored plants, some with an almost flesh like quality as if they more beast than plant. Parts of the facility seemed derelict as vegetation grew over the building and ground alike. An earthmover lay immobilized by thick vines wrapped around its massive tires. One of the images showed a blurry glimpse of a creature standing upright on two legs, its body covered in orange and black fur, yet the arms and head were almost human. Lastly, Cruwell picked up another image, this one showing a long winding rocky trail leading up the plateau from the desert.

"There is only one way in from the planet's surface. Perhaps the inhabitants couldn't get out fast enough. There is no telling what else they have in that forest of theirs," Cruwell said.

"Precisely why this mission will be unlike anything you or I have ever been on. For all we know, this laboratory has indeed been abandoned." The colonel paused to refill his glass to two fingers and quickly slammed back the contents. He winced slightly from the alcohol burning the back of his throat. He held the empty glass, slowly rotating it with his fingers. "Admiral Raus will get us there and remain on standby in orbit in case we are attacked from space. Fringe space is unpredictable—Raus may run into pirates. Our Dreadnaught warship, with no escort, will be a tempting target. Most of his battle group is still stationed around Elohim Prime. He wants this to be a smash and grab, and he will not risk prolonged exposure in orbit, given that our fleet is not the size it used to be. He will stay in orbit only while the situation is favorable to him. Therefore, we must make haste and retreat off the planet as soon as possible. Otherwise, we will have to rely on the experimental pulse drives retrofitted on the drop pod—something I would rather not do." He paused, his face beginning flush, and met Captain Cruwell's eyes. "Do you have any questions?" The colonel set his glass on the table and promptly refilled it.

"No, not at this time." The captain put down his empty glass as well. He stood up and immediately felt light-headed. He had to grasp the back of the chair to keep his balance.

"Good. Be ready tomorrow to begin training. We will emphasize close quarters combat. Each trooper will be issued a sufficient allotment of grenades and ammunition for live fire exercise."

The captain saluted and exited the colonel's quarters slightly dizzy from the drink. A sharp pain began to shoot through the left side of his head.

CHAPTER 4

Long tendrils of clouds snaked their way for miles across the azure sky. A large, brilliant sun radiated high in the sky over the desert planet. A single tear-shaped drop ship rested on the surface in a charred landing crater it had created in the dense vegetation surrounding the laboratory complex. The lone ship spilled its complement of assault troopers from a massive ramp that had dropped to the ground.

Sergeant Matthias's platoon took point and advanced seventy-five yards, tactically approaching the blast doors of the complex. The twelve troopers took up cover behind equipment crates and thick concrete walls jutting out from the complex. Two troopers carefully placed shaped charges on the blast doors and quickly retreated back into cover.

"All set here, Colonel," Matthias said via the tactical net. "No activity; this place is as quiet as a tomb."

Colonel Chuikova and Captain Cruwell walked down the ramp of the drop pod. The last platoon to exit had secured the perimeter around the landing zone. The second platoon had leapfrogged ahead, taking up a concealed position between the LZ and Matthias's platoon at the entrance of the complex.

The colonel raised the visor on his helmet to the smell of stale, damp air. What he thought from the intelligence reports was a forest actually was a dense jungle. Vines, trees, and oddly shaped flora seemed to react to his troopers' presence. A low, soft hissing seemed to emanate from all over. Even though the colonel had advanced only twenty-five yards or so, he could only make out the complex through a slight gap in the vegetation.

From his vantage point, the complex was overgrown and appeared to have been disused for quite some time.

"Copy that, Sergeant. Prepare your element for entry on my order. 2nd and 3rd platoon are moving into position now."

"Understood," Matthias replied. He unslung his slug thrower and racked a shell into the chamber.

Inside the cramped control room of the complex, a smartly dressed officer watched a single computer monitor intently as a technician busily inputted commands via a keyboard. The officer showed the marks of battle experience; a large scar ran down the left side of his face, and he wore a black patch over his left eye.

"Zoom in on the main doors," he said as the technician quickly brought a live feed image up on the monitor. At least twenty or more heavily armed troopers were taking up assault positions behind whatever cover they could find. "Patch into the satellite. I want to see their landing area." The technician quickly turned on an overhead video monitor hanging from the ceiling, and within minutes the officer had a bird's eye view of the plateau.

"Appears to be a single drop pod transport, sir," the technician said.

"Switch to thermal scan. I want to see how many we are up against."

Nodding, the technician typed commands on the keyboard, and the view quickly changed. The enemy troopers now showed up as distinct orange and red shapes. Numerous other heat signatures were visible, although they seemed to be maintaining some distance from the LZ.

The officer sighed heavily and stared at the floor. "I suppose it was only a matter of time until we were spotted. Inform Dr. Keitel that we must prep for evacuation immediately and place the facility on maximum alert. Seal the door to the genetics wing."

As the invading assault force emptied from its drop pod on the surface, an inhuman scream pierced the air in the main genetics laboratory. Three technicians in white lab coats assisted a naked humanoid form in climbing out of a large holding tank filled with a murky green liquid. When the humanoid had reached the floor and stood beside the tank, one of the technicians administered a series of injections into its right shoulder. Numerous electrodes and their wires attached the pale white body to a group of monitors, each recording and displaying vital signs.

An elderly white-coated scientist turned to his much younger assistant, who was busy sabotaging one of the laboratory's many computer systems with a sledgehammer. "A sight to behold, is it not?"

"It is," the assistant growled back, "but not a pleasant sight. We will not be able to control this monstrosity. We need more time. Why don't we just destroy this specimen and evacuate, and try to save as much research as possible instead of destroying it. We can start over at a more secure location, perhaps one closer to the home planet. It was madness leaving us out here." The assistant resumed his destructive work, sending sparks showering in the air.

"No," the elderly scientist replied. "This research could turn the tide of the war. I have been subjected to the unfortunate uncertainties of science for too long now. Finally, I have something that works. He will not be terminated. He is all the research we need. Think about the possibilities we have engineered." The scientist's voice rose in pitch with each sentence. "We can create a resurrected army of the dead to destroy everything in its path. They can sustain damage that would kill ordinary troopers, orders will be followed without hesitation, and there is an almost endless supply of dead in this war. Just think if we could administer the program on the front. We could instantly raise an army double the size of what we started with by using our dead, their dead, it doesn't matter." The elderly scientist strode purposefully to a locked refrigeration unit against the wall. He entered a numeric pass code, pulled on the handle and opened the door. He withdrew a vial filled with a pinkish liquid and turned it side to side, staring at it intently.

"This is the key," he stated. "This solution will change the tide of the war and bring victory to our side." He placed the vial back onto a shelf in the refrigeration unit and closed the door. "Can you imagine life without war, and the end of disease? We're on the cusp of performing miracles!"

The assistant leaned on the edge of an examination table and wiped a bead of sweat from his brow. "That solution wasn't even engineered by us. Its secrets were revealed by enemy agents pulling some sort of double cross. Yes, I concur that our results are incredible, but we cannot control or influence the solution. You know as well as I do that it has been resistant to our attempts. And as for disease, we have never attempted to utilize the solution as a cure for anything. It serves one dark purpose, the resurrection of the dead. Don't you know what that means?" he asked in exasperation.

"Don't lecture me! With the proper methods, we can control what we have created, mark my words. We just need more time." The elderly scientist thought back to six months ago, when he was approached by a strange man who offered the missing link to his genetic research. He at first dismissed it, but changed his mind as he performed preliminary tests on his own. The solution was unlike anything he had ever seen before. As he experimented, without government knowledge, with his newfound solution, thoughts of treason often ran through his mind. He believed that his research could have a profound impact, but he did not yet want to share his results. He wanted to be the one performing the miracles that the solution promised.

The mysterious man had given him one vial, with simple instructions on how to synthesize more for his research. He was unable to identify the compounds contained in the solution, but after almost six months of trial and error and many failed attempts, he finally made the solution work. The delay was in the application. Once applied to dead tissue, the solution revealed its true purpose. The research and experimentation had progressed quickly from there, to the recent experiments with revitalizing the dead. Of course there were setbacks. The adjacent testing room was full of them, volunteers who gave their lives in the name of science. His primary concern now was prolonging the revitalizing effect. It was far from permanent, with the host requiring periodic injections to continue to function. Replacing some of the organs with synthetic ones seemed to prolong the effects.

He felt close to a final breakthrough, but now he faced the attack on the genetics lab. The mysterious man had told him to expect an assault on the lab, but he had put it out of his mind. Now, facing the reality of the predicted attack, he recalled that the man told him he would leave for a destination he did not know, and it was there he could find the answers he was seeking.

Suddenly, the officer in charge of security's voice blared on the loudspeaker drowning out all the activity in the laboratory. The voice said in a monotonous tone, "We are under attack; enemy forces have breached the main doors. All non-security personnel must evacuate." The loudspeaker fell silent, and lights flickered as the power was interrupted. The technicians stared at the loudspeaker box on the wall. "Main power lines will be shut down in five minutes," the voice blared again.

"Why don't you contact the home planet?" the young assistant asked. "Couldn't they send a relief force?" The attack had rattled him, and he could focus only on the current threat to the facility, not the long-term effects on the research.

"There's no time!" the elderly scientist yelled in response. "We must evacuate now!"

Once the power was offline, the corridor was plunged into darkness. The blast door began to close on its own accord, and trapped a few technicians in the genetics lab. Their cries and pounding on the door died off as Dr. Keitel activated a small hand torch illuminating two technicians leading a naked humanoid covered by a blanket into a transport cart waiting in the corridor. They helped the humanoid climb into the transport cart, with Dr. Keitel getting in next to it. The cart proceeded down the corridor, which was now carved out of the earth instead of metal.

"You may commence your assault now, Sergeant." Colonel Chuikova said via the tactical net.

A thunderous explosion ripped the blast doors apart. Black smoke began to pour out. Sergeant Matthias led his platoon through the breach. The long, narrow corridor continued downward for about fifty meters until another set of blast doors blocked the way. There was currently no power, the troopers relying on their night vision to show the way. Matthias dropped to one knee and held up his arm, his hand balled into a fist, indicating to his troopers to hold position. The following troopers each took a knee and awaited further orders.

"Colonel, we have another set of doors here," Matthias said into his helmet mike. "We need cutting equipment. It's too narrow to blast."

"Copy, it's on the way. 2nd platoon is moving up for support once you get inside. If the map is correct, you should reach the main medical wing on the other side."

"Get that cutting torch over here!" Sergeant Matthias yelled into his helmet mike. 2nd platoon formed up behind Matthias's platoon, lining both walls of the corridor, and the mass of troops crowded the space. At the end of the line, a two-man heavy weapons crew placed a portable plasma cannon, mounted on a tri-pod, on the metal floor. A lone trooper weighted down with a large cylindrical tank on his back ran up to the massive blast doors from outside the bunker. He quickly unholstered his torch and activated it with the push of a button. A long blue superhot flame shot out, and the trooper set to work, sending red and orange sparks showering along the blast door.

"No frag grenades; stun only!" Sergeant Matthias shouted. "Stay to the sides and don't bunch up!" he ordered when he saw that the door was nearly cut. His men were ready for action. They were focused and alert for what awaited them on the other side.

Within moments, the torch-bearing trooper moved to the rear. The lead troopers kicked in the weakened sectioned of the blast doors and threw in two stun grenades, just in case the enemy had a trap waiting for them on the other side. After the grenades detonated, the troopers stormed into the breach, expecting their first glimpse of the base defenders. Instead, as the troopers moved up in threes as their training had taught them, they encountered no enemy contact.

Matthias was close to the front of his troops. Through his night vision, he could see that the corridor opened up into a large circular control room of sorts. The middle of the room held a large semi-circular control console. Chairs were kicked over as if someone had made a hasty departure. Beyond the control console, Matthias could see the outline of another blast door. His troopers quickly cleared the room.

"No one here, sir," a young corporal reported to Matthias. "Room is secure. The blast door on the other side is sealed."

Matthias nodded in response. He transmitted via the tactical net, "Colonel, we are still negative. We are going to have to cut another blast door." Matthias thought for a moment as his gaze saw dozens of conduit pipes snaking overhead on the ceiling. A few of them ran into a console station in the middle of the room. "Hold on a sec. We have a computer console here. It may be able to restore power. I can give Corporal Scotts a crack at it."

"Hold position, Sergeant. I want that computer analyzed first before we keep going. I'd prefer to not keep announcing our presence with every corridor we enter."

"Power is online, sergeant," Scotts said. "I don't know how long it will last. I re-routed power from auxiliary lines into the main grid." Scotts rechecked the power cables he was adjusting and closed the wall access panel. Another trooper had opened another access panel in the back of the computer console and was trying to splice into the powered lines.

"Let's see if we can get this computer online," Matthias said.

Corporal Scotts quickly moved over to the computer console and picked up an overturned chair and sat down in it. "Give it a go, Corporal," said the trooper behind the console as he stood up. "The main power line is live."

Scotts nodded and flipped a switch underneath the console monitor. A few seconds later, the console terminal and a large overhead monitor hanging from the ceiling powered on.

"OK, we are in business," Scotts said as he removed his helmet and placed it on the floor. Matthias watched over his shoulder as Scott's fingers flew over the keyboard. Matthias opened his face shield and looked around the room. The dim light was sufficient to reveal one exit at the other end of the room.

"They must have cut the power from another location," Scotts said. "This is basically a security terminal. I can pull up a layout of the facility, but the encryption is too strong. I can't do much more without more time" As he typed, lines of data scrolled vertically down the monitors. Seconds later, a long corridor with three rooms branching out took shape on one of the overhead monitors. Matthias and Scotts looked up in unison. Two rooms were labeled "Genetics," and the last room, which was the largest, was labeled "Testing."

"That's good enough. Hopefully whatever they were working on is on the other side of those doors." Matthias stroked his grey beard. "Is there enough power to open the doors?"

Scotts looked back at the dusty console monitor. He banged away at the keyboard for a few minutes before shaking his head. "They are manually locked from the other side." He looked up and met Matthias's gaze. "Looks like we cut," he said.

The enemy hastily assembled defensive positions out of desks, lockers, and whatever they could scavenge. A barricade in the main corridor was manned by a skeleton crew of lightly armed security personnel and scientists still wearing their white lab coats. Seeing the overhead lights suddenly come to life, the defenders knew time was short.

"When those blast doors are forced," a smartly dressed security officer shouted to his troops, "pour everything you have into them. Take no quarter; none will be given to you. We must give as much time as possible to the doctor so he can evacuate." The officer fingered the scar that ran down the left side of his face.

"If it is our time to die," the officer continued calmly, "let us take as many as we can with us." He stepped behind a large metal beam and withdrew a large, high-caliber pistol from its shoulder holster. He could see the marks from a cutting torch on the blast doors as they slowly were cut open. After a few moments, the circular cut section of the blast door heaved and groaned, crashing to the ground with a deafening roar.

"Cover!" the scarred officer yelled. Two stun grenades bounced off of the first barricade and detonated, causing a brilliant white flash that temporarily blinded and disoriented the forward-most defenders.

"Open fire!"

The first three-man team through the entrance was cut down by a hail of concentrated gunfire that quickly found weak spots in their armor. The second and third teams, along with Sergeant Matthias, took up kneeling positions and returned fire. Dozens of green corkscrewing energy waves exited the troopers' EMR rifles and hit the front barricade with devastating results. The ancient electro-metallic projectiles penetrated the hasty barricade with ease, along with the bodies of a few of the unfortunate defenders, and continued down the corridor with devastating results. Red mist and body parts showered and coated the metallic walls, creating a macabre work of art. At the end of the corridor, the scarred officer pulled himself up to a sitting position. He looked down and saw that his right arm was gone, blown off by one of those accursed rifles. He spat blood and fingered the hand cannon in his left hand. He could see troopers filling the corridor. He feigned death as a trooper cautiously approached. A few moments later he felt a hard kick to his ribs.

Thinking the defender was dead, the trooper began to search the body for intel. He was too slow to detect the hand cannon suddenly pointed under his chin. The scarred officer sneered as he pulled the trigger. An explosive projectile blew the trooper's head into dozens of fragments and wet mush. The headless body sank to its knees before falling directly on top of the scarred officer. With what strength he had remaining, he managed to push the corpse off and to his side. When he looked up, he was staring into the cut down barrel of an old slug thrower held one-handed by its owner. The trooper opened the face shield of his helmet, looking his quarry directly in the eye. The scarred officer broke a thin smile upon seeing the grey-haired veteran trooper.

"I am ready," the scarred officer whispered.

"The war is over for you," Matthias whispered back as he pulled the trigger. The slug thrower kicked hard, and the impact of the slug splattered the wall with brain and skull matter.

"Colonel, we have movement!" A lone trooper said over the tactical net main channel as he stood next to another trooper fidgeting nervously, his finger on the trigger of his EMR. The portable hand scanner gave multiple readings. The jungle swayed back and forth in front of them, yet no breeze could felt by the trooper. Both troopers walked backward together slowly toward the comforting hull of the drop ship.

The colonel yelled back over the net, "What do you mean, 'movement'?" He was trying to follow Matthias's breach into the next corridor, and his trooper was making it difficult by breaking into the main net channel. "Enemy personnel?" he yelled again, slightly irritated. His troopers lacked battle experience, and he didn't need them panicking at the first sign of the unexpected.

"I-I don't know sir. The scanner is reading all over the place!" Static followed the transmission.

"Sergeant, Calm down!" the colonel said. "Give me a proper report. Are you under attack?" The colonel stood by the entrance to the bunker. Looking down the entranceway, he could see overhead lights starting to flicker on and off. The remaining platoon had created a thin perimeter around the LZ. The colonel tried again to get Kortez to respond, but all he got was static.

"Damn this place!" the colonel yelled to no one in particular as he raised his face shield. "Captain!"

"Yes, sir!" Captain Cruwell ran back from just inside the bunker entrance, raising his face shield as he acknowledged the colonel.

“Take your platoon in once Matthias has the next wing secured. I’m going to take some troopers back with me and check out the LZ. Our rear perimeter might be breached.”

“Sir, I can go and secure the area—” He was cut off abruptly by the sound of automatic fire from both the left and right side of the LZ perimeter.

“Negative.” The colonel grabbed his battle sword from its magnetic sheath on his back. The sword hummed with energy in his gauntleted hand. “I’ll take care of it. Keep the assault fluid, Captain. You’re in charge until I get back.” Slamming his face shield closed, he motioned at two nearby troopers who ran to his side. “Spread out, stay within sight,” he said to them grimly. Both troopers brought their rifles up to eye level and followed the colonel back toward the LZ.

The colonel rarely felt afraid anymore; years of war had made him indifferent to death. Eventually, he surmised, when it was your time ... it was your time. As he led his two troopers into the strange jungle and toward the LZ, he felt a chill run down his spine. He sensed he was being watched by unseen eyes.

The scorched clearing of the LZ was just up ahead. It seemed easier going back, as if the jungle was letting them through. The firing that the colonel had heard earlier had stopped. He had left 3rd platoon under the command of Sergeant Kortez to secure a perimeter around the LZ. Kortez was a good trooper, and the colonel was hoping it was a glitch in the helmet comms. He couldn’t see any of his troopers around the drop pod. Another call to Kortez on the main tac channel went unanswered.

“Sir, lookout! 3’oclock!” The trooper on the right fired a quick succession of bursts from his EMR. The corkscrewing projectiles made a whooshing sound as they exited the barrel. The colonel saw, at the right edge of the LZ, one of his 3rd platoon troopers being dragged off by a strange beast covered in yellow quills. Dropping the limp body, the beast vanished into the jungle before the colonel could get a better look. The troopers gave pursuit before stopping at the edge of the jungle.

Cautiously making their way around the drop pod, the colonel and the other trooper came upon a dismembered trooper lying in a pool of crimson. The trooper’s head was missing. The three fanned out and completed the sweep of the LZ perimeter. They found three more headless corpses.

"Whatever hit them hit them hard and fast," the colonel said. He frowned; the light was getting worse as the sun began to set. "We need to get back to the bunker before nightfall."

One of the troopers standing at the edge of the LZ yelled out, his voice filled with panic. The colonel watched with awe as a ten-foot-tall purple plant with long red thorns around the stalk swayed close and spat a white viscous glob out of a large yellow orifice. More plants moved up and spat in unison, filling the air with a hissing sound like a viper snake. Within seconds, the trooper was covered head to toe in a milky white substance. He ceased his struggle and lay on the ground paralyzed. Roots and vines reached out and took hold of his body, dragging it into the jungle. The other trooper began firing wildly into the oncoming mass of purple and green. After expending his ammunition, he dropped his rifle and tried in vain to get inside the drop pod, banging on the closed ramp. The plants caught him quickly, covering him in white fluid. Within seconds, his paralyzed body vanished into the oncoming jungle.

All around, the colonel could see the LZ shrinking right before his eyes as the jungle slowly retook the scorched earth. As he watched in awe, the only thought that crossed his mind was that he would not die in battle, but become food for a bunch of mutant plants.

Matthias looked intensely at four prisoners, dressed in white lab coats, standing with their hands on the scorched wall. Four troopers efficiently frisked them.

"They were hiding in the med lab," one of the troopers said to Matthias. "Apparently they did not participate in the two-way range, sir. They were not armed."

Matthias rested his slug thrower over his shoulder, the barrel pointed at the ceiling. "What is this place?" he asked. None of the prisoners spoke, each one staring at the ground. Matthias walked through the first open door to his right off of the main corridor. A sign above the door read "Genetics Laboratory." The room was much larger than indicated on the map. The walls were lined with computers and various medical apparatus. Some of the equipment had been smashed, although the damage was negligible. Microscopes and other devices Matthias could not identify lay on metal tables. The tables surrounded six large, clear rectangular tanks that lay in a straight line in the middle of the lab.

"Scotts! Get in here!" Matthias yelled.

Scotts rushed in sans helmet. "Corridor is secure, sarge. The next door down opens into another genetics lab further to the left. There is one more door down on the right that's locked."

"OK. I am going back topside to get the colonel down here. He is not answering. See what you can make of this place. I'd like to have some kind of an answer before I return."

"Roger that, sarge," Scotts said.

"Damn radios!" Matthias yelled as he exited the bunker. He was surprised that it was dusk already. 2nd platoon still covered the entrance to the bunker. Matthias didn't see Cruwell anywhere in sight.

"Where is the captain?" Matthias asked the nearest trooper. He stiffened up, bringing his rifle to port arms.

"Sergeant, the captain went back to the LZ," the trooper replied rather stiffly.

"At ease, troop. He went by himself?"

"Yes, sergeant. There was gunfire, and he said couldn't get the colonel on the net."

Now Matthias was furious. The colonel had left on his own without telling him. Even worse, an inexperienced officer took off alone after him. He had been with the colonel through countless battles, and he would be damned if he would lose him now.

"I need five volunteers," Matthias said. Five troopers immediately stepped forward. "The rest of you maintain your position here. If I am not back with the colonel, you will report to Corporal Scotts." The remaining troopers nodded in unison.

Matthias broke into a run toward the LZ, with the five troopers hot on his heels. He could have sworn the jungle was alive, the strange plants widening the path, letting him and troopers proceed with ease.

The colonel was covered from head to toe in what he could only guess was purple blood. Several vines had snaked toward him, trying to wrap themselves around his ankles. But he was faster, slicing the vines, causing the plants to retreat. He slowly made a small circle, looking in all directions, his sword humming steadily in both hands.

The colonel saw a fleeting shadow move at the edge of the jungle before feeling two small impacts on his shoulder. Looking down, he saw two thorn-like objects embedded in his armor. *No doubt poisonous*, he thought. He looked up, and in an instant two beasts descended upon him with fury from within the confines of the jungle. Never had he seen such creatures. Standing almost seven feet tall, they were humanoid in appearance, but that's where the similarities stopped. A thick layer of yellow quills covered their heavily muscled, hairless bodies. Their heads were elongated, and as they hissed, rows of razor sharp teeth dripped saliva.

The first one jumped almost ten feet from a standstill, hurling itself at the colonel. It swiped at him with two long clawed hands. The colonel deftly sidestepped as the beast flew past. As it turned around, the colonel's massive blade stuck home, slicing the beast in half at the torso. The upper body slid to the ground; the legs remained standing for a few seconds longer before following suit.

The colonel spun around as fast as he could, but it wasn't enough. The remaining beast flew into him full force, knocking him backward against the hull of the drop ship. His helmet was knocked off his head, and his sword flew out of his grasp. As he lay on the ground stunned, he looked at the beast as it moved closer. He noticed tattered remains of what looked like military fatigues around its waist, its muscled body long having ripped them apart.

The beast now seemed to smile at him, as if it knew it had captured its quarry. The colonel regained his feet, but the beast launched a powerful right hand strike, hitting the colonel square in the jaw and sending him right back onto the ground. He slowly steadied himself against the hull of the drop ship, wiping a thin trickle of blood from his lip with his hand. The colonel waited for the next attack, but it did not come.

The beast shrieked out in pain as the colonel saw several green energy trails pierce its body in several places. Captain Cruwell stormed forward, blazing away, driving the beast into the ground, its limbs and torso evaporating into red mist. It finally ceased its cries and died. The colonel walked over to his sword and picked it up.

"I owe you one," the colonel said as he stared at the corpse.

"Don't worry about it. We should get back though. This place is starting to get on my nerves."

The captain helped steady the colonel, and as they began to make their way toward the bunker when they heard the jungle hissing in front of them. They could sense something big was moving toward them, and fast.

"You have got to be kidding me," the colonel said. He readied his sword, and the captain dropped to one knee, inserting a fresh magazine into his EMR.

After a few tense moments, they both relaxed, seeing Matthias and several troopers burst through the jungle. Matthias walked up to the colonel and said flatly, "You pull a stunt like that again, wandering off on your own, and I'll kill you myself."

CHAPTER 5

Colonel Chuikova, followed by Sergeant Matthias and Captain Cruwell, proceeded into the bunker. The remaining troopers took refuge inside the bunker entrance.

The trio approached Corporal Scotts, who waited in front of the door opening to the level's genetics lab. He ran his hand through his shoulder-length black hair, now slick with sweat, pushing it off of his face.

"What have you found out, Corporal?" the colonel asked.

Corporal Scott's cleared his throat. "This appears to be a genetics research laboratory. The enemy was working on a number of projects in here." Scotts raised his arm, motioning for the trio to enter the lab. As they entered, he followed close behind. The tech troopers inside immediately came to attention.

"At ease. Carry on," the colonel said immediately.

Scotts walked towards the center of the large room, standing in between two large tanks.

"These tanks are quite interesting," Scotts said, as he pointed to them. A tech trooper arose from his kneeling position behind the far tank, located at the back of the lab. He held a large held scanner and was busy analyzing a green puddle of liquid on the floor. Three more troopers surrounded him, each using handheld analyzers to make a concentrated sweep of the lab. Large metal cases were opened on the floor, revealing various scanning equipment and portable computers. The colonel immediately strode over, his black- booted feet avoiding as many of the green liquid puddles as possible.

"What is it?" the colonel inquired, peering into the nearest tank, trying to see if there was anything still inside the tank.

"This tank contains some sort of organic liquid," the tech trooper said. "Its composition cannot be deciphered with our equipment here; however, I have analyzed some of these large objects in the tanks and in some of the puddles in the floor."

The colonel looked down on the once-sanitized red tiled floor and noticed chunks of what appeared to be human flesh. Each chunk was in or near a puddle. He noticed that the puddles seem to be on a path that started near the largest tank, by the technician. The puddles led out of the laboratory to the main corridor, where they stopped.

"This is also of interest, sir." The tech trooper was examining a long table equipped with several microscopes. He pointed to some small, misshapen chunks laid out on metal trays. "These are all brain tissue samples, and all are in some sort of regenerative stage."

"Get to the point," the colonel said as he walked over to the table to take a look, his curiosity now piqued.

The tech trooper continued. "You can see that some of the samples are inactive, but some—." He pointed to several that were hooked up to various machines via wires and electrodes. "Well, some seem to be active."

"Active?" The colonel now listened raptly.

"Yes. Perhaps they were working on some form on neurogenesis: in other words, the reanimation of dead brain tissue. We have a limited capability to regenerate damaged, living tissue, but dead tissue—this is revolutionary."

"I want all of this prepped for movement. It goes with us."

Captain Cruwell followed the trail of puddles into the corridor. His excited voice made everyone turn toward a side door, left ajar. "There's a footprint here!" he shouted. He ran back inside the laboratory elated at his discovery. "It's barefoot, not one of ours," he continued.

"A footprint? What?" the colonel replied confused.

Scotts and Matthias hurriedly made their way to the footprint and examined the tank again more closely.

"Colonel, these are indeed pieces of flesh. And here we have a handprint on this tank." He indicated the side of the tank closest to the large puddle. "That evidence leads me to believe that there was a life-form in the tank," Scotts said matter-of-factly.

"Perhaps they have some new healing technology?" the colonel said absently, more to himself than anyone else, as he stroked his stubbled chin.

The colonel walked purposefully over to lab coated prisoners sitting on the floor under armed guard. "What were you working on here? Tell Me!" said the colonel.

The prisoner looked up in the colonel's face and uttered, "Go to Hell. We will never tell you anything."

The colonel grabbed the prisoner by the throat and lifted him off the floor with one hand. The prisoner kicked his feet wildly and grasped the colonel's gauntleted hands, trying in vain to free himself. The colonel squeezed with all of his might, crushing the man's larynx, and lowered him slowly so that his feet again touched the floor. Within moments, the body went limp, and the colonel released his grasp. After wiping a bead of sweat from his face, the colonel turned to Cruwell and said, "Captain, secure the rest of this complex. The faster the better, but be thorough. We need to find out what they were doing here." The colonel turned to the other prisoners, briefly contemplating another interrogation, but quickly lost interest. "And make sure these prisoners get topside. We will let the Auger-Seers pry what they will from their brains."

"Yes, Colonel, understood." Cruwell turned toward Sergeant Matthias and pointed to the three prisoners now sitting on the floor, with their hands bound behind their backs. "Take them up topside to the drop pod and prepare them for interrogation once we get into space. Start loading as much as can from the genetic labs also. See to it yourself."

"Consider it done." Sergeant Matthias motioned for the trooper guarding the prisoners to get them on their feet. He addressed the prisoners, looking them each in the eye. "I would suggest you cooperate. We have some rather terrifying methods to extract what we want." The prisoners said nothing as Sergeant Matthias and the lone trooper escorted them to the surface.

Cruwell turned to the remaining troopers still in the laboratory, who were busy collecting samples from the tanks and removing lab equipment, tissue samples, memory drives, and main boards from the smashed computers.

"Careful with those samples," he instructed. Cruwell did an abrupt about-face and strode out of the laboratory. Back out in the corridor, the captain walked up to Scotts and the colonel who were trying to manipulate the controls to open the sealed door. The sign above the corridor read "Testing".

Scott's was turning a large spanner set in the door, forcing it open slowly inch by inch. The door finally groaned open fully, the interior pitch black. Scott's fished out a hand held torch from his assault vest and switched it on. What it revealed made him gasp. The room was nothing more than a metal walled rectangle, half the size of the genetics labs. Stacked in a large pile on the right side were at least twenty to thirty corpses wearing nothing but their underwear. From what Scott's could see, each had a single bullet hole in the forehead.

Feeling nauseous, he stepped back and grabbed the far wall for support. The colonel stepped into the room and a second later a dim light illuminated the grisly scene. In addition to the pile of bodies, four bodies in various stages of dissection laid still on gurneys. While the genetics lab was relatively clean and orderly, this room had blood splatters on the wall. The air held the stench of death. Scott's and Cruwell entered cautiously. Scott's spied a video camera mounted on a tripod against the far wall, pointed at the corpse pile.

Scotts rewound the tape, the hit play. "Sir, you should see this," he said. Scott's backed up the video and hit play again as the colonel and Cruwell peered over his shoulder. There was no sound, but the image was clear. An underwear clad male stood in front of a smaller corpse pile, his arms at his side. An older looking technician produced a small pistol and fired, hitting him between the eyes. As soon as the body hit the floor, two lab technicians quickly picked him up and placed him on the gurney. After strapping the arms and legs down, they backed off. The older technician proceeded to inject a large syringe filled with a pink liquid into the body on the gurney. Within seconds it began to thrash and strain against its bonds. The video stopped abruptly.

"I don't have any words for this," the colonel said as his voice trailed off.

Eventually, the transport cart emerged into a vast cavern, carved from within the plateau itself and leading deep underground. Hundreds of rectangular storage containers were stacked along the walls; in addition, the cavern held construction equipment planned for use in the expansion of the base, which now was not very likely to occur. An open double door at the far end of cavern was manned by a squad of six heavily armed security officers. As the transport carts came to a halt, the elderly scientist got out, and the security leader approached him.

The pale, slime-coated figure had ceased its screaming, and it appeared it was no longer losing chunks of its fragile flesh. The figure was approximately six feet, four inches in height and appeared to weigh a bit more than two hundred pounds. The hairless body lacked visible reproductive organs. Numerous incisions across the chest cavity and the head had been stitched up, evidence of recent surgery. The facial features were unmistakably that of a human male. Chunks of flesh that had fallen off seemed to be regenerating, but in the commotion, no one noticed. Solid black eyes squinted at the bright lights in the cavern.

"Your shuttle is ready, Dr. Keitel. The pilots are already on board," the security leader said in a quiet tone, so the others could not overhear.

"Of course, I understand," Dr. Keitel replied. "I must go, do what you can to defend the base. I thought out here in fringe space we would have enough time, but I see I was wrong. No one must get out. Understand?" Dr. Keitel spoke rapidly, anxious to depart. The scientist got back into the transport cart, putting it in motion approaching a set of double doors.

Beyond the double doors, a long tunnel led upward to the surface, in a small clearing in the jungle. In the middle of the clearing sat a small, sleek silver craft capable of pulse-speed travel. The craft was camouflaged to be nearly invisible from the air.

Dr. Keitel supervised the loading of the hairless figure as it was helped inside by two technicians. Dr. Keitel noticed that he appeared to be moving mostly under its own power, with a minimal need for assistance, something he thought it would not be capable of this early. So far, this specimen had responded well to the solution and procedure. Dead tissue had been regenerated effectively. Most important was the brain. Most of the internal organs had been replaced with simpler, synthetic versions, the brain was the original. Parts of the body not deemed necessary were removed, such as the genitals. The two technicians came back out of the ship after getting the specimen inside. Dr. Keitel walked up behind them and brandished a small caliber pistol from within his white lab coat. He raised the pistol. Before either technician could react, Dr. Keitel shot them both with a pair of well-placed shots in the back of each one's head, fired less two seconds apart. They died instantly. Another transport cart suddenly emerged from the depths of the complex, stopping just inside the entrance to the cavern. Dr.

Keitel's young assistant saw the technicians' bodies fall to the ground and cried out, "What are you doing?"

Dr. Keitel spun around, aiming his pistol at his assistant. "What is the meaning of this?" the young assistant cried out once more.

Dr. Keitel approached his assistant. "I am very sorry and deeply saddened by this, Seth, but I have no choice. We must protect our research, whatever the cost. This is much bigger than you or I could have imagined, and this solution we have now is the key." Dr. Keitel now stood in front of the cart. He looked dispassionately at Seth, and fired a single shot which impacted him between the eyes. The body slumped forward against the dashboard of the cart. Dr. Keitel walked away, toward the shuttle. As he entered the shuttle, he took one last look at the bodies of the slain technicians. He closed the door to the shuttle. The engines began a slow, steady whine as the pilot increased power for liftoff.

"I am so sorry," Dr. Keitel said to himself as the shuttle lifted off into space. He shook his head slowly, a genuine look of sadness on his face.

"OK, let's get this thing out of here," he said to the pilots. His seat was behind those of the pilot and copilot. He gingerly lowered a black case from his lap to the floor between his feet. He opened it slowly, revealing a dozen vials of his precious solution, packed tightly together. Smiling, he closed the lid and stowed the box under his seat. He looked out and window. Already the complex looked like a tiny speck on the desert planet's surface.

The craft hurtled toward the relative safety of space. The hairless figure was seated in the rear of the craft. No special attempts had been made by the technicians to restrain it when it was led on board; only the life belt on the seat was utilized. Still, it managed to hold itself upright and steady against the motions of the shuttle.

The figure began to become cognizant of its surroundings. It observed the occupants of the front of the craft with keen interest as the craft rapidly gained altitude. It stored the data bombarding its senses, and it began to think of how to survive. It thought about quenching its ever-growing thirst. It could smell the flesh of the other three shuttle occupants. It vaguely recalled a time when it was a killer of men, firing weapons of flame, much like the scene it had just witnessed.

CHAPTER 6

"Has Lord Sabis transmitted a progress report?" The question penetrated the Auger-Seer's mind. His master did not use his voice to speak; he no longer had a need for it. The Auger-Seer was deep underground beneath his temple in a giant rocky chamber, monitoring half a dozen Auger-Lords who were connected permanently to the consciousness of the ancient master. They were arranged in a circular pattern around a mist-filled globe on cobweb encrusted grav-beds hovering five feet off the ground. They constantly muttered and murmured incoherent thoughts their minds received from other Auger-Lords on the planet above and other locations throughout space. The Auger-Seers job was to make sense of these utterances and keep the master informed. The ancient master felt the fatigue of his years and had lost the energy to keep tabs on his minions long ago.

"Lord Sabis has confirmed that the doctor succeeded in completing his regenerative solution—"

"*My* solution. He completed only the human factor," the master's thought interjected.

"Of course, my master," the Auger-Seer spoke aloud. Although he had been gifted certain powers of the mind, he was not yet capable of projecting his thoughts. "There is a complication. The doctor is escaping with his research. Admiral Raus was unable to stop him from leaving."

"He will not escape in totality," the master replied telepathically. "I underestimated the doctor, but it will work out in our favor. Soon he will arrive on a new world, and we can continue our expansion with our own legions, devoid of the humans above. The visions are become clearer. You must instruct Lord Sabis to compel Raus to go after the doctor."

"Of course, my master. There is one more thing—the contingency plan in case Raus never made to the facility. The mercenary force I hired is approaching and they will carry out their orders."

"That is of no longer of any consequence. They arrived too late. Inform Lord Sabis that *The Emperor's Fist* is not to leave until that research facility is razed to the ground. I do not want any survivors, lest some remnant of the research survive and fall into unintended hands."

"Of course, my master." The telepathic link was severed. The Auger-Seer placed the palm of his gloved hand on the globe surrounded by the Auger-Lords. He shuddered briefly at the grotesque sight of them. Once vital beings, they were now just withered husks. Tubes snaked from where their eye sockets and mouths used to be, connected to the base of the globe that occasionally emitted a blast of steam.

A pulse of energy surged through him as the consciousness connected to him. He issued his commands, which were translated into psychoenergy and boosted across space to Lord Sabis, one of the six Auger-Lords who were similarly connected to the consciousness on board Admiral Raus's flagship.

His commands were simple: "Destroy all ground forces and structures, and pursue the doctor."

"We have a problem, colonel." Static slightly obscured Matthias's voice as it came over the tactical net.

"What is it, Matthias?" The colonel stood outside the complex, having just observed a small craft take off into space from within the forest. Its vapor trail remained visible as it streaked into the upper atmosphere.

"Our sniper team at the base of the plateau reports a small armored column heading this direction from across the desert."

The colonel pondered this information as he stroked his chin. "What? Can you identify the force?"

After a brief pause, Matthias responded, "No sir. We cannot positively identify the column."

"Interesting," mused the colonel. "It seems another player may be seeking our prize. Very well. Recall all elements to Level One. If Captain Cruwell is ready, prep for liftoff."

The colonel walked to the edge of the plateau, where he opened his helmet's visor. Producing a set of binoculars, he scanned the area and soon spotted the approaching armored column.

"Matthias," he said into his wrist communicator, contact Raus and see if he can track that craft that took off from the forest."

"Understood."

"Let's get that door down!" Captain Cruwell yelled to his cutting team, which had nearly cut through the blast doors. "We're running out of time! And watch your fire; stick to your zones!"

He watched as light appeared in small holes which formed into jagged cracks in the door. The team leader signaled to the others, and they put aside their torches. They put their shoulders into the door and pushed with all their might. With a loud boom, the cut out section of the blast doors fell to the ground with a deafening roar. The cutting team was shot down in seconds as a hail of small arms fire hit the assault force. At Cruwell's signal, the rest of the team rushed forward and entered the vast cavern. They took positions behind any pieces of cover they could find. Cruwell could make out only five or six defenders, but they were doing a good job of keeping his element at bay. The defenders had a belt-fed projectile machine gun and were putting up a lot of fire.

Cruwell could not get all of his force inside. "We don't have time for this," he grumbled. He moved around the rock of the cavern wall that provided his cover and brandished two frag grenades. Without hesitation, he charged toward the gun crew and threw both grenades perfectly at the stack of crates they used for cover. He rolled behind an earth mover fitted with a giant drill bit just as the grenades detonated. The blast destroyed the crate barricade and the machine gun, dazing the defenders. Before they could regain their composure, the assault element rushed them, gunning down the first defender who tried to stand up.

As they realized that their primary defense was out of commission, the small contingent of defenders dropped their weapons and raised their hands, resigning themselves to be prisoners of war rather than facing certain death in battle. Cruwell emerged from behind the earth mover determined to get answers.

"Where is the exit here?" he demanded of the nearest prisoners.

Hearing nothing he said, "I'll ask one more time." Cruwell slung his rifle over his shoulder and withdrew his pistol from its holster. He switched it on, and it emitted its characteristic low whine. Still, there was no answer.

Cruwell aimed the pistol at the nearest prisoner and fired. The man's head exploded in a flash from the subatomic projectile, sending skull fragments and brain matter in a wide arc and onto some of his fellow prisoners. Cruwell stiffened briefly, in shock at what he had just done, executing a prisoner with no hesitation. After a few seconds, he snapped out of his trance.

"That blast door behind us leads to the surface," a wavering voice spoke from the end of the line of prisoners. "But you will never catch them; they have an escape craft outside."

"Thank you," Cruwell said. He activated his wrist communicator. "Colonel, this is Cruwell. We have a situation down here."

The static broke and the colonel's voice came through. "Get your ass topside and prepare to repel an attack."

"Colonel, a shuttle may have escaped," Cruwell said in earnest, trying to get his attention.

The static broke over the net again. "I know. Admiral Raus is tracking it. We have a bigger problem right now and I need every swinging dick topside. An armored reactionary force is on its way. We don't have much time." The transmission ended. Cruwell turned to his men without hesitation. "Let's go, topside!"

"You did well, Sebastian," the colonel said to Cruwell as he continued to scan with his binoculars. The armored column definitely was getting closer, each vehicle leaving a plume of dust behind it. "The pod is being loaded with prisoners and salvaged equipment. I don't want this mission to be a total waste. Fleet should be tracking the escaped craft. We still have more equipment to go; this ground force may reach us first."

Troopers formed a single file carrying various items from the genetics laboratory to the drop pod. Cruwell saw the drop pod was emitting steam and gasses from side vents as it was being prepped for liftoff. The trail through the jungle had widened considerably, almost as if the jungle had given up.

An explosion near the bunker complex entrance sent earth and shrapnel flying into the air. The lead tank from the approaching column had opened fire from its main gun. "Get that pod airborne!" the colonel yelled. Cruwell rushed down the trail to the drop pod and ran up the ramp into the pod, trying to get the pilots attention. His helmet comms were not audible since the pod was powering up. Due to the captured equipment and prisoners, space was at a premium inside the drop pod. Troopers quickly took their assigned seats and strapped themselves down. *If one of the tanks scored a lucky hit that would be far worse than a stranded infantry platoon.* Within seconds, the drop pods' engines were at optimum power. The pilot took Cruwell's incessant yelling as the signal to lift off. The pilot hit the brake release, allowing the two-story behemoth to raise, the ramp closing as it did.

"You idiot!" Cruwell yelled as strapped in troopers looked at him with curiosity. "The colonel is still down there!" He ran to the lift which was inside a center vertical tube that went straight up to the flight deck. The lift stopped and he emerged on the flight deck. Two pilots sat at the controls, strapped in. The drop pod was beginning to rattle and shake as it began to reach the upper atmosphere. The blue sky began to give way to the unforgiving reaches of space. One of the pilots looked over his shoulder and saw Cruwell standing there, his fists clenched into balls.

"Sir, you better strap in! It's going to get rough!" The pilot yelled as the noise began to get louder.

"Take this thing back down! You left colonel and some troopers down there!"

"I can't sir! The take off sequence can't be aborted. We will have to send a shuttle down once we dock on the flagship!"

By now Cruwell could barely stand, the gravitational forces working to squash him into the deck plating. He pulled out a jump seat that was stowed into the wall and sat down. He quickly strapped himself in and looked with awe through the flight deck window into space. He hoped he knew what the colonel was doing down there.

The colonel glanced up at the sky and saw the drop pod streaking for the atmosphere. He took one last look around and ordered his men into the jungle, ahead of the advancing column.

"Get your asses in the jungle, men! They will return!" As he shouted the order, several more explosions erupted all over the plateau as all three of the approaching tanks began to fire. *At least I hope they will return.*

"A sizable element is approaching ahead of us," the trooper reported to the colonel as he retreated up the rocky path from the desert, back to the jungle. "Three medium tanks in a wedge formation, plus armored personnel carriers. That incoming seems random, not aimed. I don't think they have spotted us, sir."

The colonel again looked down the plateau that his men currently occupied. Incoming rounds from the tanks still rained down indiscriminately; however, his men were now in the cover of the jungle. Luckily the plants seemed not to care and he hadn't seen any more beast men since his personal encounter a while back. The aggressors evidently saw no need for surprise. They didn't seem to be aware they were heading for a fight rather than blasting at defenseless troops. To the colonel's left, smoke began to pour out of the research laboratory's breached main doors. Through enhanced mode on his visor display, the colonel observed the reactionary force getting closer and closer. He could not yet determine who the attackers were; there were no military markings displayed anywhere. At the rear of the small armored column, he spotted three armored personnel carriers in dogged pursuit of the tanks, their dark gray armor contrasted with the dull brown of the desert.

"I thought you two made it out," the colonel said without looking at Scotts and Matthias. "It may be a while before we are evaced," the colonel noted. It was less a warning and more the colonel stating the obvious. "Raus might be getting some company up there, and he may have to leave. We will fall back into the jungle if we have to. Their armor won't be able to follow us inside."

"This is news we could have used yesterday, but for what it's worth, the captured technicians said the forest is a by-product of research on reanimation of dead plant tissues through genetic reconstruction. They started on plants first, then men. Hence your beast man that took a swing at you," Scotts said.

"I gave myself quite a chuckle." The colonel smiled sarcastically and resumed his vigilant observation of the approaching force. "I was almost eaten by a mutated flower."

As the colonel was about to turn away from the edge of the plateau to enter the jungle where his men waited, he noticed that the armored column had come to a grinding halt just shy of the plateau's base, throwing up a huge cloud of dust. The tanks had assumed a single file formation, facing the narrow road leading up to the bunker complex.

Curious. Who else wants the contents of this facility? He also wondered why there was no air response. The path from the desert was basically a rocky, rubble-strewn trail up the side of the plateau, wide enough to accommodate the medium tanks single file, but the gray beasts chose not to advance. Hatches flew open, and the faint outlines of the tank commanders could be seen conversing and pointing up at the plateau and to some of the boulders on the trail. The pursuing APC's caught up to their tanks and armed personnel began to dismount from the lowered ramps at the rear. The mechanized infantry then began to take up positions at the base of the road.

"This is very interesting," the colonel said as he raised his face shield. A com trooper running up to him interrupted his thoughts. "Sir, Admiral Raus is on the hook." The com trooper removed a handheld receiver connected to a radio transmitter he carried on his back, the large whip antennae quivering in the wind. The helmet tactical net was unable to reach into space. The colonel took off his helmet and grabbed the receiver.

"Go ahead, Admiral."

"Colonel, your drop pod is on its way here, yet Captain Cruwell informs me you are not board. Am I missing something here?"

"We got split up and that damned pod lifted off without me a few troopers. We will need an evac."

"The Auger-Lord on my ship wants me to leave orbit as soon as the drop pod is recovered. I can stall for a bit, but I cannot guarantee I can get an evac down there. Our scanners are tracking an unidentified craft that is prepping to enter pulse space. The Auger-Lord has indicated to me that this in now priority. Pulse capable craft of that small size are exceedingly rare nowadays. Also of interest is another small craft heading for the planet's surface. We are letting it go. Perhaps you can use it to get off that rock if all else fails. Whatever is going to happen is going to happen soon I think."

"I understand Admiral. Hopefully time will be on our side." The colonel handed the receiver back to the com trooper. "Sergeant!" he bellowed out.

"Yes?" Matthias ran over hurriedly, holding his helmet in his left hand.

"I wonder who else is interested in the contents of this research facility. A shuttle is also approaching our position." the colonel said. "Gather weapons and ammunition. We are going to set up an ambush and attack."

The orders didn't need to be repeated. Matthias nodded and left, then began issuing orders to the few troopers that remained. The battle wasn't over quite yet.

CHAPTER 7

The colonel stood with Corporal Scotts at his side. The colonel clutched his helmet under one arm while pointing with the other hand to the ambush spots that had been established. Sergeant Matthias directed the final placement of a short-range plasma cannon that had been retrieved from the interior of the burned out tomb that was once the research facility bunker. The cannon, with its three-man crew, covered the trail.

Matthias walked to the edge of the plateau and took up a well-concealed position behind a large boulder that still afforded a good look down at the approaching force. He propped his EMR against the boulder beside him and removed his helmet. Rivulets of sweat streamed down his face, with the hot, dry air working hard to evaporate them. The prospect of another intense action didn't set well with him, but it seemed they stood a fair chance of victory with the advantage of surprise and position.

"A small infantry force, perhaps three to four squads, is approaching from the road," Matthias spoke into his wrist communicator to the colonel. "No armor support. The tanks appear to be hanging back at the base of the road, maybe for another bombardment. I deployed our remaining sniper team with the heavy weapons crews at the trail's edge. The heavy weapons crews will be in effective range momentarily."

"Understood," the colonel replied. "Have the sniper team prepared to cover a retreat into the forest if this blows up in our face."

"Yes sir." Matthias changed the frequency on his wrist communicator and issued the orders to the sniper team leader. By now, the salvaged heavy plasma cannon was set up in a well-concealed position overlooking the road. The crew was busy loading the weapon and stabilizing it on the rocky terrain. Surrounding the weapon were two dug-in squads, each trooper armed with salvaged frag and thermite grenades from the bunker. Spare ammunition magazines and power cells were strewn in front of the hastily dug emplacements within arm's reach. The remaining squad of five troopers accompanied the colonel. They all held back near the bunker entrance, to be used as reserves.

"Matthias," the colonel said to the sergeant at his side, "your men will remain behind the firing line. Replace any man who falls and ensure that the plasma cannon does not run out of power cells."

The colonel scanned across his defensive placements with satisfaction, his helmet enhancing points of interest for him. Satisfied that he was in a tenable position, he charged his EMR, and joined Cruwell at the edge of the forest with the sniper team.

The elderly commander surveyed his mercenary soldiers with contempt and pity, from the hatch of the lead tank. Unlike their commander, most of the soldiers were devoid of feelings of honor and simply plied their skills in service of the highest bidder. The commander detested soldiers who sold out to corporations, but then again who was he kidding? He was a hypocrite, selling himself out years ago lured by the high paychecks. He had seen his share of glorious combat, winning some battles but losing most. He wore a bright yellow scarf around his neck and proudly displayed his rusting military medals on his chest, an absurd gesture to most of the mercs, who didn't care much about medals. Everyone who lived to fight the next battle received monetary compensation, and that was enough for them. The tradition of the armies they had long served had been lost. The commander was tired, as were most men in this war, but he held onto the flair and passions that had brought him to battle and had, thus far, kept him sane. He knew only how to fight, not how he could possibly assimilate back into society after his commission had expired.

The mercs were in poor spirits, having been forced to ride in the cramped confines of armored personnel carriers across the desert without opportunity for rest in nearly two days. They'd seen almost nothing of the planet's surface since being dropped there; they had gone straight from the drop zone into the personnel carriers. Secrecy of the objective had to be maintained, or so they were told by their mysterious client. As the story went, their commander had been approached in the dark, back room of a bar on some forgotten outpost in fringe space with an offer he could not refuse: payment up front, plus equipment, to assemble and run a team. All the team had to do was recover some sensitive items from some whacked out scientists on a fringe planet.

The objective was in a known pirate sector, but most of the mercs hadn't operated there before. The war didn't venture out this far and there was no need to worry about a government presence. Fringe space was filled with war deserters from both sides, trying to make a living working as mercs or pirates. Criminal gangs also operated with impunity in that no man's land of space. The few commercial ore miners who risked operating in the area invested heavily on private security and sold their cargos to the highest bidder, whether that was a military force or a criminal gang.

The mission had begun almost the moment the forces arrived on the planet's surface; they immediately received orders to move out to specified coordinates. That much of the mission was known. Barely an hour after they reached the destination, they received new orders to secure a bunker complex and await further instructions.

The mercs were as grateful for the fresh air as for the end to the constant jarring inside the personnel carriers. Their commander had received information that the bunker complex had come under full-scale assault from another unknown force but was now abandoned. News of the assault was accurate, but the assumption that the complex was abandoned would prove to be fatal.

The client was unable to spare any transport aircraft, and the forces were pushed hard the entire way, without adequate reinforcements or supplies. With only three tanks and a small contingent of mercs, the element had to assume that resupply would come from salvaging materials from the complex itself. Upon arriving at the base of the plateau, the mercs had been given orders to proceed ahead of the armor and march up the trail to the complex. The commander almost laughed out loud when he thought about the location of the complex. "A facility located in a forest on a desert planet? That's not very secret." A spiral of acrid smoke billowed high above the plateau, carrying a rancid odor. As a show of force, the lead tank fired a few high explosive rounds at the bunker for effect.

"Sir, what are your orders for the assault?" A young, bearded merc asked the commander, who was leaning out of his tank. The young merc sported an odd, mismatched kit and an impeccably clean uniform. The commander had locked his sights on the rocky outcropping, knowing that now would be the perfect time for an ambush against his forces; however, the road up to the plateau curved, making it impossible to see any further. Across the distance, he could barely see the edge of the forest; it seemed like a solid wall of green. The commander dismounted from his tank with a youthful grace, and dusted off his ancient uniform as soon as his feet hit the ground. He never took his eyes from the target.

"Take your company ahead and establish a perimeter around the bunker. The client does not want us to enter the bunker. They are sending a specialist team that should arrive soon."

"I don't like this," the young merc said. "It's too quiet. It doesn't make sense. And there's that damn forest: a forest shouldn't be here, in this desert climate. At least let me bring up a tank or an APC for support." The young merc watched nervously as the armored vehicles arranged in a single file before shutting off their engines. The tank crews already were exiting their hatches and finding relatively cool spots to drink precious water and open rations.

The commander turned and faced the young merc. "Relax. I am sure the bunker is either lightly defended or not at all defended. Either way, secure the perimeter and let your men rest. I am sure they will thank you for it. Anyway, I prefer not to send armor up the trail. It doesn't look too passable for vehicles."

"OK, it's your show." The young merc sighed heavily and walked to the front of the formation, now almost halfway up the trail. The rest of the mercs still had their weapons slung over their soldiers. Many were chewing slag root, an herbal opiate that grows wild in the desert. Many pushed up their shirt sleeves, revealing a multitude of skull tattoos and other markings on their arms, typical for galaxian mercs from their sector.

"Wait for my command!" The colonel barely whispered the order, yet in the tense silence, it was heard without difficulty.

The approaching infantry column now could be seen from the complex. The area hummed with the quiet sound of energy weapons being charged. Matthias observed that the opposing force apparently thought the bunker abandoned. They approached without caution, an infantry column in full view of the defensive line.

The colonel's steady voice crackled over all the helmet radios. "Open fire!"

The intense initial volley immediately cut down the lead soldiers of the infantry column. Masses of flesh and uniforms were melded together from the intense energy released upon them. The soldiers who were following stood in place, as if in utter disbelief of what was occurring. Some soon tried to run back down the road but were mercilessly cut down. The colonel's sniper element picked off the rear infantry at will. Within minutes, the approaching force had been eliminated without having fired a shot.

"We are under attack! We are falling back!" The panicked shout of the young merc into his helmet mike was almost drowned out by the screams of the dying and soon to be dead.

"You will advance your position until properly relieved," the commander ordered "It is probably only a rear guard. You are to charge in force." The commander issued the order from the base of the plateau. The scowl on his face showed more annoyance than displeasure with the news. By now, all of the infantry had been committed unwillingly into the fray. The commander could hear the firing and a few explosions, but he wasn't overly concerned. Suddenly, silence overtook him. The hair on the back of his neck stood up and from experience he knew something wasn't right. Rapidly approaching storm clouds partially blocked the remnants of daylight, as did acrid smoke that smelled of burned flesh.

"Michaels, report." The commander tried again on his handheld radio. "Michaels, I say again, report." He heard nothing from the infantry leader. He looked at the tank commander, who avoided his gaze, fearing that he would be forced to take his vehicles up the questionable path, to face an unknown force. His assembled crew had begun to remount their vehicles. "This could be bad," the tank commander muttered.

"Forward!" The commander ordered, as he jumped inside an APC behind the lead tank. The driver of the lead tank looked back at the commander apprehensively for a second before closing the hatch. The armored column consisted of three medium tanks and three armored personnel carriers. Retreat meant nonpayment by the client, and they all knew it, so retreat was not an option. The commander rode exposed in the turret of his APC, waving his arm forward for the remaining APC's and tanks to follow. Halfway up, the lead tank encountered the first smoking remains of the infantry. Thermite and plasma grenades dropped from above the road, along the plateau's ridge line, had done their jobs well. Fewer than a dozen of the mercs were left. The ones who remained all crouched behind a large, blackened boulder. Michaels stood up and stared at the commander, with his silly-looking yellow scarf and medals, as his APC rumbled past, the driver maneuvering carefully so as not to go over the side. The dead were pulverized beneath the tracks of the armored vehicles.

"The lead tank is approaching," the colonel said into his helmet mike. "Wait for my command." The colonel watched the lead tank approaching slowly, its progress impeded both by the dead and by the large rocks on the narrow trail. Calmly, he raised his arm. He was now positioned with the plasma cannon crew, one hand resting on the gunner's shoulder. When the lead tank and the first APC were in full view, he noticed a curious figure in the APC, wearing a yellow scarf and stoically pointing forward with his outstretched arm, as if he was leading a cavalry charge from the old days.

The colonel dropped his raised arm, signaling the gunner. The pulse cannon erupted in a massive energy discharge. The lead tank took a direct hit and stopped in its tracks, its frontal armor melted. The driver's hatch flew open, and a smoking figure, partially on fire, tried to escape the inferno inside the tank. He fell in a hail of fire from the entrenched troopers. The snipers under Cruwell's command fired and eliminated the curious figure protruding out of the top of the APC. The colonel almost wished they hadn't done that; interrogating the apparent leader could have been informative. The two other tanks tried to disengage, but there was nowhere to go. They succumbed to several well-thrown thermite grenades. The remaining APC's met a similar fate.

That ended the battle; all that remained was to take prisoners. Cruwell emerged from his concealed position, and the colonel came forward. He motioned for the reserve squad to come forward as well.

"Sergeant, find me a prisoner." Matthias and his squad quickly proceeded down the road in tactical two by two formation, covered by the snipers and the entrenched troopers. The colonel's forces had not suffered a single casualty, and he began to think of alternate plans of aggression. Perhaps there was a supply base or garrison nearby.

Matthias had no sooner rounded the bend in the road when he encountered a group of three badly mauled men, their hands raised in surrender. Their mismatched uniforms were almost grafted to their bodies from the intense heat caused by the grenades, which had burned or melted the fabric as well as the soldiers' skin. A fourth man, appearing almost unscathed, stepped in front of the others. He was weaponless, and his hands were raised. He addressed Sergeant Matthias.

"I am Michaels. We surrender and demand treatment according to the articles of war." Michaels fully expected to be shot on the spot, as was usual when mercs were captured. Sergeant Matthias gave Michaels the once over and, apparently satisfied, motioned for two of his troopers to come forward. "Search them for intel," Matthias said as he looked Michaels directly in the eyes. "Were you in charge of this attack?"

Michaels looked around before pointing to the figure slumped over the open hatch of the knocked-out APC. "No, he was," Michaels said as he stared at the ground. "I tried to warn them ..." His mumbling voice trailed off. Matthias's troopers surrounded the ragtag bunch and searched them for intelligence, going through their pockets and gear before leading them up the road. Two of the mercs needed assistance, unable to walk on their own. Two troopers removed the dead commander's body from the turret hatch and laid it on the ground. A single large bloodstained hole gaped open on his chest, and a thin trail of blood leaked from the corner of his mouth. A few pieces of brain were also on his shirt, perhaps his own or perhaps someone else's. A large part of his head was gone, thanks to another sniper round. His eyes had grayed over and stared into nothingness. Matthias knelt beside the corpse and fingered the tarnished medals, noticing that many of them were very old. The bright yellow scarf was now soaked with blood.

"The war is over for you now," Matthias muttered. He closed the eyes of the commander for the last time. After many years and many battles, the lines and creases that marked what was left of his face finally showed peace.

CHAPTER 8

The colonel sat behind a plain metal desk in a featureless room that had been hastily cleared out for use as a command post inside the bunker complex. "Was this the only attacking force we can expect?" he asked of the prisoner seated across the desk from him.

Michaels sipped water from a metal cup. One of the troopers guarding the door offer him a synthetic cigarette; Michaels pushed it away politely with his hand. He took another sip from his cup of water before responding to the question.

"No. We were given orders only to secure the bunker perimeter, not to go inside. The client told us that a special force would come by nightfall and secure the complex."

The colonel leaned in closer, with Matthias standing to his right. "Who hired you? How many will this force consist of?"

"I don't know. Only the commander had contact with the client. We were assembled only a week ago before convoying here. The reaction force likely will be another merc force; a small one, most likely, given the objective and the expected resistance. They will arrive by air. With the scarcity of aircraft and personnel in this sector, it can't be that large."

The colonel leaned back in his folding metal chair; apparently satisfied with the answers. He lit a black cigar he had liberated from the dead commander's body. The smoke gave off a peculiar odor, reminiscent of sweaty socks. "Indeed. This is getting more interesting." He turned to Matthias. "I want a report from Scotts on how much combat equipment we can salvage. We have a few hours before sundown. I want an accurate report on food, ammunition, and water," he said as Captain Cruwell saluted and exited the room.

Michaels looked at the colonel with a hint of recognition, perhaps from some long-ago campaign, or perhaps only from a photo reproduction. Michaels had read many a battle report in which this legendary officer had come away victorious under seemingly overwhelming odds. Some had even speculated that he was a creation of the enemy's propaganda machine, created to instill fear. His eyes narrowed, focusing more intently on the colonel, trying to place him, and with more curiosity. "Were you present on Alsace Sigma? That was my first platoon command when I served in the cluster militia. The regiment was routed even though we had superior numbers and equipment."

The colonel smiled and sat back, slightly amused. "I was there. Your commanders made many foolish decisions. It was easy to anticipate their movements."

"How did you escape the pincer envelopment? Your forces from your previous counterattack were stretched very thin. We thought we had you for sure." Michaels questioned the colonel much as an eager student might question a respected professor.

The two men conversed about military history and strategies as the preparations were made outside, becoming more urgent as darkness took hold outside.

"What do we have, Corporal?" Matthias asked Scotts, who was supervising his troopers at the end of a corridor as they brought equipment and supplies up from within the bunker. They had tried their best to clear a path down the hallways; however, blood and brains remained splattered on the walls and floor, and the occasional small body part had been missed by the cleanup crews. The bodies had been cleared and placed in adjacent rooms.

Matthias turned to address his superior. "Sarge, we have seventeen thermite and six frag grenades. We have six power packs remaining for the plasma cannon. Food and water are sufficient; this bunker was adequately stocked probably for at least the next three months. The troopers have one to two cells left for their EMR's, and maybe one magazine each."

"We will make do with what we have," Matthias said.

The defensive lines were reoccupied and the troopers re- suited in full armor. The drop pod LZ was nearly overgrown with vegetation, leaving no evidence it was used earlier. The knocked out mercenary vehicles on the trail leading up to the plateau might give away the trap, but Matthias determined that it was worth the risk. Michaels stated that his group of mercenaries had been ordered to observe strict radio silence, so that the new force may not have been alerted. This almost seemed to be too easy.

Matthias roamed among his troopers in the defensive line around the perimeter of the bunker. As darkness descended, the sergeant and his men found themselves frequently looking into the dense forest, trying to identify strange sounds from within it. The distant approach of engines could be heard getting louder and louder as the ship approached. It appeared that Michaels had been honest, and an attack force was approaching. He confirmed a delta shaped shuttle craft descending from the clouds visually. Matthias dared not use his radio for fear of interception. He grabbed a trooper next to him and sent him into the bunker to report to the colonel.

"Tell the colonel we have a space craft approaching. It is too far away to tell the class. ETA possibly five to ten minutes." The trooper hurried inside the bunker, where he ran headlong into the colonel and Scotts. Seeing the two apparently in important conversation, he didn't speak right away.

Corporal Scotts monitored the approaching craft. The colonel was behind him, staring intently at the data displayed on the overhead monitor. "What am I looking at Corporal?"

"Sir, I am downloading the bunkers' transmissions from the last 72 hours. Anyone they were in contact with, we will know and maybe we can find out who sent in the merc force.

"Good work," the colonel said. Seeing the trooper standing in the doorway of the bunker he asked, "What is it troop?"

"Shuttle approaching sir!" the trooper said.

The colonel turned to Scotts and said, "Have our captured merc meet them outside. Hopefully we can take this shuttle without firing a shot.

Scotts nodded in agreement. He exited the security room and walked back towards the genetics lab. The surviving remnants of the mercenary force were sitting against the wall under the watchful eye of a lone trooper.

Scotts spotted Michaels kneeling down, tending to his wounded comrades. Michaels stood up, straightened his uniform, and looked at Scotts as he approached.

"I don't think you are telling us everything about your contract," Scotts stated matter-of-factly. "I think you know more about this bunker than you are letting on."

"What I told your colonel is the truth." Michaels looked Scotts directly in the eye as he spoke. "I will say one thing. When the client approached the commander and me with the contract, I had heard other firms turned him down. It was rumored the man was an Auger-Seer from Hellenheim."

"An Auger-Seer? That is absurd," replied Scotts.

"Is it? When was the last time you were in fringe space? Your Auger-Seers are everywhere, working out their own plans as they see fit." Michaels sat down on the concrete floor, his back against the wall. "Anyway, I just said it was a rumor. It was a large contract, one that could set us up for awhile. We didn't question who he worked for."

The colonel had been listening for the past few minutes. "Whatever was on that shuttle wasn't meant to be found by us," he said.

Scotts and the colonel locked eyes briefly, both of them thinking the same thought. Maybe it was en route to the highest bidder, whoever that may be.

The colonel and the Scotts both headed to the surface, with Michaels and the lone trooper trailing them. Matthias met them just inside the door of the bunker. Matthias nudged Michaels towards the LZ with the barrel of his slug thrower as four troopers followed closely behind. Michaels looked up and waved to the approaching craft as if everything was just fine

"I see the ground forces, preparing to set down." The pilot began the landing sequence, and within minutes, the craft had touched down, throwing up a huge cloud of sand and burnt vegetation. Michaels stood alone in front of the lead craft, shielding his eyes from the debris with one hand.

After the pilots shut off the engines, Michaels dropped his arm. The ramp to the rear of the craft opened. The craft's pilot and copilot were followed by a twelve-man security squad, armed with submachine guns.

Four scientific personnel wearing white overalls followed them out. The squad leader approached Michaels with a puzzled look on his face.

"Are those your casualties on the road? Where is the rest of your unit?" Michaels casually eyed the squad leader. "I am the last of my unit. I implore you to drop your weapons. You are surrounded."

The squad leader looked around, bewildered as he noticed heavily armed troopers aiming the rifles at them. He quickly realized the situation and unslung his submachine gun placing it on the ground, then motioned for his squad to follow suit.

"Wise move." Michaels said.

"The shuttle is secure," Matthias said. All the personnel that had exited were kneeling on the ground with their hands up. The rest of the troopers from the perimeter had made it to the LZ.

"Sergeant," the colonel ordered, "prepare for an immediate evac. No sense on waiting for Raus to give us a ride."

The colonel approached Michaels, who leaned against the hull of the shuttle, two troopers guarding him. The colonel relit the stub of his strange-smelling cigar.

"I cannot take you with me. You and your wounded comrades are on your own." He gestured to the security squad from the shuttle, "They will accompany us for interrogation." Michaels nodded, straightened out his uniform, and smartly saluted the colonel. "There are enough provisions for you to hold out for some time."

"Yes sir. It has been an honor and a privilege."

The colonel returned the salute. "Good luck to you." The colonel walked to the rear of the last shuttle. All of the troopers had loaded up, Scotts was behind the controls with Matthias in the co-pilots seat even though he had no clue what he was doing.

With one last look at the bunker, the colonel climbed the shuttle's ramp and disappeared inside, the ramp closing after him.

Michaels, from the safety of the bunker entrance, watched the shuttle turn into a tiny speck in the atmosphere, marveling that he was still alive. He made a promise to himself that if he ever made it home, he would quit the merc life and open a bar on some remote planet.

CHAPTER 9

"This is Colonel Chuikova's commandeered shuttle requesting landing clearance," Scotts said into his headset. He watched as the rendezvous coordinates came up on the computer screen almost immediately.

As the shuttle began its approach to Admiral Raus's flagship ship, the colonel emerged from the cargo hold.

"We have you in our grid," Scotts heard the reply in his headset. "We will take care of the rest. Welcome back and please relay to the colonel his presence is wanted upon the bridge upon arrival." Scotts surrendered control as the craft headed toward the flagship.

The colonel made his way to the bridge of the flagship. *The Emperor's Fist* was the last of the massive battle dreadnaughts that once were used to quell planetary uprisings. At one time, the ship and its weaponry could turn rogue planets into lifeless rocks. Now, the war necessitated that the pride of the fleet act as little more than a troopship. Many of the original laser cannon batteries had been removed and redeployed for defensive positions on Hellenheim. Multiple missile launchers now constituted most of the ship's offensive firepower. Nonetheless, *The Emperor's Fist* remained a symbol of pride for the navy.

When the colonel reached the bridge, he received an enthusiastic greeting from the dreadnaught's aging commanding admiral. Captain Cruwell stood behind the admiral and came to attention. The small, slightly stooped, white-haired admiral removed a monocle from his left eye and grasped the colonel's gloved hand in his. The men contrasted each other sharply. The admiral appeared more like a professor than the most powerful and successful naval commander of the United Consortium of Planets.

"Please, gentlemen, let's retire to my quarters," the admiral suggested. He indicated a door opening from the side of the massive bridge. The colonel put his hand on the captain's shoulder.

"Relax, captain. You got the bulk of the men and equipment out. You did well." Cruwell relaxed a little, letting out a deep breath. He wasn't sure how the colonel would react knowing he was almost left stranded.

The three men walked past two marine guards posted outside and entered. Artifacts gathered throughout the admiral's extensive military campaigns filled the space. The captain took a keen interest in several items, including a large collection of exotic swords.

The admiral took a seat in a large leather chair behind a cluttered black desk. He produced a box of cigars and opened the lid, offering the contents to his guests. The colonel immediately removed one from the box and put it in his breast pocket. The captain nodded politely and took one.

"Gentlemen, sit down." Each of them took a comfortable chair in front of the desk. "I speak on behalf of Marshal Von Jesonik. He is very pleased at the success of your mission."

The colonel nodded, secretly relieved. The marshal wasn't in league with the Auger-Lords. His gaze stuck on a strange piece of ancient art behind the desk, depicting a crucified woman being burned alive by a large mob.

The admiral turned to the data terminal on his desk and activated it. "The marshal has sent your next orders via secure transmission. I will play it for you. I will make sure you get a hot meal and that your equipment is loaded on your shuttle." The captain opened his mouth to speak, but instead the admiral started playing the transmission, cutting him off. Projecting from the terminal was a holographic image of Von Jesonik sitting behind his oak desk.

"Greetings, Johann. Your mission is going well. Time is now critical. Admiral Raus has informed me that the escaping shuttle is being tracked, and he has locked onto its pulse signature. The next phase of the mission will have you pursue the shuttle and bring back its crew and whatever was taken from the facility. We must have it. Assemble your team. The admiral will brief you on the rest."

The hologram disappeared. The colonel appeared to be deep in thought but made no comment. Cruwell, however, was about to burst at the seams.

"Pursue where, exactly? Further into fringe space?" Cruwell addressed Raus directly, rising out of his chair. The colonel reached over and pulled him back into his seat.

"It is not your place to question, Sebastian, only to follow orders," The Colonel said unperturbed. "Please continue, Admiral."

Raus seemed unfazed by the captain's outburst as well. He continued, "You will select a squad of your best men. You will track the shuttle and recover the weapon. If it is human or an alien, you should capture it alive. If you end up on an inhabited planet, it is important that you remain undetected; however, you need to assess the planet's defenses in case we are running into another enemy-held planet. As such you will leave the shuttle in orbit behind a chameleon field and utilize the transmit disks. Your ship is ready. We didn't have time to test the pulse drive, but the Auger-Seers onboard confirmed that it will work. Once the escaping shuttle comes out of the pulse beam, the Auger-Lords should be able to pinpoint a destination point; however, our technicians have discovered that the signatures deteriorate rapidly. You must get ready to depart immediately, or the pulse drive will be useless."

Admiral Raus leaned closer and whispered, "The Auger-Lords are excited. I have never see so much chattering around that globe of theirs. I fear that if you fail, we are all done for."

"Understood," the colonel replied. His heart sank. This new mission was fully supported by the Auger-Lords. What was their involvement? "Admiral, this shuttle has a pulse drive, a chameleon field generator, *and* we are to use transmit disks? I am quite frankly unsure we will survive. Pulse drives and chameleon field generators were prone to overheating and destroying entire starships. They haven't been used in years. Don't even get me started on those transmit disks." The colonel's confidence in the mission seemed to disappear in a split second.

"Your concerns are duly noted, colonel. However, I have been assured that you have nothing to fear. Just focus on your mission. The technology is sound," the admiral said reassuringly.

"Very well. Is there anything else you can tell us about our mission, Admiral? I hate going into situations blind, especially when ancient technology is involved, going to an unknown destination." The colonel smiled, looking at Cruwell. The captain knew as well the orders came from the Auger-Lords, and not the marshal. The mere fact they were being given the use of a pulse capable craft and ordered to go into unknown space indicated perhaps the Auger-Lords witnessed some prophetic vision through their sightless eyes.

"I can tell you that what my technicians have analyzed from what was recovered from the planet's surface has the home planet extremely eager for your success."

The colonel rose out of his seat, pulling Cruwell up with him. "OK. I will pick my team, and we will make ourselves ready as quickly as possible."

"I have taken the liberty of informing Sergeant Matthias and Corporal Scotts to begin prepping the shuttle," Admiral Raus said. "That corporal of your is a pretty resourceful troop, his piloting skills are quite useful. My technicians informed me he checked out on the shuttle with no problem. I could use a good pilot if you want to leave him behind."

"I am afraid I need every capable man, admiral," the colonel said as he looked over at Cruwell. "We will do our best, admiral."

The colonel and the captain saluted Admiral Raus, who saluted back. He turned his attention to the data terminal, leaving his two guests to show themselves out. The marines posted at the door escorted them to the hanger bay where their ship awaited them.

As the men headed toward the hangar bays, Cruwell asked, "Who else are you selecting for the squad?"

The colonel responded in a steady tone. "The craft is not big enough to hold a complete squad and equipment. I must select most qualified for the mission, of course: myself, Matthias, Scotts, and you, if you wish, even though it appears that you pick and choose which orders to follow."

Without breaking stride, Cruwell replied, "Yes, that would be a good team, and I would be honored." The two exchanged no further conversation as they entered the cavernous hangar bay. The small, stubby shuttle that they were to use was parked amid stacks of equipment and a team of about a dozen technicians. They saw Sergeant Matthias loading small crates inside the shuttle, and Corporal Scotts working on a small piece of equipment. Scotts had a big grin on his face as he studied a pair of circular disks, each with a small box attached to them. Matthias saw the corporal's grin and punched him hard in the shoulder, nearly knocking him over. Matthias turned in time to see the colonel and Cruwell approaching. He immediately came to attention, as did Scotts, trying to conceal a small grimace on his face from the pain of the sergeant's punch.

"At ease," the colonel told them. "How are the preparations going? Are we almost ready?" The colonel surveyed the busy technicians and rested his gaze on Matthias and Scotts.

Matthias replied, "Yes sir. We are almost ready. The crew had the shuttle prepped before we arrived, just finishing loading the rest of the gear now. Where we headed?" The colonel strode over to the shuttle, climbed inside for a quick look, and quickly stepped back out.

"Wherever that escaping shuttle leads us. Those are our orders." He looked at Scotts, who had resumed his examination of the disks. "Corporal, are you sure think you can fly this antique?"

Scotts looked up and resumed his grin. "Yes, I can. The controls are not much different from the Class II freighters I used to fly. The pulse drive is easy enough to operate. And you will need me to operate these." He indicated the disks he had been studying.

After a brief pause, Cruwell stated impatiently, "Well, go on."

"These are trans-matter disks, another holdover of ancient technology, much like our pulse drives. Very little is known about their construction, I uploaded a sim program from the ship's computer and should be able to operate them with no problem.

Cruwell interjected, "I have heard of those, but they didn't work. Men appeared at the destinations as a giant mess, turned inside out and the like." Scotts set the disks down on the ground and replied, "Yes, I am aware of that history. These, however, are modified with a more stable and constant power source. They were tested just before you arrived and should work. It's not like we have a choice, right?" The corporal chuckled a bit.

"How do we get the disk to the destination without flying the shuttle to it?" the colonel asked, his interest piqued. He had heard little about this technology.

Scotts replied, "First off, the master disk stays in the shuttle, and the other gets projected to the destination on the planet with one lucky volunteer. Once we can determine the coordinates where we want to arrive, the master disk will fold space, allowing us to cross over to the destination in a split second, think of it like taking a step over a line. From there, it's really pretty simple. Once the point man is at the destination, he sets the other disk up to receive the rest of the men. The only drawback is that repeated uses will overheat the unit. It must be used sparingly."

"Sparingly," the colonel repeated. "And what if it overheats?"

Scotts turned to Cruwell with his ever-present grin, relishing his role as purveyor of knowledge about this extraordinary technology. "You get turned inside out, I imagine, and the unit eventually detonates into a small thermonuclear explosion." He began to laugh, but Sergeant Matthias intervened and pushed him roughly into the shuttle.

"Wait a second," Cruwell said seriously. "Why do we need to set up a second disk? Can't we all just go through the master disk together?"

"Well, I wouldn't try it," said Scotts. "And the problem is that you won't be able to get back. You will be stuck at the destination point."

In a dark corner of the hangar bay, a robed Auger-Seer observed the colonel and his men. His observations were quickly converted into thoughts and read by Lord Sabis, who was connected to the consciousness. The master's wishes were, so far, being carried out. The escaping shuttle was a nuisance, but he had it under control. Now it was only a matter of time.

Hours later, after the promised hot meal, the colonel's select team was under way. "Preparing to engage pulse drive," Scotts said, looking at a computer monitor, which showed *The Emperor's Fist* shrinking rapidly in the distance. The shuttle accelerated quickly. Scotts checked and rechecked the core power indicator. According to the computer, the pulsar core was almost at full power, at which it could make the jump. The navigational computer had received the destination coordinates from the flagship's computer just moments before.

Scotts looked over his shoulder at the crowded crew compartment. Much of the cargo was in the crew area because the containment core for the pulse drive took up much of the cargo bay. Most heavy equipment had been removed just prior to departure. The team had only what the colonel expected would be needed. The retrofitted shuttle hummed throughout with the power of harnessed pulsar star particles becoming agitated within the core. The colonel, Matthias, and Cruwell were strapped into their seats, weapons and crates packed in around them.

A voice came back from *The Emperor's Fist.* "Engagement of pulse drive acknowledged. Good luck."

Scotts switched off the communications link and activated the pulse drive, praying that the craft didn't disintegrate right then and there. *The Emperor's Fist* and the surrounding stars blurred behind them as the drive kicked in. An electromagnetic beam fired from the shuttles core, and exited the ship through its external exhaust port. Deep hues of purple and red enveloped the ship as the incredible force of the beam jolted the men into the backs of their seats. The blocks of color turned into thousands of perfect lines projected in front of the shuttle. A monitor began beeping loudly as it displayed characters written in an ancient script. Scotts looked at the display but could not read it; he knew how to run the drive but not all of its details. He had no need to know, and there had been no time for him to learn. He was powerless to affect operation of the drive: either it would work, or it wouldn't. He had been briefed that such a display would occur once the shuttle locked onto the destination, and seeing it provided some comfort to him.

CHAPTER 10

When the stubby shuttle's pulse engines disengaged, Corporal Scotts immediately began the process of tracking the fleeing craft. Its pulse signature led to a blue planet, the third one out from the single sun in the system. Images of the planet that showed on the corporal's monitors indicated that it was fertile and lush in flora, and largely covered with water. The planet also appeared to be heavily populated, with what appeared to be cities dotting the landscape, giving off heat signatures characteristic of urban areas.

The renegade shuttle's pulse signature faded as the ship penetrated the planet's atmosphere, but Scotts was able to track it to the planet's surface. He turned away from the computer terminal, faced the colonel, and said, "Sensor sweep is completed. The computer has identified the location, but with a margin of error."

"What is the margin of error?" the colonel asked as he unbuckled himself from his seat.

"The margin should be small, but it depends on how far we are behind the ship. The sim program indicated that tracking a pulse beam produces a time distortion effect."

"Just spit it out, kid," Sergeant Matthias interrupted, standing up from his seat.

"That shuttle might have an hour head start, or a few days. It's hard to tell."

"No matter," the colonel said. "The data is the best we can get; we'll have to work with it. Get the trans-mat device operational, and we'll set up a base once we pinpoint the craft's planet fall. Matthias will go first.

Leaving the shuttle on automatic controls, Scotts retrieved the two large, black ovoid disks of the trans-mat device from the cargo hold. He set the larger of the two disks in the middle of the steel-grated floor of the hold. He took the smaller one back to the pilot's seat and detached a small handheld computer from its side. He began to punch buttons on it in sequence.

"All set," he indicated a few minutes later.

He set the smaller disk on a shelf next to his seat and keyed a sequence of commands into the ship's computer. The large disk on the floor began to rotate and whine. The top surface of the disk opened outward, spreading like a flower's petals. A brilliant column of purplish light shot from the disk. The light column began to rotate slowly and took a funnel shape. Corporal Scotts replaced the handheld computer on the side of the smaller disk.

"Just step into the funnel," he instructed Matthias. He handed him the smaller disk. "As soon as you arrive, you must set up this disk before the master unit overheats. Activate this switch," he said, indicating a small switch within a black box on the side of the disk. "I've already programmed it; just turn it on."

"I'll see you on the ground," Sergeant Matthias said nervously. As he eyed the column of light, beads of sweat formed on his forehead. He stepped into the funnel of light and immediately vanished. The funnel increased its speed of rotation, and the high-pitched whine from the disk became louder. Scotts watched a monitor for a few seconds, before seeing the uplink message indicating that the slave disk had been activated. "Next man up!" he shouted, to be heard above the whine of the disk.

Cruwell stepped into the swirling light and vanished. "You're next," Scotts yelled to the colonel. "The unit has to cool down, or the shuttle will blow!"

"Roger that! Meet us on the surface as soon as the unit is ready!"

Scotts nodded. The rotating disk and funnel of light now generated a strong breeze inside the shuttle, lifting smaller unsecured objects into the air and spinning them in the air above the disk. The colonel turned and stepped into the funnel of light. Scotts waited a few seconds after the colonel disappeared before disabling the trans-mat device. The disk quickly powered down to a barely audible hum. As its rotation slowed, the wind decreased, and airborne objects crashed to the steel-grated floor. The disk ceased rotating in less than 30 seconds, and Scotts could see a fine trail of smoke emanating from underneath it. He ran a quick diagnostic on the disk and was pleased to see no problems.

"They should be safe," Scotts said quietly. "I can only hope."

CHAPTER 11

"Follow the preset coordinates," Dr. Keitel told the shuttle pilot. He watched the pilot's movements as he stood behind the man's seat. "When we reach our destination, I will send an encrypted communication back to command. It is too risky right now." The pilot nodded and continued to adjust the controls on his computer terminal. Stars appeared as continuous streams of multicolored light as the shuttle traveled through pulse space. Dr. Keitel turned around and walked toward his own seat. He had no desire to send any communication to anyone just yet, but the pilot didn't need to know that.

The doctor gasped as he saw his experiment sitting straight up in his seat, blinking his black eyes rapidly. "What am I?" The figure spoke with difficulty, the words escaping slowly past his pale lips. The figure looked at his hands, which were devoid of fingernails, and began to slowly clench and unclench his fists. Dr. Keitel sat down slowly, confident his experiment wouldn't unlock the seat restraints. He spoke softly, as a mother would speak to a child.

"You are my creation."

The figure looked Dr. Keitel directly in the eyes. "I remember that I was like you before, but I died." He began to access his fragmented memory. Scenes from his past slowly filtered in and out, but it was a difficult process. His past was filled with pain; that much he could make out.

"You were once a soldier." Dr. Keitel paused, considering if he should say more. He continued, "You were killed in battle."

"Yes. I think I remember. War. I remember war."

Dr. Keitel put his hand on the figure's arm. "You are my son now. When you have recovered fully, we will return home and bring about a glorious end to the war. Peace will finally be achieved."

Dr. Keitel suddenly screamed out in pain and rose to his feet as his pale, black-eyed experiment grabbed his hand and squeezed hard.

The pilot turned around. One of them commanded harshly, "We are exiting pulse space. Sit down!"

Dr. Keitel continued to scream in pain until the figure released its grip. His creation spoke angrily, "There will be no peace, only war." He grabbed Dr. Keitel's forearm and pulled him closer. He could sense the fear inside the doctor. He could smell the flesh.

"I can feel myself getting stronger," he said, abruptly changing the subject. He began to strain against the life belt restraints.

The shuttle came out of pulse space in the vicinity of a large planet, mostly blue from the water covering the majority of its surface. "We have arrived, Doctor," one of the pilots announced. "Initiating stealth run and landing sequence." He shouted the last few words to be heard over the engine noise as they reversed thrust.

Dr. Keitel collapsed back into his seat, clutching his sore hand. He faced his undead creation. "There is much for you learn. You have enormous strength and immunity. However, you must learn to control it," he whispered in pain.

"I feel weak now." The figure's head dropped forward.

"You're not fully healed. Your body is a lot different from what it used to be. It is powerful, but exercising that power uses energy."

The copilot turned around to face his passengers. "We are preparing to land. Stand by."

The sleek silver craft penetrated the planet's atmosphere. The pilot and copilot looked with curiosity out the windows as they flew over an obviously populated planet. They cruised low and fast, entering the airspace over a metropolitan area rife with tall metal buildings and numerous roadways. Lights from the buildings provided some illumination, but visibility was low. Rain splashed on the craft's windshield, forcing the pilots to rely on their instruments. Although not entirely invisible, their craft possessed a stealth coating on its airframe that rendered it nearly invisible to most tracking systems, aiding in their secrecy. The copilot pointed to a large tract of land cluttered with debris as the ship continued to slow. "There, that looks good."

"There appears to be a landing gear malfunction," the pilot noted. A red indicator light flashed, and the pilot tried to reset the system.

"It must have been damaged in the pulse," the copilot countered. "Prepare for hard impact."

The pilot nodded and eased the craft downward. Nose first; the shuttle impacted the soft soil with a dull thud, sending mud and debris into the air. The front half of the shuttle buried itself in the soft, muddy ground, leaving the rear section of the craft exposed at sharp angle.

The pilot and copilot undid their seat restraints and carefully got up out of their seats. They had to grab handholds built into the walls of the craft and find footholds because of the steep angle. Fortunately, the equipment brought on board was secured in the rear by a large cargo net, although the load now strained against it.

Dr. Keitel also got up carefully and retrieved a stasis bandage from the first aid kit for his hand. As he applied the bandage, he noticed that his creation was awake. It clumsily undid its harness and fell forward, knocking both pilots off their feet. They both crashed into the main control consoles. Dr. Keitel cursed under his breath. He thought the creature was secure; it must have seen how to open its harness by watching him.

The creature grabbed the stunned pilot by the throat. It savagely bit off a large chunk of flesh, causing the pilot to scream in agony. The copilot grabbed hold of the black-eyed assailant, but it was futile. A pistol report rang out, and the copilot's body jerked, tumbling backward into the main window. The lower portion of the body splayed horizontally across the control console.

Dr. Keitel slowly lowered the pistol he carried in his good hand. He reached for a panel on the wall of the ship and activated the cargo door. When the door slid open, a wisp of damp air entered the craft. The figure savagely broke the pilot's neck and tossed his lifeless body forward in the ship. It landed at the bottom of the control console. The creature's mouth was stained red, and bloody streaks ran down its chin and onto its chest.

"Well done," Dr. Keitel said.

The creature slowly turned to face Dr. Keitel, looking up as the doctor braced himself in the cargo door, planning his exit from the craft.

"We must disguise this craft quickly before we are discovered. Wait here and I will scout out the area." Dr. Keitel surmised quickly that perhaps if he appeared to be cooperating, he wouldn't be threatened. It seemed to work for the moment. The figure said nothing, just staring ahead blankly. Dr.

Keitel returned his pistol to the holster concealed in his waistband. With a little difficultly, he carefully removed retrieved two heavy hardened plastic black cases from the small cargo storage area, being careful not to undo to the cargo net. Both cases came up to his waist and weighed about 100 pounds each. He pushed both cases out of the craft and jumped out himself, landing with a grunt. Fortunately for him, the jump was only a few feet. Looking around, he saw what he appraised to be stacks of crushed metal vehicles and numerous large metal shipping containers. When he looked back at the craft, it seemed to fit in with its surroundings. As long as no one had witnessed the impact, he stood a good chance of avoiding discovery for a while. He figured that the darkness and the light rain lessened the chance of there being a witness.

He made his way inside a long metal container with the word "Hanjin" painted on the side. The inside was empty, and he quickly surmised the container would serve as a good base of operations. He quickly recovered the two black cases he had thrown from the ship and began setting up his new lab. He opened the first case, which contained several syringes filled with a bright pink liquid. Seeing that the syringes had come through undamaged, he closed the case and opened the other one. It revealed several scientific apparatus and a portable computer terminal.

Dr. Keitel hurriedly ran back to the open door of the shuttle. "Wait inside here," he told the creature, who was leaning against one wall. "I will be back after I make an assessment of the area." Dr. Keitel didn't expect a response, and he didn't get one. He closed the shuttle door from the outside, hoping his creation wouldn't try to discover how to get out.

The colonel and his team had transported into a back room of a condemned one-story house. A bent street sign outside read, in faded letters, "Orleans Street," with "3400 block" in smaller characters below that. Plywood boards covered most of the windows, and the yard was filled with trash. A faded orange sticker affixed to the front door read, "Condemned by the Metro Housing Authority: Do Not Enter."

When Sergeant Matthias had materialized inside the rancid dwelling, four occupants had looked up, surprised, from where they sat on the floor, but none of them had moved or put up resistance. He quickly and silently dispatched them with his combat knife. When Colonel Chuikova and

Captain Cruwell arrived, they quickly searched the rest of the house but found no one else present. They stripped the bodies of clothing, and placed them in one of the smaller rooms, and shut the door.

The colonel surmised that the four were vagrants or common criminals, and that they therefore would not be missed. The staging area room was bare, save for a small table and single chair and two filthy, mold-covered mattresses. The room reeked of stale urine and mildew. The team quickly cleared the room of its litter of spoiled food, hypodermic syringes, filthy clothing, and various other bits of trash. They put the clothing in a pile with the clothing they had stripped from the occupants of the house.

More than fifteen minutes had passed since the colonel's arrival. The team members had selected clothing from pile that fit them best, broken open a few of their equipment crates which were sent after them down the trans-mat. They stood and now watched the slowly rotating trans-mat disk.

"Should we wait for Scotts, or should I go back?" Matthias asked the colonel. Matthias knelt down and opened a small panel on the box on the trans-mat disk. He looked inside briefly not quite sure he knew how to activate it.

"It doesn't appear overheated yet," he announced, satisfied as he closed the panel back up.

"Maybe he didn't make it," Cruwell suggested.

No sooner had he spoken than the disk began to rotate more quickly. The top of the disk opened outward, and the purplish light radiated from it once more. The three stepped back, and immediately the unmistakable lanky outline of Corporal Scotts materialized before their eyes. His veins, followed by his muscles, became visible in the swirling light show. The lights finally dissipated, and the corporal collapsed in a sweaty heap onto the ground. Cruwell and Matthias gently raised him to his feet. Scotts put one arm on a wall to support himself.

"We thought you weren't going to make it," the colonel said. He put a hand on Scotts' head. "You look like you are all here."

Scotts turned away and vomited on the wall, sinking to his knees in the process.

"It'll pass," the colonel said. "We all suffered some vertigo. Hell of a way to travel."

Scotts slowly rose to his feet, unsupported. "How long have you been here?" he asked.

"Not long, maybe twenty minutes," the colonel answered. "We were worried about you, but Cruwell said the transmit beams get twisted and pulled apart sometimes, making reassembly take longer. Take off your utility overalls. We have some clothes we acquired from the inhabitants here, so that we'll fit in better." Scotts nodded and reached over, deactivating the trans-mat disk.

The colonel turned and pulled Matthias off to the side. "You and Cruwell need to obtain transportation," he said.

Matthias nodded slowly. He put on a long black trench coat from the pile and drew the collar tight around his neck. He found a side window that was only partially boarded up, pulled another board loose, and exited through the hole.

"Scotts," the colonel said, "monitor the radio frequencies in this area and keep me informed of anything that might resemble our target. Also, keep alert for any unusual power surges. That shuttle might still have power and they may be attempting to liftoff again."

Cruwell said, "I'm going to see if I can track the alien on foot until Matthias can secure transportation. The shuttle's signature terminated around here somewhere, we could get lucky." He had selected tattered jeans, black Chuck Taylors, and a dirty white T-shirt that bore the single word "Relax." He put his hand cannon down the back of his pants and retrieved a small black box from one of the equipment crates. He activated a small switch, and a 3-D holographic image was projected in the middle of the room. The image slowly rotated and gave a display of the immediate area. A strap was attached to the box, allowing him to wear it on his wrist. He grabbed an L. A. Raiders jacket and headed for the window Matthias had used as an exit.

"Happy hunting," Scotts said, managing to crack a smile. He powered on the computer terminal, sat down, and began to adjust frequencies. Within seconds, he was on an active frequency, and traffic could be heard emitting through the speaker.

"Sir, this appears to be a military or civil order channel. I will commence monitoring," Scotts said.

The colonel nodded and watched the captain depart. He loosely replaced the board over the window.

"Corporal, I'm returning to the shuttle to maintain contact with Raus and monitor the shuttle's long-range scanner. This could be just a short stop for our quarry, perhaps for fuel."

Scotts nodded and stood up, and walked back to the trans-mat disk. He activated it, and within moments, the colonel stepped through. After he vanished into the room's musty air, Scotts powered down the disk and sat back down. He quickly unpacked a computer terminal from a crate and set it up on the table.

The rain had increased to a downpour, and water began to leak through several small holes in the ceiling. A loud crash suddenly occurred outside the house, startling Scotts. He could hear several loud voices. He stared at the front door of the house and grabbed his pistol, which was sitting on the table next to him. He aimed its laser sight at the door and powered up the sub-atomic projectiles. The pistol made a slight whine as he hit the activation switch.

I hate this planet already. He stayed frozen, his weapon aimed at the door. After a few minutes, with no further loud noises from the outside, he deactivated his pistol. He quickly resumed his work scanning frequencies.

A few minutes later, he heard a panicked voice on what he had determined as a police frequency. He listened for a moment before contacting Cruwell. "Captain, I have something interesting here."

"Go ahead," Cruwell replied, over a buzz of static.

"I think we may have found our science experiment. I am going to patch the radio communications through to your handset. The transmission is from a policeman."

"Good work."

Cruwell was riding shotgun in a lime green 1990 Ford Mustang that Matthias had found with its keys in the ignition. After a quick familiarization he was now driving. As he listened to the radio broadcast patched through to his wrist box, the holographic 3-D map of the surrounding area also was projected, illuminating the dark confines of the vehicle with a pale green light. The holographic map was able to display other vehicles and pedestrians through a link to the shuttle's sensors, high above in the sky. Humans and other living creatures gave a faint red outline, indicating heat. He heard an excited voice yelling over the radio, "He's not falling! Where's my backup?"

"If they are shooting him and he's not falling," Cruwell said, "that may be our alien.

"Let me give you a fix on the transmission," Scotts said. A moment later, a flashing blue dot appeared within the hologram.

Cruwell saw it and quickly determined the quickest course toward it. He gave Matthias a direction, and the sergeant pressed harder on the car's accelerator, but with little response other than the pedal going all the way to the floor and a slight increase in acceleration. The car appeared to have reached its top speed, and it belched acrid black smoke from its bent tailpipe. A few minutes later, the car was within a block of the source of the radio transmission.

"Go slow," Cruwell said, watching the holographic map intently. "We are here." According to the hologram, the source of the radio calls appeared to be leaning up against a vehicle, and the captain correlated the holographic image with the scene outside the car. "That's him right there, but I don't have any sign of our alien, or whatever it is. We may be too late."

"What do you want me to do?" asked Matthias.

Cruwell withdrew a monocular from a pocket, switched it to night vision, and stared at the policeman through it for a moment. "He is holding a pistol with the slide locked to the rear. I think he is talking on a handheld communication device of some sort." Cruwell put down his monocular and noticed the arrival of several cars with flashing lights on their roofs. The policeman sat down in the car he had been leaning against, with the door open.

"Let's hang back and see where this takes us," he suggested. "It's all we have to go on for now. I'm also interested in taking a look around here when the area clears out."

Matthias parked the Mustang on a side street, behind an overflowing trash dumpster.

"We should get hold of Scotts," he said, "and try to get a sensor sweep of this area from the shuttle. If our quarry landed around here, we should be able to lock onto it."

"I should have thought of that," Cruwell replied. "I'm a little exhausted right now. Make the call, sergeant."

A lone figure wearing a soaked white long sleeved shirt and gray pants was also watching events unfold, from a concealed position down the street. Dr. Keitel hoped his creation had enough sense to flee if these indigenous life forms approached the shuttle. Its sense of self-preservation seemed to be developing faster than he had anticipated.

PART TWO

CHAPTER 12

As Johnny Roman sipped strong, black coffee out of a Styrofoam cup and reading the sports page of the *Morning News*, he found his mind drifting to his promotion to homicide detective. He still could not comprehend how he had made it up the promotion ladder so quickly.

With barely 22 months on the force, he had put in for lateral reassignment to the Southwest Division as a detective based on nothing more than a whim. You won't know if you don't try. That's what his dad told him anyway. Roman scored very well on the aptitude test so was not too surprised to be invited before the interview panel, but notification that he was on the final selection list came as something of a shock. With several homicide detectives on administrative leave pending internal affairs investigations resulting from various civil rights violations and evidence tampering, vacancies needed to be filled. Roman's limited but effective street experience made him a prime candidate. He was also a former Army Ranger and a veteran of the war in Iraq, and he had prior experience as a gun for hire working for the U.S. State Department, which helped his resume. He figured he could bring a fresh outside perspective to a rapidly sinking department. Being awarded the department's Medal of Valor last month hadn't hurt either, or so the newly appointed deputy chief over investigations thought when he had approved Roman for assignment to detective one week ago.

As he waited in a chair outside Detective Captain Martinez's office, he turned his attention back to the sports page. *What the hell is up with the Cowboys, losing 38 to 6 against the Texans*? He took another sip of his coffee.

The door to Captain Martinez's office opened. A short, stocky Hispanic man with gray hair parted to the side and a gray moustache appeared in the doorway. "Are you John Roman?" he asked, seemingly rather annoyed.

"Yes sir," Roman stated as he jumped to his feet, discarding the paper and Styrofoam cup in an overflowing trash bin next to the door that appeared not to have been cleaned in days.

"Get in my office." Martinez retreated back into his office, not waiting for Roman. Roman followed him in.

"Close the door and sit down."

Roman shut the door and sat down. He briefly looked around and saw various plaques and awards on the wall. A couple of photos with the mayor and the recently fired police chief caught his eye.

Martinez sat in an oversized leather chair behind a desk. Roman looked up at Martinez with curiosity as Martinez read from a police personnel folder. He could see that the vertical label had his name on it.

Martinez spoke from behind the folder. "You have an impressive record so far in your short career. I see you have three letters of commendation plus the Medal of Valor for pulling a woman out of a burning car." Martinez closed the folder and dropped it on his desk. He reclined back in the chair and addressed Roman with a look of contempt.

"You made detective. That's real nice. And you are assigned to my homicide unit. That's also very nice. Let me ask you something."

"Yes sir?" Roman replied, unable to even guess at what was about to hit him full on like a freight train.

Martinez rose out of his chair and shouted nearly at the top of his lungs. "What do you think gives you the right to make detective when I have guys on the street busting their ass for 15 years who don't get as much as a 'thank you' for trying? Huh? Answer me that!"

Roman said nothing; he just stared at an old picture of Martinez, apparently taken shortly after he had graduated out of the police academy. That probably was before he had even been born.

Martinez sat back down in his chair and adjusted his solid black necktie. "I guess you wouldn't know the answer to that, now would you? You are assigned to homicide. I can't change that right now. I run a hard-charging unit. You may have heard that. My detectives' records speak for themselves. You stack us up against anybody, and we have more convictions on the books than any other unit, or even department, for that matter." Martinez appeared to relax a little more. He took a pencil from the desktop and twirled it between his fingers.

"You're sorry ass is here because I requested another detective. I have a massive backlog I need to clear. I asked for an experienced officer, and I got you. Your probationary period starts right now. I was Special Forces in 'Nam, so I respect your service with the Rangers, but that's all I respect as of right now. You report to Detective Sergeant Seebolt. You screw up, he reports to me, and I have you back writing speeding tickets or working as a transit cop. You got that?"

"Yes sir," was all Roman could think to reply. He stared the captain right in the eyes, and Martinez looked away immediately. Roman stole a quick glance at his watch and saw that it was only 7:10. *Damn, when can I get out of here?*

Martinez rose out of his chair again and walked around the desk to Roman, a set of keys and an old flip style cellular telephone in one hand.

"These keys are for your ride. It's a take-home, your responsibility. Go to the motor pool to sign for it. Here is your phone. Go draw a radio from supply. How many mags you carry?"

Roman checked his concealed magazine pouch, even though he knew the answer. "Two," he replied.

"You might consider three. They don't take kindly to rookies where you're going to be working." He took notice of Roman's sidearm. "What are you carrying? That's not the department issue Beretta, is it?"

"No," Roman replied. "It's a Glock 19. I'm qualified to carry it." Martinez looked back up into Roman's eyes. "Brush up on your Spanish; it will save your ass." He reached to a spot on the desktop near his phone and picked up a yellow sticky note. He gave Roman the note, which had an address written on it. "Detective Seebolt is already on scene. You're going to assist him with whatever he needs. You have questions, ask him. This job is not for rookies. No one is going to hold your hand. I will be watching you. It's that simple. Now get out of my office. As a matter of fact, I don't want to see you in my squad room at all unless you're writing something up. In homicide, your car is your office." With that, Martinez walked back around the desk and sat down. He picked up the telephone and began dialing. Taking that as a dismissal, Roman got out of his chair and left the office.

"Asshole," Roman muttered to himself. "Special Forces, my ass. Maybe the grass isn't always greener on the other side."

Roman signed the property form for his unmarked black Crown Victoria and other miscellaneous gear. He retrieved a Remington 870 tactical shotgun from the counter along with a box of 00 buckshot and picked up the duffle bag he had brought from his locker. *I get my dream job, and I am assigned to this prick. How much worse can it get?* He hadn't bothered to check out his desk or introduce himself to any other detectives in the squad room. It seemed to him that he was on a one-way ticket back to traffic duty, so what was the point?

Roman went to the garage and found his black Crown Vic parked amongst rows of marked police vehicles covered in dust. Popping the trunk, he tossed the duffle bag inside. He unzipped the bag and retrieved his ballistic vest. He thought about putting it on, but changed his mind and put it back in the bag. He quickly loaded the Remington and put five additional shells in the side saddle holder mounted on the shotgun. He closed the trunk, walked to the driver's side door, and placed the shotgun in the roof rack. He sat behind the wheel, and inserted the key into the ignition. The 4.6-liter V-8 engine roared to life. *OK, here goes my career.* He adjusted the seat, backed out, and exited the garage with red and blue lights flashing.

CHAPTER 13

Yellow tape marked "Police Line—Do Not Cross" blocked off a small area behind a Diamond Shamrock gas station, and two police cruisers were on the scene as Johnny Roman pulled up. One officer was busy keeping a few curious onlookers back, and another, a corporal with bulging biceps exploding out if his shirt sleeves, was writing notes in a pocket-sized notebook as he stood near the body of the apparent victim, which lay at an awkward angle on the pavement. Roman got out of his car and walked up to the corporal.

"Hey, what's up?" he greeted the corporal. I'm Johnny Roman, newly assigned to homicide. I'm supposed to assist for a Detective Seebolt until he gets here." He extended his hand to the corporal, who looked up from his notebook and saw the detective's shield hanging from Roman's neck.

"Seebolt? Right, he radioed in. He's on something else. He said for me to tell you to hang on. The lieutenant is coming over to work this one."

"OK. Tell me what you have. I can help you out until he shows up." Roman looked at the pool of crimson surrounding the corpse.

The corporal sighed heavily. He placed his notebook in a breast pocket and walked over to the body.

"All right." Pointing to the left, he stated, "Dispatch received a 911 call from the gas station owner about a body. He was taking out the trash or some shit. Russo over there was first on scene." The corporal pointed to the other officer, on the perimeter. The corporal continued, "The station owner says it's been real slow all day, and he didn't notice anyone hanging around.

I found one guy who apparently was sleeping back here by the dumpster. So far, he claims he didn't see anything either."

"OK. So the owner says he neither saw nor heard anything?" Roman asked.

"Correct. He stated he just found the body as is. Forensics and the meat wagon have been called. We're just waiting on the lieutenant to show up so I can get my ass back 10-8."

"All right. Thanks, corporal." Roman headed toward Officer Russo, who was taking notes as he interviewed the witness. As Roman approached, Russo detached the mike from his epaulette. "Ryan!" Roman exclaimed as he approached Russo. Russo turned around, surprised, holding his mike in midair.

"Johnny, how's it going?" Russo replied with surprise. Replacing the mike on his epaulette, he offered his hand to Roman, who shook it. "I see you're on homicide, man. That's great! That's got to be a world record. Don't even tell me what you did to get promoted so fast!" Russo laughed rather loudly. By now, more officers had arrived, and they began to widen the perimeter around the crime scene.

"Well, good luck on this one," Russo said rather sarcastically.

"Why do you say that?" Roman replied.

"Well shit, man, you get a murder—or anything else, for that matter—in these parts, and suddenly everyone's is deaf and blind. Nobody sees anything. These people think that if they give a statement, we're going to call immigration. Good luck with this, man, this is a dead end. My business card is as good as toilet paper around here." Russo closed his notebook and returned it to his pocket.

"Well, I have my own problems right now. I have a hard-ass dinosaur captain who wants me out. You got an ID on the deceased?"

Russo looked back toward the body, but before he could say anything, a white Chevrolet Astro coroner van slowly pulled up to the crime scene perimeter. Russo nodded towards the driver.

"Victim is a Hispanic male, early thirties," Russo said after regaining his train of thought. "The funny thing is the nature of the wounds. It looks like an animal bit a chunk out of this guy. Hey, maybe it was a pit bull or something. But that's your job, *Detective,*" Ryan said with a sarcastic grin. "Not quite like our time at the academy, right?

"Did either of you examine the body?" Roman countered, trying to keep the conversation on point.

"No," Russo answered. "Like I said we are just waiting on the lieutenant. We haven't touched anything."

"Well I guess I can take some notes then." Roman walked over to the body and produced a pen and a small notebook out of his jacket pocket. Russo followed him closely.

"Hey man, the lieutenant said not to touch anything."

"Relax, I'll be a few minutes," Roman said slightly agitated.

As he sketched the crime scene, he noticed that the body did indeed appear as if something had bitten or torn a large portion of flesh from the throat area. He fished some white latex gloves out of his back pocket and put them on.

"You guys check to make sure he was dead?" Roman asked as he put two fingers against the carotid artery. No pulse.

"Not my job man. Listen, I'll catch up with you later, I need to log in the arriving units." Roman shrugged as Russo walked back to the perimeter. "We should get a beer sometime and catch up," Russo said over his shoulder as he walked away.

"Sure. Call me," Roman said. He quickly resumed his inspection of the body.

He lifted the man's wallet from where it was lying next to the body. He went through the contents of the wallet and discovered a phone calling card in Spanish and a Mexican Matricula Consular ID card, which many Mexican immigrants in the area carried. He also found a few business cards for landscaping and house painting businesses, but that was all.

"I would say the motive could be robbery," Roman muttered to himself. "He seems to be a working man, doesn't look like a gang banger." He lifted up the man's bloodied T-shirt. "I don't see any tats." He checked his pants pockets, turning them inside out. Nothing.

"Hey, Detective Roman," the corporal at the perimeter called out. Roman looked up.

"Since you're hanging around you should talk to this woman. She says she is the man's wife," the corporal said. She was attempting to enter the crime scene, but the corporal had a strong grip on her arm. Roman walked over and gently laid his hand on the hysterical woman's shoulder.

"All right, let her go," he told the corporal. Turning to the woman, he said, "Cálmate, señorita. Por favor." His request had an unintended effect, as the woman collapsed to her knees on the ground and began to weep. She looked up at Roman and began to speak to him in rapid Spanish.

"What is she saying?" the corporal asked.

"She's speaking too damn fast. Mas despacio, por favor," Roman pleaded. The woman nodded. She wiped tears from her red swollen eyes with her right hand. Roman was able to translate after she resumed speaking, this time much slower.

"She said she was going to buy some milk for their baby just now when she saw him on the ground. I assume they live nearby."

The woman started speaking again. "She says he got paid earlier today from a landscaping gig and he should have a few hundred cash on him," Roman translated.

"Make sure you keep her here until the lieutenant arrives," Roman said. Probably best to get a Spanish speaking officer over to take her statement." Without looking at the corporal, Roman walked over to the coroner's van, now parked. The portly driver got out of the vehicle with some difficulty and addressed Roman.

"How long you going to be?" The driver removed a handkerchief from his back pocket and wiped sweat off his forehead.

Roman answered, "As long as it takes. This crime scene is still being processed. The lead detective hasn't shown up yet, and neither has forensics. You in a hurry or something?"

The driver took a step back and raised his hands in a defensive manner. "OK, Chief, no problem. I have a job to do too, you know."

I am surrounded by assholes today. Roman turned around and surveyed the scene one more time, trying to take in every detail. Sometimes he wondered why he chose this line of work. Seeing death and mayhem on an almost daily basis was probably going to be the norm from now on. He quickly reassured himself as he headed to his car. If it wasn't for people like him, the world would descend into chaos, right? He liked to think so anyway. It helped the day go by a little faster. His stomach rumbled. Roman realized he had been drinking coffee all morning and he was starving.

CHAPTER 14

"Lincoln 78," Roman heard his call signal over the car's radio.

"Go ahead," he replied as he picked up his radio mike. He was in the drive-thru lane at McDonald's. After almost an hour at the murder scene, there wasn't anything left for him to do since Detective Seebolt's whereabouts were currently unknown to him. Seebolt wasn't answering his cell, so some breakfast was definitely in order.

"Lincoln 78," the radio dispatcher responded, "code 27 at the 600 block of Dawson and 128th. Detective Seebolt is requesting assistance."

"10-4," Roman replied. *Shit, another dead body. So much for breakfast.* Roman exited the drive-thru lane while activating the red blue emergency lights on his vehicle. He got on the South Central Expressway and exited a few miles later, at Hickory Street, entering an older residential area. Moments later, he was on scene, pulling his vehicle into a rundown strip mall parking lot. Only two businesses remained in the strip mall, a pawn shop and a Laundromat with the letters written upside down on the sign. Several officers were keeping a small crowd back. Roman parked his vehicle and approached the nearest officer, a burly African American sergeant. "Where is Detective Seebolt?" he asked, while holding up his shield. The sergeant pointed towards two plainclothes detectives conversing with one another.

"All right, thanks." Roman turned and walked toward the two plainclothes officers. As he walked inside the scene, he could see the exposed body behind the Laundromat, near a dumpster overflowing with cardboard boxes.

The detectives stopped talking as he approached. "Sorry to interrupt. Is one of you Detective Seebolt?" he asked.

One of them answered, a man who appeared to be about fifty years old and had the look of a veteran detective, with hard, chiseled features and a neat crop of short gray hair, parted to one side. "You must be Johnny Roman. Good to meet you. Sorry to have you working like this on your first day. I wished I could have gotten you to ride with me, but it's been too damn hectic already. No better way to learn, though." This friendly introduction, coming from a detective who appeared so down-to-business, took Roman completely off guard. Seebolt extended his hand, which Roman shook. His tweed sport coat and wrinkled khakis looked like he had slept in them. Roman noticed that he carried a .357 revolver with a 6-inch barrel instead of a semi-automatic. *Old school.*

"Anything I can do to help, sir?" Roman answered.

"You can help the uniforms get statements. Start with that homeless guy over there," Seebolt said, indicating a disheveled man sitting on the curb. "It seems like there's a pattern developing this morning. We had another body this morning that apparently is similar. Looks like an animal bite or something, although the homeless guy claims it was no animal. He says he saw another man attacking this one. This guy is torn up pretty bad. I just talked with the lieutenant who was at the scene with you. He said the earlier victim is in pretty much the same condition."

"Yeah, the Mexican was bitten or slashed. Is there anything else about this victim that may indicate an animal attack or an assault?" Roman asked.

"Not much," Seebolt replied. "The guy over there states he saw a brief struggle, he tried to intervene, and I'm guessing he scared the suspect off." Seebolt pointed again to the disheveled man sitting on the curb, a slim white male with the tattered white T-shirt of a U.S. Marines Khe Sahn 2/5 Battalion veteran, and he sported a long, gray, unkempt beard. "Anyway, I'd be interested to hear your theories. It's not every day someone gets bitten to death out here, let alone twice in one day. I figure it would be much easier just to shoot or stab someone. Maybe the suspect had a dog or something no one saw."

Roman nodded and walked over to the man sitting on the curb, who now had his head buried in his hands. He was visibly shaken.

"What happened to your friend?" Roman asked, as calmly as possibly. The unkempt man looked up and met Roman's gaze with his own.

"First off, that motherfucker wasn't my friend," he spat.

Roman put up his hands in a defensive posture. "All right, sorry. Did you know the man?"

The homeless man looked away from Roman. "You got a cigarette?"

"Yeah, here." Roman produced a pack of L&M's. The man took one from the freshly opened pack, and Roman offered him a light.

"All right, man," he stated as he took a big drag. "I knew him. We used to be friends, before he stole some shit from me." He looked toward the body. "But that ain't a way for a vet to die; you know what I mean, man?"

"Yeah, I hear you. What did you see?"

The man stood up and took another big drag on the cigarette. "I saw this big motherfucker, looked like he was naked. Wasn't wearing no clothes or nothin', but I didn't see a pecker. The dude was, like, bald everywhere. Looked like he had blood on him, too. They had some words, then the dude just up and bit him or something on the neck. The dude took his clothes. Had these black eyes too. I started yelling at him. He ran off after that."

"All right. What clothes did he take?"

"Dude had a black leather jacket and some busted ass jeans. That's all I seen, man." Roman wrote the description in his notepad. "What direction was he headed in?"

"I don't know, man. I saw that shit going down, but it happened real fast. Next thing I know the guy is gone. Sorry."

"That's OK," Roman replied. He reached into his wallet and removed a business card. "If you think of anything, you call me. Alright?"

"Yeah, sure. Whatever, man." He took the card and sat back down on the curb, taking another drag off of his cigarette.

Roman walked over to the body and did a cursory examination. *Sure as shit, no clothes. Who steals a homeless guy's clothes?* He looked around for Seebolt and spotted him by his car, on his cellular phone. Roman put on a fresh pair of latex gloves he retrieved from his inside jacket pocket and, being careful not to touch the victim, traced an outline with his finger around what appeared to be a large bite mark on the throat. *This is no animal, unless a bear is on the loose in the middle of the city*, Roman thought to himself. *Damn, two cases already. Welcome to the new understaffed homicide.*

"Let us know when you are finished, detective." A short Asian female spoke from behind Roman. She was holding a rather expensive looking camera. Another female behind her carried two pelican cases in either hand.

Their windbreakers both stated "*Forensics*" vertically on both jacket sleeves Roman stood up and moved away from the body. "Don't mind me, do your thing."

Roman was suddenly distracted as his cellular phone started to vibrate in his pants pocket. He turned and walked away, just as the Forensic tech began to take pictures.

"Is this Detective Johnny Roman?" The voice on the other end of the cellular phone asked.

"Yeah, who is this?" Roman replied, as he lit a cigarette. Roman stepped under the yellow police tape and walked towards his car to get some privacy.

"Ok, this is Maynard Fontenot, coroner tech. We met briefly this morning," the reply came over the cellular phone.

"Yeah, ok. What can I help you with? You looking to pick up another body before the crime scene is processed again?" Roman replied with a hint of sarcasm.

"Ok, sorry about that. This is a little serious. I'll get to the point. The body was released to me not long after you left. I transported the deceased to the Coroner's Office. I just started to prepare the body for autopsy for the coroner, nothing out of the ordinary, just logging property and prepping the body." Maynard paused and sneezed hard into the phone, causing Roman to pull it away from his ear.

"Uh, ok right." Maynard resumed, "I think you should come down here. I have something you should check out; maybe it will help you in your case, ok?"

"I am not the lead detective on this one, Doc. You have the wrong guy." Maynard came back on the phone after a brief pause. "I know, but I can't get a hold of anybody else right now. This is serious. Your dispatch patched me through to you."

Roman suddenly seemed invigorated with curiosity and he asked, "Do you think the wounds were caused by an animal?"

"Animal? Possibly. But this is something way above you or me. Just come down here and check it out." Maynard seemed to be getting a little antsy.

"Just tell me on the phone."

"I really think you need to see this. I don't really want to explain this over an unsecured line, ok?" Roman could now detect a bit of panic in Maynard's voice.

"Yeah, ok," Roman replied. "I'll be over as soon as I can." With that, Roman ended the call. He headed towards Seebolt, who was engaged in an apparently heated conversation on his cellular phone. He stood around for a few minutes eyeing for an opening. Seeing Seebolt pause on the phone, he took his opportunity. "Detective, is it ok if I follow up a lead on my own? I want to head down to the Coroner's Office and compare the wound marks of the first vic."

Seebolt put up his hand, and turned to face Roman. He nodded his head in approval and resumed his conversation. Roman ran to his car and got inside. The engine roared to life and he hit the accelerator

When Dr. Keitel left the crash site, he made a simple reconnaissance of the area. His conclusion was that further testing could commence. He had the bulk of his equipment with him in the crashed shuttle, and the surrounding neighborhood was devoid of heavy traffic and curious onlookers. Upon returning to the crash site, he found the shuttle door removed forcibly from the shuttle, lying on the ground. His creation was nowhere to be found. Dr. Keitel worried that he would not be able to survive without his care, even though he had shown learning, strength, and adaptation that he had not anticipated. On the plus side, he could conduct a field study to determine how quickly his creation was able to integrate itself in its new surroundings, as well as test the survivability of his re-engineered body. To do this, however, he must first find his creation, and he must keep it supplied with the necessary regenerative solution.

Dr. Keitel entered the storage container and retrieved two syringes filled with the pink compound that was essential to keeping his creation functional away from its fixed life support equipment. He placed the syringes in his pants pocket and made some last-minute adjustments to the crude laboratory he had set up. He had located a chair out in the junkyard and quickly affixed links of chain to be used as restraints. He had set up two computers, each connected to a large control box. Snaking from the control box were the many cables and electrodes that would need to be attached and inserted into the body to effectively monitor any anatomical and physiological changes. He was satisfied with the setup of his equipment; the only thing missing was his patient.

Back inside the crashed shuttle, Dr. Keitel gingerly descended downward toward the main control console. The shuttle still had power. He began to take sensor readings and was pleased to locate a source of high heat moving slowly, not that far away from his location. With some creative engineering, he devised a way to fabricate a crude but effective tracking device. One by-product of his experiment that Dr. Keitel had noted was the intense core temperature generated by his patient. Up to this point, it had been virtually impossible to sustain dead organs for long periods of time, but science had perfected many replacement limbs and organs. The war wounded many soldiers and civilians, many critically. Evolution in the research and production of artificial limbs and organs enabled the recipients to survive, albeit forever dependent on their newfound source of life. His patient was no different. Instead of just one limb or organ, however, virtually all internal organs had to be replaced, and this was unprecedented. Replacing the majority was a risk, but for the longevity of the patient, it was worth the risk. These synthetic organs and limbs were fueled by their own power source, and as such they gave off heat. This heat had to be removed from the body, and an exhaust port was created in the lower abdomen. As long as this port remained functional, heat levels could be brought down rapidly, especially when connected to equipment designed to enhance the cooling effect. The bigger problem was the brain. It was too complex to replicate or synthesize. Keeping the brain at an optimum temperature was essential in controlling his test subjects. The other test subjects registered minimal brain activity or none at all, resulting in a painful death all over again. This one was different. In order to regenerate dead soldiers so that they could fight as they had been doing before, they needed brain function, and they needed their former knowledge and abilities. They were of little use if they could no longer fight and follow orders.

Before the research base had been attacked and overrun, Dr. Keitel's staff had made startling discoveries about what happened once the solution interacted with dormant blood. Once the solution was administered, the blood began to change, almost taking on a parasitic quality. The solution began to combine on a cellular level with the red blood cells. Once this occurred, the new red blood cells consumed the white blood cells and platelets, behaving like a virus. These new super cells began to multiple rapidly and grow in size. Subsequent blood tests showed the new cells were resistant to traditional viruses. A curious by-product was that the blood took on a black color, and its viscosity was increased tenfold. That was where the research was terminated. Dr. Keitel salvaged what he could in fleeing from the lab; his most fortunate souvenir was his most advanced patient

The initial test subjects had been criminals and prisoners of war, and they had proven to be abject failures. The laboratory testing room was full of corpses. Although they initially showed positive results in regeneration, they were completely devoid of thought and eventually ended up in a comatose state, with most ended up dying within an hour of injection. This one, however, was different. The solution Dr. Keitel devised and administered prior to the research facility being overrun seemed to be succeeding. Why did it work on this one subject and not the others still mystified him although he had a theory. Not only did the body successfully regenerate itself, but the brain followed suit, becoming reactivated, allowing the thought and learning processes to effectively become "turned on" again. This test subject had been a successful soldier before he met his demise. Perhaps his past training and will to simply survive allowed him to persevere and learn at an accelerated rate.

His patient had been a frontline special assault soldier and had partaken in numerous behind-the-lines operations. Soldiers like this were trained for years in the art of war. When he was killed in action, his body was immediately flagged for research and development. Dr. Keitel had convinced the military authorities that highly trained soldiers were critical for his experiments if he was create a solution that could effectively render deceased soldiers fit for duty again. He now realized he was correct. Not only had the solution worked in rejuvenating dead tissue, it also would allow the soldier to once again think independently and be returned to the front. Dr. Keitel expected to be forever immortalized in the annals of science for his research. One major problem remained: Those that could help him had no idea where he was, and that he was currently stranded because of the wrecked shuttle.

Dr. Keitel finished constructing his tracking device and emerged from the crashed shuttle. The device was a little larger than he had anticipated, but it would serve its purpose. Fortunately, according to the device, his patient hadn't traveled too far. He checked his pocket for the two syringes filled with the pink solution and ensured he still had his pistol in the back of his pants. He set off as fast as he could, letting his tracker show him the way.

After about ten minutes, he arrived at a large gathering. Vehicles with flashing blue and red lights and several uniformed persons were in his path. Numerous heat signatures were now pinged on his scanner. Narrowing it down would be difficult now. His patient would have to wait a little longer.

Dr. Keitel watched as a corpse was enclosed in a black bag and loaded into the rear of into a large white vehicle with the words "County Coroner" displayed prominently on the sides. He saw enough to determine it wasn't his test subject. An obese man loaded the victim and entered the front of the vehicle. After a few minutes, the vehicle departed the area.

Dr. Keitel's patient was operating completely on its own, which was significant. Obviously it felt threatened and fled. Self-preservation was taking over. Dr. Keitel had not yet decided how long he would allow it to remain free, but he had to bring it back soon. He considered this a test, and his subject passed. As the white vehicle rounded a corner and left the area, Dr. Keitel realized that he needed to examine that body himself before anyone from this planet was able to. If his subject had been responsible for this murder, he needed to determine cause of death. Was it savage and barbaric, like an animal? Or was it precise and quick, like an ex-military professional? He realized he couldn't chase the vehicle on foot. The tracker was emitting a barely audible beeper. A simple view screen with displayed a direction and estimated speed. He hadn't the faintest idea how he would be able to catch up to it until a yellow painted vehicle with the word "taxi" written on the door slowly approached. He waved towards the driver. As the taxi pulled over, he fingered the pistol in his waistband.

"Beginning Y- shaped incision," the coroner dictated. "There is no visible evidence of chest trauma … HEY! You are not supposed to be in here!" The tape recorder fell to the sanitized tile floor with a loud crash.

"Don't do anything foolish," Dr. Keitel told him, aiming a pistol at his head. "I know how to use this. I implore you to drop your scalpel. We have much to talk about and very little time."

The coroner slowly lowered the bloody scalpel onto the corpse lying on the examination table. He raised both hands in the air. His name tag read "J. Jewell, M.D"

"Are you alone here?" Keitel asked.

"My assistant will return any minute. You will never get away with whatever you are trying to do," Dr. Jewell said. With one hand, he lowered his surgical mask and took off his plastic safety glasses.

"Oh, I think I will. But as of right now, I can't have you conducting any examination on that body that was just brought in. You have a means of transportation outside, correct?"

"Yes-s. A b-black Mercedes," Dr. Jewell stuttered.

"Good. I am going to conduct a cursory examination, then we will walk outside slowly, and you are going to drive. If you alert anyone, I will kill you and them as well." Dr. Keitel retrieved his tracking device from a bag he had slung over his shoulder, and gave it a quick glance. The machine registered 100.1 degree body temperature of the recently brought in corpse, rather than the 98.6 degrees of this planets inhabitants. Now he could dial in an exact heat signature rather than relying on a heat range.

"Sit down and don't move," Dr. Keitel said as he motioned with this pistol to a nearby chair. Dr. Jewell sat down. Dr. Keitel moved over to the next examination table. His eyes immediately gravitated to large gaping neck wound. It was savage and beastly, definitely not the work of a skilled assassin. Either this wasn't caused by his patient, or it was and his patient was resorting to some kind of animalistic behavior.

A chime went off in the room, startling Dr. Keitel.

"What is that?"

"Front door. My assistant is undoubtedly returning."

"Let's go. I am not quite finished with you yet," Dr. Keitel responded as he aimed the pistol once more at Dr. Jewell's head. "Back door, let's move."

Dr. Jewell raised his hands and exited the room with Dr. Keitel close behind. He needed to do a full examination of the body, but he didn't want any more interactions with the local populace for the time being. The taxi driver he shot a couple blocks away would undoubtedly draw attention. He did note one positive, tracking his patient would be much easier now.

Maynard Fontenot?" Roman asked, as he offered his hand. He saw that the coroner tech was sweating profusely and holding onto a large styrofoam cup with both hands.

"Yes. You must be Detective Roman. Sorry about earlier. Please follow me," the portly coroner tech responded, shaking Roman's outstretched hand weakly. He tossed the cup into an overflowing trashcan. "I'm glad dispatch gave me your number. I was running out of options." Maynard Fontenot was in his mid-thirties, had a short, stocky build with black oily hair that ended in a ponytail, and wore thin wire frame glasses perched on the end of his nose, which Roman noted was sporting a nice large patch of untrimmed nose hair. He was dressed in the typical white lab coat, with a crooked name tag over the breast pocket. Numerous stains from old, greasy, heart-stopping lunches dotted the coat as well.

Fontenot led Roman down a nondescript white hallway and finally came to a door with a glass pane that read "Autopsy." The coroner's office appeared to be devoid of any other staff. Inside the autopsy room were two bodies, one partially dissected, with a prominent hole on the left side of the skull, and one that was not, but had most of the throat ripped away. Roman instantly recognized it as the victim from earlier in the morning. It was this body that the coroner tech escorted Roman to see.

"First off," Fontenot said, "the chief coroner is on vacation, and the deputy coroner is nowhere to be found at the moment, so I am pretty much in charge. Anyway, this is the body that I picked up from your crime scene. I know that you were one of the investigating officers, so I felt compelled to tell you of my findings before I put it in the freezer."

Roman took a step back, defensively putting both hands in the air, and replied, "Again, I am not the investigating officer. This is my first day on the job, and I don't want to get messed up working the lieutenant's case without his knowledge. Please omit me from any of your paperwork, OK?"

Fontenot looked at him for a moment, slightly irritated. "Just look at the goddamn body." His face was quickly turning a bright red.

"What do you have?" Roman asked, oblivious to Fontenot's rising blood pressure. He viewed the corpse with morbid fascination; working patrol he didn't visit the coroner's office. Detectives always did the follow up investigations. Numerous tools of the coroner's trade were neatly laid out on a metal tray, but the tools had barely been touched, except for a large, bloody scalpel lying carelessly across the corpse's chest. A Y-shaped incision had been started, but abruptly stopped. He peered into the skull at the partially exposed brain.

"Not that body. It's the same one from earlier, remember?" Fontenot said.

"Yea, sorry. Lost my train of thought for a second," Roman said.

"Well, the thing is, I brought the body in and started prepping it like I usually do," he said as he indicated toward the body with an apparent animal wound. "Anyway, I have to inventory property, scrub the body, and all that crap. The bite or whatever is still there, except now there is some black ooze leaking out. It's not blood. Also, feel the body."

Roman looked at him with a puzzled look. "Feel the body?" he asked. "What the hell for?"

Fontenot grabbed Roman's hand and placed it on the corpse's abdominal area before he could react. He withdrew it in an instant.

"Holy shit!" Roman exclaimed. "That's hot!" Roman calmed down and poked the corpse with the end of his pen. "You sure he is dead?"

Fontenot stared at the body as if expecting it to sit up at any moment. "Well, he is dead now, I think. Besides missing most of his throat, he has no vital signs. He was pronounced at 8:10 and it's now..." He checked a wall clock, and said "10:36." Maynard produced a handkerchief and wiped some accumulated sweat off of his brow.

"You told anybody else about this?" Roman asked. He again placed his hand on the corpse.

"That's where it gets interesting. The deputy coroner was here, but now I cannot find him anywhere. He must have started the autopsy." Fontenot indicated towards the bloody scalpel on the neighboring corpse. "It's like he just decided to go home for the day; won't answer his cell or anything, plus his car is gone. I would call EMS, but this guy has no vitals. I mean, he was already pronounced at the scene, he should be dead. No pulse, no heart rate, nothing. I was an Army medic in Iraq back in '03, so I am not a complete moron." Fontenot paused, expecting Roman to make a comment about his weight and military service. Hearing none, he continued, "It's like he no longer has any blood, just this black ooze, which I cannot identify. I would like to perform some more tests, but that's not my job, and the boss would probably fire me for doing this on my own. I can probably send a blood sample to the lab, but that's probably a 48-hour turnaround or longer. Anyway, I just wanted you to know."

"Maybe your boss will be back in a few minutes?" Roman offered.

"Maybe so, but the fact is this corpse isn't acting like a corpse. If this guy wakes up and it turns out someone screwed up and he is really alive by some miracle, I don't want to get blamed for it and sued. That's why I called you, got it?"

"OK, black ooze and hot body," Roman said. "I got it."

Fontenot looked at Roman quizzically and asked, "Exactly how long have you been a cop?"

Seeing he wasn't going to get a response, he continued, "This black ooze just started leaking out when I called you." Fontenot's face revealed his confusion. "Like I said, the deputy coroner was already in here getting ready. I brought this new body in and left. I came back in no more than ten minutes later to see if he wanted a sandwich, and he was gone."

Roman watched with fascination as some sort of black ooze seeped out of the corpse's neck. The ooze was beginning to pool on the side of the table and slowly drip onto the floor.

"I'm no doctor, but that is much thicker than blood. It's almost like honey."

Fontenot opened a cabinet and retrieved a petri dish. He squatted with some difficulty and, using the lid, scooped up some of the ooze into the dish. Satisfied that he had enough, he put the lid back on. Black ooze was all over the outside of the dish and on his hands. Fontenot wiped them on his white lab coat.

"Sounds like you have a problem," Roman said. "Let me know when that blood or whatever it is gets identified. I just came from another crime scene with the same cause of death, dude torn to pieces. I thought I saw blood, but seeing this, it may be the same kind of ooze," Roman replied. "Any info you can give me will be appreciated."

"No problem. Just remember, I scratch your back, you scratch mine." Fontenot's cell phone emitted the first few notes to the *Knight Rider* theme song. He pulled out his phone from his pocket and read a text message. He replaced the phone and walked past Roman back into the hall. "Find your own way out, OK? I have another pickup to make."

"Wait," Roman said abruptly.

Fontenot stopped and turned around in the doorway. Roman walked over to the partially dissected body and knelt down. He picked up a handheld voice recorder.

"It's still on." Roman stood up, showing the recorder to Fontenot, who went back inside as Roman pressed the stop button. He hit rewind, and hit stop again. Pressing play, he heard part of his previous conversation with Fontenot. He rewound the tape a few more times until he heard an unfamiliar voice. He backed up a few seconds at a time, until Fontenot stopped him. "There. That's sounds like the beginning of his report," Fontenot said.

Roman let the tape play, and a firm, confident voice spoke evenly and calmly.

"Cursory examination of the deceased shows the projectile has penetrated the left frontal lobe of the brain in a lateral direction, proceeding to the pons, ventral to the cerebellum. Visual examination of the base of the skull indicates a possible fracture of the temporal bone. Cerebrospinal fluid is pooling in the left ear and leaking out of the nose." Following an audible click, the recording continued. "Beginning Y-shaped incision. There is no visible evidence of chest trauma ... HEY! You are not supposed to be in here!" They could hear a crash, most likely the recorder falling to the floor. A slightly muffled voice said, "Don't do anything foolish. I know how to use this. I implore you to drop your scalpel. We have much to talk about and very little time."

"You will never get away with this," the first voice replied.

"That's my boss!" exclaimed Fontenot.

"Oh, I think I will. But as of right now, I can't have you conducting any examination on that body that was just brought in." The conversation became inaudible. Roman fast forwarded the tape and pressed play again. The conversation resumed.

"Back door, let's move." There was more conversation, but it was muffled. Footsteps could be heard fading away, and the recording went quiet. Roman fast forwarded, checking periodically for any other conversation, until he heard Fontenot's voice talking to him. He clicked the recorder off.

"Now we know what happened to your boss," Roman said.

Fontenot looked terrified. "This is getting way out of hand. I'm out of here."

"Relax. I'll call this in. We'll find him, but you need to stick around. I'll have some uniformed officers over here in a minute."

CHAPTER 15

"Any unit in the vicinity, 41-25 in progress, corner of Orleans and Louise," Roman's car radio announced.

"This is Lincoln 78. I'll take it, E.T.A. five mikes," Roman said over the radio as he threw his recently lit cigarette out of the window. He didn't give two shits about smoking in a government vehicle today. He didn't think until after he had already answered the call. *What am I doing? I'm a detective now. I don't take assault calls. Oh well, some habits will die hard.* He had put an APB out for the deputy coroner based on information he'd obtained from Fontenot, but there was nothing else to work with. The deputy coroner's Mercedes was missing out of the parking lot, and he hoped it would turn up before the day was out, giving them more information.

"10-4, Lincoln 78," dispatch replied. No other responses to the assault call came over the radio.

After a five-minute drive, Roman pulled his vehicle into the driveway of a dilapidated, boarded up house. In the front yard of the house, with his back to the street, was a heavily muscled bald man standing at least 6'4", wearing a leather motorcycle jacket. He fit to a tee the description of the homicide suspect that he had obtained from the homeless guy earlier in the day. When the man turned, Roman could see that he was strangling a rather heavy female weighing at least 200 pounds. He had her at least two feet off of the ground and was holding her throat with both hands. He appeared to be trying to bite her on the face but she was putting up a spirited defense. Despite her screams, no one came to her rescue. A couple of bystanders watched from neighboring yards and through windows, but no one attempted to intervene.

He quickly removed his worn brown leather bomber jacket and tossed it on the passenger seat. He exited his vehicle and drew his Glock 19 from his hip holster. He took cover behind the driver's side front wheel and aimed at the suspect from over the hood of the vehicle.

"Police officer!" Roman shouted. "Drop the woman, put your hands up, and don't move!"

Upon hearing Roman's voice, the man threw the woman to the ground. She landed in a heap at his feet. Roman didn't detect any signs of her being bitten, which was good. The woman didn't move. The man turned to Roman and began to walk toward him, his right hand outstretched. His mouth was bloody, and chunks of flesh could be seen dangling between his teeth.

"You take one more step, and I will open fire!" Roman shouted. He took aim, lining up the sights on his Glock. He had about 25 yards to the suspect. He could feel the adrenaline starting to course through his body.

Three loud pistol reports emanated from Roman's pistol. The man spun around from the impact of the 9mm Hydro-shock rounds, all which struck him in the upper chest. He dropped to one knee, but didn't fall.

What the hell!

The man unsteadily got back to his feet and took another step toward Roman. Roman fired two more times, center mass. The Hydro-shocks expanded as designed; creating a large wound area on the man's chest. Roman watched with disbelief as the wound area seemingly closed up before his eyes. Roman holstered his Glock and jumped back into his vehicle, got on the radio, and shouted into the mike head, "I've got shots fired, send backup!" He dropped the mike head and reached for the 870 Remington shotgun that was secured in the roof rack on the ceiling.

"Eat buckshot!" He moved tactically towards the suspect closing the distance to fifteen yards, lining up the ghost ring sights center mass.

Roman fired, the shotgun bucked hard into his shoulder, sending eight pellets downrange. Roman was sure he hit him, he saw him flinch hard after the impact. Roman held his breath for what seemed like an eternity before the man fell face first on the pavement, letting out in inhuman scream. Roman flinched at the sound, quickly racked the action, sending another shell into the breach. By this time, sirens could be heard in the distance, rapidly approaching. Roman walked back behind his vehicle, resuming a cover position behind the front wheel, keeping his eyes on his suspect the whole time.

Without warning, the suspect abruptly raised himself off the ground, stood, and faced Roman. He did not advance any closer. The buckshot had done some damage, tearing a few gaping holes in his chest. There was no blood; instead the wound looked almost as if it had been burned. Roman noticed that his eyes were solid black, just as described by the homeless guy in his statement. No whites could be seen. His face was heavily scarred, and Roman noticed what looked like blood on his lips. Black veins snaked through his pale, almost translucent skin. The image reminded him of some sort of twisted interpretation of Frankenstein's monster. As he stared with awe, the man's lips parted, and raspy words escaped his dry, cracked lips.

"I have killed before, and I will kill again." The deep, crackling voice emanated from a twisted, evil grin. Having issued his prophecy, the man turned and ran down the street at a breakneck pace. Roman fired another blast before the man turned into an alleyway, but he couldn't tell if the rounds hit or not. Roman ran over to the woman, lying on the ground. She had a weak pulse and was breathing heavily but appeared unhurt.

One marked police cruiser pulled onto the scene with sirens blaring and lights flashing. Roman frantically yelled at the officer to pursue the suspect down the alley. The cruiser pulled away and headed in the indicated direction. Roman ran back to his vehicle and radioed for EMS. By this time, bystanders had crowded closer to the scene, leaving the safety of their homes and yards. Roman leaned on his open vehicle door, trying to figure out how his rounds could have failed to stop the big man.

Even if he had body armor … no way, Roman thought to himself. His cellular phone vibrated in his pocket. He grabbed it and recognized Captain Martinez's phone number.

"Yes sir," Roman answered, in a defeated tone.

"Drop what you're doing and get to my office now," Martinez said in a clipped, irritated tone.

"Sir, I was just involved in a shooting," Roman answered calmly. "I think it was the suspect from the Seebolt's homicide I was at this morning." There was not much else he could do now, other than taking statements and seeing if the pursuit would catch the suspect.

There was a long pause on the line, and Roman could detect other voices in the background. Martinez finally replied, "Understood. Get here as soon as you can." The line went dead. By now, two other units had arrived, and the unit that had gone in pursuit the assailant returned. The officer got out of the vehicle, shaking his head.

"He just vanished on me," he reported to Roman. "He's around here, though, and we'll find him."

Roman gave the officer his card. "I have to go back downtown. Let me know if you get any leads."

The officer nodded and took the card before walking off.

I won't be taking this one. He was pissed off that the savage assailant had gotten away, at least for now. Roman fired up the Crown Vic and hit the accelerator hard, leaving two skid marks on the potholed pavement. A beat up, rusted lime green Ford Mustang slowly pulled out from a space halfway down the block and followed him.

"You are making quite a name for yourself already," Martinez told Roman. "So far, I've heard about two bodies, a missing coroner, and a shooting, all involving you in some way or another. Do you actually have anything to report, or are you just dicking around out there, playing John Wayne?" Martinez slowly walked behind his desk and grabbed a cigar from a box in a drawer. He clipped off the end, produced a lighter from his pants pocket, and lit the cigar, taking a few deep puffs. He walked to the window and looked at the scene below.

"Seebolt seemed impressed with you," he continued, "so I'm giving you the benefit of the doubt. It's your first day; don't dig yourself any deeper into a hole. Pending the outcome of this shooting, I don't want you running around all over town getting involved in everything you come across. What the hell were you doing responding to an assault, anyway? I want a report on my desk no later than 8:00 a.m. tomorrow regarding you discharging your weapon. Internal Affairs will be looking for you, so don't go far." He waved his hand to dismiss Roman, who left the office with a befuddled look on his face.

Roman walked to the cubicle that had been assigned as his work station. A laptop computer and a telephone sat on a battered metal desk that had a torn desk chair behind it. That was all the furniture. With a heavy sigh,

Roman sat down in the chair. *Might as well take a break for a moment.* He dropped his L&M's and car keys on the desk and hit the power button on the laptop. As the Windows XP splash screen loaded, he didn't feel like spending the next couple of hours writing the report. The vibration of his cellular phone in his jeans pocket interrupted his thoughts.

He got out the phone and answered while he waited for the computer screen to load.

"Yeah, Roman, this is Maynard down at the coroner's office. We have a big problem now." Fontenot's voice sounded shaky.

"OK. What happened? Did you figure out what that black stuff is?" Roman asked.

"Uh, no. It seems as though you may have been right after all."

"Right? What do you mean?" Roman started typing on the laptop, not yet very concerned about what Fontenot was saying.

"The Mexican guy from this morning is gone—just *gone*." The pitch of Fontenot's voice rose with every word. "He just up and vanished."

Roman stopped typing and closed the lid on his laptop. "What do you mean, vanished?" He grabbed his cigarettes and keys, got out of his chair, and headed out of his cubicle and toward the parking lot.

"Exactly what I said—he's gone. When the cops came in here and did their thing, I never put the guy in the freezer. I mean, I just forgot."

"OK, so what?"

"Well, I stepped out, went to down the street to grab a burrito. I took my time. I mean, it's a little stressful, you know. I got the coroner calling me, yelling that he has to end his vacation early and all this—"

"Get to the point!" Roman interjected sternly.

"Sorry. Well, I picked up another body, same cause of death, massive trauma to the neck, massive blood loss—"

Roman was already on the stairs that led to the parking lot. "Yeah, I know. I was there," Roman said, cutting him off.

"Yeah, well he also had contusions and a broken nose, and some cuts to his face, not to mention the chunks of flesh bitten from his body. Like I said, I went to the scene in the van to collect the body after forensics did their thing. I brought it here, and the damn thing is twitching, right before my eyes!"

Roman could hear the panic in Fontenot's voice. "I'm fifteen minutes away," he told Fontenot. "Anybody else know about this?"

"Hell no, are you crazy? No, no one but me knows. Luckily, I'm alone here. All your cop buddies took off, but I can't keep it quiet much longer. I rigged some restraints, so the body should stay put. Either someone stole the first one, or it came back to life too and is walking around somewhere.

Who knows? Maybe the same guy who kidnapped the doc stole the body. It sounds like *Day of the Dead*. Get your ass down here, fast!" Fontenot hung up the phone. Roman ran down the last few stairs, taking two at a time.

First day on the job and I've got walking corpses at the coroner's office. He got in his car and gunned it out of the parking lot.

CHAPTER 16

Half a block before Roman reached the parking lot of the coroner's office, his cellular phone vibrated. He quickly pulled to the side of the road and parked his car and fished the phone out of the right pocket of his worn leather jacket.

"Roman," he answered, a lit cigarette in his mouth.

"Roman, this is Maynard." Fontenot's voice than began to waver. "Uh, look. Plans have changed. I need you to meet me at the corner of Hickory and St. Paul, at the Williams Chicken."

"What the hell for?" Roman almost shouted in the phone.

"Look, you can't go inside now. Just get over here. I am not playing around, OK?" The line went dead and he threw the phone in the passenger seat. *Jackass,* Roman thought to himself. He looked down the street at the building housing the coroner's office. He noticed three fire engines and an ambulance, and at least three police cruisers. *What the hell?* Either the vehicles had been there for a while, or he had been so deep in thought that he hadn't noticed their flashing lights.

He threw his Crown Vic in reverse, backed up enough to leave enough room to turn, checked traffic, and pulled a fast U. He hit the accelerator and turned a corner before he was noticed.

A few minutes later, he pulled into the parking lot of the Williams Fried Chicken on the corner of Hickory and St. Paul, as Fontenot had instructed. He parked his car, grabbed his cell phone, and entered the restaurant. The place almost came to a standstill as he walked in, but he was quickly ignored. He saw Fontenot in the back, stuffing his face as fast as he could.

"What did you do, man?" Roman said as he slid in the vinyl booth across from Fontenot.

Fontenot wiped some gravy from his mouth as he replied. "It's what *didn't* I do, you know?" He resumed eating. "Look, that homeless guy that you sent in—he got up not five minutes after I got off the phone with you, and he walked out and tried to come after me. He busted right out of those restraints." He dipped another chicken tender into his little Styrofoam cup of gravy.

"What? You mean to tell me that dead guy got up and left?" Roman replied as he leaned closer.

"Yeah, that's exactly what I'm telling you. You deaf, or what?"

"No." Roman sat back down in the booth. "I've seen some weird shit too."

Fontenot wiped his mouth on his shirtsleeve and took a big swig of Fanta orange soda out of his Styrofoam soft drink cup "All right, like I said, I hung up the phone with you, and I heard this bloodcurdling scream, like the ones you hear in movies."

"Go on."

"Anyway, I go over, thinking maybe he is alive or something and he gets off the table, charges me, and sends me flying into the wall. Anyway, he takes off out of the autopsy office. I have the cleaning crew freaking out. They see me and think I'm doing some weird sex acts or something; I don't know, so I bolted. I didn't know what else to do. I followed the guy over to Old City Park in my car before I lost him. He ran fast, man. You'd think a jacked up looking guy like that would stop traffic and someone would call 911. Wrong. What kind of sick town do we live in?" Fontenot paused, taking a gulp of his Fanta. "Anyway, it looked like he ran into a nearby junkyard maybe, I don't know. Anyways, that's it. I can't show my face now, I know that. If I would have hung around, I would have gotten jammed for sure. That's two bodies gone now, plus the coroner missing."

"A junkyard?" Roman asked.

"Yeah, a junkyard. I can't be sure, but it looked like he went in through a hole in the fence. He hardly hesitated looking for it; it was as if he knew where he was going. I didn't go in after him. He could have lost me easily in there, or he could have ambushed me. I'm not crazy, you know."

"All right. I believe you, man. I just shot this big guy like thirty times, and he kept going. Maybe it was PCP or something."

Fontenot ate the last of his tenders and reached for his corn fritters. "I have two bodies that are gone, and the coroner. I am so screwed. I know they're all connected. You got to check out that junkyard."

"Where are you going to go?" Roman asked.

Fontenot wiped his mouth as he finished the last corn fritter. He took his last swig of Fanta and sat back in the booth. "I don't know. I got a couple places I could go. This is heavy, man, real heavy. You're the police—you help me."

Roman looked out of the window toward his car and saw a police unit going by, running code 3, lights and sirens. He looked back and stared Maynard directly in the eye. "I need this, trust me. I'll do what I can. I'm going to check out that junkyard before it gets dark. Stay out of sight and keep your phone on."

"Yeah, all right. You call me, OK, Roman?"

"I'll call you." With that, Roman got out of the booth and headed for the door.

CHAPTER 17

"Matthias, report." Colonel Chuikova's crackling voice was barely audible over the headset.

"Colonel, another human has entered the perimeter. This one is not emitting a heat signature either. It is a very abnormal reading. No sign of any other activity inside the perimeter."

"OK. Keep surveillance, Matthias. What happened to the main target you and Cruwell were following?"

"Sorry, sir. We tried following a policeman, but vehicle was too fast. We could not keep up."

"Understood. I'll leave it up to you to follow your instincts. You need to get a faster vehicle it would seem."

Matthias was about to reply in the affirmative when he noticed a black vehicle pull off to the side of the road and stop. "Wait a moment, sir, we might have something. Stand by." Matthias observed a lone figure exit the vehicle and approach the same hole in the junkyard fence as the two other humans had entered just moments before. Matthias noticed that the figure approached methodically and took what appeared to be some sort of weapon from within the confines of his jacket. Cruwell pulled the monocular up to his eye and looked out of the window. The figure looked around a few times before entering the hole.

"Colonel."

"Go ahead," crackled the reply.

"Colonel," Cruwell replied, "I have just observed another person enter. He appears to be different. I think it is the policeman we tried to tail from earlier. The heat signature is normal. He appeared to be brandishing a weapon."

"Stay on target. I am sending Scotts to back you up. Understood?"

"Yes, sir." Cruwell resumed his observation of the hole in the fence. He could see Corporal Scotts down the road. He had just opened the door of the policeman's vehicle and was examining its interior.

"Captain, this is Scotts."

"Go ahead."

"This vehicle appears to belong to be the policeman you were following. There is a radio, which is active, and what appears to be a slug thrower here," Scotts replied. He had exited the vehicle and taken up a concealed position behind the burned out remains of a liquor store, adjacent to the vehicle.

"OK. Recover the weapon. In case we have to engage him, I don't want him having any advantage. I am sending Matthias on foot to cover the junkyard hole and observe the policeman if he comes into contact with our alien or those other two anomalies."

"Understood."

Cruwell observed Scotts quickly go back in the vehicle and emerge with the weapon. Matthias silently exited the old Mustang and ran across the street to the junkyard entrance. He looked around for a good cover position before finally deciding on some nearby bushes growing out of control. Scotts hit his position on the opposite side of the street from Matthias and concealed himself as well. Cruwell slid into the driver's seat of the Mustang and turned the key, hoping it wouldn't backfire. It started with no unusual noise, and he began to circle the block slowly. His holographic map showed no heat signatures within the fenced in area, except for that of the policeman.

Scotts drew his sidearm and rechecked the ammunition magazine. About two minutes later, he heard six loud reports from within the junkyard. Matthias and Scotts observed the policeman emerge, with his weapon raised. He was also carrying another object, in his other hand. The policeman fired three more shots through the hole in the fence before running to his car. The vehicle fired up and sped away, right past their concealed position. Sergeant Matthias and Corporal Scotts resumed watch on the hole and observed nothing more. The duo, upon seeing no other activity, exited their positions. Cruwell put his monocular back inside his pants pocket and emerged from around the corner in the Mustang, and they all piled in, with Cruwell relinquishing the driver's seat to Matthias. Scotts was still holding the recently acquired projectile weapon. An eerie quiet set in around the junkyard as the three sped off. A steady rain resumed from the cloudy gray skies.

"What's our play?" Matthias asked. "You want me to try to catch up with him, or are we going in the fence?"

Cruwell watched the policeman's vehicle on his holographic map. "No, let's return to base. We can monitor his location from there, and we probably won't be able to catch the policeman anyway, in this vehicle. We already lost him once today."

"There is one other thing I failed to mention, captain."

"What?"

"The policeman's name is Johnny Roman. I intercepted his voice communications. He apparently has upset his boss."

Great, Roman thought angrily as he sped away from the junkyard. *Who jacks a police car?* He was still on an adrenaline high, but now he was getting just plain pissed as he kept glancing at where his shotgun used to be. *Most officers never fire their service weapons in the span of their whole career, let alone twice in two days!* He also began to wonder if he should even bother to call it in. He was supposed to be training on the job with Detective Seebolt, but his instincts got the better of him.

After going through the hole in the junkyard fence 20 minutes ago, he had wandered around for a few minutes trying to see if the owner was around. The junkyard appeared not to be under good care, and he wondered if it had been abandoned. He could not remember ever seeing the place before. He saw nothing out of the ordinary, just stacks of crushed cars, rusting shipping containers, lots of trash, and overgrown weeds, accompanied by a stench of dead animals. He stopped suddenly, seeing a large structure. He thought it could be the junkyard office. He would not have noticed it if he hadn't caught a glimpse of a shadow moving in that direction.

The object, though large, was well camouflaged in the context of the junkyard. He approached the object, which was nestled between stacks of crushed cars on either side. Instead of an office, it looked like an inverted shipping container partially buried in the ground. As he got closer, he could tell it was something different. There was an opening on one side; just low enough to that he could look in. The opening appeared to be into a room of some sort. He drew his surefire flashlight from his belt holster and activated it, carefully hoisting himself up into the doorframe.

The flashlight beam illuminated a small compartment containing four seats. There appeared to be a windshield at the end that was buried in the earth. A nauseating stench, much worse than outside, immediately hit his nostrils as he stepped inside. He shined his light around the compartment and was briefly frozen with awe. Lights blinked on and off near the windshield. He noticed two figures lying at awkward angles across the windshield, seemingly lifeless. They appeared to be wearing uniforms of some sort. He inched himself forward from the doorway for a closer look, and his foot kicked something. He shined his light down and saw the remains of a dog wedged behind a forward-facing seat. Its insides had been savagely pulled out from a gaping hole in its midsection. The head also appeared to have a large chunk of flesh removed, as if it had been bitten by a large animal. Roman drew his hand over his nose and pointed his pistol in the direction of the two figures slumped against the windshield.

"Police," Roman said weakly, his voice barely audible. Sensing no movement, he carefully entered the confined space and made his way down toward the front. He poked one of the bodies with the barrel of his Glock. Its neck was savagely broken, and the body looked as though it has been dead for a couple of days at least. Roman noticed that the eyes were wide open, as if the poor bastard died from fright before being so savagely attacked. Dried blood covered most of the face, but Roman could see chunks missing from the face and throat, as if someone or something had gnawed off pieces of it, much like the other two bodies from earlier. Roman could not determine the cause of death of the other body, but its face also was covered in dried blood, with pieces gnawed off.

Are they really dead? Nothing seems to want to die these days. He tried to laugh at himself, but it didn't work. He grasped the medallion of St. Michael he wore around his neck and continued to examine the two bodies. He noticed a massive large caliber sidearm resting in the thigh holster of one of them. He drew the weapon out and was amazed at its light weight.

Suddenly, he heard a scratching sound behind him. A deep growl came from the opening he had just passed through. He spun around and saw the homeless man whose apparent death he had witnessed earlier. The body was just like he remembered; the guy still wasn't wearing any clothes. Roman also noticed that he was holding a severed leg from a dog in his right hand.

"What the— don't move, police!" Roman cried as he stumbled backward, his back crashing into the dead pilot's body on the console. The homeless man bumped his head as he made his way inside, clumsily falling face first into the back of the nearest seat. Sensing fresh meat, the homeless man hissed at Roman. Roman raised the weapon he had recovered from the second pilot and squeezed the trigger. The weapon emitted a high- pitched whine, blasting a high-powered projectile out of the barrel. A bright green smoke trail exited, following the round as it struck its target. Roman wasn't expecting the recoil and was knocked backwards. The weapon fell out of his hand and clattered onto the console, out of reach. The homeless man staggered from the force of the rounds and fell outside, his right arm hanging from his shoulder by a few strands of rotting skin.

Roman grasped what handholds he could find and headed toward the hole. He pulled himself out and fired three more shots from his Glock. The last two 9mm Hydro-shocks blew the homeless man's right arm completely off at the shoulder. His right hand still clutched the severed dog leg. Black ooze spurted from his shoulder, where his arm previously was attached. He was still moving, struggling to push himself off the ground, and his eyes met Roman's. Roman charged past him, heading straight for the hole in the fence, without looking around.

The gaze of his solid black eyes had been almost hypnotic. His hands shook so much that he had a hard time inserting the key into the ignition of his vehicle. After yelling into his radio mike, he finally got his car started and hit the accelerator. It took about five minutes before his adrenaline rush subsided and he noticed his shotgun was missing out of the rack.

CHAPTER 18

"911 Emergency. Do you require police or fire assistance?" The female dispatcher's reply to the caller was short and to the point.

"I need the police!" the caller excitedly repeated. "This is Leroy, down at the Ambassador Hotel on Hickory, right by the expressway. I got this big mother that just killed a girl out back of my establishment. You better send somebody!"

"OK, sir," the dispatcher replied. "I am dispatching units to your location. Is the suspect still on property?"

"How the hell should I know? He out back. Who do you think I am, TJ Hooker? I think they was doing drugs or something."

"Sir, please remain calm and get to a safe area."

"Yeah, whatever you say. Just make sure they get here today, OK?"

Two police units responded to the 911 call, arriving 28 minutes later. Both cruisers parked in front of the dilapidated Ambassador Hotel with no emergency lights activated. As the units pulled up, several people loitering outside immediately ran in the opposite direction.

Two officers stepped into the lobby, and one approached the desk. "Are you the person who placed the 911 call?" he asked Leroy. The officer scanned the lobby of the hotel, his hand on the holster of his weapon.

"Yes, I did." Leroy looked at the two officers with disgust. "What the hell took you so long? I called that shit in over a half hour ago."

"Where is the suspect?" the officer at the desk asked, sidestepping the question. He looked at the staircase leading up from the lobby. The few people in the lobby when the officers entered had gone outside.

"Gone, I would imagine. If this was a white neighborhood, you would have been here in two minutes."

"Give me a break, OK?"

"Look, Officer *Russo*," Leroy replied as he read the nameplate on the officer's uniform. "I told that woman on the phone they was out back in the alley. You need to go out back. That's where he was biting her and shit, man. They was shootin' up heroin or something."

Russo looked over at his partner in surprise and nodded. "All right, we will check it out. You stay put."

"You ain't got to tell me twice, man. Shit, that mofo is one scary dude. 911 my ass," Leroy replied, his voice heavy with sarcasm.

The two officers moved to the back of the hotel and drew their Glock 17 service weapons. Russo slowly opened the back door and pushed it open, revealing a trash-strewn alley. The rain that had sprinkled off and on throughout the day had ended for the moment, leaving large puddles in the alley. Both officers stepped into the alley. Initially, they saw nothing, but an arm hanging out of a dumpster near the hotel's back door caught Russo's eye. Russo ran over to the dumpster, shouting to his partner, "Kevin, over here!"

Kevin ran over to Russo. They both slowly opened the dumpster lid and saw a naked female laying on top a mound of bags of garbage. She was covered in fresh blood, making it difficult to identify the cause of death. Several chunks of flesh were missing from her shoulder and buttocks regions. Her head was lying at an awkward angle from her body, and her right breast appeared to have been bitten clean off. Russo quickly closed the lid and turned to Kevin, a hand raised to cover his nose.

"You'd better call this in. I'll see what else I can find around here." Kevin immediately got on his shoulder mike and called dispatch. Russo noticed blood dripping from the exposed hand onto the ground. *This is fresh. The killer is still around here.*

"You make the call?" he shouted to Kevin over a loud thunderclap.

Kevin turned around and replied, "Yeah, I made it. We're looking at fifteen for a response, maybe longer. You know how it is here."

"He's still here," Russo said matter-of-factly. "This is fresh. I think we can get him."

A sudden scream further down the alley diverted the attention of both officers. They both ran in that direction, weapons raised and pointed in the direction of the scream. Another scream pierced the heavy air. They were getting closer. The darkened skies opened up with another bout of rain. The officers turned down a side alley and saw a massive individual holding a rather waifish female around the throat, lifting her about three feet off the ground. Both officers immediately reacted and aimed their weapons at the figure.

"Put her down, now!" Russo yelled in a loud commanding voice. The imposing figure turned and stared at Russo. He dropped the female to the ground and immediately charged the two officers. "Stop, or we will fire!" Russo yelled. The figure did not stop; instead, he broke into a sprint toward the two officers, only thirty yards away.

Three loud reports emitted from each of the two weapons. The figure slowed down a bit and sank to one knee, but raised again, his pace noticeably slower. Two more reports bellowed from the guns, and the figure dropped into a large, trash-filled rain puddle, face first. His body did not move.

"Check the body, I'll cover you," Russo commanded.

Kevin slowly approached the body and pushed him with his foot. There was no response. Kevin holstered his weapon and turned back toward Russo.

"He's dead," he said.

No sooner had he finished his sentence than the figure rose from the ground and grabbed Kevin from behind, putting him in a headlock and lifting his 200-pound, six-foot, four-inch frame like a matchstick. Kevin barely managed a scream before his neck snapped. Russo stared in disbelief. His arm wavered as he brought his weapon to bear once more upon the figure. He was only feet away. Russo seemed almost paralyzed as he stared into the figure's black, cloudy pupils. He managed to fire a single shot into the figure's midsection. A piercing cry rang out, and the figure dropped to both knees. Both of his hands grabbed at his midsection. The rain had increased, and the thunderclaps had gotten louder and more frequent. It was getting dark, and intermittent lightning flashes lit up the alley. Russo ran over to his partner and checked for a pulse as he kept his weapon leveled at the figure. He was still on his knees, clutching his midsection in obvious pain. He pulled something silver out of his body and held it out in front of him, staring at the object. Russo detected a very weak and fading pulse from his partner.

Russo feebly grabbed at his shoulder mike, and in a voice that was nearly a whispered, said into it, "Officer down. 10-100, officer down." He dropped his mike and leveled the pistol at the figure, not waiting for a response.

"You are going to die for this," he said in a quiet, steady voice.

The figure slowly rose, looking at the dying officer, a twisted, evil smile on his face. "I cannot die," his guttural voice proclaimed. Rain cascaded down his pale, bald head.

The figure reached down and picked up Kevin's service pistol. He looked at it with the curiosity of a child before putting it down the front of his pants. He turned around suddenly and ran back toward the hotel.

Russo's gun wavered in his hand. He fired the remaining rounds in his weapon, but they did not strike the assailant, slamming harmlessly into a wall. The assailant turned abruptly and ran down the main alley, out of sight. Russo ran to Kevin's dying body and knelt down beside him, among several spent shell casings. He cradled Kevin's head on his lap as he waited for help to arrive. His hands trembled uncontrollably. He dropped his weapon, the slide locked to the rear. Kevin stared up into Russo's eyes one last time as a steady flow of blood cascaded out of the corner of his open mouth. Kevin raised his head and took one last gasp of air and sank back into Russo's lap. Still no one arrived. Russo could hear traffic on his radio, but he was desensitized and did not care. Kevin's life force slowly left his body in the middle of the trash-strewn alley. Russo's tears intermingled with the cold rain cascading down his face.

The man on the sidewalk was obviously hurt. He was running as fast as he could, but he was beginning to feel pain. He had been hit several times by bullets.

"Get in!" Dr. Keitel yelled out of the open passenger window of the black Mercedes, as he pulled up alongside the curb.

The man on the sidewalk instantly recognized the man yelling at him. He realized that this man was the only one on this world who could help him. He needed to heal; he wasn't ready to die just yet, and for all of his bravado in the alley, he realized that death truly was a possibility. He opened the back door of the Mercedes and dove inside. He slammed the door closed as Dr. Keitel hit the gas and sped off.

CHAPTER 19

"Look at me, man. Tell me what you saw!" the detective demanded.

"I already told you," Russo responded defiantly. "We found the dead woman. Kevin pursued. He got taken out. I fired my pistol at the suspect, and he wasn't even fazed. All right? What else do you want from me?" Russo was now totally soaked from the rain. Someone had placed a fire department blanket over him, but that too was now soaked.

Detective Roman lifted up the yellow police tape and strode purposefully toward the investigating officers. He opened his jacket, revealing his badge on a neck chain, to the officer on the perimeter. Recognizing Officer Russo, Roman immediately quickened his pace toward him. Officer Russo, seated on the ground, buried his face in his hands. Another detective was trying in vain to extract any information he could get. The alley had transformed into a major crime scene. Tarps protected the crime scene from the rain, and forensic technicians busily marked evidence around the woman and the fallen officer, who was further up the alley. Numerous placards on the ground identified shell casings and other evidence by number, so they could be tagged and photographed. The rain continued, but only as a light sprinkle. Darkness forced the technicians to set up portable lights to illuminate the immediate area.

Roman put a hand on the detective's chest and lightly pushed him back from Officer Russo. "Take a break, man."

The detective looked at Roman in profound shock. "Who the hell do you think you are?" he asked, his voice rising.

Roman turned and stared him in the eye, exhaustion and determination emanating from his own eyes.

"I said take a break, jackass. What part of that do you not understand?" His voice was almost a yell, causing a few nearby officers to stop what they were doing and glance toward Roman.

The detective raised his hands in defense. "Fine. The captain will hear about this." He turned his back and walked away.

"Prick," Roman muttered to himself. He knelt down and put his hand on Russo's shoulder. "Ryan, I'm sorry about what happened, but we have to talk, OK?"

Russo looked up at Roman and nodded. "All right, just keep those assholes off of me for now, OK?"

Roman sighed. "Let's take a walk inside and get out of this rain."

Russo got up, and they both retreated into the hotel. It was mostly devoid of cops, save for a couple interviewing Leroy. They both sat down in adjacent puke-green pleather chairs, each chair exhibiting a multitude of rips and tears.

"Tell me what happened," Roman requested. "What did you and Kevin see?"

Russo rubbed his face with his hand and looked up. "We got the call. The guy inside said we were twenty minutes late or something, I dunno. Anyway, he says the guy is out back doing drugs. We go out in the alley and find the first girl. She is almost half-eaten. Nasty."

"Tell me about the girl's wounds."

"She had chunks out of her body, almost like she was bitten by some big animal. Her neck was broken too. Anyway, the body was fresh. Her blood hadn't coagulated yet. She was still warm, man."

"What happened next?" Roman put an L&M to his lips and lit it. He offered the pack to Russo, but he ignored the offer.

"This big guy was there, wearing a leather jacket and pants. Bald dude. He had this other chick held up like three feet off the ground. We heard her screams and ran over. He was strangling her. That's when we opened fire. We thought he was down, but he grabbed Kevin. I emptied my Glock, but he got away. We never did get any backup." Russo paused for a moment, staring at the floor. He looked back up at Roman and said, "I'll take that smoke now."

Roman offered him his pack of L&M's. Russo removed a cigarette and put it to his lips. Roman produced a zippo lighter and lit the cigarette. "I think the man that killed Kevin is involved with three other murders that happened in this area," Roman said. *Well, four, if you count that jackass I shot like seven times at the junkyard.*

"I'm close to breaking this," Roman told Russo. "I can feel it. I've got to get with Detective Seebolt and have him help me sort this mess out."

Russo put out his cigarette in a full ashtray and stood up.

"One last thing," Roman asked. "What happened to the other girl?"

"I don't know. She was taken by ambulance; I think she was still alive." Russo got up to leave. "Didn't you get suspended or something?" he added.

"Something like that. Have you seen Detective Seebolt around?" Russo shook his head, "No, haven't seen him."

Roman briefly shook Russo's hand and went back outside to the alley. He wanted to get a look at the deceased female. He didn't care about the crime scene; he just wanted to look at her wounds.

The open dumpster lid exposed the body. As a photographer snapped pictures of the scene and the body, two technicians examined something on the side of the dumpster. Roman carefully stepped over a large pool of blood and peered into the dumpster.

The woman inside looked like the guy at the junkyard. Parts of her body showed traces of that same black ooze, possibly emanating from the wounds on her shoulder, but he could not be sure. It may have come from the assailant. Roman noticed that her left breast appeared to have been bitten or torn off, and her throat area was deeply bruised. He noticed a small purse in the bottom of the dumpster. He looked at the nearest technician, who was prepping an amino black reagent test to check for fingerprints in the blood.

"You guys retrieve anything out of here yet?"

"No. We are under orders not to touch anything until Captain Martinez and Sergeant Alvarez from Homicide arrive to take charge of the crime scene."

"Is that so?" Roman mused out loud. "Well, I don't have all day." He withdrew a pair of latex gloves from his jacket pocket and put them on. He grabbed an evidence bag from the technician's kit. "I'll just be a moment."

Roman heaved himself into the dumpster, trying hard not to land on the woman. The surefire flashlight illuminated the dumpster sufficiently. He examined the body quickly and paid particular attention to the black ooze around the hole where her breast used to be. He reached down and retrieved the woman's purse. He heaved himself out of the dumpster and opened the purse, trying to take as less time as possible. Its contents seemed ordinary enough until he found a kit junkies use to shoot up and some heroin. He put both back in the purse, which he threw back in the dumpster. The technicians stared at him in disbelief.

"Thanks," Roman said as he walked away from the dumpster. He looked at the crudely sketched map he had drawn earlier and noted the direction Russo said the assailant was said to be headed.

Toward the junkyard. Roman exited the crime scene just as several vehicles made their way in. *I really don't want to go back there alone.*

Roman saw a black RV with what appeared to be a large radar dish on the roof, followed closely by two green camouflaged military Humvees. Trailing behind the strange convoy were Captain Martinez and Sergeant Alvarez in a white unmarked Crown Vic with emergency lights in the grill and dash flashing red and blue.

This is getting too weird. What the hell is the military doing here?

"I am receiving, Matthias," Cruwell said. "Go ahead with your transmission."

"Captain, the policeman is on the move," Matthias replied. "Our target has struck again, this time drawing a large contingent of other police. Our target appears to be heading toward the place we were earlier, with the hole in the fence."

"OK, we will rendezvous at base. The police might be planning an operation at the junkyard. It's just a matter of time before they realize they are dealing with an alien. If they fail to kill it, we must ensure that the target does not escape."

Matthias switched off his mike. From his position across the street from the Ambassador Hotel, he observed the activity with keen interest. He had maneuvered himself toward the alley in back of the hotel, but the police perimeter stopped him. He observed Roman's conversation with an obviously distraught officer who was sitting on the ground, their exit into the hotel, and Roman's emergence a few minutes later.

Roman headed directly toward him. They locked eyes for a brief moment before a small convoy of vehicles pulled into the alley, forcing him to one side and Roman to the other. Matthias noticed Roman pull his jacket up ever so slightly, so as to hide his face, as the last vehicle pulled in. Roman quickly turned up the street toward the junkyard.

Matthias turned his mike back on. “Scotts, do you have a fix on the target’s position?”

Cruwell’s staticky reply came back. “No. He is becoming more difficult to track with this weather. Don’t forget that he’s dead, he omits no heat signature.”

“Thanks for the science lesson,” Matthias said. “Keep trying.” He realized he was beginning to get cold; he was drenched head to toe from the slight by steady rainfall. He pulled his coat around his body and hurried off after Roman. The mission was beginning to feel like another day in the trenches. The darkness swallowed him as he followed the detective, keeping close enough to monitor him but far enough away to be inconspicuous.

CHAPTER 20

I have you now. Roman peeked around a corner of the junkyard fence, expecting that this was where Kevin's killer was taking refuge. The rain had slowed to a light drizzle, almost a mist, and the clouds had cleared so that the moon helped Roman see in the newly arrived nightfall. He put his left hand against the fence to support himself. He hadn't run this far and this fast in quite a while, and he was exhausted and lightheaded. He was pretty sure he hadn't been spotted or trailed, but with the way things had been going, he couldn't take that chance. As he debated whether to call in for backup or not, his cellular phone played the opening theme to *CHiPs.* He was going to ignore it, but out of habit he glanced at the screen, and he recognized Maynard Fontenot's number. He put the phone to his ear.

"Roman."

"This is Maynard Fontenot. I haven't heard from you. What's going on?"

"Look, I can't exactly talk right now. I'm about to bust this guy right now. Let me call you back."

"All right. Look, I turned myself in to my boss. I am suspended and under investigation. I didn't mention your name, though. I could really use your—"

Roman cut in. "*Look,* I'll call you back. I have to go." He ended the call and put the cellular back into his pocket. He drew his Glock and press checked the slide, verifying that he had a round chambered. He thought about using his flashlight but quickly decided against it.

As he edged closer to the hole in the fence, a black Mercedes passed by, driving at a high rate of speed, briefly startling him. It struck him as odd that a car like that would be in a neighborhood like this. Once the car passed around the corner, he looked around again. Seeing no one, he entered the hole in the junkyard fence.

"Come here, you asshole," he muttered under his breath. The rain picked up again, becoming a steady torrent. Roman looked up at the night sky and cursed the rain. Typical Texas weather—you couldn't count on a reliable forecast. He headed toward the location of his last encounter.

Roman had taken about half a dozen steps when he was suddenly flung into a stack of crushed cars. His Glock flew from his grip. The impact momentarily knocked the wind out of him. Although he had difficulty catching his breath, he managed to stagger to his feet. A deafening thunderclap erupted as he looked around the muddy ground for his pistol. As he leaned over to see the ground better, a heavy hand fell on his shoulder, spinning him around. He came face to face with the homeless guy from earlier that day.

The homeless guy was holding his severed arm, which Roman had blown off with the gun from the shuttle. The walking corpse paused and tore a piece of flesh off of the arm and began to chew. The Hispanic guy from earlier that day approached from out of the shadows, moving in very slowly but deliberately. The entrails of someone or something dangled out of its mouth. Each man had a massive chunk of flesh removed from his neck, and they were both devoid of clothes. Several bite marks and pieces of missing flesh covered each of their bodies. Each also had unusual, solid black eyes.

The men's mouths moved as if they were trying to form words, but nothing comprehensible came out, just low, almost inaudible growls. Roman felt hands around his throat, choking the breath out of him and holding him tight. The mouth of his assailant opened, belching forth a god-awful stench Roman likened to that of an animal that had been dead for several days. The man leaned in closer to Roman, as if to bite him. Before he could, two sharp, loud cracks pierced the sound of the rain. He released his grip around Roman's throat and dropped him to the ground.

Roman gasped, struggling to find his breath. Standing in front of the hole in the fence was the man he had made eye contact with in front of the hotel, holding a large caliber handgun. He recognized the trench coat and the Chuck Taylors. The two walking corpses both approached him, the smell of flesh seeming to drive them into action. The man by the fence hole reached into his jacket pocket and removed a magazine with blue ammunition that contrasted sharply with the surrounding darkness. He calmly ejected the magazine from his weapon and replaced it with the new one.

The two living corpses were now no more than ten feet away. Roman crawled away from his attacker and located his Glock on the muddy ground. The man by the fence took aim at the nearest living corpse and fired. The projectile lodged in the chest of the Hispanic guy and erupted from within. Chunks of dead flesh showered the immediate area. The man dropped to his knees and fell face first into the muddy earth. The bulk of his body was consumed by a blue fire that the rain could not douse. The homeless guy seemed unfazed he continued his slow advance toward Roman. The man by the fence aimed again and fired, achieving the same results. The body of the homeless guy dropped to the ground, to be consumed quickly by blue flames.

Roman reloaded his Glock and fired at the nearest prone corpse. "Die you bastard!" He fired half a dozen shots as he rose to his feet, the 9mm Hydro- shocks striking center mass.

The man in the Chuck Taylors ran toward the armless corpse. Behind him was another similarly attired man armed with a large rifle, unlike one Roman had ever seen. Roman ignored them and ran around the back of the pile of stacked cars, looking for Kevin's killer. He found no traces of anyone else in the area. He turned and saw the two men approach him cautiously, each brandishing their similar weapons of amazing firepower. He looked at his Glock and back at their weapons, wondering why he wasn't having much luck shooting bad guys. The three men stared at one another for a moment in silence. A radio transmission coming from somewhere on one of Roman's adversaries broke the tension.

"Hurry up! You are going to have company. Multiple vehicles are arriving at your location! Get out of there!"

The two associates stopped and spoke to one another. "We have to hurry, or we will be surrounded!" Yelling over a deafening thunderclap, both men ignored Roman, leaving him standing there. Their primary target was nowhere to be seen. Sirens could now be heard in the distance.

"We are out of here! Destroy the landing craft!" a voice bellowed from the unseen radio transmitter.

One of them ran back to the hole in the fence and disappeared through it to the street. The other was about to follow when he turned to Roman, who was still standing there in shock.

"I would be careful around here if I was you," the man advised. He carefully made his way toward the half-buried shuttle craft and tossed two round objects with blinking red lights into it from the open door. He ran toward the hole in the fence and jumped through. Roman stood by, holding his pistol by his thigh. He watched with awe as the interior of the shuttlecraft was incinerated and melted beyond recognition, the structure collapsing onto itself. No surrounding objects were affected; the fast but intense blaze was entirely self-contained.

Within moments, uniformed officers swarmed through the hole in the fence. Roman raised his hands, his pistol in his right and his shield in his left.

"Police officer, don't shoot."

"Sit down," Detective Captain Martinez told Johnny Roman. The captain sat in the oversized leather chair behind his desk, and he faced a wall that was plastered with the many decorations and commendations he had acquired over the years. Roman sighed and took the seat he had occupied not that long ago. The morning sun streaked through the open blinds, lighting up the office. Martinez withdrew his cellular phone from his shirt pocket and activated the vibrate mode, before swiveling in his chair to face Roman. He ran his right hand through his gray hair as he leaned his chair back.

"Roman, your caseload seems to be getting beyond your control. I'll cut right to it. As of now, you are to no longer assist Detective Seebolt. As a matter of fact, you are to take a few days off, and in that time I hope you can calm down. As I see it, you're running investigations on your own with some questionable judgment. That junkyard thing was the last straw. I also heard you were at the scene of the hotel murder last night, tampering with evidence." Martinez spoke calmly and evenly, which surprised Roman; he expected to have a piece of his ass chewed off and devoured.

Martinez carefully chose his next words before he spoke. "And don't get me started on your involvement with the missing coroner. I'm having to draft extra officers on overtime for that mess."

"Sir, with all due respect," Roman interrupted, "Seebolt asked me to follow up on some leads, which I did. I think we're close to cracking this, and pulling me off now would severely limit our resources." He paused, not sure that Martinez was paying attention to him. Finally, Martinez broke the silence, much to Roman's relief.

"I know about you and Seebolt working together, but I take my orders from higher up. What is going on is bigger than you or me. I also thought I had made myself clear. You are being placed on administrative leave pending investigation of your discharge of your firearm. That means you are off the street. Don't worry, you won't lose any pay. Anyway, it will give you time to get some sleep. You look like hell."

Roman stared at his interlocked hands, resting in the lap of his Levi's, which still had dried mud on them from the previous night. He had been up for nearly twenty-four hours straight. He figured there wasn't any reason to say anything more, and now that he thought about it, he was very tired. The speaker phone on the captain's desk sounded, breaking his thought.

"Captain, there is a Colonel Little in reception to see you," a female voice said.

Hurriedly, Martinez hit a button on the phone and replied, "Tell him I'll be right down."

Martinez looked up at Roman with his "What are you still doing in my office?" look on his face. "We'll call you when we need you. You are dismissed."

Roman nodded and got up. He had reached the door of the office when he stopped and turned to face Martinez.

"What is the military doing here?"

"I'm late for a meeting, and I don't need to answer your questions. You are suspended. I suggest you stay that way." Martinez retrieved his blazer from a coat rack and nudged Roman out of the way as he left his office.

CHAPTER 21

Roman entered his small one-bedroom apartment and turned on the light, which illuminated a cluttered room. His watch showed 9:02 a.m., indicating that he had been up considerably more than 24 hours now, and he was beginning to feel it. His answering machine, on a cluttered table by the front door, showed one missed call. Curious, Roman hit the play button. Within a second of hearing the annoying, high-pitched voice on the recording, he wished he hadn't.

"I don't know what your problem is, John. We were supposed to have dinner with my parents last night. Not only did you miss that, you have missed just about every other thing I have asked you to attend with me. Don't bother calling me back, since you're obviously too busy anyway." The recording abruptly ended. Roman shrugged in indifference.

He turned and headed across the near end of the living room toward the kitchen. The craving for a cold beer overtook him, blocking any thoughts relating to his sometimes overbearing, and now former, girlfriend.

At least I can get some sleep, I guess. Caught up in the activity of the past day, he hadn't stopped to consider how tired he really was. He tossed his jacket onto a worn black leather couch in the living room; it promptly slid off onto the floor, landing on a half-eaten bag of pork rinds. Several empty beer cans sat on his cluttered glass coffee table. The latest issue of *Hustler* magazine rested on the arm at the opposite end of the couch. Everything from clothes to dirty dishes littered the floor.

Roman walked into the kitchen and opened his refrigerator. Devoid of any food, the refrigerator was nevertheless well stocked in beer. Roman reached in and grabbed a can of Natural Light. After popping it open, he took a long chug. Inhaling deeply, he reached in and grabbed another can and closed the refrigerator door. He stood a moment in the kitchen finishing his first beer. As he was about to set the empty can on the counter, he heard a series of meows and felt his cat rubbing against his leg.

"Hey, Morris, sorry I forgot about you. Hang on, buddy." The meows intensified, and his gray tabby jumped on the counter. Roman opened a can of tuna fish and dumped the contents onto a paper plate, which he set on the counter. Morris immediately went to town, eating hungrily. Roman stroked the cat's back, watching with a smile as Morris's tail pointed straight up and his butt lifted in the air.

A light knock sounded at the front door.

"Who is it?" Roman asked as he unholstered his Glock.He put the pistol behind his leg as he approached the door.

The muffled voice on the other side replied, "Relax, its Maynard, Maynard Fontenot. I ... I don't know where else to go." Fontenot stammered out the last sentence, seemingly rather distraught.

"How did you find my apartment?" Roman asked.

"I ... I followed you from the station. Sorry. I got lucky you were there." Roman holstered his pistol and undid the dead bolt. He sighed and opened the door.

"It doesn't matter. Come in."

Fontenot nodded and walked his large, odorous frame past Roman into the apartment. Roman looked past him into the parking lot outside the door. Satisfied that Fontenot hadn't been followed, he closed the door.

"Stinks in here," Fontenot commented, pulling his shirt over his nose.

Roman walked into the kitchen and retrieved another beer from the refrigerator.

"Are you sure you're not smelling yourself? You smell like a stale fart half the time." The remark made Fontenot's face drop slightly, and Roman silently reminded himself to watch the jokes.

"You'll get used to it," Roman continued. "I forgot to clean out the cat box, and I haven't been home long after a long day out. Beer?"

Fontenot nodded, and Roman tossed a Natural Light in his direction. Fontenot caught it, pulled the flip top, and took a long pull. Eyeing the couch, he turned around and sat down, taking a moment to flip to the *Hustler* centerfold.

"What are you doing over here, anyway?" Roman asked his guest. He crushed his empty can and tossed it into the sink. He walked over to the couch and sat down. Morris ran over and jumped into his lap, purring loudly the moment Roman started scratching his back.

Putting down the *Hustler*, Fontenot replied, "I got fired. I consider myself lucky, though. It could have been worse."

"Are they going to investigate you or anything, or is that it?" Roman asked.

Fontenot took another pull from the beer. "No. That's just it. It's weird, because two bodies have vanished on my watch, and they hardly asked me any questions. It was two suits that caught up with me. They didn't say they were police or anything. I think someone or something else is involved."

Roman continued to rub his cat, now scratching behind his ears. Morris began to drool, in obvious ecstasy. "Well, I found your bodies."

"Say what?" Fontenot finished the rest of his beer and sat the empty can on the cluttered coffee table.

"Yeah, they looked dead enough although they both tried to kill me before these two guys dressed like thugs came out of nowhere and shot both of them with some high tech weaponry I have never seen. The bodies were incinerated, as far as I could tell. No trace left. They saved my ass."

"This is getting too weird. Sounds like CIA or something. I have read about these things." Fontenot shook his head in disbelief. "So what's happening with you? Are you still on the case?"

Roman pushed Morris off of his lap and stood up abruptly. He sighed heavily and stared at a picture hanging above the fireplace, showing his long-deceased father playing golf. "I'm officially on suspension for an officer-involved shooting. The media has been trying to get answers, so the brass is telling me to take a walk for a while." He paused for a second. "Well, at least that's what my boss said to me as I headed to my car."

"Sorry to hear that," Fontenot said.

"Yeah, me too. And when they told me I was suspended, they made no mention of any event that has transpired. I was told not even to worry about doing a report, just to go home and get some sleep. It's all B.S."

Fontenot looked hard at Roman. He removed his glasses from his round face and cleaned the lenses with his shirt. "This is heavy, man. You think the Feds or somebody is in on it? X-files stuff?"

"You know, I would normally tell you no. I mean, this isn't supposed to happen. The dead aren't supposed to walk the earth. But with the weird shit I've seen, I wouldn't be surprised."

Fontenot looked around the apartment, taking in its disarray and peculiar smell. "Can I get another beer?"

Roman nodded, and Fontenot headed into the kitchen. Roman noticed that he seemed to be adjusting to the odor in the apartment, and he decided to let Morris's cat box be for a while; he wasn't in the mood to clean it just yet. He was about to head to the bathroom to take a leak when he heard another knock at the front door. Again he withdrew his pistol from its holster and put it behind his leg, his paranoia getting the best of him. He glanced at Fontenot, in the kitchen, who had found a nearly empty bag of Cheetos and was busy finishing the remnants.

"Are you expecting anyone?" Roman asked Fontenot, who shook his head from side to side. He took a pull from his beer, apparently not concerned about who might be there.

"Who is it?" Roman asked.

The response was slightly muffled by the door. "I need to speak with you. I think we can help each other out."

"With what?" Roman countered. He looked through the peephole in the door but couldn't see anybody.

"I have been following you. I saw you shoot the alien. Perhaps I can make things a little clearer for you."

Roman creased his brow when he heard the word "alien." He undid the dead bolt and opened the door a crack. "Did you say *alien*? Do you think I'm an idiot?" He put on a tough front to put the visitor on the defensive, but deep inside he was curious. A well-built, tall man stepped from his position beside the door to stand in front of it, where Roman could see him. He wore a black FUBU jersey, with the number 00 across the front, and baggy jeans. Roman was taken aback when he gazed into the man's eyes. The pupils were a bright green, with specks of blue. The man's face had a long scar running from the bottom of his left earlobe to the corner of his lip. His short grey hair was spiked straight up.

"Who are you?" Seeing that the man was unarmed, Roman opened the door and lowered his guard. He noticed another man walking from the parking lot toward the apartment. He was smaller in stature that the first but similarly attired, wearing a Houston Astros baseball jersey that seemed to be about two sizes too big.

The first man held out his hand. "I am Colonel Johann Chuikova, Spearhead Corps Commander. This is my associate, Corporal Scotts." Roman holstered his pistol. He shook the colonel's outstretched hand. "I'm Johnny Roman. I am afraid I am a little confused. Are you some kind of special ops unit or what? I was under the impression it was illegal for the military to conduct operations on US soil."

Scotts replied, "We know who you are. And yes, he said, *alien.*" Scotts smiled after the last sentence. "We are not of your planet either."

Roman opened the door wider, stood aside, and let the two men enter his apartment. He again looked around the parking lot and thought a beat-up Ford Mustang parked across the street looked familiar from the last couple of days, but he didn't think anything more of it. He wasn't sure why he trusted these two strangers, or even why he believed them, but somehow he did. As both men entered the apartment, Scotts exclaimed, "Wow, it smells in here!"

Upon seeing the two new visitors, Fontenot pushed past the three men to the door. He looked at Roman and nodded toward the colonel and Scotts. "I hope you know what you're doing," he said to Roman. "These guys have "Fed" written all over them. Later." He quickly stepped outside and closed the door after himself.

Roman dead bolted the door behind Fontenot and faced his new guests. "Uh, sit down," he said, waving toward his couch. The colonel sat down first, at one end, and Corporal Scotts sat next to him. The corporal immediately noticed the *Hustler* magazine and picked it up, and starting thumbing through the well-worn pages.

"I'll get to the point," the colonel said. "We are tracking an alien that has escaped from our sector of space. It just so happens he has landed here on your planet." The colonel paused, observing Roman for any reaction. Seeing nothing besides the expected stunned surprise, he continued. "We have been watching you for some time, and we feel we can be of assistance to you, and you to us. This creature has the potential to create unimaginable havoc upon your population."

"I knew something wasn't right," Roman said. "I emptied my weapon into him, and he wasn't even fazed. And there's the matter of dead people walking out of the coroner's office. If that's connected, I'd agree with you that this has the potential for havoc, all right. But your space alien concept is a little hard for me to take in. I'd buy it if it was a virus or something."

"Well, he *is* an alien to you. He is not of your planet. That is the reality of it. For that matter, so are we. We want to move on him soon, and we could use your help. As for your virus theory, it may not be too far off. He is capable of transferring something to his victims, rendering them incapable of functioning normally."

Roman reached into his jeans pocket and removed an ID card he had found earlier, lying on the ground in the junkyard.

"I found this before the shuttle was blown. Maybe you know what it is."

Scotts reached forward and took the ID. After giving it a quick glance, he announced, "This is a security badge for a Dr. Keitel."

The colonel leaned forward and peered at the ID. "I saw an intelligence report awhile back in which he was rumored to be the enemy's top genetic researcher. Perhaps we are after his experiment. It seems the good doctor was unable to control it."

"He was at the research facility we hit," Scotts added.

Roman walked back to the refrigerator and withdrew three beers. Walking back, he opened two and handed one each to the colonel and to Corporal Scotts.

"You said you are a colonel, yes?"

"That is correct."

"And you're not from this planet?"

"No."

Roman opened the remaining beer and took a small sip before sitting down on the hearth of fireplace. Corporal Scotts eyed his beer with curiosity and smelled the open can. He took a small sip. A slight smile broke across his face. He took a longer pull and gave an approving nod in Roman's direction. The colonel drained his entire can in three successive gulps. He set the empty can down on the coffee table.

"You have anything harder?" he asked.

"Yeah, hold on." Roman walked back into the kitchen and retrieved a half-full bottle of Jim Beam. He grabbed a glass from a cabinet and walked back to the couch. Setting the glass down in front of the colonel, he poured several fingers of the amber liquid into it. The colonel grabbed the glass and took a hearty swig.

"Not bad. It's hard for me to find good rotgut these days."

"I know it's not top shelf, but I wouldn't call Beam rotgut." Roman paused as he watched the colonel finish the glass and pour another. "OK, maybe for you it is. I'm not familiar with what aliens drink." His lip curled up sardonically at one corner.

Roman eyed both men again, noticing their clothing. "I wouldn't mind seeing some proof you guys are from outer space, like maybe a ray gun, your ship, something like that. You could just be some psychos off the street, for all I know—or Feds, like Fontenot thought." Although he asked for the proof, Roman somehow didn't really care if they were aliens or not. He knew, however, that there was something just not normal about these two.

"Of course." Scotts pulled a familiar looking, larger caliber pistol from the back of his pants. He removed the ammunition magazine, exposing the rounds. "These are tipped with high explosives. This weapon also can fire smoke, incendiary, and acid rounds."

"I saw that before, except the ammo was blue," said Roman, remembering the two guys who had saved his ass at the junkyard.

"Actually, our main battle rifles are much better than these pistols. We have a few on the shuttle, but we're trying to avoid using them, as we are trying to minimize our technological footprint on your planet."

"You're what?" Roman asked.

"Our technological footprint. If we all were to die here on your planet, our technology would give an unfair advantage to whoever found it and would upset the balance."

"I see. So it's probably not a good idea to have a crack head running around eating people either. Anyway, I'm not sure I can be of much help to you. I got suspended an hour ago. I'm off the case and off the street. Plus, I haven't slept in something like thirty hours."

The colonel rose from the couch, setting his empty glass on the table as he stood. He walked over to bookcase against one wall, overflowing with books. He withdrew a well-worn copy of the paperback *Doctor Who and the Genesis of the Daleks* off the top of a stack. The cover intrigued him, and he studied it for a moment before replacing the book on the shelf. He turned and faced Roman and withdrew a small black box from his pants pocket. He activated the box and a holographic map appeared, complete with people walking and cars driving.

"Is that in real time?" Roman asked, stepping closer to the image.

"Yes, this is a map of our base of operations. As you can see, there is a lot of traffic around us."

Roman noticed that the neighborhood was run down, and there was indeed a lot of foot and vehicle activity. "You guys could have picked a better part of town."

The colonel shut off the hologram and smiled. "That's why we would like you to help us, Mr. Roman." The colonel put the box back into his pocket. "We need a new base of operations. Plus, you have seen the alien and engaged it. Your knowledge of local customs could help us."

Roman looked around at his place for a moment. He replied, "Well, this place is a little small. What are you offering?"

"Help us catch this alien, and we will be forever in your debt."

Roman considered the open-ended offer for a moment. "I'll tell you what," he said. "You let me borrow that hand cannon, and one of those rifles and some ammo, and you've got a deal. My pistol isn't very effective against your alien. I just want to get that asshole."

"Done, but we will need those back when the time comes."

Scotts handed over his weapon and a couple of extra ammunition magazines. Roman eyed the weapon with satisfaction.

"There is one other thing, Mr. Roman," the colonel said.

"What's that?"

"We have two others in our group. I hope that is not a problem."

Roman was engaged in removing the ammunition magazine and re-inserting it. He enjoyed hearing the whine of the weapon as it powered up.

"No problem."

"Good. Scotts, go fetch Matthias and the captain, and bring our gear in."

Scotts got up, opened the front door, and went outside. Roman went to the door to watch. A few moments later, the corporal returned with Cruwell and Matthias behind him. Both men carried black cases and duffle bags. Matthias handed his equipment to Scotts. Roman put the hand cannon in his waistband at the back his pants. He was amazed at its light weight; he couldn't even feel it in the back of his pants. He looked at Matthias.

"I know you," Roman said.

Matthias nodded.

"I guess I owe you one for saving my ass at the junkyard."

"I expect you would do the same for me," replied Matthias.

Roman turned to Captain Cruwell, who was still standing in the doorway.

"You can put your gear in the bedroom," he said. Scotts and Cruwell both nodded. "Not much space here, sorry," Roman added.

Roman turned toward the colonel and said, "You guys have anything else to drive besides that shitbox parked outside?"

"It is the only vehicle we've appropriated."

"Ditch that heap when you get a chance. I'll drive."

CHAPTER 22

"Glad you make it," the gray-haired man said to the biker standing at the front door of his modest, one-story house. "Please come in and sit down." He moved his wheelchair to the side of the door and pointed to a black leather couch against one wall of the living room immediately inside. He wore a red flannel shirt and sported a gray, unkempt beard that reached the middle of his chest. An oxygen mask hung over his shoulder, within easy reach.

"All right," the visitor said. "This had better be good, Dean." The biker, dressed in biking leathers, entered the house, smoking a cigarette. He saw two televisions on in the living room, one tuned in to CNN and the other on FOX News. The biker closed the door behind him and followed Dean into the living room, which was cluttered with grouped arrangements of newspapers, boxes of dialysis bags, and oxygen canisters. He took a seat on the couch.

"I think it will be worth your while. Hold on, let me get the specs." The host opened his laptop and powered it on. He adjusted his thick-lensed glasses as he waited for the computer to load.

"You got any beer around here?"

"Come on, Cyrus, you know better than that." He looked up from his laptop and lifted his shirt, exposing a tube protruding from his side. "Get yourself a Sprite."

Cyrus retreated into the kitchen, sending several cats scurrying across the counter. He opened the fridge and pulled out a half-full two-liter bottle. "OK, I've got it," Dean announced.

When Cyrus returned from the kitchen with a glass full of the soda, he leaned over and looked at Dean's laptop.

"Here it is," Dean said. "My boy Stevie sent me this as a favor for some equipment I built him. He's a damn good hacker. I've been watching it, and it's good. The pickup is for next Wednesday."

"What the fuck are you talking about?"

"Oh, sorry, I still get excited sometimes." Dean pushed his glasses farther up his nose. "This particular bank normally does cash transfers via armored car on Wednesdays, just prior to opening."

"OK. So what? I'm not hitting an armored car, too much risk. I did four years for armed robbery, you know that."

"No, listen, this job is different. This particular branch has missed the last three transfers to the cash depot. That's almost three weeks." Dean shifted his weight in his wheelchair. "They changed armored companies, which created a delay at a few branches. But this one—" Dean tapped the laptop screen for emphasis. "This is one that can set you up for a while."

Cyrus drank the rest of his Sprite and said, "Cut the shit, Dean. How much are we talking about?"

Dean took his glasses off and retrieved a red bandanna from his shirt pocket. He wiped a few beads of sweat off his forehead and hit a few more keys on the laptop.

"Here, look at these last few cash drops. You're looking at an easy 400 to 600 thousand."

Cyrus stood up and started to pace the room. "That's a good score, but that's a lot of risk. I don't know. What about going in at night?"

"I can't help you at night. Look, it's a regional branch. That's the only way to get that kind of score, and even then it's only because the cash is piling up awaiting pickup. I mean it's a helluva lot better than the normal one or two thousand score you usually get in a smash and grab.

"Yeah, well ... OK, I see your point. What do you need upfront? I'm not saying I'll do it, but what do you need?" Dean asked, his interest piqued.

Dean closed his laptop and turned his wheelchair around so that he was looking toward Cyrus. "I need twenty-five grand up front and another twenty-five after you complete the job."

Cyrus stopped pacing and faced Dean directly. "Wait a minute, check me on this. You want us to do this in daylight, with witnesses, and maybe have to shoot it out with the cops? Why can't we get in the night before, disabling the alarms, cracking the vault overnight?"

"I can't help you there. I'm getting old and haven't been in the game much lately. All I can guarantee is that the money is there. You hit it fast and hard, and you should be good. There's a teller on the inside that just started working. She'll make sure the manager is identified and can help with opening the vault. Also, Stevie told her how to disable the silent alarm."

"A teller on the inside? Sounds like you assumed I would say yes."

"No more than two guards, probably old farts that aren't even carrying ammo. Twenty-five grand also gets your crew some serious firepower, police scanners, cell phone jammers, and whatever else you need. I'm talking machine guns like they have in Afghanistan, the big ones. You're in and you are out fast if you don't screw up."

"OK. You got a deal."

"Good. I'll get you the rest of the specs and a phone number for the weapons. You know the way out."

Cyrus set down his glass, walked to the door, opened it, and paused. He turned around and asked, "Why do you do all this? I mean, you're about to croak. No offense."

"None taken," Dean said as he started to cough. He grabbed his oxygen mask and inhaled deeply from it, and replaced it over his shoulder. "I do it because I have nothing else to do. It excites me, and it keeps me busy."

"Yeah, whatever, man. See you around."

CHAPTER 23

After the black Mercedes E350 sedan passed through the gate of the underground parking garage, Dr. Keitel hit the button on the small transmitter again, closing the gates behind him. He replaced the transmitter in the glove box, closing the little door. He had been through here three times already. The first time was with his unwilling hostage, whom he had abducted earlier from the county coroner's office. After a brief moment of intense persuasion, the hostage had led him to his loft apartment, in the small downtown building above this garage. The underground parking garage was excellent for concealment.

On a second trip, Dr. Keitel removed his salvaged equipment from the shipping container and transported it here. The crash site was becoming too dangerous, and it was too risky with the attention his patient was bringing. The solution was having a side effect he had not counted on: Its properties could transfer from the host to another body, and the effects were similar.

His third trip, just ending, was the most rewarding, as he finally recovered his patient, and just in time. While he was driving to the apartment, he kept looking into the back seat. What he saw was not very promising. The solution's effects were indeed short term, and he needed to find out why.

The doctor quickly pulled into the parking space assigned to his hostage and the Mercedes. He parked without a problem; there was nothing complex about operating the vehicle, and he had mastered it within minutes. He exited the vehicle and scanned the garage. It contained only three other vehicles. He quickly opened the driver's side rear door, grabbed his patient by the arm, and pulled. He arose slowly, with difficulty, and did not protest or struggle. The unlikely duo slowly made their way into the elevator. Dr. Keitel used his hostage's key card and activated the lift by swiping it in a card reader. He pressed the number for the third floor and within a few seconds, the doors opened. He put his shoulder under his patient's arm and guided him down the hall to the apartment. Using the key card once again, he opened the door and entered.

"I must work quickly," Dr. Keitel told his semiconscious patient. "Yes, you have sustained much damage. There is so much for you to learn, especially about protecting yourself. If only you wouldn't have taken off on your own." Dr. Keitel helped his patient onto the island in the spacious kitchen and had him lie on his back. He opened his patient's perforated leather jacket and began making an assessment.

"The rate of healing has slowed; there are multiple wounds consistent with a small-caliber projectile weapon. Yes, yes. Oh my." Dr. Keitel stopped as he examined the metallic port in the lower abdominal area. "The waste port is damaged; most likely one of these projectiles hit it at an angle. It is folded shut. No wonder you're beginning to overheat. You can't dissipate heat fast enough."

Dr. Keitel put on a pair of surgical latex gloves he had found in a box in the apartment. He wiped away some of the black blood that had begun to seep from the damaged port in the abdominal area. He retrieved a large clamp from one of his cases, along with a simple pair of pliers. Holding one tool in each hand, and with each attached to a different part of the waste port, he pulled and grunted until the port opened. Satisfied, he replaced the tools and removed a surgical kit from one of his cases. Some of the lacerations were deep, and he stitched up those. Once that was complete, he loaded a syringe from a bottle of the pink solution. He was about to inject it into his patient's arm when he noticed bruising and a distinctive puncture mark at the bend of the elbow.

"Curious. He must have tried to self-administer something." He shrugged and inserted the needle into the black vein. Depressing the plunger, he watched all of the pink liquid disappear into his patient's arm. He placed the syringe on the counter behind him and began to check for any other physical signs of damage. Seeing none, he sighed and pulled off the surgical gloves. He opened another case which had a small computer terminal and a coiled hose apparatus. He switched on the computer and connected the hose to the newly repaired exhaust port. The computer terminal initiated a diagnostic check of the implanted organs and tissue. Seeing that the check would take some time, he poured himself a cup coffee and walked into an adjacent room, most likely a study, as it was lined with numerous books on various subjects. His hostage was sitting in a black leather office chair, his hands and feet duct taped. He still wore his surgical scrubs, which were now soaked in blood. His throat had been cut from left to right, with the blood pooling on the floor underneath the chair. His head was slumped forward, his chin resting against his chest. Dr. Keitel briefly thought he may have been overzealous in killing his captive so soon, but he quickly reassured himself. He had acquired what he needed from the man, and he did not need any more witnesses. He reached for a stereo receiver and hit the play button. Turning up the volume, he smiled as he sipped his coffee with Beethoven's Symphony Number 5 in C Minor reverberating throughout the apartment.

"Feeling better?"

It took a moment for the patient to process the question. After a moment, he understood. Yes, he was feeling better, much better. He wearily opened his eyes. He felt cool, actually very comfortable. He sat up and looked around, immediately realizing he was in a tub filled with water. His jacket and pants had been removed, leaving him feeling vulnerable. He stood up with ease, chilled water running off his body and down into the tub.

"Take this and dry yourself off. When you're finished, I have much to tell you. Your clothes have been cleaned and are here for you. I couldn't find anything here for you to wear. The previous owner wasn't very large in stature."

The patient watched the man, whom he remembered from earlier, depart the bathroom. The man had saved him, that much he remembered. His body was nearly healed; most of the lacerations had healed themselves or were covered with adhesive bandages. He looked in the mirror and noticed the patchwork of black veins snaking across his chest and down his arms. Grabbing the towel, he dried off and quickly put the jeans and leather jacket back on. Most of the blood and other stains had been cleaned off. He walked through the main living area of the apartment and into the kitchen, where he sat down in a chair that was pulled out from the table.

"I hope you recognize me now. I am Dr. Keitel. I have been working on you for quite some time. Do you remember me?"

"Yes."

"Good. I am preparing a field kit for you. Show me your arm."

He obeyed, retracting the sleeve of his jacket, exposing his pale forearm. Dr. Keitel secured the end of a strip of duct tape to his patient's arm and pressed a syringe filled with pink solution against the forearm, parallel to it. He pulled the tape across the syringe and pressed it down on the skin on the other side. He placed two more syringes against the forearm and secured them similarly with the same length of tape. He wrapped that section of arm, holding the three syringes, running the tape twice around the arm. Satisfied, he pulled the jacket sleeve down.

"That's in case you get into trouble again. Take a syringe and plunge it anywhere on your body. Once the solution wears off, I think that is when the blood lust begins and you lose control. I apologize for the cold bath, but ice helps bring your core temperature down to manageable levels in an emergency. You were overheating because the port was broken, but it's repaired for now. As long as you keep your core body temperature down, you should be ok. Otherwise your body will begin to shut down and you will die eventually. Your brain is the key. You have been generating entirely too much heat, and your body cannot regulate it fast enough. While you were unconscious, I took some blood, and somehow a synthetic opioid got into your system, something similar to what I would prescribe for pain. I must implore you to inject only the solution into your body—nothing else. Any outside substance you introduce can amplify the effects of hyperthermia, leading to brain tissue destruction."

He sat there trying to remember something—anything. The events of the past kept coming to him in gaps while he was unconscious. He remembered fighting in a war, in different places, and he also remembered being shot multiple times and feeling almost no pain. It dawned on him that he was extraordinarily powerful, but with limitations. His body could endure only so much … and he was tired no longer.

"You're not saying much," Dr. Keitel commented. He sat down across from his patient, sipping on a cup of coffee. "I have a plan." He took another sip, carefully eyeing the other man, who sat passively, black eyes unblinking. "We are going to create an army of followers, but we need to do it the right way. Your methods, while instinctive, are creating too much attention. Once you are at 100%, we will proceed."

"An army," the words escaped his dry, chapped lips, "that I can lead once more."

Dr. Keitel smiled and set his coffee cup on the table. "Yes, you will once more lead an army on the field of battle. With my help, you will be unstoppable."

The black Mercedes pulled into the parking lot of a T&A Truck Stop, just off of the interstate. Dr. Keitel drove the vehicle into a parking spot, halted the car, and placed it in park. Across the road was a large, nondescript wooden building, but what was behind it, nestled inside a gated compound, intrigued the doctor the most. The smaller, one-story building held a faded, hand-painted sign reading "Dean's Automotive and Body Shop." Even at first glance, it didn't seem like much of an automotive shop. A large party appeared to be taking place inside, and loud music blasted out whenever the front doors were opened. A long line of motorcycles of various makes and models fronted the building, and a few pickup trucks were parked haphazardly in the dirt lot.

"This might be a good place to try," Dr. Keitel said to his passenger. "The city is getting too dangerous, with the police attention. Go in there and see what you can do. We need soldiers. I'll be close by."

With a grunt, the passenger exited the car, closing the door behind him. Dr. Keitel backed the Mercedes out of its spot and left the lot rapidly. His passenger walked purposefully across the street, anticipating a battle. He was ready.

Two bikers, each drinking a bottle of Lone Star beer, looked at the strange man walking through the front door, and one commented "Get a load of this fucker." The man, built with a solid frame and wearing a brown motorcycle jacket marked with numerous holes, entered the smoke-filled, crowded bar. The jacket was unzipped, and he was bare-chested beneath it. His jeans, torn in several places, featured numerous stains that appeared to be blood.

The man stopped a few feet inside of the crowded bar and began to look around. A large sign over the bar read "Meine Ehre heißt Treue." The crowd was pretty rough; the majority wore their colors on the backs of their cuts. The words "SS Viking" were emblazoned on a top rocker on the backs of their leather cuts, complementing a large distinctive skull and crossbones of the Waffen SS. "Texas" was stitched on the bottom rocker patch, with a small rectangular "MC" patch and diamond shaped "1%er" patch completing the cut. Several bikers noticed the newcomer and eyed him with keen interest. The area around the pool table emptied as Cyrus walked toward the bar's entrance. He was wearing black leather chaps with the same distinctive SS Viking cut and several additional patches, the most notable reading "Club President." He displayed several SS-inspired tattoos; most noticeable was a large red swastika on his left shoulder.

Cyrus slowly walked toward the unwelcome visitor, holding a pool cue with both hands. "I think you're lost, friend. This is a private bar."

Motörhead's "Ace of Spades" had stopped playing, and the bar was all but silent, with all attention on the newcomer. The bikers had surrounded the man. Some held knives, and a couple had drawn pistols.

The pale man did not speak. His black eyes were fixated on a redheaded waitress with curly hair standing behind the bar. She was frozen in position, unable to move as her gaze met his. He seemed to be staring at her large breasts, which were barely contained in her low-cut leather halter top.

Cyrus stepped down from the elevated platform holding the pool table area and stood directly in front of the man. "You deaf or what? If you want trouble, you've come to the right place."

The man turned and faced the bar. "I'm thirsty."

Howls of laughter erupted from the crowd. Cyrus stepped closer, now face to face with the man.

"You got some balls, buddy. This is my clubhouse and bar, and I say who gets to stay and who gets to drink." He looked out at the crowd and continued, "Should we let him stay or make him go?"

A chorus of boos and other noises emanated from the crowd. A couple of beer bottles arced across the room and struck the man across the back of the head. He remained in place, unfazed.

"The people have spoken, my friend. Now get the fuck out!"

Cyrus raised a fist and landed a tremendous blow on the man's face, knocking his head backward. Still, the man did not flinch. He stared at Cyrus with his black eyes and spoke very softly. "Do not do that again."

Cyrus stepped back, holding his hand in pain, almost in a daze. He felt like he had just punched a concrete wall. The man grabbed him by the throat, picked him up, and held him three feet off the ground. He tossed Cyrus into a group of other bikers, sending the bunch crashing to the ground. A pistol shot rang out. Mayhem quickly ensued, as several terrified women ran out of the bar and the remaining bikers grabbed whatever weapons they could find. The pale man turned around, grabbed the nearest biker, and threw him through the front door, sending wood splinters flying in every direction.

Within minutes, the battle was over. Smashed tables and chairs littered the entire floor, and bikers lay in heaps. The pale man turned back to the red-haired waitress, still standing behind the bar. He strode purposefully toward her.

"Give me beer," he commanded in a low tone. The terrified waitress retrieved a mug and filled it with beer from a tap.

"Here," she responded nervously, her hand shaking as she set the mug on the bar.

The man looked at the glass and lifted it and drank the contents in one gulp. A small smile crossed his face. "More," he said.

The waitress refilled the mug, which the stranger again drained in one gulp. He paused and turned around. The bar was pretty much empty, save for the gang leader and a few of his disciples. The rest had managed to crawl or walk out. The remaining few managed to extricate themselves from the debris and stand. Two drew pistols but did not aim them at the stranger. Cyrus regained his composure, stepped forward, and spoke. "When someone enters my bar and they are not welcome, they die." Seeing no reaction from the man, he continued, "I like your style. I think perhaps we may be able to help each other." The waitress filled the man's mug again, and he again drained it in one gulp.

"You ever hear of the Viking Motorcycle Club?" Again, the man provided no response or reaction; he just stared straight ahead, blankly. The waitress continued to refill his glass. Cyrus shifted from one booted foot to the other nervously. He continued, "You should join up with us. It would be worth your while."

The man finished his beer in one gulp once again and slammed the glass to the ground, shattering it into several pieces.

"I need an army, weapons."

Cyrus responded matter-of-factly, "We have lots of guns. Whatever you want, we have or we can get, but this army is mine."

The man turned around and looked at the waitress. "I want her." The waitress didn't react; she just stared into the depth of his black eyes.

"She's yours, man."

"Randy, I swear I shot that guy," the skinny biker said, as he took a long pull off a fat joint. He sat on a stack of worn out tires, with Randy standing beside him; both of them stared in the direction of a nearby mobile home. The night sky was dark and cloudy, but so far there had been no rain. "I hit him right in the back, and he didn't even flinch. There is something seriously weird about that dude." He passed the joint back to Randy, who was standing next to him.

"You shouldn't shoot people in the back anyway, you pussy." Randy took a hit off the joint and started to hack as he inhaled the smoke and broke out into laughter.

The SS Viking Motorcycle Club compound sat in a four-acre tract of land a few miles north of the city, in a rural area. The men talking were just outside two run-down, double-wide mobile homes, parked side by side. A giant red flag bearing a black swastika fluttered on a flagpole nearby. Below it was another flag, displaying the club colors. Several customized Harley-Davidson and Triumph motorcycles were parked haphazardly all over the compound. Beer cans and bottles littered the ground, almost as if they had fallen from the sky like rain. Several scantily clad women, ranging from jailbait to middle-aged and varying in build from anorexic looking to obese, lounged around. A few bikers with AK-47 rifles slung over their shoulders guarded the compound's gates. Inside one of the mobile homes, an initiation of sorts was taking place.

"I can't believe you don't have any ink, man," Cyrus said to the man sitting on a stained couch, looking at his naked upper body. "We got to change that." He waved at one of his bikers, who disappeared into a back room and reappeared moments later with a tattoo needle gun.

"We're going to put some ink on you. The crowded mobile home erupted into yells and cheers. The man said nothing. Someone had cranked up the stereo, which blared Skrewdriver through the speakers. The man allowed himself to be led to a kitchen table and chair by the red-haired waitress from the bar at the other end of the mobile home. He sat down, and one of the bikers began to tattoo on his shoulder. The red-haired waitress sat in the man's lap and raised a joint to his lips. He inhaled deeply. Swallowing the smoke, he began to cough but immediately took another hit. An image of the Nazi swastika began to form on his shoulder as the steady buzzing of the needle gun continued. The night was just beginning.

The sound of automatic fire ripped through the air. Several bikers were lined up side by side, shooting at an old washing machine and refrigerator. Both were liberally perforated.

Cyrus handed his new SS-Viking member a SAW M-249 light machine gun and said, "Try this on for size."

The man took it, examined it for a second or two, and aimed at the washing machine. He let the machine gun rip in bursts of ten to fifteen rounds. Expended shell casings flew out the side of the gun. Within moments, the box magazine was expended. The washing machine had a neat three-inch hole in the center of its front.

Seeing the smile on the man's face, Cyrus said, "You like that? That's what the Marines are kicking ass with in Afghanistan."

"It will do."

"Good. You're carrying it tomorrow when we hit the bank."

The other bikers on the firing line ceased shooting. Cyrus put his arm around the man's shoulder and led him to the other mobile home which served as the club headquarters. "There is something I want you to be a part of." Two of the other bikers attempted to follow inside the mobile home but were turned away. "I need to speak with our brother alone," Cyrus said to the two bikers.

As the door slammed shut, the first said to the second, "That's bullshit. Since when does Cyrus discuss plans without us?"

The second biker replied, "I don't know. That new guy just ain't right. It would be a real shame if they both had an accident tomorrow."

"Yeah, I see what you mean. It would be a real shame. I ain't cutting up my share for that fucker. There needs to be some changes around here. Who does Cyrus think he is letting someone in, bypassing our laws? I was a fuckin' prospect for two years before I got in. This ain't right."

"Sit down," Cyrus said. He reached into an ice chest and retrieved two Busch tallboys. He tossed one to his new member. "You need a name, man. I don't know what to call you."

The other man opened his beer and began to chug its contents. He responded, "Call me whatever you like. I remember I was a corps captain once. I was killed in action." His voice drifted off as he sat down on a worn-out, stained cloth couch. The fresh swastika tattoo on his shoulder caught the dim light from a grimy window.

Cyrus rubbed the back of his shaved head around the tattooed image of the SS runes. "Whatever. Your name is the Reaper. And tomorrow you're going to reap some souls." Cyrus took a big chug from his tallboy, and added, "And a shitload of money too." He threw his head back and slammed the rest of his beer. Tossing the can in the corner, he continued, "We are going to take down a bank. There's a huge amount of cash being transported out. I have someone on the inside that got us all the details. It's easy in and out. I want you in on it, man. I want you to back me up. It's going to be a big score, you can count on that."

Reaper stood up and pulled a bag from his jeans pocket, filled with a green, leafy substance he got from another club member. He grabbed some rolling papers off of the counter by the kitchen sink and began to roll himself a joint. This new activity probably was the most enjoyable aspect of his new existence. "Enjoy it tonight," Cyrus said, "but have a clear head tomorrow." He stood up and headed for the door. He stopped and turned around. "What happened to Susie? I haven't seen her all morning. I know she was all over you last night."

Reaper finished rolling his joint and looked up. "She is around. She serves me now."

"Yeah, OK. If you want her for your old lady I have no issue with that. She's too old for most of the guys anyway. We're going to gear up tonight, so make sure your shit is wired tight."

About 30 minutes later, Reaper stumbled out of the club headquarters trailer. Once he disappeared into the darkness, two bikers strode purposefully inside. Cyrus was sitting on the sofa, smoking a joint staring at the ceiling.

"What the fuck do you two want?" Cyrus asked absentmindedly.

A tall, lanky biker pulled a chair from the kitchen and faced it backwards before sitting down. A rectangular patch on the front of his cut read, "SGT AT ARMS." The other one took a seat at the end of the couch.

"I will tell you what I want. First off, you can't admit new members without a club majority vote. This guy could be a Fed, for all we know, and you just let him in."

"Is that all?" Cyrus responded calmly.

"No, and you letting him onto our score. That was supposed to be kept quiet. Who knows who he might tell?"

Cyrus leaned forward and extinguished his joint into an ashtray that hadn't been emptied in days. He sat back against the couch, interlocked his fingers behind his head, and let out a large sigh.

"OK, listen, Skinny. I know what you are saying, but I think we have an opportunity here." Cyrus removed a Marlboro Red from a pack from his shirt pocket and lit it. "This guy ain't no Fed. He's fucking insane. He was shot and stabbed, for Christ's sake, and there's hardly a mark on him. He can take the heat." He took a long drag and continued. "This score Dean put me onto is going to set us straight for a long time. But there's a reason I have only you and Randy on it. I know I can trust you. We were part of the original five. Shit, we did four years together in Huntsville."

Skinny bowed his head and rubbed the back of it, and Randy nodded solemnly. "Yeah, we have seen some shit," Randy said.

"Do you trust me?" Cyrus asked.

Skinny raised his head and looked Cyrus directly in his eyes. "You're my brother, man. I trust you, but—" His voice trailed off slightly. "Sometimes I question the direction you are taking the club in. I mean, we don't know this guy. He isn't normal, man."

Cyrus leaned forward and put his hand on Skinny's shoulder. "You gotta trust me on this one. This guy is crazy, and if we keep him high and drunk he will take the fall or get wasted. That's why I originally had those two other prospects in. But damn, why waste two prospects when we have this guy? He's an animal, and when we get the score, I'll put a bullet in his head personally." Cyrus stood up and looked at Randy. "Are we good?"

Randy looked at Skinny nodding in the affirmative. "Yeah, we're good man, but good luck putting him down with one bullet." The two bikers stood up and gave each other a quick embrace. Cyrus stood up, and Skinny embraced him as well.

"I'm good," Skinny said. "The club is going to ask questions, though. We can't let on he is in the club, prospect or not. You know they will get pissed if we made a decision without a club vote."

Cyrus lit another cigarette. "I'll handle the club. As far as he knows, he's in. He ain't gonna be around long enough to earn a cut. You guys just get everything prepped. Tell Melvin and Notch they ain't goin' on this run with us. Don't tell them why."

"I'll handle the prospects," Randy said.

"When the time comes, I'll take care of him. You have my word," Cyrus said.

Mozart's Symphony 40 in G Minor filled the interior of the Mercedes. Dr. Keitel took no notice of the flashing red and blue lights behind him until an amplified voice brought him out his trance.

"Black Mercedes, pull over. This is the Highway Patrol, pull over now."

"Oh my." Dr. Keitel quickly pressed the brake and eased the Mercedes onto the shoulder of the interstate. He looked out of the rearview mirror and watched a policeman inside a cruiser wearing a curious looking hat talk into a handheld radio. After a few moments, he exited the car. A spotlight was turned on, briefly blinding the doctor. He cursed silently under his breath and quickly palmed a scalpel from a bag of equipment on the seat next to him, concealing it under his right thigh. The trooper approached the Mercedes and tapped on the glass. After a moment of looking for the right button, Dr. Keitel lowered the driver's side window.

"Texas state trooper, sir. I clocked you doing 89 in a 55. License and registration please." The state trooper rested his right hand on his holstered pistol, and his left hand skimmed a flashlight over the back seat.

Dr. Keitel made a pretense of looking through Dr. Jewell's wallet. "I—I'm sorry. I seem to have lost my license. I know I had it yesterday."

"How about the registration, sir?" The State Trooper asked.

Registration. Dr. Keitel considered this. He had Dr. Jewell's wallet, but his identity card had his picture on it. That wouldn't work. He thought about the glove box. The gate opener for the apartment was in there, and he had seen a bunch of papers. He reached forward and opened the glove box, retrieving a black folder. He opened it and showed it to the trooper.

"OK, that's your insurance, and that is your registration. Are you James Jewell?"

"Yes, I am," Dr. Keitel replied nervously.

"OK. Sit tight. I'll be right back." The trooper turned off his flashlight and began to walk back to his car. His head was down as he checked the registration. *Probably just some rich old fart out for a joy ride.* He didn't hear Dr. Keitel quietly open the driver's side door and step out. Passing traffic, coupled with his dispatcher talking to other troopers in the area, provided enough background noise that he didn't hear the approach of the man behind him. Dr. Keitel pressed the scalpel into the palm of his hand and moved quickly. In one quick motion, he reached around the trooper's neck and sliced from ear to ear. The sharp blade cut easily through the carotid artery and into the trachea. The trooper dropped the papers and fell to his knees, choking on his own blood. Dr. Keitel watched him struggle, holding his neck with both hands as his blood poured out. Within seconds he ceased his struggle and fell face forward on the asphalt. Dr. Keitel quickly dragged the trooper's body off the shoulder of the interstate. Fortunately, no passing vehicles had slowed down or stopped, and he figured he had not been observed. He removed the trooper's pistol from its holster and quickly climbed back into Mercedes. The trooper's dash-mounted camera recorded the black Mercedes spinning its tires and merging back onto the interstate.

CHAPTER 24

Roman sat at the weathered dining room table, eating a peanut butter sandwich while holding a half-quart carton of milk. "You guys picking anything up?"

Corporal Scotts looked up from his terminal and removed the headphones from his head. "Nothing. It's been two days, and the activity has been minimal. Matthias and the captain have been unsuccessful as well. The junkyard has been sealed off. It's as if our target has vanished."

Roman finished his sandwich and took a pull from the milk carton. "A guy like that doesn't stay quiet for long."

From downstairs, the colonel yelled, "I'm going back to the shuttle to report. I might be a while. Raus was letting me have it last time telling me it was taking too long. I fear that if we don't find our alien, we will be forced to leave. He is taking a tremendous risk staying in his position. It's a matter of time before he is discovered."

Scotts got up from his chair. "I'll prep the trans-mat," he replied.

"No, I can get it. Just find our target," the colonel said as he headed up the stairs.

Scotts nodded and sat back down.

Roman set his milk down on the table and picked up the headphones, putting them on his head. Familiar police and fire traffic could be heard. He took keen interest in a series of police transmissions involving multiple codes; a robbery in progress, shots fired, and an officer down flooded the net. Roman recognized the locations as not too far away. He got up and looked at the voice communicator that Corporal Scotts used to talk with

Sergeant Matthias or whoever else was in the Ford doing scanner sweeps for the alien. He spoke into the transmitter.

"Hey, does anybody read me on this?"

"This is Cruwell. Is that you, Johnny?"

"Yeah."

"What is it?"

"You may want to check your position. There is some heavy activity up your way. Sounds like a bank robbery or something. Our guy might be involved. It seems like his style, a lot of shooting that seems excessive for a typical bank robbery in this area."

The voice transmission replied, "OK. Do you have an exact location?"

"Stand by; I'll try to get a location for you."

Roman put the headset on and listened for a moment. He picked up the voice communicator again. "It's a bank at the intersection of Anderson Road and Marsh Lane.

"Yeah, OK, I got it. I see it on the holomap. We aren't too far away. Ask Scotts to patch the radio traffic through to us."

Scotts begin to type feverishly on his portable computer terminal, patching into the computer on their orbiting ship which was in a sense acting like a satellite. He immediately brought up a live 3-D schematic of the bank, outlined in green against the black screen. Red squares representing cars drove up and down the street. Nothing seemed out of the ordinary until Scotts pointed to a larger red square, possible representing a small van or truck parked directly outside the front door of the bank. Now Roman could see orange and yellow heat signatures of three people running to the van from the bank. More red green shapes started to pull into the bank parking lot. Now Roman could see orange flashes pulsing intermittently towards the direction of the smaller shapes.

"Gunfire?" Roman asked.

"A lot of it from what I'm seeing," replied Scotts. "You receiving this Matthias?" he asked through the headset.

"That's a good copy," Matthias replied. "Enlarge your image and look at the back of the larger vehicle. That may be our alien."

Roman and Scotts looked closer to the back of the larger vehicle and saw pulsing red flashes, with much faster frequency than the others. "Definitely a larger caliber weapon," said Scotts. He typed a command into the terminal keyboard, enlarging the image. Roman immediately knew what he was looking at.

"He has no heat signature, just a black outline." Roman sat back in his chair and let a deep breath. That guy is not right."

By now the image began to show the vehicle moving in the parking lot, the volume of fire increasing. Within seconds it broke through the perimeter the other smaller vehicles had attempted to set up.

"Matthias you better hold back. There is too much firepower out there."

"Copy that, get some heavier weapons and meet us. We will take him out together."

Roman was already loading shells into his shotgun. "Let's get this asshole," he said grimly.

CHAPTER 25

The white van was filled with cigarette smoke as it circled the block for the third time. Skinny was keeping an eye out for the cops and the armored car in case it was early for the pickup. Randy, Cyrus, and Reaper were in the back loading bullets into magazines and checking the actions on their rifles.

"Skinny," Cyrus said, "idle the van out front. If you see any heat before three minutes, hit the horn." Cyrus fastened his bullet proof vest and put a plain black leather jacket on over it.

Skinny nodded as he parked the windowless cargo van outside the bank. The bank had just opened, but it already had a lot of customers inside.

"Lock and load," Cyrus said. "Try not to shoot any civilians if you can avoid it. Dean said there are always two security guards on site when they have drops. Take those fuckers out first, they will be armed. I'll get the key from the manager. Reaper is going to stay by the door with the machine gun. He will keep the cops off of us if they get too close. Randy, you watch my back and sack up the cash. The insider is a woman, and she is supposed to have a tattoo on her right arm of a dragon. Skinny, keep an eye out for the armored cars; they should be here soon for the pickup. We should be long gone before they get here. Everyone clear?"

The crew nodded, save for Reaper. He was busy loading an ammunition belt into his M-249. His hands worked expertly, even though he could not recall ever having working with this kind of weaponry.

"All right, let's get it on!" Cyrus shouted.

Each of the men but one pulled a black ski mask over his face. With the exception of Cyrus and Reaper, they each wore a Vietnam-era military flak jacket, covered with extra ammunition magazines they had duct taped on. The crew burst out of the back of the van, straight into the bank. Once through the front door, Randy leveled his AK-47 and immediately shot the first security guard point blank with a three-round burst. The other guard drew his revolver and fired, missing the robbers and striking the front door glass, which spiderwebbed but did not shatter.

"Get him!" Randy yelled.

Cyrus opened up with his AK-47 and dropped the guard with one shot to the head causing the busy bank to erupt into screams and frantic yelling from the customers and employees. Most of the people inside were on the ground for safety. Randy jumped on top of the teller counter, firing two rounds into the ceiling.

"Nobody moves!" yelled Randy. "We don't want to kill anybody else. We're just here for the money. Cooperate and you'll live to see your families and all that bullshit!" After completing his announcement, Randy jumped behind the teller counter. A pale-skinned woman with black lipstick and black eyeliner was sitting down in a desk chair, apparently not too frightened. She deftly moved the sleeve of her blouse just a bit for Randy to see the dragon tattoo hidden underneath her sleeve.

"Empty the drawers, sweetheart," Randy told her, the ski mask covering his face concealing his grin. *This is too damn easy.*

The teller got up and began to empty the cash drawers from the teller lines into a large canvas sack. Across the counter, Cyrus had quickly identified the manager, who had been sitting behind his desk.

"Give me the vault key," he told the man.

"I don't know what you're talking about," the manager replied. "The vault is on a time lock. I cannot open it."

Cyrus punched the manager square in his beaky nose, knocking his wire-framed glasses onto the floor. The manager's nose began to bleed profusely down his face and onto his shirt. Cyrus leveled his AK at the man.

"I won't ask again. I don't give a rat fuck if you live or die. The key, if you please."

The manager promptly removed a chain from around his neck, with a cylindrical key dangling from it.

"Thank you," Cyrus said sarcastically, hitting the manager with the butt of his rifle, knocking him to the floor, unconscious.

Holding the key in the air, Cyrus yelled, "Got it! Randy with me, Reaper watch these fuckers."

Reaper made no move to disguise himself with a ski mask. He was also shirtless, his upper body displaying two fresh tattoos in addition to his original Viking Club insignia. Two large syringes filled with a bright pink substance were duct taped to his right arm. He surveyed the panic-stricken people in the lobby. He held his M-249 machine gun at eye level, scanning for targets. He maintained his position by the front door. In a matter of minutes, Randy and Cyrus were at the vault. Cyrus inserted the key into the lock, and the vault slowly swung open on its own power. Both men quickly entered the vault and saw four large five foot tall metal racks, loaded with several trays of banded cash.

"Fuck me!" Cyrus exclaimed.

Skinny frantically began to sound the horn outside.

"Cops, we gotta hurry," said Cyrus.

Randy opened a duffle bag he was carrying and pulled out two more. Cyrus took one and opened it. He dumped money laden trays in it and closed the bag. Randy did the same with the other two bags.

"What about the rest?"

"No time! Let's go!" Cyrus yelled.

Both robbers ran to the front door and looked outside. A Metro police car was pulling into the lot lights flashing and siren blaring.

"Cops!" Cyrus yelled.

Skinny and Randy jumped into the back of the van. Reaper exited the bank last and fixated on the police car. He had a wide grin on his face as he opened up with his machine gun. The front of the squad car was peppered with bullet holes as the officer tried to jump out through the passenger door. Reaper got into the van, closing the side door behind him. Skinny gunned the engine, but slammed on the brakes when another police car arrived from the opposite direction and attempted to block the van's progress.

"Reaper, clear us a path!" Cyrus shouted.

The back doors to the van opened and Reaper hit the ground. He fired at the police car as the first obvious enemy and prepared to shoot anything that moved.

Destroy, he thought. *Kill and destroy*. He had no idea where those thoughts came from.

"What do you think?" Matthias asked his partner, in the passenger seat of the Mustang.

"There is definitely a lot of firing going on, let's get a closer look." Cruwell looked at his map, which had multiple heat sources indicated on it. Matthias pulled into a parking lot across the street from the bank. Several police cars were arriving on the scene and had blocked off the street. A helicopter also flew overhead. A white cargo van drove slowly around the bank's parking lot, its rear doors open. A heavily armed figure walked next to it, firing indiscriminately. Two police cars already had been disabled. A few officers tried to return fire with their handguns, but it was no use. The other occupants of the van were also firing automatic rifles, out of the front windows and open side door. As the van slowly circled the parking lot, the figure on foot began to walk toward the hastily set up police perimeter, holding his large machine gun in one hand. The figure paused and aimed up at the helicopter, causing it to fly out of the area. The words "Channel 5 News" could be seen on the side of the helicopter.

"I would definitely say that is our guy," Cruwell stated as he looked through his monocular out of the passenger window. Cruwell watched the figure walk straight up to two of the disabled police cars. Two officers rose up from behind the rear of the car and opened fire with semi-automatic pistols. The figure jerked left and right under the bullet impacts, his upper chest peppered with dark spots. Both officers ran out of ammunition at the same time and were in shock the figure was still moving towards him. Cruwell looked away with disgust as the figure opened up with the machine gun dropping both officers to the ground into a mess of blood and body parts. He picked up his voice communicator and relayed the unfolding scenario to Corporal Scotts via his wrist communicator.

"The colonel is on board the shuttle," Scotts replied. "I can send him a message, but it takes a few minutes to get up there."

"We might not have a few minutes," Cruwell replied. "The police are outgunned, and their numbers are dwindling. They only have small arms. You and Johnny try to meet us and bring all the weapons you can. This might be our only chance to get him."

"What do you want me to tell the colonel?"

"Tell him to load the equipment and prep the shuttle for departure."

"Understood. Watch your back; you don't want to die on this planet."

The transmission ended. Sergeant Matthias drew his pistol and checked the magazine. "I hope they don't go far. This is drawing entirely too much attention from the police."

The white van finally drove out of the bank parking lot, albeit very slowly. A lone, shirtless figure continued to let loose automatic fire peppering the already disabled police cars with more holes. The pinned down officers has no choice but to seek cover. The police were hopelessly outgunned. As the van quickly accelerated and left the bank, several bullet-riddled police cars and civilian cars now littered the roadway. Sirens could be heard in the distance, but it was simply too little, too late. Several bodies lay in the street and in the parking lot. Panic-stricken motorists had abandoned their cars, leaving a surreal sight for the evening news.

"Damn! That was intense!" Cyrus said. The bikers took off their ski masks and began to remove their body armor. Reaper sat in the back seat, reloading his M-249 with another belt of ammunition. Randy opened up a large black duffle bag and smiled.

"How much we get, Cyrus? This is insane."

Cyrus turned around from the front passenger seat as he inserted a fresh magazine into his AK-47. "At least half a mil. The rest of the money would have made it a million easy. Dean was right on, this time."

Cyrus looked at Reaper, who was staring out of the back window. "You kicked major ass, Reaper. Major ass!" Reaper said nothing. He looked down and saw where several bullets had penetrated his body. He noticed that he wasn't healing like he had from previous injuries. He started to feel very hot, and the machine gun started to feel very heavy. He fumbled with one of the syringes duct taped to himself, and after freeing it, he plunged it into his thigh. He didn't get the immediate sense of vitality he usually felt.

"I—I need to cool down," Reaper stuttered. He was having an increasingly difficult time focusing, and his head felt like it was on fire.

"Holy shit," Randy said, "he's been hit like twenty times!" Randy inspected the Reaper more closely. Black ooze began to seep from his nostrils. "We got to ditch this guy, man. He ain't gonna make it!"

The van accelerated onto the expressway, heading north out of the city. "We'll ditch the van," Cyrus said. "That's our next step in the plan—don't forget the plan." He faced forward and looked up through the windshield. "Dude, they have air support on us again. Hurry up!"

Traffic was slow on the expressway, so Skinny stayed in the shoulder. He accelerated, passing cars in the regular traffic lanes. He exited at the next turnoff and entered a heavily congested warehouse district. Matthias and Cruwell followed as close as they could without arousing any suspicion.

"I have them on the holomap," Cruwell said. "I'm also reading a very abnormally high heat source. Our alien might finally be fried." He looked ahead for a moment. "They pulled into that building over there." He pointed at a large warehouse with several tractor trailers parked in the lot. "I have them on the map; let's wait until Johnny and Scotts get here with some weapons."

Police cars began to enter the area, and police and news helicopters hovered overhead. A large blue van and an armored personnel carrier, complete with a fixed battering ram, entered the newly established police perimeter. Both vehicles had the words "County Sheriff SWAT" painted on their sides.

Cruwell said, "It looks like they aren't playing around with this one."

"Hurry up," Scotts said. "We'll never make it."

"Relax," Roman said calmly as he activated his dashboard emergency lights. He accelerated, weaving even more as he negotiated through traffic. He had never bothered to turn in his cruiser or any of his equipment, as he had been instructed to do, and no one had tracked him down to ask for its return. He figured it would take the police bureaucracy a while to catch up with him, but he still did have a sense of duty. He still wore the badge and he was determined to catch this maniac. They had hastily filled the back seat with whatever weapons were easily at hand. Scotts sat in the passenger seat, loading up his EMR. Underneath the barrel was a grenade launcher, which Corporal Scotts loaded with short, stubby rounds.

Roman, a lit cigarette in his mouth, drove as fast as he could, swerving from the shoulder back into traffic. "You better put your seatbelt on."

Scotts complied and buckled his seatbelt. He held up the holographic map and shouted directions to Roman. The black Crown Vic approached

100 miles per hour as it sped along the expressway. "There. Take the next exit!"

Roman swerved and barely made the exit ramp. Up ahead, the flashing lights of numerous police cars were everywhere caused him to slam on the brakes.

"Great. This won't be easy getting in," he commented.

Roman slowly drove the Crown Vic closer as he saw officers clearing traffic. Scotts pointed to a nearby Shell gas station. Roman hit the accelerator and pulled in. The familiar lime green Mustang was parked in the back; Matthias and Cruwell were outside the vehicle looking at the scene through binoculars.

"It took you guys long enough," Cruwell greeted them. "You bring weapons?"

"We're set. What are we going to do?" Scotts asked as he exited the Crown Vic.

Roman opened the trunk of his vehicle and retrieved his ballistic vest. He put it on over his white T-shirt and proceeded to unload buckshot and insert slugs into his recently re-acquired shotgun. He also took out a Houston Astros baseball hat and placed it on his head backwards. He closed the trunk.

"We need to find a way in," Cruwell said, lowering his binoculars and looking at Corporal Scotts. "There is a massive heat buildup. Our guy might finally be dying. If they get him, we'll have lost our chance."

The police had effectively cordoned off the area. Inside the warehouse, the situation had become tense.

"We are totally screwed," Cyrus said. "You took the wrong turn!"

"Back off!" Skinny replied nervously. "I followed your directions, exactly like you said. How was I supposed to know there would be an army outside?"

Skinny had parked their van inside a massive warehouse, seemingly empty, save for them. He and Randy dragged Reaper out of the van and laid him on the floor.

"I must cool down," Reaper said again, repeating the words he had whispered dozens of times. He stared in dismay at the remaining cracked syringes he had retrieved out of his jacket pocket. The precious pink, strength-giving liquid was all but gone. He was dying, and he knew it. He needed to find the doctor quickly.

"This guy should be dead. He is not right," Skinny said.

"Shut up," Cyrus answered tersely. "He saved our asses back there. Find the exits and cover them. We need to see what the cops have facing us."

Skinny and Randy looked at each other quizzically, before heading off in different directions. Cyrus looked at Reaper. He put a hand to Reaper's pale head and noted that he was hot to the touch. He looked around and saw a sign above a door that read "Break Room." With one hand, he dragged his brother into that room.

"You're lucky, man," Cyrus said, spotting an ice machine sitting in the corner. He propped Reaper against a wall next to the machine and began to scoop out ice and drop it onto his brother. After a few minutes, all of the ice was gone, but Reaper's skin had cooled down. His black eyes opened very slowly, and he sat up straighter.

"Where are we?" he managed to say. His wounds began to close up, much to his relief.

"We're trapped. Skinny took a wrong turn, and we're boxed in. They have SWAT teams out there. I ain't going back to the joint, man. This is it. Hang in there. We still need you, man."

Cruwell frowned over his holographic map. "What's wrong?" Matthias asked.

Cruwell began to tap the side of the box that projected the map. "The heat signature is fading away. This thing is running out of power or something."

"No, I think our alien is attempting to heal himself."

"So what does that mean?" Roman asked, dropping his cigarette to the ground and grinding it out with the toe of his boot. He stared up at a passing helicopter.

"It means they could try to escape the police perimeter," Scotts answered. "If he is healed, he will be ready to fight."

Roman sat down in his Crown Vic and listened to the radio transmissions. "It looks like they're going to send in the SWAT teams any minute now. This should be interesting."

The warehouse was completely surrounded, and the police had barricaded the only entrance into the industrial park. Two camouflaged

Humvees, a black RV and three unmarked Crown Vics entered the perimeter and came to a halt.

The doors to the vehicles opened, and several figures emerged, wearing black trench coats. Camouflaged soldiers got out of the Humvees, each carrying an M-4 rifle. The last figure to exit the Humvee adjusted his blue beret and returned the salutes of his waiting men. One of the trench- coated figures walked toward the man and pointed to the warehouse. A marked sheriff's car pulled up to the perimeter, and a seemingly agitated sheriff got out and began yelling at the assembled group, which largely ignored him. One of the trench-coated figures spoke a few words to the sheriff, who, still seemingly very agitated, quickly got in his vehicle and drove off.

"This is horseshit!" the sheriff shouted into his cell phone as he drove to his command post. "I am the county sheriff, and this is my county. I was called to deploy my tactical assets, and I have. I don't need any feds or military telling me what to do! When the chief of police shows up, he will tell you the same thing."

"I am sorry, sheriff, the voice on the other end of the phone said. "This is now a US government operation. We all have our orders. The chief of police has assured us his complete cooperation. Colonel Little is in charge of this operation here, and we will need your tactical team and equipment. This is now a matter of national security, and you need to give him your full and utmost cooperation."

"Fine. But my SWAT team is pulling out," the sheriff replied sternly. "He can use his soldiers for a suicide mission if he wants. Matter of fact, I should just pull all of my men out and let him handle it by himself."

The calm voice on the other end of the phone replied, "Sorry, sheriff. You will cooperate and give Colonel Little access to all of your men and equipment. If you don't like it, I will find someone to replace you. I have a press conference to attend to now. This type of incident doesn't get ignored for very long. Good day."

The sheriff placed the cellular phone onto its dashboard-mounted cradle. He soon reached the mobile command post and jerked his car to a halt. He got out and walked toward the post, shaking his head, muttering under his breath. "Damn politicians."

The sheriff turned and walked back to his vehicle. He reached inside and retrieved the cellular phone from its cradle mounted on the dash. He quickly dialed a number and put the phone to his ear. He spoke as soon as the call was picked up, not giving the other party a chance.

"This is the sheriff. Commander Glover, pull your SWAT team out. All deputies will also pull back. This is now a military operation."

"Sir, Colonel Little has given us orders to initiate an assault."

"Dammit, Glover, do what I say! That is an order! I am on my way!" The sheriff ended the call and got into the driver seat. Firing up the ignition, he quickly U-turned his vehicle and headed back toward the black RV. By now, more soldiers wearing blue berets manned the perimeter. The sheriff attempted to drive up to the black RV but was stopped by one of the blue beret wearing soldiers brandishing an M-4.

"Your vehicle may not pass," the soldier said.

"Get out of my way before I run you over!" The sheriff hit the accelerator and broke through the yellow barrier tape. He parked his cruiser in front of the lead Humvee and got out. He was quickly subdued by two soldiers.

"Get your hands off of me!" the sheriff yelled. He looked around, and much to his satisfaction, his SWAT vans were pulling back, along with the rest of his deputies. Only the Metro Police remained. The military now had an overwhelming presence. The black RV had a large radar dish and antenna array on its roof. As the sheriff approached, several soldiers got out; their distinctive blue berets perched on their heads. An Army veteran of the Gulf War, the sheriff recognized different military unit patches and ranks when he saw them. He noted with interest that these soldiers bore no insignia or name patches on their uniforms.

"Unhand the sheriff," Colonel Little commanded as he walked from his Humvee towards the RV. The sheriff brushed off his uniform and straightened up to face the colonel. He noted the distinctive full-bird silver insignia on his collar but saw that his uniform was devoid of any unit patch. "Sheriff, you disappoint me. You were to leave your tactical units in my command. They are now pulling back. We are going to lose a valuable opportunity, as you have the only tactical asset here."

"Listen, Colonel," the sheriff answered. "My men responded to a bank robbery in which several officers were hurt or killed. I do not know why the military is here, but from what I understand, it is against the law for the military to be conducting police operations."

"These men that killed your officers are wanted terrorists. I am empowered by the President of the United States to arrest them and contain this situation before any more lives are lost. That is all you need to know," the colonel replied curtly.

"Terrorists? Are you kidding me? What is really going on here? The military just doesn't show up for a bank robbery."

"Sheriff, there are three things I ask of my men. I ask that they lead, follow, or get the hell out of way. You are doing none of these things. So if you don't mind, please, get out of my operation and direct traffic." The sheriff shook his head angrily and got back into his car. Seeing the sheriff exit the military perimeter in his car, the colonel walked inside the RV.

"Get those tactical teams back here at once," he told his staff. "That sheriff has interfered for the last time, if necessary detain him." He looked at a man wearing a black suit and tie, along with sunglasses, standing in the corner.

"Instead of standing there, why don't get off your ass and do something?"

The man in black spoke. "I am only here to make sure you contain the situation, Colonel. Handling local law enforcement is of no interest to me." The colonel's attention was diverted by a soldier who sat at a terminal and shouted an alarm.

"Colonel! They are attempting to escape!"

The colonel moved behind the soldier's shoulder to watch a camera feed on the computer terminal.

"Damn. What is the status of the tactical teams?"

"They are regrouping now, but they are not in position anymore, since the sheriff ordered them out."

The colonel pounded his right fist into his left palm. "That's great. I want our reaction force ready to go when they arrive. Orders are to shoot on sight."

"Yes sir." The soldier relayed the command through a microphone.

CHAPTER 26

"It's now or never," Randy said, peeking through the blinds of a window. "The SWAT teams are pulling back!" The crew had driven their van into an open garage door leading into a large warehouse and closed the door behind them. Skinny now stood next to the button on the wall to open it up again. They fired a few rounds into the ceiling, chasing out the few employees in the warehouse. Reaper sat up now; most of the ice that had been placed on him had melted.

Cyrus stood alone, contemplating his next move, when Randy yelled out, "What are you gonna do, just stand there?"

"Don't yell at me!" Cyrus yelled back. "I'm thinking."

"Oh, that's just great. Listen, they're pulling back! We need to make a break for it!"

Cyrus nodded, and ran over to Reaper helping him into a standing position. He walked him over to the van and helped into the side door. He picked up the SAW and put it in Reaper's hands.

"We gotta break out, man. I need you to cover us."

Randy ran back to the van and got in through the driver's side door. He inserted a fresh magazine into his AK and stuck it out the window. Cyrus got into the passenger seat.

"Hit the door and let's go!" he told Randy.

Skinny slammed the red button, and the garage door began to retract upward. He ran back and jumped into the van's open side door. Reaper was poised at it, with his SAW hanging out of the open door. Skinny stood slightly behind, his AK at the ready. Randy hit the gas and sent the van hurtling toward the police perimeter.

"Here they come! Open fire!"

The few Metro police who had not followed the sheriff's order to pull back opened fire with shotguns and pistols. The van took several hits, but it kept coming. The sudden withdrawal of the two SWAT teams created a gap in the perimeter, and the crew exploited it to the best of their ability. Randy and Cyrus fired through the windshield, sending several officers scattering for cover. As soon as the van passed the first set of cars, Reaper and Skinny unleashed a devastating broadside salvo. The van broke through a chain link fence behind the warehouse and turned down into a residential neighborhood.

"Where are they headed?" Roman asked. Corporal Scotts intently studied the holomap. "If they continue, they will most likely come out here." He raised a section of the map, which rotated and flashed the two likely exits.

"That's not too far from here," Roman said. He surveyed the scene at the warehouse. "Looks like we could catch them before the cops will."

The warehouse area had turned into a giant traffic jam, as police cars and military vehicles tried to get to the back of the lot. Others tried to get to the main road, but they were blocked by disabled cars and empty cars whose drivers had fled and were being held back by the police perimeter. Roman got back into the driver's seat.

"Whenever you're ready, ladies, we can go, I'm driving."

Captain Cruwell jumped into the passenger seat, his EMR jutting out of the window. Scotts and Sergeant Matthias jumped into the back of the Crown Vic, each also sticking an EMR out his window. The car roared to life, and Roman eased it out onto the roadway. Using his emergency lights and siren, Roman managed to negotiate through the gridlocked traffic via the sidewalk. Using directions from Scott's holomap, he quickly approached the van as it weaved through traffic at a steady but high speed. There were no police cars currently following it.

"Wow. Hard to imagine they missed it," Sergeant Matthias commented.

"Actually, not really," Roman replied. "The police will be trying to minimize civilian casualties. Hopefully, he will go north and get to a less populated area. I'll try to hang back until we can find a good area to take them down."

The van continued north on a four-lane road and finally got to the outskirts of the city. The jurisdiction of the Metro police ended here, and they didn't have many units in the area. Only the county sheriff had assets outside the city limits to use, but it seemed he wasn't letting that happen. Roman thought they were all alone until Scotts looked over his shoulder out of the rear window and said, "I think they found us again."

Police sirens could be heard faintly in pursuit, and they could hear a helicopter overhead again.

"It's now or never guys. Make the call, Sebastian," said Matthias to Cruwell.

Cruwell looked behind him and up at the helicopter. He turned around and stared ahead at the fleeing van. "OK. Let's take it out now. We will disable the vehicle. Kill the others if you have to, but try to get the alien alive."

Everyone rechecked their rifles. Roman leaned over, took his hand cannon out of the glove box, and press checked it.

"Locked and loaded. Let's do it."

Roman slammed down hard on the accelerator and pulled up to the van's bumper.

CHAPTER 27

"We're being followed!" Skinny yelled. He reached into a small duffel bag on the floor of the van and pulled out a pipe bomb with a short fuse protruding out of it and a Zippo lighter bearing the inscription "1st Marine Division-Fallujah '04."

"Eat this!" Skinny lit the fuse and tossed the pipe bomb out of the side of the van. It hit the pavement and detonated a second later, causing the black sedan in pursuit to swerve to the right. The sedan straightened out and continued its pursuit. Reaper leaned out of the van's side and squeezed off a short burst with the M-249, causing the black sedan to swerve to the left of the van out of his sight.

"What's going on back there?" Cyrus leaned out of the front window and looked behind the van but didn't see anything.

"We got company!" Skinny yelled back.

Suddenly, the van jerked violently to the left. Randy tried hard to keep it straight, but the rear tires had been shot out. The van went off the road and plowed through a two-strand barbed wire fence. A couple of cows grazing near the fence line barely made it out of the way as the van hurtled through the fence, finally coming to rest at the edge of a large pond after hitting a large tree stump with considerable force.

Reaper got out of the van but had to hold onto the side door for support, he felt lethargic and weak still. He raised the M-249 and waited for the black sedan to follow the van through the fence. Skinny retrieved another pipe bomb and poised himself to light the fuse and throw it. Randy and Cyrus staggered out of the van, blood streaming from a cut on the left side of his face and walked to the side sliding door. Smoke began to curl from underneath the hood. The van was covered with bullet holes but had severed its purpose well.

"Too far; I was careless, foolish." Dr. Keitel spoke aloud to himself as he haphazardly removed clothes from a closet and piled them on the bed. Satisfied that he had enough, he stuffed them into a large Samsonite suitcase he found in the bedroom closet. He had already gathered most of his necessary medical supplies and equipment, stacking it by the front door of the apartment. There was only one problem now: He knew he could not continue to use the black Mercedes, because the police would surely be looking for it, and him. He finished packing, his thoughts now turning to acquiring a new vehicle. It would be easy enough to wait in the parking garage and wait for a tenant to return and appropriate another vehicle by force. A sudden shout from outside in the hallway interrupted the thoughts racing through his mind. He picked up the Glock-17 pistol that belonged to the state trooper he had murdered earlier. The sleek pistol fit comfortably in his sweaty palm.

"Metro police! Search warrant!" The shouting and commotion outside the door indicated the presence of many policemen. Dr. Keitel looked briefly out the window. There was no escape; he was on the third floor, with one exit out of the apartment.

"Metro SWAT! We are coming in!"

"Oh my, how I have failed." Dejected, Dr. Keitel walked into the study and sat down on the floor next to the decaying body of the coroner, Dr. Jewell. Weeping a single tear, he placed the pistol against his temple and pulled the trigger as the SWAT battering ram smashed the front door inward.

"Nice shooting, Roman."

"Thanks. I've always wanted to shoot out the tires of a moving car." Roman eased the Crown Vic off the road. A couple of passing cars had stopped, but Roman waved them on. He continued driving through the gap in the fence. Up ahead, he spotted the smoking van. Roman immediately stopped the car. Scotts and Matthias immediately jumped out and ran into the brush, out of sight.

"What the hell?" Roman exclaimed. "Where are they going?"

"Relax," Cruwell replied. "They've done this sort of thing before." Suddenly, the front windshield of the Crown Vic was peppered with bullet holes, causing Roman and Cruwell to duck. Both men were showered with shattered glass.

"Get out!" Roman shouted.

Roman and Cruwell each rolled out of the car. Up ahead they could see a large, pale-skinned, tattoo-covered biker firing a machine gun in long bursts. They could also see a couple other bikers firing behind him. Cruwell let loose with short, controlled bursts from his EMR, causing the bikers to take cover. The machine gunner, however, stood his ground. His grip on the weapon seemed to weaken, however, and its bullets started kicking up dirt in front of the Crown Vic. Electro-magnetic rounds, leaving their distinctively colored vapor trails, erupted from the side as Corporal Scotts and Sergeant Matthias opened fire. Skinny was hit immediately, and he fell to the ground screaming, dropping his lit pipe bomb.

"Fire in the hole!" Randy yelled as he tried to get out of the way. Matthias rose up from his position and cut him down with a volley of well-aimed shots. Cyrus returned fire with his AK-47, striking Matthias in the shoulder and right arm. Matthias cried out in pain and dropped his EMR. Scotts pulled him down to the ground just as the pipe bomb detonated. The explosion ignited the bullet-riddled van, which had been leaking fuel from its perforated fuel tank. A ball of fire erupted, and a small mushroom cloud of smoke rose from the wreckage. Charred $100 bills began to swirl up in the warm draft from the fire before floating to the ground. Roman and Cruwell helped Scotts drag Matthias back to the car. They could hear sirens approaching.

"Get him in the car!" Cruwell yelled.

Scotts and Roman dragged Matthias into the back seat of the Crown Vic. He had slipped into semi-consciousness and was bleeding profusely from his wounds. Scotts ran back to Cruwell, leaving Roman to attend to Matthias. Roman made his way to the back of the vehicle and opened the trunk. He retrieved a first aid kit and set to work.

"Where is he?" Scotts asked as he approached Cruwell, who was looking around near the burning van. They circled the area cautiously, their weapons aimed at the ground but at the ready. Suddenly, Scotts cried out, "There he is!"

The pale skin of the Reaper had changed to a bright red. Sweat cascaded down his bald head, clearly stinging his black eyes. He dragged himself slowly away from the wreck. His right leg had been sheared off by the pipe bomb blast, and black ooze flowed freely from the stump. His right arm also was badly cut. Black ooze leaked from his ears and his nostrils as well.

His progress was halted by a boot stepping on his back, pressing him to the ground.

"That's far enough," he heard.

Reaper slowly turned onto his back. He saw Cruwell and Scotts staring down at him, their rifles aimed at his midsection. He coughed, sending droplets of black ooze into the air. A smile slowly broke over his scratched face.

"So it ends." He coughed again.

Cruwell looked over at Scotts, who nodded. They both shouldered their rifles, reaching down and picking Reaper up by the arms and dragging him toward the Crown Vic. Over Reaper's cries of protest, Cruwell replied, "We're not done with you yet."

Roman ran toward them and yelled, "Hurry up!"

Seeing the tangled, bloody mess they were dragging, he said, "How is he still alive?"

"Yeah, a sight to behold," Cruwell said. "Get him in the trunk!" The three quickly put Reaper into the trunk of the Crown Vic. Roman got into the driver's seat, Captain Cruwell in the passenger's seat, and Scotts in back with Matthias. Roman threw the engine into reverse and backed the car through the hole in the fence. When the vehicle hit the pavement, Roman U-turned southbound. Headed north directly at them were several police cars and two Humvees. A few police cars U-turned and gave chase.

"Where are we going?" Roman asked as he gunned the engine, weaving in and out of traffic.

"Back to your place," Cruwell answered. "We can activate the trans-mat and get out." Cruwell looked into the back seat. Matthias was now unconscious; his shoulder and arm bandages were soaked through with blood.

"He doesn't have much longer; might have hit an artery," Scotts said. "He's lost a lot of blood." Cruwell looked at Scotts, who pointed to Matthias's bandaged side.

"He'll make it," Cruwell said. "We just need a little more time."

"Where are they headed?" Colonel Little asked.

The soldier pushed a series of buttons on his terminal. "Colonel, they appear to be headed back to the detective's apartment."

"Good. We will intercept them there. We need to try to get a team ahead of them if possible. Relay a different location to the police; I don't want them to bear witness to our methods of cleanup."

CHAPTER 28

"I'm almost there, hang on!" Roman yelled as he sped toward his apartment. He took a corner with tires sliding and rubber burning and drove the vehicle up the curb and onto the tiny patch of grass that was his front lawn and came to a halt. Corporal Scotts jumped out and ran to the other side of the vehicle to help Captain Cruwell, who was busy pulling the now semi-conscious Sergeant Matthias out. Roman popped open the trunk and grabbed Reaper's overheated body, dragging it to the front door.

"Scotts, get the trans-mat online!" Cruwell yelled frantically.

Roman opened the front door to his apartment and ran back to help Cruwell and Matthias. Scotts ran inside the apartment to the trans-mat. Roman noticed a pair of Humvees turning into the apartment complex's parking lot.

"Damn. We have company."

Roman pushed Cruwell inside and ran back to the Crown Vic to retrieve his shotgun. "Get inside," he told the others. "I'll hold them off!" Cruwell nodded and disappeared inside, dragging Reaper by his arm. A couple of curious neighbors stepped out of their apartments to see what was going on. They quickly ran back inside as Roman opened up with two slug rounds from his shotgun aimed at the nearest Humvee, causing it to swerve and come to a halt. Six soldiers wearing blue berets jumped out, their M-4s at the ready. The other Humvee stopped close by. Five more soldiers got out and took up positions among the cars parked in the parking lot.

A strong wind began to swirl in Roman's upstairs bedroom as Scotts activated the trans-mat. Cruwell nodded to Scotts, and they both heaved Matthias into the swirling mass of multicolored lights. He disappeared in an instant, leaving no trace behind.

"You're next, Scotts! The alien goes with you!" Cruwell yelled over the increasingly high-pitched whine of the trans-mat. Cruwell had dragged Reaper upstairs, and his apparently lifeless black eyes stared blankly at the wall.

Scotts looked at Cruwell and shouted, "Hurry! It will overheat! Go get Roman!"

Cruwell nodded as Scotts picked Reaper up under his arms. Scotts took a deep breath and stepped into the lights, immediately disappearing from sight.

"Roman, let's go!" Cruwell yelled down the stairs. He could hear the gunfire outside.

Roman quickly emptied his shotgun and closed the front door and locked the deadbolt. Rounds from an M-4 impacted the outside of the wall and door, penetrating in some areas sending wood splinters flying. He ran upstairs and immediately froze upon seeing the awesome light display emitting from the trans-mat. The whine was now almost deafening.

"We must go now!" Cruwell yelled over the high-pitched whine. Stupidly, Roman replied, "Where?"

"Back with us. You must decide now!"

An explosion tore through the front door, and they could hear soldiers enter the apartment, preceded by sounds of flash bang grenades detonating in the entryway. The trans-mat slowly started to slow its rotation.

"Hurry!" Cruwell jumped into the light and vanished. Roman stared at the swirling lights before spotting his cat, Morris, cowering under his black futon. Roman ran over and lifted up the futon, grabbing Morris by the scruff of his neck in the process. With one hand holding his shotgun and the other holding Morris, he jumped into the light a split second before it powered off. He vanished just as the soldiers reached the doorway to the bedroom. The lead soldier looked around the empty room and activated his throat mic.

"Colonel, we have a problem."

The room was a mess from the swirling wind of the trans-mat, and it started to fill with smoke from the overheated trans-mat disk and the flash bang grenades from main room.

With the extra passengers, the shuttle was a bit cramped. Colonel Chuikova had seen the trans-mat activate on the shuttle and grabbed Matthias as he materialized. Taking note of the sergeant's wounds, he quickly put him into the life support stasis pod. Matthias's body was instantly frozen, halting the creeping death that was trying to overtake him. Scotts came next, with Reaper. The colonel immediately took their prize and pulled him to the back of the shuttle. Scotts quickly recovered from his trans-mat journey and helped secure Reaper, placing him in the shuttle's other stasis pod. A few moments later, Cruwell materialized. He stepped back from the trans-mat and stared into it.

Scotts walked up to Cruwell and said, "Is Roman coming?"

"I don't know, but the trans-mat is almost spent. He'd better come quickly, if he's going to come."

The colonel walked up to Scotts. "We need to erase all evidence of us being there."

"What about Roman? We can't do that!" Scotts protested. "I have my orders."

Suddenly, Roman appeared in the trans-mat beam. Cruwell ran over and caught him before he collapsed. Roman clutched Morris tightly to his chest. The cat seemed to fare the trip a lot better than his owner. Scotts looked at the colonel, who simply nodded.

"Do it."

Scotts hit a sequence of buttons on the shuttle's trans-mat, and the swirling lights began to reverse themselves. Scotts had accelerated the overheating of the unit on the planet. Smoke began to emit from underneath the device on the shuttle.

Cruwell helped Roman to a bench in the back of the shuttle. Scotts opened a case on the steel-grated floor of the shuttle to show a large, cylindrical device. He twisted the top of the device to activate it. Upon hearing it beep, Scotts tossed the device into the trans-mat beam. He immediately shut off the trans-mat. The swirling lights stopped suddenly, briefly throwing the shuttle into an eerie quiet. The colonel grabbed Scotts by the shoulder.

"What was that?"

"Insurance. In case the trans-mat unit on the planet doesn't detonate, that bomb I just sent down will ensure it does."

"Good work. We must leave now. Raus says they have been detected and will soon be engaged."

Scotts nodded and began to initiate startup of the pulse drive. After everyone was secured for the pulse jump, Scotts activated the drive. The tiny shuttle instantly became a blur as space and time contracted for a split second, hurtling the crew back toward the other side of space.

"Team leader, give me an update," Colonel Little said into the handset. The black RV in which he rode slowly made its way back toward Roman's apartment.

"Sir, they are not here. They vanished!" The voice on the other end was very excited. The last transmission came through from the assault team.

"What the hell do you mean, they vanished? Nothing can vanish into thin air!"

The transmit disk began to rotate in the opposite direction, and within a few seconds it stopped. The team leader knelt down beside the trans-mat and noticed there was a cylindrical device with a flashing red indicator on the top. The team leader observed curiously as the flashing light increased its frequency.

"Sir, our situation just got worse." The excited voice suddenly turned serious with the intense realization of what might soon happen. Colonel Little's frantic calls over the radio were suddenly forgotten.

"Oh my god."

Dean activated his wheelchair and went into his television room, where both sets showed breaking news. Dean turned down CNN and turned up Fox News. He listened with intense curiosity as a reporter spoke from the studio.

"We have breaking news just in. An entire apartment complex was destroyed in what police and federal officials are calling an act of domestic terrorism. A Metro spokesman issued a statement that police detective John Roman, who lived at the destroyed apartment complex, was affiliated with the notorious white supremacist motorcycle gang calling itself the 'SS Viking.' Apparently, Roman and members of his outlaw gang robbed a bank this afternoon. Upon being chased by police, Roman and his gang detonated an ammonium nitrate fertilizer bomb. The police department has also stated that Roman was under investigation and that they were about to move on him with federal authorities. The bomb that was used apparently was meant for City Hall. Stay tuned for more on this breaking story."

Dean put the volume back on mute, and his house resumed its normal silence, save for the occasional meow from one of his cats. Dean guided his wheelchair back into his study, where he resumed painting a miniature figurine of a dragon. He began to highlight the red around the eyes. He paused and muttered to himself, "I guess Cyrus screwed up. At least I got fifty grand out of the deal.

CHAPTER 29

The Emperor's Fist emerged from the electromagnetic corridor prematurely, with large, powerful gravitational waves emitting from its pulse core. Those who weren't braced properly were knocked off their feet or chairs. The elongated strands of starlight immediately shrank to points of singularity as the ship slowed to cruising speed. Unfortunately, it was not alone.

"M class warship sighted, Admiral," a helmsman reported from his viewing screen.

Admiral Raus stared out through the massive panoramic view screen. *The Emperor's Fist* had emerged near a small, uninhabited water planet. Massive ion storms erupted all over its surface. The enemy warship that the helmsman had picked up was the only thing keeping them from returning home, and the admiral wasn't about to let that happen. The gravitational waves produced a distortional effect around *The Emperor's Fist*, pulling the enemy ship closer, into attack range.

"The ship is closing rapidly, sir," the helmsman continued. "I am detecting multiple torpedo launches."

"Very well. Prepare for impact. Shut off the pulse core and initiate conventional thrusters. Hard starboard turn and prepare a retaliatory strike."

The initial salvo hit *The Emperor's Fist* hard, head-on. The massive, aging battle barge was most heavily armored in the front; it buckled under the impact but held together. Several computer banks emitted electrical sparks, and a few crew members were tossed to the deck. Immediately, alarm klaxons resonated throughout the ship. The helmsman turned the battle barge to starboard, exposing its deadly banks of laser batteries. Once the maneuver was complete, the admiral gave the order: "Fire!"

The gunnery control officer immediately relayed the order, and gunnery crews stationed on various parts of the ship let loose with salvos, striking the enemy warship in several places. The enemy ship lurched to its port side and dived in a feeble attempt to escape the laser batteries. The gravitational waves from pulse space began to dissipate slowly, giving *The Emperor's Fist* more room to maneuver. It increased its speed and completed its turn to port to expose its intact complement of broadside batteries.

"Prep all weapons for concentrated fire on my command," Admiral Raus ordered.

The massive ships drifted closer and closer, starboard side facing port side. The enemy warship opened up with another volley. Again *The Emperor's Fist* took several direct hits under the laser onslaught. Sections of armored hull broke free from the battle barge and floated off into space. The exposed sections began leaking precious atmosphere. Damage report alarms went off throughout the ship, sending crew members scurrying around to terminals, trying to get assessments from affected parts of the ship. Concussion booms reverberated throughout the ship.

"Damage report," Admiral Raus requested calmly. He stroked his chin, seemingly oblivious to the damage to the bridge and to the medics assisting wounded crew members.

"A concentrated fire, sir," an ensign reported. "They have created a hull breach on decks nine through eleven. They are trying to target the pulse core."

"Seal decks and return fire. All fire containment teams should be deployed."

"Aye, sir."

The Emperor's Fist groaned and creaked under the damage strain on its ancient hull, but it complied. The helmsman carefully monitored the crewman who was responsible for maneuvering the ship manually, now that it no longer was in pulse space.

The two behemoths were now directly side by side, the gap between them growing ever smaller. *The Emperor's Fist* loosed another tremendous, concentrated salvo. Anti-ship missiles streaked from its launch tubes as complementing volleys of multicolored laser fire ripped through the enemy warship's hull, sending even more fragments floating off into space, adding to the increasingly dense debris field around the two ships. Long, thin trails of the coolant for the massive engines of the attacking ship leaked into space, signifying the end. Within moments, the enemy ship lost all thrust capability and was dead in space.

"Ensign," Admiral Raus ordered, "load boarding hooks, prepare for boarding assault."

"Aye, sir."

The ensign activated a serious of switches and began shouting orders into a microphone built into his control console.

Admiral Raus turned his chair to face Colonel Chuikova, who was standing by the blast door to the bridge.

"Colonel, if you will take command of the boarding party, I would appreciate your help."

"Of course." The colonel saluted and disappeared out of the bridge. He quickened his pace to the crew quarters, where he encountered Corporal Scotts, Captain Cruwell, and Roman.

"We're going to board the warship," he told them. "Let's move out." Without a word, Cruwell and Scotts each grabbed his EMR and magazine bandoliers, which they had retrieved from the ship's armory earlier. Roman got up to follow, but the colonel stopped him.

"This is not your fight, Johnny."

"Like hell it's not! I came with you, and wherever you go, I go." Roman was still carrying his shotgun, the hand cannon was stuffed down the front of his pants.

The colonel looked him over and nodded. "Fine. Stay with Cruwell and Scotts, and do as they say."

A loud crash sounded, and a concussion knocked everyone off balance. The ship listed to the starboard side. After a few seconds, it stabilized, and people regained their footing. The colonel headed out into the corridor, which was starting to fill with armed crew members, security personnel, and two squads of heavily armed Marines in battle armor.

"Follow me!" he commanded.

"This is Star Admiral Raus, Commander of the UCP warship *The Emperor's Fist*," the admiral broadcasted over several common radio frequencies. "Surrender your vessel and prepare to be boarded."

The panoramic window on the bridge turned partially into a video transmission screen, on which the enemy warship's commander appeared. His bridge apparently had taken a direct hit. Several crew members lay dead or dying in the background. Electrical conduits dangled from the ceiling, sending sparks showering onto the floor.

"Raus. Old friend, we meet again." The opposing commander's voice was hoarse, and blood streaked his worn face. He stood straight and brushed off his uniform.

"Admiral Horth," Raus replied. "A valiant attack, but it has failed. We are preparing to board. You have sustained much damage. Surrender and we will treat you as prisoners of war accordingly."

Admiral Horth nodded wearily, his face clearly showing signs of defeat. He glanced behind him at the carnage unfolding. He turned back around and faced the screen.

"Yes, we have sustained major damage, but the honor of dying in battle will be achieved. I am going down with my ship. This war will end for me today. I pray it ends soon for you, my friend. Surrender is not an option, as I know you are well aware."

Raus nodded slowly in understanding. He switched off the video feed. The screen reverted to the view of the enemy warship precariously attached to *The Emperor's Fist* by many harpoon cables. Raus slumped back into his chair, longing for home.

"This brings back memories," Cruwell said as he watched the cutting team breach the airlock of the enemy ship from the umbilical. When the circle was completed, the massive airlock door crashed into its ship with a deafening roar. The cutting teams and the soldiers behind it braced for an attack from the other side, but no resistance was forthcoming. The boarders could see that the enemy warship was full of internal fires and rapidly filling with smoke. Screams of the wounded reverberated throughout the main corridor.

The colonel turned and faced his complement of heavily armed marines. "Make way to the bridge before this ship breaks up. The ship's engine core has been damaged, and we do not have much time. Look for intel and the ship's commander."

The marine leader nodded and moved into the warship. Roman stepped into the breach and looked around in awe.

"Damned Star Wars battle. This is crazy."

Scotts followed him in, powering up his pulse rifle.

"Keep on your guard," Scotts warned.

Cruwell brought up the rear of their little group, as they followed the Marines toward the bridge. They occasionally encountered small arms fire, but it was quickly suppressed. The warship's crew were quickly taken prisoner and sent to the rear without their weapons. Many simply walked toward the boarders with arms raised in surrender, sensing the futility of prolonging the battle. Crew members from *The Emperor's Fist* helped the wounded evacuate the doomed ship, protected by the ship's security detachment. Within minutes, resistance had ceased altogether. The loudest sounds were occasional sparks of electricity and the constant drone of the alarm klaxons.

The colonel and his men reached the bridge. Its massive blast doors were open, revealing many dead. Admiral Horth was slumped in his chair; a pistol had fallen onto the floor from his outstretched hand. A thin trickle of crimson ran down his face from a single hole in his temple. The colonel closed Horth's eyes.

"Scotts," he ordered, "uplink the main computer to *The Emperor's Fist.* Once you have initiated the upload, we will fall back."

Scotts nodded and set to work. Roman and a few Marines roamed the bridge, checking for survivors. Upon seeing none, they waited for Scotts to finish. Cruwell watched the main corridor for any signs of resistance. Roman knelt down besides a dead female lying prone on the grated floor. He retrieved her sidearm from its holster and eyed the elongated silver weapon with curiosity.

Ray gun.

"Got it!" Scotts said from the terminal where he was working. He got up and headed toward the door. The colonel looked around one last time and double-timed down the corridor back toward *The Emperor's Fist* behind his men. He activated his wrist comlink and spoke. "Admiral, we are returning. Only light resistance encountered. Prisoners and wounded being brought on board."

"Understood. Make haste. The enemy ship is beginning to break apart. We must break contact as soon as your party is back on board."

The colonel stood together on the bridge with Admiral Raus and watched as the massive grappling hooks and the boarding umbilicals from *The Emperor's Fist* were disengaged from the enemy warship. The distance between the two ships increased, and Raus gave the final order.

"Open fire."

The Emperor's Fist opened with a last concentrated salvo from its laser batteries and missile tubes, targeting the rear of the ship, which contained its volatile power source. Within moments, the enemy ship erupted into a huge ball of fire and debris.

Raus slumped back into his chair. "Helm, set course for Hellenheim," he ordered. "Full power."

"Aye, sir."

The mighty engines of *The Emperor's Fist* roared to life, and the massive battle barge headed for home.

CHAPTER 30

"This is truly impressive," Roman said as he stared out the view port of his quarters. Corporal Scotts, standing next to him holding a small cup of water, nodded his head. "I've imagined such things, but I never thought they could be reality, at least not for a few centuries. I thought the space shuttle was cool. But this ..."

The Emperor's Fist had entered friendly territory, and the industrial planet Hellenheim laid below them. Hundreds of small space faring craft, some merchant, some navy, surrounded the planet like bees surrounding their hive. The planet was dull gray and seemed to be covered almost entirely by a thick black cloud cover.

"Do you have oceans here?" Roman asked.

"No," replied Scotts. He continued, "Water is brought from off world, and because of the war, it is strictly rationed. There are water-bearing planets in our empire, but the oceans are very dangerous places."

Roman continued to take it all in. "It's just so dark and gray."

Scotts nodded. "It's our industry. Since the early days of the war, almost all of the factories are producing arms and equipment, as quickly as possible, and with the best resources devoted to production for the war. Our shipyards are here also, but they no longer produce commercial vessels, only warships. We had to resort to archaic forms of energy such as coal for basic necessities." Scotts sighed heavily before continuing. "We're running out of resources. If we don't find a solution soon, the situation could get a lot worse."

Roman took a step back and sat down on the edge of the metal bed. "Maybe I should have stayed home," he mused. "It seems like I traded one hell for another. At least I wasn't facing extinction back on Earth."

"There is a bright spot, in that the enemy is in the same predicament. The war has been equally hard on them. There have been rumors of peace negotiations."

The two were interrupted by the flash of the video screen mounted by the view port. The image of Captain Cruwell took form.

"You two come down to the hangar bay. We're taking a shuttle down to meet the marshal. That means your dress blues, Scotts," Cruwell said.

"Damn! I hate that uniform," Scotts protested.

"Deal with it." Cruwell looked like he was about to sign off, but he resumed. "Roman, you're going to have to wear one of our uniforms. I hope you don't mind. You will be meeting our top military commander, and your clothes are, well ..."

"Well, *what*?" Roman looked down at his crusty Levi's. His brown leather jacket had developed some kind of odor he couldn't identify, and his T-shirt had several blood stains on it.

"Your appearance is unacceptable. Also, if you wouldn't mind taking a shower, that would be good."

"OK. What do I do with Morris?"

"What?"

"My cat."

Cruwell thought for a moment. "Right, that furry thing you have. I am getting you temporary quarters at the training academy. We will take you there first to get settled in, and you can drop your cat there."

Cruwell lastly turned and faced Scotts through the video monitor. "Don't be late, Corporal."

Scotts came to attention and saluted the video monitor as it powered off. "Well, that's that," he said. "I wonder if we'll meet the supreme chancellor himself."

"Who is he? Your leader?"

"Yes, he's our leader, although he's only a shell of the man he once was, say twenty years ago. The war was his idea. Our planet was overpopulated, and the only way to relieve the pressure was to seize surrounding worlds." Scotts strode over to the food dispenser and programmed a request for another glass of water. "Our war is actually a civil war. Technically, we were part of the same empire many millennia ago. I guess eventually somebody just gets too ambitious, and not everyone can get along any more. Peace doesn't last too long around here."

"I know about civil war," Roman said. We had one where I am from."

Scotts walked over to the view port and looked out toward his planet, slowly sipping the water. "I forget how the war started, to be honest. But we all followed the chancellor and still do … well, most of us anyway. Our empire has begun to fall into ruin. What was promised to last only a year or two has dragged on for twenty more." He drank the last of the water and set the glass down on a nearby metal table. "Perhaps it will end soon."

Roman stared at him in silence. Scotts stood motionless for a moment, absorbed in his own thoughts. Turning to Roman, he flashed his smile and said, "Get your cat. Not all is bad on our planet. After this little meeting, I'll take you to my favorite club. They have the best spirits in town!"

Roman scooped up Morris, who was lazily resting on the bed. Scotts put his arm around Roman, and the two exited the room, heading toward the hangar bay to board the shuttle that would take them to Luriana, Hellenheim's capital city.

CHAPTER 31

"I hate this damn thing," Scotts said as he pulled the high collar of his seldom-used dress uniform away from his neck. "And these damn pants are too stiff." Gold stripes ran down the sides of his pants, and his rank was displayed on both sleeves of his tunic. His left shoulder displayed the infantry patch of the United Consortium of Planets ground forces, and he also wore the silver winged insignia indicating his status as a pilot, although he was primarily an infantry grunt now.

"Corporal, shut up." Sergeant Matthias sipped from a glass filled with a bright green liquid, holding a cigar in his other hand. His right arm was in a clear sling that suspended his healing arm. He was doing much better, albeit still very sore. Like Scotts and the others, he wore his dark blue dress uniform. Medals from various campaigns decorated the jacket, rivaling those of Colonel Chuikova. Captain Cruwell and the colonel stood just outside the oaken doors that led into the office of Marshal Von Jesonik, with Matthias, and Scotts close behind them. The colonel casually smoked a cigar, pausing every few seconds to look at it and inhale the smoke. He was the only one wearing battle armor, as he often did, just in case he were to be called away at a moment's notice. Roman stood by himself, looking out through the window over the industrial landscape. The dominance of the grey buildings in the landscape shocked him. Most were devoid of any architectural significance, just plain, block buildings. Scotts had explained that the society was now based on functionality, as opposed to aesthetic beauty. Some buildings, such as those of the national university, remained worth visiting, and Roman made a mental note to take a tour whenever he got settled in.

Everything that had happened to him since leaving Earth had been something straight out of a science fiction book. His situation reminded him of old *Doctor Who* episodes he used to sneak downstairs to watch late at night on public access television while his parents slept upstairs. Regardless of the outcome, he was happy to be on this adventure; it truly was a once in a lifetime opportunity. He raised a glass filled with bright green liquid to his lips and let the smooth contents run down the back of his throat. Ernst, Von Jesonik's attendant, had said the strange brew was called Torol, for its origins on the jungle planet Torol, and that it was the finest ale he had to offer. Both the planet and the drink were said to be named for an ancient explorer who had charted many of the worlds that made up what once was all of the United Consortium of Planets. The drink's main ingredient was derived from a toxic plant. Whatever it was, Roman already felt a heavy buzz coming on, and he was only on his third sip.

The massive doors opened suddenly. Ernst stepped out in traditional robes, with golden symbols embroidered on the sleeves.

"Please, come in. The marshal will receive you now." Ernst bowed deeply as the men filed past him into the grand office. Roman set his glass down on a table before going through the doors, and he straightened the blue dress uniform issued to him from the training academy supply room. It briefly brought back memories of his time served in the Army back home.

"Gentlemen! Please come in." Marshal Von Jesonik stepped out from behind his desk and shook everyone's hand, pausing after shaking Roman's. "You must be Mr. Roman. It is an honor to meet you. I hope we can make your stay as comfortable as possible."

"Thank you," Roman replied humbly.

Von Jesonik stood directly in front of Colonel Chuikova and put his gloved hand upon the colonel's armored shoulder.

"Johann, I am so pleased. The chancellor himself sends his regards." He dropped his hand and walked back behind his massive desk. "I cannot tell you how crucial your mission was. Our science teams are busy analyzing the specimen you have brought back, and the initial reports are very favorable."

The all stood frozen, side by side, and said nothing.

Von Jesonik continued. "Johann, you and your men deserve a much needed rest. In two weeks' time, we will meet again to discuss the future. As of right now, consider yourselves on leave."

Scotts and Matthias turned toward each other, smiling. "I have one other thing before you are dismissed," Von Jesonik said, nodding to Ernst, who retrieved a large ornate box, inlaid with gold and jewels, from the desk. He slowly opened it, revealing the contents.

"I know how much you detest these things, Johann, but it will be done." He walked in front of the assembled men and issued the order, "Group, attention!"

The men came to attention, Roman following suit. Von Jesonik walked around his desk and stood in front of Roman.

"Mr. Roman, for unwavering service and commitment to the chancellor of the United Consortium of Planets, I hereby bestow upon you the honorary rank of lieutenant." He reached into the box and pulled out a pair of silver shoulder boards with a single gold stripe on them, and he put the gaudy rank into Roman's left hand, shook his right hand and moved down the line, leaving Roman staring at his newfangled decoration.

"Corporal Joachim Scotts, for unwavering service and commitment to the United Consortium of Planets, I hereby bestow upon you the rank of Flight Officer, 1st class. You will get your orders for assignment to a fighter wing in the near future. Congratulations." Scotts broke into a huge grin as Von Jesonik placed a silver shoulder board into his hand and pinned an insignia onto his collar. The marshal moved to the next man, with Ernst trailing behind with the box.

"Sergeant Roger Matthias, for unwavering service and commitment to the United Planets, I hereby bestow upon you the rank of Command Sergeant of Infantry." Seeing Matthias's jaw drop, Von Jesonik continued, "That is the highest non-officer rank, and with it comes many responsibilities. Your years of service and your impeccable service record have not gone unnoticed." Von Jesonik handed the chevron stripes to Matthias and pinned the rank to his collar. He moved on and stood in front Cruwell.

"Captain Sebastian Cruwell, for unwavering service and commitment to the United Consortium of Planets, I hereby bestow upon you the rank of major." He reached into the box and retrieved the insignia of gold star and crossed swords, which he pinned to Cruwell's collar. He placed gold shoulder boards, carrying an image of the star and crossed swords, into his hand. Cruwell shook Von Jesonik's hand and stared at the shoulder boards with a blank look on his face. Many thoughts crossed his mind at the moment, one of which was his rapid ascent through the officer ranks. He thought he might be the youngest major ever appointed.

Von Jesonik stood face to face with the colonel. He reached into the box and retrieved a gold baton, covered with many jewels and intricate carvings. "Johann, I will make this short. You are elevated to Ground Marshal of Army group Dreadwolf. Congratulations." He placed an ancient baton, which had been presented to dozens of general staff officers in the past, into Chuikova's gloved hand, his face cracked with a rare smile. Von Jesonik stepped back and surveyed, one more time, the men assembled before him. He stood stiffly and saluted. The men each returned the salute. Von Jesonik lowered his arm and declared, "Dismissed!" The men filed out of the office single file, with Ernst trailing behind. Ernst closed the doors to the office, leaving the men to themselves in the foyer. "That wasn't so bad, was it?" Scotts asked.

Chuikova looked down at the baton he had received. "No, I guess it wasn't that bad." He looked at Cruwell and nodded approvingly. "You've earned it, major." He walked over to Matthias and Scotts. "None of this could have happened without you two, either, that's for sure." Scotts and Matthias each laughed and slapped Chuikova on the shoulder. Chuikova turned to Roman, who was standing off to the side. For the first time in a while, he felt like an outsider—almost.

"Johnny. Welcome to the brotherhood." He shook Roman's hand and ushered them all down the corridor toward the turbo lift, trailing behind. Roman couldn't help but think that the colonel had forced that statement and handshake on him, but the feeling was short-lived as Johann shouted, "Tonight, drinks are on me!"

The men erupted in yells and cheers, sending many robed people scurrying out of their way, wondering what was going on.

Scotts yelled over his shoulder toward Roman just as they started to enter the turbo lift. "Don't think you can tell me what to do, lieutenant!"

The turbo lift doors sealed shut, silencing the corridor. The lift descended, taking the men to some much needed rest and relaxation.

Roman spotted the sign riveted above the large, steel double doors, reading *Bloody Hell's Tavern*. The tavern was a small, square, windowless building three stories high. Monoliths of varying size dwarfed it on all sides;

one almost had to know exactly where it was to find it. Roman looked at the sign and shrugged. This was where Scotts had told him to meet everyone for drinks. Everyone had split up taking care of their own business, leaving Roman exploring the city on his own for most of the day. In front of the tavern, a few soldiers in utility coveralls milled about, talking to one another. Overhead, an occasional monorail car passed by in a whiz of speed, kicking up a fast breeze. The lack of anything resembling cars on the street intrigued Roman. All the transportation appeared to done by monorail, or people simply walked. Everyone also seemed to be in good physical condition. Of course, having to walk a few miles to get someplace (the tavern was two miles or so from the barracks); it would be difficult to be lazy or out of shape. As Roman walked toward the double doors, they slid open silently, beckoning him inside. He stepped into the threshold, and the doors slid closed silently behind him. A scanner built into the wall briefly searched him for contraband. Once the scan was completed, a female computer voice spoke. "You may proceed."

Roman stepped down into a large sunken area, filled with all types of people. He found it difficult to see very far in the pale light. He recognized the grey military uniforms of the infantry, the blue uniforms of the navy, and the loose-fitting robes favored by most people in the civilian sectors. Video screens suspended from the ceiling showed news broadcasts from other planets. Roman noticed a large eagle, carved out of what appeared to be wood, hanging above the bar. It clutched what appeared to be a real, and still bloody, sword in its talons. Various artifacts lined the walls, including what appeared to be unit insignias of various military units. The bar area was fairly crowded, with most of the patrons either standing around tables in the middle, drinking and talking, or sitting in booths surrounding the circular bar. Roman straightened his newly cleaned leather jacket and walked toward the bar. The hot shower he had taken earlier had left him refreshed and completely recharged. He watched those seated around the circular bar enjoying after-work drinks, some of them playing a game of chance on the numerous video screens. Few took notice of Roman's strange attire, save for the bartender.

"What can I get you?" The purple-haired bartender eyed Roman up and down. Roman noted her hair, tightly wrapped in a bun behind her head, and numerous tattoos, one of the familiar eagle and sword, on her left arm. Situated below that tattoo were the words "XXX Corps Dreadwolves" and the phrase "Death Never Dies." Roman caught himself staring at her silver prosthetic left arm, which reminded him of the Terminator movies back on Earth.

The woman made eye contact as she wiped the counter with a damp rag. "Never seen a girl with only one arm?"

"Sorry," Roman stammered. "I didn't mean to stare. It's just that I saw your other tattoo and …"

"Don't worry," she cut him off. "I lost it in the war. I was one of the lucky ones."

Roman sat down on a recently vacated stool and looked at the various bottles behind the bartender. He honestly had no idea where to start.

"I don't suppose you have any beer or whiskey?"

"Excuse me?"

He remembered the drink Scotts had told him about in Von Jesonik's waiting room earlier, although the name escaped him at the moment. "Actually, I forgot the name, but it comes from a jungle planet. It's green in color."

Without pause, the bartender reached under the bar and retrieved a slim glass bottle. She quickly poured a glass of the familiar green liquid. He was about to drink it when he remembered something.

"Shit."

"What?"

"I don't have any money to pay for this."

The bartender eyed Roman more with curiosity than the contempt she would have for any other non-paying customer.

"I can see that you're not from around here, so it's on the house." She turned to refill a drink for a nearby soldier.

Roman was about to make a smartass comment like "How did you figure that out?" but decided against it. Instead, he said, "I didn't realize I stood out that bad." She had been pretty cool so far. What's the golden rule? Don't piss off the bartender, right? "It's kind of a long story on how I ended up here."

The bartender looked back at him, over her shoulder. "I figured that much. We all have long stories around here." She pushed two purple drinks in the direction of a slightly inebriated soldier to Roman's left.

Roman was about to say something else to her when he felt a slap on his shoulder. Looking back, his gaze met Scott's usual jovial self.

"I see you've met Natasha. You're lucky; she's in a good mood tonight!"

Natasha flashed Scotts a "go to hell" look and walked to another part of the bar and a group of rowdy academy cadets whose drinks needed refilling.

"We thought you got lost," Scotts said. "We have a table in the back." Roman followed Scotts through the maze of patrons into the rear part of the bar, which had filled up even more since he had arrived. Perhaps it was happy hour, Roman thought to himself. No video broadcasts played in the back section, just a slow ambient rhythm. Chuikova was seated in the middle of a large booth, with Cruwell and Matthias on each side. Two rather attractive black-haired women sat on either side of Matthias in the booth, laughing at his jokes, one of them massaging his shoulders. As Roman scanned the rest of the back part of the bar, he found similarities to strip clubs back home. Several women in various stages of undress chatted and danced with the customers, male and female alike. A striking contrast however, was a large, painted mural on the wall featuring a fanged, grey wolf. The word "DREADWOLF" was painted in red script under the wolf.

"Sit down!" Matthias roared at Roman. The alcohol was working just fine tonight, Roman mused. Chuikova nodded in his direction. Not surprisingly, he smoked a cigar and had a glass of rather rusty-colored liquid in front of him. From his experiences as a cop back home, Roman was pretty sure Chuikova (and Matthias, for that matter) was three sheets to the wind. Cruwell, on the other hand, appeared to be drinking water or vodka (if they had vodka on this planet). Cruwell sat quietly, rotating his glass in his hands, not saying anything. He gazed up at Roman and nodded in his direction. Roman noted that Cruwell's shoulder-length black hair was tied into a ponytail, a more casual style than he usually sported. Roman chuckled to himself as he turned his gaze back to Matthias. Although his arm was still in the sling, he managed to use it to lift his glass to his lips.

"I didn't think you could have places like this here," Roman said over the noise of the music.

Matthias replied, "Just what kind of society do you think we have?" He started to laugh, and the others joined him.

Chuikova interrupted, "Anything you want, it's on me. Well, actually, it's on the army!" Scotts summoned a waitress and ordered a round of drinks for everyone.

"I have a job for you if you're interested, Johnny," Chuikova said as he finished the last of his drink and set the empty glass on the table. Roman could tell that Chuikova was trying his best not to slur his words.

"I'm listening."

"I have a friend who is in command of the police force in this sector. There is a job there if you want it. It will at least give you something to do for a while."

"I haven't seen any police presence here," Roman replied." He reached for his glass and took another small, cautious sip of Torol.

"Well, it's actually a military unit, attached to XXX Corps. The XXX Corps has been in control of the police for a while in this sector. Now that I am basically in command of XXX Corps now, it's no problem. With the war still going on, the police don't really have any manpower. Anyway, I prefer not to talk business. Come by my quarters tomorrow, and we'll pay my friend a visit." Chuikova received his fresh drink from the waitress and raised it up in the air.

"Let's have a toast to the end of war!"

Everyone at the table stood up and raised their glasses. All of them except Roman shouted in unison, "Dreadwolves! Death never dies!"

Scotts looked over at Roman after he slammed the rest of his drink and said, "See any girls you like?"

"Well, actually, I like the bartender," Roman said half jokingly. He found himself looking back toward the bar area, trying to could catch a glimpse of her.

Matthias started laughing as he overheard Johnny's response. "Natasha will kick your ass, man. Very tough. I fought alongside her on one campaign. She's got a couple other bionic implants to go along with that arm. But I think everything else works, if you know what I mean." Matthias laughed again, and continued. "Last one of her platoon to survive an ambush up on Chairia's second moon, I think. Infantry lieutenants don't last long, you know. She got lucky."

"Yeah, you'd better be careful, man," Scotts added. Good luck to you, though!" He stood and headed toward a side door. "I gotta take a piss."

Cruwell stood up, finished his drink, and set the glass on the table. "If you will all excuse me, my new rank has burdened me with many new responsibilities. I have an early start tomorrow."

Matthias blurted out, "We *all* have an early start tomorrow!"

Cruwell nodded and headed toward the exit. Roman finished the last of his Torol and set the empty glass on the table. The drink's effects were kicking in; he felt very relaxed. Watching Cruwell leave, Roman sensed he was bothered by something, but he wasn't sure what it was.

Roman unsteadily stood up trying to get his legs under him. He said the group, "I'm going to try my luck." He thought he sounded under control. But then again, drunks usually think they are.

"Good luck to you," Matthias said, "and lad, watch out for the right cross!" He erupted in laughter and signaled for the waitress to refill his empty glass.

Roman walked toward the front of the bar, pushing his way through the crowd. He felt a slight buzz beginning to develop, but it was nothing he couldn't handle. He finally made it to the bar, but instead of Natasha, he was confronted by a burly, bearded man with a bionic eye.

"Damn. Where's Natasha?"

"She's on break, be back in fifteen," the barkeep said gruffly.

Roman nodded and began to walk back toward his friends. He spotted Natasha, sitting at a small table by herself, having a drink and smoking a cigarette. Matthias was right. Along with her bionic left arm, she also had a bionic implant on her left upper thigh, her black skirt not quite hiding the implant from view. He quickly looked up from her otherwise muscular legs and caught her staring directly back at him. She had let her long purple hair down, so that it fell down the sides of her face. Letting out a heavy sigh, Roman walked over.

"I'm sorry. I wasn't staring this time."

Natasha took a drag on the cigarette and looked him up and down, keying on the backside of his faded Levi's. Pushing her hair away from her face, she said, "Those look comfortable." Exhaling the smoke away from Roman, she pointed to the chair opposite her. "You don't have to stand all night."

"Thanks."

"So tell me, what sector are you from, anyway? Did you get discharged already?"

"I am from a planet called Earth," Roman said a little nervously. He continued, "I arrived a couple days ago." He remained deliberately vague because he had been warned against mentioning any mission parameters to prying minds. The information was strictly classified.

"Really." Natasha opened a flat black case to reach for another cigarette. As if on cue, Roman reached into his own jacket pocket and pulled out his pack of L&M's. He offered the pack to her, and she pulled out one of the cigarettes, eyeing it with curiosity. Roman pulled out his chrome Zippo and lit the cigarette. Natasha inhaled deeply, sitting back into the chair.

Eyeing the cigarette held by her thumb and index finger, Natasha said, "Sure beats synthetics. Thanks."

"I'm Johnny." Roman offered his outstretched hand. She shook it with a surprisingly firm grip. Roman couldn't help but notice her muscular build, among other things, showcased by her tight, black sleeveless shirt.

Taking another drag off of the L&M, Natasha continued, "I have never heard of Earth." She took another long drag off of the cigarette. "I don't know what to make of you, Johnny." Her dark grey eyes stared into his. "I am Natasha," she continued, not displaying any outward signs of emotion.

"I know. Matthias and Scotts told me a little about you."

"Did they, now? Matthias is a good man, damned lucky if you ask me. He saved my life. I think he's been shot more times than anybody else I know—at least anyone living."

I can attest to that, Roman thought to himself, recalling the three AK-47 slugs pulled from Matthias's shoulder.

Natasha finished her cigarette and put it out in a chrome ashtray sitting on the table top. She stood up and tied her hair into a ponytail. "Well, if you know those two, you hang around with good company." She looked back toward the bar. "Sorry, Johnny, but I've got to get back to work."

A brief uncomfortable silence ensued. The pair stood from their chairs, facing each other. Roman finally broke the awkward silence. Natasha seemed to be waiting for him to. When they stood up fully, Roman was surprised that she was almost a foot taller than his six feet. He had thought she was standing on a platform behind the bar.

"Any chance you would like to go out sometime?" he got composure back quickly as he lit another cigarette and took a long drag. He felt like an idiot, hearing his voice breaking between words.

"You seem like you're squared away, but I don't play around anymore." Natasha looked at her bionic arm, and back into Roman's eyes. "I am scarred for life, you know. It's enough I have to live with this day to day." She headed back to the bar, leaving Roman staring after her, wondering if he had said something wrong. Maybe she was just another psycho woman. Of course, having limbs blown off and serving in a seemingly endless war might do that to a person. She hadn't said no, though.

The tavern began emptying out at the last call. By the time Roman was ready to leave, most of the people exiting were staff. He thought for a moment that he might be making a mistake, but what the hell did he have to lose? He thought he had perhaps missed Natasha leaving the bar, but he checked himself. He wasn't sure it was possible to miss a woman like that in a crowd, anywhere. He was pondering that, smoking his last L&M, when Natasha finally stepped outside. She was wearing a see-through jacket over her clothes. She saw him waiting off to the side and walked over. Her knee-high black boots made no sound on the pavement.

"You stand out pretty good in those clothes," she said as she approached him. "I wouldn't miss those pants anywhere." A slight smile formed on her lips.

Roman smiled back. "All they had for me was army issue. I didn't feel right wearing that to a bar."

"Are you waiting for someone or what? The tavern's closing up."

That sounds like a trick question, Roman thought to himself. He cleared his throat and said, "Yeah—I was waiting for you. I thought maybe I could walk you home or something."

She looked directly at him and wasn't sure how to respond. Her tough girl routine wasn't holding up very well right now. It was not every day she met a man who had the nerve to come up and talk to her. She answered the only way she knew how. That had been the safest way up until now. "Thanks, Johnny, but I thought I told you I have enough problems."

Roman cut her off and put his hands up in defense. "Look, I just wanted to talk. That's all. I am sorry if I overstepped myself." Roman began to back away, feeling more than a little pissed off. Talking to members of the opposite sex was not exactly his strongest point, especially those from other planets, and rejection wasn't a good feeling. Roman started to turn around and began the long walk back down the street to the training academy.

"Wait." The voice was flat, and Roman sensed a little falter in it. Roman turned back and looked up into those grey eyes, causing Natasha to blush and look away. Natasha continued, "I'm sorry." She walked toward him, closing the distance. The wind picked up, causing her hair to swirl about her face. "I don't mean to come across like that. It's nothing personal. It's just the way it's been for me since I got all scarred up."

"Don't worry about it." Roman felt better already and was mad at himself for getting flustered.

Natasha nodded in the direction opposite from where Roman was heading. "My place is about two clicks from here."

As they walked side by side, Natasha asked, "So where are you staying again? Sorry, I forgot if you mentioned it." She hated forcing conversation.

"Over at the training academy," Roman replied. "They have a bunch of empty rooms."

"Ouch, sorry to hear that. I remember those accommodations being pretty rough."

Roman looked up at her as they walked. The cool night breeze whistled as it blew. "The barracks aren't half bad. The air is a little stale, though." He fired back a question at her. "How long did you serve?" The conversation began to flow a little easier for both of them.

She continued looking straight ahead as she answered. "One year. I signed up for a career; I wasn't drafted. I was commissioned as a lieutenant. I didn't last very long, though, for reasons you can see." She raised the silver bionic arm and flexed her hand. Most of her hand, save for a few fingers, also was bionic. She lowered her arm and continued. "I was discharged and really didn't feel like doing anything until I got a job at the tavern. I was hopped up on painkillers most of the time. The job helped. I was in the psych hospital for a while. It was a rough time for me, as well as many of the others who ended up wounded and discharged. The tavern is run by vets and staffed by vets. I get by OK."

Roman looked straight ahead as they walked, occasionally looking up at the surrounding monoliths. He could see no other pedestrians. The darkness of the night was held at bay by numerous streetlights.

"Well, this is me," Natasha said. The pair stopped in front a dull grey building, ten or twelve stories high. It reminded Roman of an apartment building from the old Soviet communist regime. Natasha activated a video screen next to the glass door and swiped her entry key. The doors opened silently. She stepped into the building and turned around. Roman remained standing outside the door.

"Well, good night," he said.

"Thanks for the escort." Natasha began walking toward a turbo lift inside. "I'll see you around, ok. You know where you can find me," she said over her left shoulder.

"Oh, and one there is more thing," Roman said.

Natasha stopped and turned around, looking at him as she activated the turbo lift control. "What is it?"

"You know, you're not as bad looking as you think." She smiled and entered the turbo lift, leaving Roman feeling like a schoolboy.

CHAPTER 32

Three months later, Roman sat at his desk at the Police Detachment Headquarters of XXX Corps. A knock sounded on the metal door of his office.

"Come in," he answered.

The metal door slid silently open in response to his pushing a button on his desk. Scotts entered the room and gave a low whistle.

"Not bad, Lieutenant, not bad at all."

Roman looked up from the news video feed playing on the monitor on his desk. Stacks of paper and a few books cluttered the rest of the desktop. Open boxes of various papers covered the floor, leaving only a narrow trail from the door to the desk. Roman's trusty Remington 870 stood propped against the wall behind him. A pistol belt holding his newly acquired departmental issue sidearm draped over his chair.

"Good to see you, man," Roman said, standing up and extending his hand. "It's been a while. How is everyone else doing?" He waved Scotts to a chair opposite his desk.

"They're keeping us all busy, that's for sure." Scotts looked at the stacks of papers all over the office. "It looks like they're *really* keeping you busy here. And I thought I had it rough."

Roman turned around and activated a switch on the wall behind him. A dark opaque cover on the wall slid upward into a slot, out of sight, revealing a clear window and the cloudy sky outside. A few pale rays of sunlight could be seen in the distance.

"I heard you were a pilot again, he noted. "That's great, man."

Scotts moved around a couple of boxes and sat down in the only other chair in the office besides Roman's. "Yeah, it's more suited to me. I used to be a pilot before all of this." Scotts paused and looked at his friend, who was still staring out the window. "Are you doing all right? You seem worn down."

Roman turned around and sat back down. He was wearing his lieutenant's uniform, which now had the XXX Corps Dreadwolf insignia over the right sleeve. He also wore a gold, five-pointed badge over his right breast, indicating his position of police lieutenant.

"I'm just a little tired. When I signed on, I didn't realize this planet's police force was almost non-existent." He eased his chair back onto two legs and continued. "I'm going through all of the policies and procedures to see what changes I can come up with. There's a lot to be done, almost like starting from scratch. The police force really should be run by civilians, for example. The colonel in charge here is very receptive to my ideas so far. He has me writing up a training protocol for new cadets." Roman paused and scratched his head. "The types of crimes that go on here are a lot different from what I am used to. The cops here are pretty heavy handed, so policing my own force and educating them on suspect rights has been a challenge. I haven't had a single murder, shooting, or robbery yet. Mainly just a lot of fights, public drunks, and missing persons due to that fact they were drunk and got lost. I'm far more used to being on the street, though. This office stuff sucks ass."

"Well, Johann said you were doing a good job over here. Apparently, your hard work has not gone unnoticed." He paused for a moment. "And it looks like you're going to have your hands full in the coming weeks."

"Oh? Why is that?"

"The war is over," Scotts said decisively.

Roman looked his friend directly in the eyes. "Over? I have the news on all the time. Why haven't I heard that?"

"It was announced just a couple of hours ago, and the news still hasn't trickled down from the highest levels. A peace settlement was finally reached. I wanted to tell you before you found out otherwise. You're going to get a lot of recruits as the military demobilizes, that's for sure."

"Wow. I sure am glad for you guys."

"Hey, you helped put an end to the war. Without your help on your planet, we may not have succeeded."

"I suppose so." Roman sat back down in his high-backed leather chair.

"The alien we brought back was studied, taken apart, and who knows what else. To make a long story short, with the knowledge gained, we were able to put more troopers on the field of battle than the enemy."

Roman tilted his head and studied his friend's face for a short moment. "You mean you sent an army of *corpses* out there?" He was more shocked than anything else, and he did his best not to lose his cool. "If just one could create so much havoc, who knows what hundreds could be capable of?" The mere thought was too much for him to comprehend.

"Not exactly an army of corpses," Scotts countered. "I believe we were able to isolate his rapid healing qualities. That made our casualties much less serious, close to non-existent. Guys would get hit but heal almost immediately. I've heard reports of side effects, but nothing to be too concerned about." Scotts glanced at his wristwatch and abruptly stood up, straightening his uniform. "I also wanted to tell you that your presence will be required soon. I am sure Sebastian will get in touch with you about the details."

"Fair enough."

"Oh, and one other thing I wanted to ask you. I hope I'm not probing into your personal life."

"We'll see. What is it?"

"How are you and Natasha doing? I had heard you two were spending a lot of time together."

"You sure hear a lot!" Roman answered with a chuckle. "We're doing fine. I work a lot; she's still at the tavern. We don't see each other that much, but we enjoy each other's company, so I guess it's working out."

Scotts nodded and extended his hand over Roman's desk. As they shook hands, he said, "Take care, friend. I'll see you in a few days."

Scotts exited the cluttered office and headed down the deserted corridor toward the turbo lift, Roman trailing behind him. Once inside the lift, he activated the ground floor button. As the doors slid shut, he added, "Just looking after you, buddy. See you soon."

The doors closed, leaving Roman in the empty corridor. He glanced at his watch and headed back to the office to lock up. He couldn't help but think to himself that Scotts just wasn't the same anymore.

The next three weeks passed quickly for Roman. Per his usual pattern, Roman woke from a fitful sleep at 5:30 a.m., in response to the dull blare of an alarm clock. Ever since arriving on Hellenheim, he had been unable to get more than three or four hours of sleep at a time. He slowly got out of bed, stretching his arms. Morris stayed in place, lying on top of one of the pillows, licking his paw. The tiger-striped cat displayed no intent of moving anytime in the near future. Roman walked over to the window. The sun actually looked like it might break through the cloud cover later, a break from the routine of gray days.

His apartment wasn't much, barely better than the one he'd had on Earth, but it beat the barracks. When his commission with the XXX Corps police services detachment was made official, he had started drawing a paycheck, and he immediately moved into the first modest apartment that he could afford that had a really good AC system. Utilities were included, which was nice. He missed a couple things from his home, but for the most part, he didn't mind the beginnings of his new life. He was surprised at the similarities between his old life and life on this new planet. Morris didn't seem to mind the change, either. Domestic cats weren't native to the planet, so cat food was non-existent. Instead, Morris enjoyed an upgraded steady diet of imported, off-world fish.

Roman activated his shower and stepped in. Water rationing meant that he was done thirty seconds later. He'd found that hard to get used to. Fortunately, the soap was integrated into the water, making showering more efficient, but it was disgusting if any got into your mouth. He stepped out of the shower and put on a black T-shirt with the XXX Corps police insignia on it. He made a small pot of coffee and sat on a kitchen chair, looking out of his window, watching the sun try to break through.

The ceremony marking the end of the war would be held that evening. By the chancellor's decree, Roman and his friends were to be decorated with the United Consortium of Planets' highest medal. Cruwell had contacted Roman a couple of days earlier with all of the details. For the last several weeks, the news had been full of reports of troopships coming home. The streets became much busier, and housing almost impossible to find. Roman was glad he'd found his apartment when he did. He was still sipping his coffee when a wall- mounted video monitor activated itself. Natasha's familiar figure stood outside on the street.

"Hey, you awake yet?" She held a white bag in each hand and held them up to the camera. "I thought you could use some breakfast before your big day."

It took Roman a second to respond; mornings just weren't his thing. "Yeah. Come on up."

A few moments later, his front door chime played to indicate a presence outside his apartment. He walked over and opened the door. Natasha had her long purple hair in a ponytail today. She smiled at Johnny and gave him a big hug, which he reciprocated.

"You're a lifesaver," Johnny said. Taking the bags, he set them on his table. "Coffee?"

"Sure."

He poured another cup for himself and one for Natasha, emptying the pot, and sat down at the table. Natasha removed the meat and egg burritos from the bag. They tasted OK, although Roman tried not to think about exactly where the meat and the eggs actually came from.

"You just got off not too long ago, I'm guessing?"

Natasha nodded. "Yeah, around 5:00. Just about every place in our sector is seeing a huge influx, with all of the troopships returning. I haven't earned this much cash in a very long time."

Roman took another bite from his burrito and washed it down with some coffee. He liked the easiness of his routines with her. Since the night that he had met Natasha, they had remained in fairly close contact, with only a few short breaks. She now seemed more comfortable around him, and she told him more about her past as the days went on. Roman enjoyed her company, even though it was taking a while for her to open up. He could respect that; he knew he was a private person too. He was in no hurry, anyway. Adjusting to life on a new planet gave him enough to do without rushing into a relationship. For now, Natasha was more like a friend, and he reflected that one needs all the friends one can get.

"Are they treating you all right?" Roman knew how men in uniform could be, especially if they hadn't been on leave in a while.

Natasha laughed. "You crack me up. In case you may have forgotten, I can handle myself very well."

Roman had no doubt of this and quickly changed the subject. "I just want you to know that I'm still holding that position for you down at the H.Q. I mean, you were a XXX Corps front line platoon leader. Especially with troop demobilization happening soon, the police force is going to be one of the top employers. I know I can get your officer's commission reinstated."

"Johnny, we've talked about this before. I just don't think I'm ready for government service again. They left me high and dry last time. I'm still waiting on my disability pension."

"I'm sorry." Johnny reached across the table and took her hand in both of his. She looked at him in surprise; the move shocked both of them. He could feel her hand tremble through his. He quickly released his grip, sat back in the chair, and resumed his blank stare out the window. "I just worry about you. Anyway, it's there if you want it."

Natasha nodded and decided to change the subject to something more neutral. "I think the cloud cover is breaking for good now that the factories are slowing production."

Roman said nothing. He took another sip from his coffee and resumed eating his burrito.

"Are you ready for today?" Natasha asked.

Roman wiped his mouth with his hand. "A dog and pony show, from what Matthias told me a couple days ago. But tonight, after the assembly, I get to meet the chancellor."

"I'll watch the chancellor's speech at home. All other programming has been suspended. I appreciate you inviting me to your ceremony tonight, though. I'll be there. I think you look sharp in your uniform."

They both shared a laugh and finished their coffee while watching the sunrise.

CHAPTER 33

The gathering of uniformed troopers, representing all branches of service, was on a scale Roman had never before witnessed. Massive foundations of white stone appeared at regular intervals across the parade grounds. Protruding out of the foundations were forty-foot swords, constructed out of a smooth rock resembling obsidian. Members of the various divisions of the military stood in mass block formations in front of the stone foundations. A wide pathway passed through the middle of the great assembly, ending in front of a giant platform. Flanking the platform on both sides were the great eagles of the United Consortium of Planets. Large torches burned with bright red flames on either side of the stairs up to the main platform. The entire spectacle took place on green grass beneath a humongous bioshield that protected the greenery, rarely seen on the planet, from the polluted air.

Roman stood at the head of a company of newly recruited police cadets that was a part of the XXX Corps. The company all but vanished among the many thousands of military and police forces that had come from all over Hellenheim and the nearby planets still subservient to the supreme chancellor. Over the next hour, the remaining divisions marched into their designated positions. As the last of them found their positions, the supreme chancellor finally appeared, followed at a respectful distance by Marshal Von Jesonik; Chuikova, dressed in full regalia, including his jeweled baton; and three other high-ranking officers. The military leaders walked purposefully toward the platform. As they passed the assembled men, the divisions raised their standards in honor. The standard bearers began to pound their standards in a rhythmic manner.

When his group reached the base of the main platform, only the supreme chancellor, dressed in a simple black suit, continued up the giant steps. Red flames licked up out of the torch dishes lining the stairs, like great wispy fingers. The supreme chancellor reached the platform and turned to face his massed armies. He raised one hand, and the rhythmic pounding of the standards ceased. He slowly lowered his hand. After surveying his commanders below him, at the base of the steps, he began to speak into the voice projector, in powerful, deep tones appropriate to the solemnity of the occasion.

"Throughout the twenty-two years of this war, we have all suffered. The trooper has suffered at the front; the civilian has suffered at home. Today begins a new era in which our grand empire is once again reunited. I speak to you as our troops stand along a great line from Hellenheim to the capitals of the conquered planets, and as columns of the defeated enemy march as prisoners. They are giving up by the thousands. Throughout this long war, I know that one thing has remained true: I have shown our people the light and the path to victory. At this moment, our thankful hearts go to our noble troopers. We have conquered, and we have prevailed!"

Cheers erupted from the formations. The supreme chancellor stepped back and pushed a couple of strands of hair off of his face. He nodded and stepped back to the voice projector. Raising his hand, he quieted the masses and continued.

"I did not want this war. It was propagated by greedy and corrupt governors of the outer worlds of the empire, as I have said time after time. Those of you who have been with me from the beginning know that I have tried to achieve nothing but peace and good relations with our outer world governors. I say again that I tried, in every possible way, to bring about the end of this terrible war." The supreme chancellor paused briefly, taking a deep breath. He continued in a calmer, quieter tone. "Justice will be served to those who are guilty. The people of these regions have suffered much, and I do not desire to prolong their suffering. Today is a day of celebration and remembrance. Today is a day for heroes. With that in mind, I request that Ground Marshal Chuikova join me on this platform and receive the empire's highest award, the Star Cluster of the Empire."

The standard bearers resumed the rhythmic thumping of their standards as Ground Marshal Chuikova ascended the steps. He bowed before the supreme chancellor and accepted a brilliant blue medal, beset with eight jeweled stars, hanging on the end of a gold braided necklace. As the supreme chancellor hung the medal on Chuikova's neck, the masses erupted in cheers. A few moments later, while the cheers continued, a curious entourage of black-robed figures seemingly appeared from nowhere at the base of the steps. The supreme chancellor and Chuikova descended the steps, joined the robed figures and other military leaders on the ground, and began the long walk out of the grounds.

"Are you ready?" Natasha's voice broke the silence of Roman's apartment later than evening. She entered the apartment and replaced the key card in her overcoat pocket.

Roman stepped out from the bathroom, adjusting his black bowtie. "Just let yourself in and make yourself at home, why don't you?" He grinned at her, and she smiled back as he struggled with the tie.

"Dammit," he swore at the strip of cloth.

She walked toward him, grabbed the tie, and within minutes fixed the problem. She took a step back and looked him over. His knee-high leather boots were mirror polished, as were his belt and shoulder strap. He adjusted his badge and grabbed his peaked hat off of a nearby table. Turning around, he finally took in Natasha.

"I … wow."

Natasha looked herself over, trying to see herself through his eyes. "Is there something wrong?" she asked nervously.

"No. Quite the contrary. You are absolutely stunning." Roman smiled as he complimented her. She wore a long, black flowing evening dress complete with gloves that went up her arms, covering the bionic appendage. Roman was surprised to see that she'd gone as far as applying makeup, fairly generously. He had never seen her wear it before. The scar on her face was barely noticeable. She blushed from his comments.

"Thanks, Johnny. It's been a while since I've been out to anything nearly this formal."

"No prob. Let's go, shall we?"

Roman offered her his arm, which she accepted without hesitation. He secured the apartment on the way out, and they made their way to the busy street below. Nightfall had set, but the streets still teemed with activity.

After a short walk, they arrived at the number seven light rail station. Sifting through the dense crowds entering and exiting the light rail, they boarded for the trip to the government section. They attracted quite a few stares in the light rail, but no one said anything. The daytime assembly and the gathering at the supreme chancellor's residence had been the talk of the town, but only a relatively small number of people had actually been invited, and their fellow rail passengers could only guess that Roman and Natasha, dressed as they were, were among those lucky few.

The light rail stopped at the government section a few minutes later, and Roman and Natasha exited. The government section truly was a separate section of the city, walled off from the rest, housing various government bureaus, both military and civilian. Through one of the gates, Roman and Natasha saw the supreme chancellor's residence illuminated by several columns of white light that split the night sky. The brilliant columns reached upward and touched the bottoms of the clouds overhead. After a short time, Roman and Natasha reached the first set of security checks, where a long line of similarly dressed guests waited to get in. The security guards had been trained well to handle the crowd efficiently, and Roman and Natasha soon reached the front of the line.

Roman showed his paper invitation to the private manning the security station. The private nodded and said, "Please submit a retinal scan." He lifted a small scanner to Roman's face. Roman looked down into the screen and waited. The scanner beeped once and announced in a robotic voice, "Roman, John J., lieutenant, sector 7 police administration. Confirmed."

"Go ahead, sir," the private said. Roman nodded and took a few steps forward, and waited for Natasha to clear the retina scan. After a few moments, she joined him.

They followed the crowd toward the main structure that served as the chancellor's residence, at the end of a half-kilometer pathway, lined on each side by alternating shimmering mirrors, stone columns, statues, and sculptures. The columns and the pathway were constructed out of bright red stone, inset with lights to help show the way. Guests stopped every so often to admire the beauty and workmanship of the artwork.

When they reached the steps into the main building, Roman and Natasha found another security checkpoint. Several armed troopers lined the steps. They submitted to another retinal scan and were scanned for weapons or any other contraband. After the second scan was completed, he again showed the paper invitation he had received earlier in the day, imprinted with his name and Natasha's. He nodded in acknowledgment when the private waved him through. He stood at the top of the steps, watching Natasha look down into a scanner. She undertook the same contraband scan.

As another private passed a scanner over her body, the machine beeped rapidly. The private waved the handheld scanner to clear it, targeted her upper thighs and forearms. Two more troopers, holding large rifles at the ready, approached her.

"Is there a problem, private?" a soldier with three chevrons on his sleeve asked.

"I have a positive scan, Sergeant."

The sergeant looked at Natasha and asked, "What do you have?"

"Bionics." Natasha pulled off her right glove, exposing her bionic arm.

The private waved the scanner over it, confirming the positive reading. The sergeant nodded and pointed to her right leg. Natasha leaned over and raised her dress over her thigh boots, exposing part of her upper thigh and the bionic plate. The sergeant reached out to touch her thigh and found his wrist gripped tightly.

"Is there a problem, sergeant?" Roman sneered. Security was one thing, harassment was another. "I have no problem having you arrested for your unprofessional behavior."

"No, lieutenant," the sergeant said, recognizing Roman. "No problem here." The sergeant nodded nervously to the other troopers, who cleared the doorway. Roman had made a name for himself in his short time on the planet, and his closeness with some of the most powerful men in the military was well known. Natasha dropped her dress back down and walked up the stairs with Roman in pursuit.

"I am *so* sorry about that," he told her. "It's OK. Let's go in, shall we?"

Nodding, Roman took hold of her hand, and they walked into the main building. Two attendants ushered them through the massive double doors into the ballroom, which already held several hundred guests.

"Wow, this is impressive!" Natasha noted. "I've seen this building before, on news feeds, but I never thought it was this big in person." She looked around in awe, especially at the geodesic dome above. A mural painted on the ceiling of the dome depicted naval fleet ships, once numerous but now depleted by war. Roman found himself caught up in the grandeur as well. He managed to grab two glasses from a passing waiter and gave one to Natasha. As he sipped the bubbling liquid, he heard his name called from behind.

"Johnny." The low voice was almost imperceptible over the crowd noise. Roman spun around and saw the familiar face of Sebastian Cruwell, who had a plump blonde woman in tow as he made his way toward Roman. Roman extended his hand, which Cruwell shook.

"It's been a while, Sebastian."

"Indeed it has. Listen, we need to talk." Cruwell's hushed voice had a sense of urgency.

Roman nodded quickly. "Sure, whenever you want."

Cruwell looked around the crowded ballroom. He told his companion, "We'll just be a moment." She nodded and took Natasha by the arm and led her off, as if on cue, as Cruwell guided Roman toward a nook in the wall. Natasha looked back over her shoulder at Roman. He nodded and waved, giving Cruwell his attention.

"We need to talk *right now*?" Roman asked.

"Listen, there are a lot of things going on that you are not aware of. I know you think you are working for the good, but be warned." Cruwell paused, turned, and scanned the crowd once more. "All is not what it seems."

Roman set his glass on a small table. "What do you mean 'all is not what it seems?' Are you OK?"

"Look, Johnny, I won't talk about it here. There are eyes and ears everywhere. But I need to speak with you. This is just a heads-up. I'll get in touch with you and set up a meeting, OK?"

"OK."

Cruwell was about to speak when an attendant approached. "Sirs, your presence is requested upstairs in the supreme chancellor's study, if you will follow me please." Roman looked at Cruwell, who nodded and shrugged. They both followed the attendant. Roman spotted Natasha and gave her a small wave to let her know that he was leaving the main ballroom.

Roman trailed behind Cruwell and the attendant as they ascended the staircase to the second level, which was off limits to the guests except by special invitation. They passed through a large passageway coming to a stop before a large door. Two ceremonial guards heavily armed with red plumes sticking out of their helmets stood outside.

"This way, please," the attendant requested. The guards stepped aside in unison as the attendant pushed upon the door into the chancellor's study, a massive room that appeared even larger with its furniture all placed near the walls. The supreme chancellor sat behind his large desk, which had the words "blood, honor, loyalty" carved boldly onto its side. Ground Marshal Chuikova and Sergeant Matthias were already seated in large chairs in front of the desk.

The attendant bowed and left the study, closing the door behind him. Chuikova and Matthias stood up and looked at the new visitors.

"My friends," the supreme chancellor spoke, "please come in." Roman and Cruwell approached the desk. The supreme chancellor smiled and held up his right hand, acknowledging his new guests. He quickly dropped his left hand below the desk, out of sight.

"Please come in, yes." The supreme chancellor repeated himself and stood up. He placed his left hand behind his back and walked to the front of the desk. The only insignia was a gold cross bearing a silver eagle on his left breast pocket. Roman, who had never met the supreme chancellor, found himself surprised. The man's voice seemed a little weak and quavered slightly, very much unlike his presentation at the afternoon's assembly. Roman supposed that his voice had been altered through the public address system.

"I thank you for coming," the supreme chancellor said. "You have each played an important part in the conclusion of the war, and I wanted to thank you personally." He reached over the surface of his desk and picked up two medals by their neck chains. Roman noticed that even though the supreme chancellor held his left hand behind his back, the arm trembled slightly. "Major Cruwell, please accept this medal of bravery for your actions on the blue planet."

The supreme chancellor placed the medal over Cruwell's lowered head. It was the same design as the insignia on the chancellor's jacket. Cruwell shook the supreme chancellor's hand and stepped back. Roman noticed with keen interest that Chuikova looked coldly at Cruwell, his eyes piercing him like two daggers. The supreme chancellor interrupted Roman's quick observation.

"I have wanted to meet you for some time, Lieutenant Roman. I have heard a great many things about you and your work helping to rebuild the police force in sector seven. That is a noble task." the supreme chancellor shook Roman's hand and continued, "I am especially interested in hearing about your home planet, but for now, I wish to recognize you for your service toward our victory." Roman lowered his head, and the supreme chancellor placed the second medal around his neck.

"Keep up the good work, and enjoy the rest of the banquet."

As if on cue, the attendant opened the doors to the study from outside. Cruwell came to attention, executed an about face, and exited. Roman looked at his old friends, but they said nothing. Matthias nodded slightly, but that was it. Shrugging, Roman exited the study and caught up with Cruwell, who was waiting outside. Once they were out of earshot of the guards, Roman asked, "What the hell was that? They totally ignored us."

"I'll try to explain later, when we meet again. It's not safe to talk here. Enjoy the rest of the evening, but be very careful of your surroundings." He paused, as if considering his words, and asked, "What time do you have?"

Roman looked at his wristwatch. "10:15."

"Remember that time Johnny, remember."

Cruwell said nothing more and walked toward the stairs leading back to the ballroom, leaving Roman looking at him curiously. He followed Cruwell, a few steps behind, and they soon found their female companions chatting with a group of half a dozen other women. Natasha immediately noticed Roman's medal and congratulated him on it.

The two couples enjoyed the rest of the evening together, through the cocktail hour, dinner, and dancing. A few hours later, after the chancellor gave his final speech of the day, the four left with the main crowd of guests. As Roman and Natasha exited the government sector and headed toward the light rail station, Roman found himself looking over his shoulder more than a few times. Cruwell's words had spooked him.

They boarded the light rail. When it was in motion, Natasha whispered into Roman's ear, "What are you doing?"

"What do you mean?" The others in the carriage did not seem to notice the sharpness and volume of his response.

"You keep looking around. You seem very tense."

Roman looked Natasha directly in her eyes. "How do you know all that?"

"Trust me," she said. "I know."

"Well, I would be lying if I said I wasn't feeling something. I can't explain it now. I don't know what to think."

Natasha said nothing more but gripped Roman's hand tightly. Within moments they arrived at their destination. A short walk brought them to Roman's apartment building. He retrieved his access card from his pocket and swiped it at the terminal, opening the door to the ground floor. Still holding Natasha's hand, he said, "Do you want to come up?"

"Yes. I would like that."

Roman smiled and kissed her lightly on the cheek. They entered the building, and the door silently slid shut behind them.

CHAPTER 34

Two weeks after the banquet at the supreme chancellor's residence, Roman sat behind his desk, looking over dossiers of potential recruits. During those two weeks, he had kept aware of his surroundings but hadn't been able to detect anybody following him. Further adding to his caution, his boss and mentor, Colonel Seib, had notified Roman that he was retiring and to be wary of his replacement. Even though Colonel Seib's retirement was still a few weeks off, he kept his ears open for any sign of political machinations that might affect him. His experience as a police officer on Earth had taught him that. He eyed the corridor outside his office and saw it bustling with activity, much of it taken care of by his two new assistants.

Roman sat back in his chair and activated his video monitor. After a few seconds, an image of Natasha appeared. He stared at it for a few minutes, until he received an incoming call alert.

"Roman," he answered.

The caller did not appear on screen. "Roman, I am sending you an encrypted file. Follow the directions."

The call ended abruptly, leaving Roman wondering what it was all about. A few seconds later, another alert went off, indicating that his system had received a file. He got up and closed the door of his office. Sitting back down, he opened the file, which contained video. Major Cruwell's face appeared. The video appeared to have been taken on a street using a public video feed.

"Johnny, I need you to meet me at the bio park on the southwest corner of Sector Nine. Remember that time we discussed?" The file ended and promptly deleted itself. Roman looked at the blank screen quizzically.

4:45. He had five and a half hours to wait.

He quickly pushed Natasha's icon on the video monitor. Within a few seconds, she answered.

"Hey, what are you doing?" she asked.

"Listen, I have to work a little late tonight, so I'm going to have to cancel dinner. I'm really sorry, I'll make it up to you next week."

"I understand. I know they have you working like an ore miner over there. I'll just see you tomorrow. Perhaps we can get lunch. If i'm off work that is."

"Will do. Your boss lets you get away with murder down there."

He ended the transmission and looked at his watch again.

Roman went back to his apartment after work and changed out of his uniform. He found himself checking his watch every few minutes while he tried to distract himself with video entertainment and news feeds. He headed out a little past 9:45, knowing that the bio park was about a twenty-minute walk. The precinct had issued him a personal vehicle, but he decided an official vehicle might arouse suspicion. Rain continued to fall, causing Roman to draw up his black overcoat as he headed out. The streets were almost devoid of people.

He arrived at the park soaking wet, even though the rain had let up a bit. The bio park contained a few trees and some grass. It was actually covered by a small magnetic shield. The shield not only blocked out the elements, but blocked out the industrial pollution as well. It seamlessly integrated itself into the air. Seeing no one around, Roman walked into the park and sat down on a bench, relieved to be under the shield's protection from rain.

10:15. That was the appointed time, and no one was in sight.

He no sooner looked up from his watch than Cruwell sat down next to him.

"Right on time; that's good. Were you followed?"

"I didn't see anyone." Roman looked at Cruwell curiously, wondering how he had appeared so suddenly and silently.

"Neither did I. I followed you here," Cruwell replied.

"What?" Roman asked with surprise. "Sebastian, you are going to have to start telling me what is going on, OK? This cloak and dagger shit is getting a little weird."

"Relax, Johnny. I will. Look at this."

Cruwell retrieved a small video monitor from within his coat. "I work in the Intelligence Security Service Bureau. I have a privileged access code, and I saw this footage I think may have some bearing on your future here."

"You work for the ISSB? I've heard of that—very secretive."

"Actually, I have always worked for them. Not all of the powers that be are on the same team. Anyway, you need to see this footage."

Cruwell activated the video monitor, which Roman peered at with interest. The video looked like it was taken with a handheld camera. It seemed to be shot inside some kind of research lab. Row after row of medical stasis pods lined each side of a long, white corridor.

"What am I looking for here?"

"Just watch."

The video continued to roll. Two white-coated scientists came into view, walking down the corridor, checking each pod. The camera filmed the nearest pod and panned through to several others. Inside the pods, human forms appeared to be in some sort of suspended animation.

"What is this, your army or something?" Roman asked. Cruwell didn't respond, and Roman continued to watch the monitor. Suddenly, he gasped at what he saw.

"You've got to be kidding me!" Upon closer inspection of the pods, Roman could make out the faint outlines of the biker tattoos he had seen on the Reaper. Every form in the pods had the identical markings, all the way down to the track marks on their arms.

"I'm afraid not kidding, Johnny. The alien we brought back from your planet has been cloned hundreds, if not thousands, of times over. How do you think the war ended so fast? What is even more disturbing is the planet on which these things were let loose are out of control. They spread some kind of virus that renders the host into a primitive animalist state."

"Yes. Before I met up with you guys, there were a couple walking around. I cannot believe Chuikova would let that happen." Roman sat back on the bench, averting his eyes from the video monitor.

Cruwell closed the video monitor and placed back into his jacket. "Johnny, Johann is not the same person you knew from before."

"What do you mean by that?"

Cruwell stood up and looked around. "You need to be aware of some things. I will be in contact with you. But there are things you must do right away."

"What are—"

"Just listen, Johnny," Cruwell interrupted. "Never go a direct route when we meet. Try to draw out anybody that may be on you. Go into shops and restaurants, dead ends. Things like that. Don't be predictable. They even have the capabilities to watch you from space. You need to check your office for listening devices. They may already have you tapped."

"Why are you telling me all of this? I have a low-level job at the Sector Seven police HQ. So they have some clones. Albeit, they've neo-Nazi biker clones, but why should I really care, Sebastian? Apparently, these clones helped win the war for you."

After a heavy sigh and a brief pause, Cruwell continued. "I'm telling you because they will come for you soon."

"What?" Johnny asked, both confused and astonished. Cruwell hesitated, as he looked up at the night sky through the magnetic shield. "War is coming again, Johnny."

"And? It seems like you guys like war. Like you're all mad and pissed off at everything."

Cruwell continued staring straight up into the night sky. "The war is coming to your home planet."

Roman's face went ashen as he realized what Cruwell just told him. "You're kidding," was all he could say, but down inside, he knew that Cruwell was dead serious. A twisted realization slowly began to dawn on him. He remembered the supreme chancellor saying that he wanted to learn everything about Earth. Everything that had happened so far was for a reason that could fit into this pattern. They kept tabs on him by giving him a job. Hell, Natasha might even be in on it.

"No, I'm not kidding," Cruwell said. "Johann is in charge of coming up with an assault plan. Because he is now a marshal, he has immense power. Because we have re-absorbed the rest of our small empire, we have a fairly sizable naval force now. The enemy saw the effects of our new weapon and wants no part of it."

"I can't believe it. I mean, Earth is kind of a dump anyway, but it's still home. I have friends and family there. I couldn't imagine those things running around eating people and destroying everything in their path."

"Believe it. It's going to take a while, but preparations have been made. The supreme chancellor wants to extend his reach as far as he can before he dies."

"What do you want me to do?"

Cruwell turned to face Roman, who was still sitting back on the bench. "You have to be careful, Johnny. They will try to use you for information. If the Auger-Seers are locked onto you, they may even use that girl of yours against you. They are capable of many things, and their sight is far reaching. I'll be in contact when I can."

Roman stood up and looked directly into Cruwell's red, bloodshot eyes that made it appear as though he hadn't slept in days. "Thanks for telling me. It means a lot."

Cruwell simply nodded and walked off, leaving Roman alone on the bench, his mind racing at a hundred miles an hour. He thought about his family and friends and what might happen to them. It was too overwhelming. He slowly got up and headed back toward his apartment. Keeping Cruwell's cautions in mind, he took a detour into a bar that had opened recently. As he entered, he noticed that it was pretty much empty. He sat at the bar and asked the barkeep for the strongest thing he had. Roman smiled with irony as the barkeep poured him Johann's beverage of choice. He looked for second at the tall glass, filled with murky, rust-colored liquid. He paid the barkeep and took a sip, flinching a little as the liquid burned his throat going down.

Roman pulled the blanket over his head as Natasha raised the sunshade and let the morning sunlight creep in. Roman groaned as he felt the consequences of the previous night are drinking.

"You sound pretty bad there. I'll put some coffee on for you."

Roman pushed Morris off of him and sat up in bed, his face buried in his hands. "I don't remember coming in last night." He looked up at Natasha. "When did you get here? I didn't do anything stupid, did I?"

Natasha returned with a cup of coffee and handed it to him. "You asked me to come over. It was late, but you looked bad on the screen, so I came. You were rambling on about your planet being destroyed. It was pretty incoherent before you passed out."

"I'm really sorry to have put you through that." He set his coffee down on an adjacent table and lay back down on the bed. Morris jumped up on his stomach and began to purr. Roman stroked the cat behind his ears as Natasha scratched his back. She looked at Roman, staring into those hazel eyes she loved getting lost in.

"Are you OK, Johnny? I've never seen you act this way before."

Roman sighed heavily and peered out of the window, watching the day outside grow brighter. He looked at Natasha and brushed her hair out of her face.

"Yes... Everything is fine." Roman stroked her hair and smiled. "Everything will be OK."

CHAPTER 35

Lately, sleep hadn't come easily for Johnny Roman. He was wide awake, staring at the numerous cracks in the ceiling, when his intercom alarm went off. He grabbed the video screen lying on his nightstand and activated the video monitor switch. A Gestapo-looking figure stood outside his apartment building in the rain. Roman wasn't sure if it was intentional or not, but the figure's face was obscured by his trench coat collar turned up and his hat pulled down. Roman threw off his sweat-soaked sheet and sat on the edge of the bed. His bedside clock read 4:23 a.m.

The figure on the video screen spoke, the urgent voice slightly obscured by thunderclaps and the sound of torrential rain.

"I am Colonel Brenneke. I apologize for this disturbance, but I am afraid you will have to come with me."

The request, and at such an unusual hour, took Roman by surprise. "4:23 in the morning? This can't wait?" Roman waited for an answer, but the dark figure outside just stood patiently. "What the hell for?" he continued.

"Please comply. I do not wish to use force."

"Whatever," Roman muttered. He stood up slowly and stretched. Placing the video screen back on the nightstand, he walked to his front door. The lights came on, activated by his movement. "Dim," Roman said to the system, and the lights instantly reduced their intensity. He activated the video screen mounted by the door and pushed a green access button that opened the main lobby door. He hit the intercom button. "It's open." The figure outside gave no reply but entered the apartment building.

Roman noticed that he was followed by several other figures that had not been visible on the video earlier, arousing his curiosity even further. A few minutes later, the door buzzer rang. Roman activated the door, and it slid quietly to the side. The man who had called himself Colonel Brenneke stood in the doorway. Although he called himself a colonel, his black peaked cap and trench coat showed no military insignia. Roman had a sickening feeling he was dealing with an officer of the ISSB, the same intelligence organization that his friend Sebastian Cruwell worked for. He wondered if he had any friends left anymore. He also wondered why he was asked to let them in when they could simply have bypassed the security grid and entered unannounced.

"May I enter?" the man asked quietly.

Roman looked beyond him to see six other masked and helmeted troopers in the hallway, waiting by the turbo lift, wearing tactical armor with rifles at the ready. They wore matching uniforms, but none of them displayed insignia.

"Is all of this necessary?" Roman asked. "This isn't a crack house." The words rolled off of his tongue acidly, but the colonel did not respond. The two men stared silently at each other for a moment. Roman felt his shoulders tense, noticed that the colonel had his right hand inside his trench coat, no doubt fingering a hand cannon.

"Be my guest," he said, gesturing inside the apartment with his hand. Roman stepped back and walked to the kitchen. The colonel followed him in slowly, looking around the small efficiency apartment as he did. Roman stood behind the kitchen counter and removed a cigarette from a pack on the counter. He had a pistol in a top drawer just in case. The colonel removed his hat and shook it, sending beads of water flying. The remaining troopers did not enter, but Roman could still see them, just outside the door. The colonel replaced his hat on his head, covering his short flattop haircut.

Roman remained silent as the colonel spoke. "I am afraid I do have to take you with me to answer some questions regarding your relationship with your girlfriend."

Roman placed his hand on the drawer handle. "Do you care to explain why?"

The colonel turned to the doorway and nodded. The tactical troopers entered and immediately spread out. Roman saw one of them remove a pair of hand restraints from his belt. The men did not aim their weapons at him, but they looked ready to do so in an instant.

"I hope you do not try to fight your way out of here, Mr. Roman. We just want to talk. Your girlfriend has ties to a terrorist cell that is under surveillance as we speak. We were hoping we could appeal to your, ah ... sense of duty. Please, come with us."

"I don't suppose I have any rights here, do I?" he asked the colonel sarcastically. He already knew he had none, especially if the ISSB had business with him. It seemed that they needed something from him; if they didn't, he would be dead already.

Still, he thought, the situation was not favorable. He might get a shot or two off at the colonel, but he was most likely wearing armor. The troopers had him, though; there were too many of them. Sebastian was right: Nothing was what it seemed anymore. There was no way in hell Natasha was a terrorist. Roman removed his hand from the drawer handle.

"OK. You win. At least let me put some pants on."

When he turned toward the bedroom, Brenneke's troopers rushed Roman, taking him to the floor. Within seconds he was handcuffed, with a hood placed over his head. He yelled and cursed but was quickly silenced by a shock baton to the head, rendering him unconscious. As two of the troopers dragged Roman out, holding him upright between them, the rest of them followed, with Brenneke in the rear. The entourage quickly boarded the turbo lift, left the building.

"Cigarette?"

Roman slowly came to. The first thing he noticed was a throbbing pain on the back of his skull. The bright desk light shining in his face didn't help one bit. He noticed that he was handcuffed to metal chair in which he was propped. He didn't recognize the man sitting on the desk, facing him, although he recognized the black ISSB uniform.

"Yeah. Sure. And maybe you could explain why I'm here."

"Of course. Your service to our society hasn't gone unnoticed." The man unlocked the restraints. Roman rubbed his wrists and took the offered cigarette from a silver holder. After the man lit it, he inhaled deeply, and sat back into the chair. He grimaced as he exhaled, still not quite used to synthetic smokes.

"We need information from you regarding your home planet."

"Information? All you had to do was ask. What do you want to know, who won the World Series last year, or what?"

The man got up from the desk and walked to a mirror. He dropped his cigarette and put it out under his boot. "I want you to tell me about your planet's military capabilities, weapons, and space capabilities. These are the subjects I wish to discuss with you."

Roman looked at the man with disgust. "I thought this had to do with Natasha being a terrorist." Seeing the blank look on his interrogator's face, Roman was more confused than ever. Why had Colonel Brenneke told him that story?

"Fine," he said. "I'll play your game for a bit. I've been asked all that before. I told you, I don't have those answers. I was a police officer, same as I am here."

The interrogator turned away from the window and again sat on the desk, opposite Roman. He withdrew another cigarette, lit it, and inhaled. He continued, "Mr. Roman, I know you are lying. You have been under observation for quite some time. If you do not tell me what I need to know, I can make things very difficult for you."

Roman stood up and walked to the mirror, knowing quite well someone was on the other side. "Very well, I will tell you. My planet is quite advanced. We have a massive space fleet of star destroyers. If by chance you managed to get through that, we have armies of robots as well as vampires, and we can raise the dead as well."

A robed figure stood in the shadows in the next room, looking through the one-way mirror at Roman. He spoke to two uniformed men also watching the interrogation. They listened as Roman continued to spin tales about Klingons and an orbiting battle station called the Death Star.

"He is lying," the robed figure commented dryly.

"Of course he is. He does not have the knowledge you seek."

The robed figure replied, "Yes, I have read your report that is in the archive. I am still quite curious as to the extent of your relationship to Mr. Roman while you were on planet X713 Delta. I sense your report is lacking … something, Sergeant Matthias."

Matthias stepped forward, putting his face close to that of the robed figure. "That's *Command* Sergeant Matthias, if you don't mind; I think I've earned it. I disclosed everything that went on while on X713 Delta. The others spoke the truth as well. Our faith in the supreme chancellor is unwavering, as is evidenced by our service to him!" The second uniformed man put a hand on Matthias's shoulder to hold him back. Matthias relaxed a little, and continued. "At any rate, Roman was an insignificant policeman on a primitive planet. He knew nothing when he was brought here a year ago, and he still knows nothing. He is a good man, and I will stand by that. If his girlfriend is indeed a member of a terrorist cell, I am convinced he has no knowledge of that."

The robed figure stepped backward, into the light, and hissed at Matthias, "I am not concerned about his friends! The invasion of X713 Delta has been ordered, and given that, Roman is now an enemy of the state and of the people. I would watch what I say when talking about him, if I were you. I know you and your friends were corrupted and seduced by temptation on X713 Delta, and if that has clouded your judgment, I will make you pay with your life." The robed figure exited the room, his long robes billowing around him.

Matthias called out after the robed figure, "What about Roman?"

The robed figure stopped and turned around. "Once he tells the truth and is fully interrogated by my Auger-Seers, send him to the ore mines. His brain will be liquefied anyways. It makes no difference to me what happens to him. His citizenship is hereby revoked." He turned and continued walking away. The other uniformed man stepped into the light and stood next to Matthias.

"What do we do now?"

Matthias turned and faced the two-way mirror, in which Roman could now be heard describing firebases on Mars and Uranus in great detail.

"My friend, I don't know. I didn't think this would happen. We must get Roman off our planet, the seers will lobotomize him. These shadow guys are everywhere now, watching everything we do." He turned around and faced Scotts and said, "Go find Cruwell. He will know what to do. And be quiet about it. The ISSB is everywhere. "

CHAPTER 36

"Roman, get up," the guard said from outside Roman's cell. "You have a visitor." The guard opened the cell door with his passkey and activated the overhead lights, illuminating the sparsely furnished cell. The heavy door slid open silently. Roman threw his blanket off and sat up on his bunk. He rubbed his face with his hands and looked up. A look of recognition instantly washed over his bearded face.

"Sebastian. What are you doing here? I thought you had forgotten about me, along with everyone else."

Sebastian Cruwell walked into the cell, and the door slid closed behind him. He wore his major's uniform of the ISSB, indicating that this probably was an official visit of some sort. Roman couldn't help but notice that his calf boots held a shine so bright he could probably shave off of them. He also noticed that Cruwell wore a pistol.

"I heard that you had been arrested. You have to believe me; I knew nothing about it, although I sensed it would happen in time."

Roman said nothing. A thought of being executed by his old friend rushed into his mind quite unexpectedly.

Cruwell continued, "A lot has been going on in the few weeks you have been imprisoned. The supreme chancellor is surrounded by robed seers now. I think they just didn't know what to do with you; they aren't yet mass murdering undesirables. I think the supreme chancellor still wishes to be popular among the people, and executions rarely help in that regard."

"What do you mean they didn't know what to do with me?" Roman stood up and reached for his synthetics cigarettes. "I suppose I should feel lucky. I still haven't been tortured or anything, which is a plus." He was wearing only his boxer underwear, and after he stood up, he brushed his testicles off of his sweaty leg. What Cruwell said kind of made sense. He had been in this humid, barren cell for just more than three weeks, and no one had offered any explanations. He was fed regularly and was allowed his synthetics (which he kept meaning to quit smoking, but he hadn't quite gotten around to that yet), but that was the extent of his contacts with his jailers.

"Well, I have secured your release," Cruwell said. "You have two options. Your official release has assigned you to an off-world mining facility reserved for political prisoners."

Roman took a drag off of the synthetic cigarette. He had gotten a little more used to them over time, and there just wasn't much else to do.

"What's the unofficial release?"

Cruwell walked toward the cell door, and knocked twice. The jailer opened the door. Cruwell stepped out of the cell and returned, holding two large duffel bags. He dropped them both on the floor of the cell.

"Option two may not be any better, but at least you would be free."

"Go on," Roman said.

"I have secured your transfer into a penal battalion that is going to your planet, Earth. You could join the fighting, or perhaps you could escape, if you desired."

Roman put out the cigarette in an ashtray almost filled to capacity. "So you did invade my planet after all?" He wasn't surprised.

"It will happen. The invasion is currently being planned."

"I'm in. If it gets me away from here, I'll go."

Cruwell walked out through the open door. "Get dressed. You'll be taken to your unit by an assistant of mine in exactly one hour. Good luck, Johnny."

As the jailer moved to close the cell door, Roman called out, "Wait. There's one more thing."

Cruwell stopped and turned around.

"What about Natasha?" Roman asked.

Cruwell shook his head. "I'm sorry, I don't know. I think she may have gone underground. I'll try to find out what I can." He paused as if to say something more but he caught himself. He quickly changed the subject and said, "I have your cat now. He's an interesting creature. I'll give him a good home." Cruwell left abruptly, leaving Roman to stare blankly at the two duffel bags.

CHAPTER 37

Roman stood among a large group of other prisoners who, like himself, recently had been reassigned to this penal battalion. The penal battalion consisted of three companies, and Roman found himself assigned to the first company. Everyone had two large duffel bags, seemingly identical to the ones Roman had recently acquired, and they talked loudly among themselves. They were assembled in a large hangar, mostly empty except for the men and their bags of gear. They each wore an orange jumpsuit with a large white letter "P" hastily marked on the back. Roman made his way to one side of the hangar and casually leaned against a large support column as he smoked a synthetic cigarette, observing his surroundings. It didn't take long to find out who was in charge.

"Fall in!" A loud, booming voice echoed throughout the hangar. The assembled group looked for the source of the voice, quieting only slightly, earlier conversations changing mostly to questions to each other about what was happening. Six smartly uniformed men walked down the massive granite steps that led from the main entrance to the hangar itself. The group of six halted just in front of the group. Five of the men wore purple berets. The sixth, a youthful man wearing a yellow beret, took a step forward from his companions. Roman eyed him closely and spotted the rank of infantry assault captain, also noting numerous medals and badges on the breast of his uniform. What stood out most was that the captain had only one good arm, the other was bionic. There was no synthetic skin covering the metallic appendage. Roman also noticed that he carried two unusual canisters hanging off of his belt.

The captain strode across the front line of the group, his one hand fingering the top of one of the canisters on his belt. As he got closer to Roman, his heavily scarred face was revealed in clearer light.

"What a miracle of modern science," Roman muttered to himself.

The captain stopped abruptly and spoke in a low, raspy voice that somehow projected across the entire hangar. "For the next four weeks, I will be your senior training officer. You will be divided into two platoons and you will be trained by my veteran staff." As the captain spoke, several in the group made obscene hand gestures in his direction; others continued to ignore him, still engrossed in their own conversations. The captain continued seemingly unaware of the disrespect being shown toward him. "Your training begins now." He casually withdrew from his belt the canister he had been fingering and pushed a plunger at its top. It began to hiss and emit a red vapor.

Roman immediately opened one of his duffel bags and withdrew his canteen. He unzipped his overalls and removed his white T-shirt. He quickly soaked the T-shirt with water from his canteen, and covered his nose and mouth with it. The captain tossed the vapor canister into the center of the group. Within seconds, the group was enveloped in the red vapor. The men began to cough and gag. Roman's eyes watered, but other than that, his crude air filter protected him. He remembered the same dirty trick pulled on him as an Army recruit at Fort McClellan, way back in the day. Back then, he had had no warning and no experience, and he succumbed to the gas.

Some of the group tried to break for the exit, but the five men in purple berets guarded it. Whoever got close to them got a vicious shot from a shock baton. The captain and his men seemed unaffected by the red vapor; Roman wondered if they had bionic lungs. Within five minutes, most of the group lay on the ground in a fetal position or were contorted in pain from strikes from a shock baton. They all had tears and snot streaming down their faces. The captain began fingering the second canister on his belt, as if he were going to toss that as well.

"Now that I have your full attention, I will continue. You experienced a training gas grenade. Judging by the way you acted, you won't live very long in a hostile environment." He took off his beret and wiped a bead of sweat from his forehead. His hair was close cut and parted to the side. He continued, "You will be assigned numbers, and from here on out, you will not use your names. You will address the staff by their ranks. You have no rank and will receive no pay. You are here because the government has deemed you worthy enough to repay your debt to society by serving in the supreme chancellor's penal battalion. If you survive your term of service, you will receive a full pardon." The captain replaced his beret smartly. "It is fortunate that your government wishes to train you at all." He turned and addressed one of the other men. "Senior Corporal."

The large, muscular man stepped forward. His rolled up sleeves barely contained his massive arms. The senior corporal saluted the captain.

"Assign the platoons," the captain told him, "and get with Assault

Sergeant Rimanek. She should be arriving shortly to take command of the

1st platoon." The captain turned around and exited the hangar, leaving the other five men behind. The senior corporal gave orders to the other four men, and all five began shouting at the penal battalion recruits. This time, they all listened.

"Get up! Get off of your asses and recover your gear! Fall in four ranks. Let's go!"

With a bit of confusion, the group organized into four ranks, each one a duffel bag in each hand. Those who moved slowly received a shock baton strike to the back of a leg.

"You have got to be shitting me," Roman muttered to himself. "Maybe I should have slaved in the mines after all." Shaking his head, he picked up his duffel bags and fell in with the rest of the men.

Roman dropped his duffel bags as he found himself in the first rank of the four that formed up. Two corporals walked down the front of the first rank, one carrying a data pad and the other a can of spray paint.

"Name?"

Roman faced the corporal, his hands firmly in his pockets.

"Roman." He casually removed a synthetic from his overalls and put it between his lips. He refrained from lighting it and thrust his hands back in his pockets. The corporal took no apparent notice and surveyed his data pad intently.

"Political detainee. Low risk. Assigned 1st Platoon." The corporal looked up from his data pad. "Your number is 769. Don't forget it." The corporal moved on to the next man. The other corporal crudely sprayed the number 769 on each of Roman's duffel bags.

"Turn around."

"Wha–?"

The corporal grabbed Roman roughly by the collar and spun around, and sprayed the number 765 on Roman's back, just above the letter "P." He spun him around again and did the same across his chest.

The pair of corporals walked up and down the formed ranks until the last of the men had been identified and numbered. They returned to the front of the assembled group. The one with the data pad addressed the men.

"All of you assigned to 1st platoon, fall out and reform to the left."

About half of the line fell out and reformed. Roman silently wondered if the other group that remained was considered "low risk" as well, or how the men had been divided. He was again near the front of the line of the newly formed 1st platoon, a position he knew from past experience often led to bad results.

A group of five soldiers made its way into the hangar and stood surrounding Roman's platoon. Another group of five soldiers marched the other platoon out of the hangar. A tall female (or what was left of her, Roman mused) took the lead. The sleeves on her tight, form-fitting uniform were rolled up, exposing scarred, muscular arms. Her left wrist was bionic, and she made no attempt to hide it. Roman looked up into her eyes and shuddered for a split second. The left side of her face showed heavy burn scars, and she wore an eye patch over her left eye as well. Like the others members of the formal military that she accompanied to the hangar, her uniform displayed numerous medals. She wore a yellow beret, which Roman surmised indicated leadership status among a group, and three inverted chevrons on her shoulder indicating the rank of assault sergeant.

"Damn, that's a tough looking bitch." Roman thought he had used his inner voice, but apparently he had not, as his new sergeant removed a small whip from her belt and hit him squarely across his chest. The whip seemed to have an electric charge, and the blow knocked him off his feet. He lay on the concrete for a few seconds, until his neighbors lifted him up slowly. "Must have a bionic ear as well," he muttered to himself under his breath.

The whip left a neat tear in his overalls and an inch-long scratch that cauterized itself on impact. He stared his new sergeant face to face.

"Insubordination will not be tolerated, 769." Roman's olfactory senses detected the faint aroma of something resembling gun oil and rubbing alcohol. The sergeant moved closer, so that their faces were only inches apart. She was about a half an inch taller than he. She looked him up and down, and spoke softly, "Back in line, 769." Roman shook off his helping neighbors and straightened his collar. He tried his best to match her piercing gaze. As she turned away, he swore he saw a faint smile break across her dry, cracked lips.

"Fall out for chow," the sergeant ordered. She left the hangar as the other members of her cadre removed their shock batons from their belts and began herding the group out of the hangar toward the mess hall.

CHAPTER 38

"You really need to watch what you say, you know," Roman heard a high-pitched, whiny voice say from his right side as he stood in the chow line. He turned his head to identify the speaker, a thin, bespectacled man about five feet, six inches in height, sporting a pencil-thin moustache. Roman eyed him curiously.

"Thanks for the advice, but I think I can handle myself," Roman said in a clipped tone.

The thin, balding man offered Roman his hand, unaware that Roman perceived his overtures as annoying rather than friendly. "I'm Petor. I was an engineer at the university before I was arrested." The thin man retracted his unshaken hand as he and Roman reached the serving counter. Following Roman's lead, Petor picked up a plastic tray and plate. The greasy cook on the other side of the counter unenthusiastically spooned something resembling Silly Putty onto both of their trays. The men in the chow line, with the exception of Petor, talked amongst themselves in low, guarded whispers, despite the fact that the corporals overseeing them appeared far more concerned with the display on a large video screen mounted on the far wall than with what the prisoners were doing.

"I was in a camp, you know," Petor continued. "They called it a re-education facility." He nodded at the greasy cook, whose gaze remained on the pan of Silly Putty as he spooned it out.

Petor continued, "You should never use first names, or they will get you with those nasty batons. My number is 711. My guess is they want to dehumanize you or something, take away your individuality."

They reached the end of the serving line. Roman took his tray and abruptly walked away, heading to an unoccupied table set against the wall. Petor followed spiritedly and sat down across the table from Roman, who buried his head in his hands upon seeing Petor sit down. Petor continued talking, using a tone a father might use when his telling his teenage son the ins and outs of dating girls for the first time.

"Individuality breeds corruption and perversion—at least that's what they told me during my arrest. Of course, most of the intellectual elite, such as me, were arrested almost immediately, and the youth of appropriate age were immediately drafted into the military."

Petor was about to continue when Roman interrupted, his voice rose in irritation. "Anybody ever tell you that you talk too damn much?" Just about everyone in the chow hall, including the corporals, turned to look at the seated pair.

Petor sat back in his chair, a defeated look on his face. "Sorry," he muttered. He looked down at his food and began to eat in silence.

Roman looked at his companion for a moment. He looked around and saw that they already had lost the crowd's attention. "Look, man. I'm sorry. I didn't mean it. It's been a long month."

Petor looked up, a small smile on his face. "It's OK. I do have a tendency to talk too much. I apologize." He resumed eating.

Roman felt a little better. It wasn't his goal to upset anybody, but some people just don't get it. "Well, sometimes the less you talk, the longer you live. It's a pleasure to meet you, 711." Roman extended his hand, which Petor readily accepted.

Petor turned his gaze to the ceiling for a moment, thinking hard about Roman's statement. He looked Roman square in the eye. "Perhaps you're right, 769. I'd like to live for a good long time, so maybe I should be quiet from time to time."

Roman nodded. The two resumed their bland meal in silence.

The rest of the evening passed calmly as the recruits settled into their new life. Petor remained next to Roman most of the time, by his choice and by circumstance; they even were assigned spaces next to each other in the rows of cots laid out inside another old hangar. Roman didn't mind Petor's company, now that the man talked more quietly, chose his words a little better, and didn't ramble on about things Roman did not care to hear. Roman actually started taking to the odd man.

After chow the battalion replaced their orange jumpsuits with military fatigues. Roman was surprised to see a rather attractive woman during uniform issue; he had thought all the prisoners were men. He tried to talk to her because everyone else seemed to ignore her for some reason. She had looked back at him with profound sorrow in her eyes and said nothing.

"Lights out in five!" a muscular corporal Roman overheard was named Henri shouted across the hangar bay. "Get your rest; tomorrow will be a lot worse for you!" Corporal Henri exited, leaving the hangar bay devoid of any training staff. Roman scanned the exits, looking for any sign of Henri or anyone else in authority. Petor sensed what he was doing.

"Don't even think about escape. There is nowhere for you to go."

Roman looked at Petor for a moment. "Yeah, I suppose you're right. I don't even know where we are," Roman said.

Roman changed the subject and asked "What's the deal with that girl over there?" He rose up from his bunk and subtly indicated with a nod of his head towards the end of the row of bunks the female he had tried to talk to earlier. She lay curled up in the fetal position, on a cot set off by itself.

Petor looked up and sighed as a hint of recognition washed over his face. He answered with a tinge of sadness in his voice. "I don't know her name. She doesn't speak. She came from a camp close by mine, for females only. I think she used to be in the military, but she deserted. They cut the tongues out of deserters. I cringe to think what else they may have done to her." Petor looked away and began to polish his newly issued combat boots.

Roman noticed that he was doing a pretty bad job of it. "Look. Like this," he said. He grabbed Petor's boot and placed it between his legs. He wrapped a large strip of his old T-shirt around his index finger. He dipped it in a container of water and in the polish, so that wet polish covered his fingertip. He rubbed that fingertip in circles on the surface of the boot. As he demonstrated, he continued the conversation. "She may be useful to us if she was ex-military. We can use people around us who have fired weapons before."

Seeing the boot begin to shine, Roman handed it back to Petor, along with the polish and strip of cloth. Petor nodded appreciatively, and tried his best to duplicate what he had just observed. "I think very few here are ex-military. Military men usually were executed on the spot for infractions, except for certain circumstances. You may not be able to rely on too many people here knowing what they're doing."

Roman grunted. "You're probably right."

"Lights out!" Corporal Henri yelled and hit a switch. The hangar bay lights slowly dimmed until total blackness enveloped the area.

Roman dreamed he was on a beach somewhere, perhaps one of the Philippine islands. While awake, he often fondly remembered the island of Bohol and the time he spent there with a beautiful Filipina while he was on leave during the war in Afghanistan. Now he dreamed he was lying in the sand on an island much like that one, in the sun, drinking an ice cold beer. Ah, ice cold beer …

"Get up, 769," a voice hissed in his ear.

Roman slowly opened his eyes, his dream quickly fading into memory. He squinted as a bright flashlight shined in his eyes. Two soldiers stood over him, their faces invisible to him.

"Let's go. Sarge wants to see you," he heard from one of them. They each grabbed an arm and dragged him forcibly out of his cot. He struggled to keep his footing under the rough handling. It seemed to Roman that they were taking him toward a side door leading out of the hangar bay.

"Can I at least grab my pants?" he asked, still wearing his boxers.

Both soldiers laughed quietly. The one on the left snickered, "You may not need them for very long."

They exited the hangar bay and walked through a serious of metal walled, brightly lit corridors. The air was humid, some the walls were slick with moisture. It reminded Roman of the time he stayed at the academy barracks when he first arrived on the planet. The soldiers finally released Roman, allowing him to stand up straight. The three of them stood in front of an unmarked door. One of the soldiers hit the call button next to a speaker by the frame of the door. A voice from the intercom responded, "You may go. Your presence is no longer required."

"As you wish," one of the soldiers responded. Both of them took a step back, turned, and went back around the corner of the nondescript, poorly lit hallway.

The slightly rusted metallic door slid open silently. Roman instantly recognized the sergeant he had met earlier in the day and winced slightly as he remembered the sting from her shock whip. “It’s OK, 769,” the sergeant said as she grabbed his I.D. tag, which hung on a chain around his neck. “I won’t bite.” Pulling at the tag, she led him by its chain into her quarters. The door closed silently behind them.

Roman tried not to stare, but he couldn’t avert his eyes. She still hadn’t made any attempt to hide any of her bionics. She had her boots off, and he could see that part of her right foot and three its toes were bionic. She wore a skin-tight black sleeveless shirt and shorts with the UCP logo visible. She had a very muscular body, albeit scarred and half machine.

“I can see that my appearance disturbs you,” she said. “Please, sit and have a drink.” She gestured toward a simple table and two chairs. A decanter of clear liquid sat in the middle of the table. She returned with two shot-sized glasses “It’s on the tip of your tongue. You may speak freely.”

Roman looked at her square in her good eye, avoiding the bionic eye. “OK. I want to know—just what the hell happened to you?”

She threw her head back, and her blonde hair, still damp from a recent washing, flew back and settled on the backs of her shoulders. She met his gaze. “I’m a by-product of war, I suppose. I stepped on a land mine and was shot several times during a battle in the early stages of the war. They patched me up and sent me back in. I was *so* lucky to be the beneficiary of modern medicine, don’t you think?” She threw her head back again and laughed. “I wished I was dead. I am an abomination hooked on painkillers and rotgut.” She slowed down, thinking back to that day that destroyed her. “You should have seen me. I was quite a mess.” She watched Roman’s face to see that he caught the sarcasm. Her own face hardened for a moment. “Perhaps that moment of agony was my rebirth.”

“Perhaps.” Roman threw back a shot of the strong alcohol and winced as it burned the back of his throat. Instantly, a warm feeling washed over him. “So what can I do for you, Sergeant? Why was I brought here?”

The sergeant threw back her own shot and placed the glass on the table, rotating it in her fingers. “Off duty, you can call me Rima, on duty you will call me Sergeant,” she said. “I know who you are. You were a lieutenant with the police. And I know you are not of this world.”

“OK. You got me. So what?”

“‘So what is that the ISSB, or better yet the Shadow, thinks you are on an ore mine off world somewhere.” Seeing Roman flinch at that comment, she smiled. “Relax. Your friend Sebastian is a good friend of mine. He had you assigned here, and I agreed to watch over you until you ship back to your planet."

Roman sat back in his metal chair. "I feel so much better now," he noted sarcastically. "You know, my chest still burns from that damned whip of yours."

Rima laughed again. "I had to make it look good, you know." She poured another shot, and quickly downed it. She stood up, directly in front of Roman. "There are still certain parts of me that are human. Perhaps we can come to some sort of arrangement while you are here in training."

Roman smelled the strong odor of rubbing alcohol, or maybe it was the liquor. He wasn't sure.

"Maybe you could throw the eye patch back on or something," he suggested.

Rima smiled widely as she put her muscular arms around Roman's neck. "You know, if I had my way, I would keep you around and not let you ship out.

Petor woke up at the sound of the corporals walking up and down the aisles, yelling and flipping random sleeping bodies out of their cots and onto the floor. Petor rubbed his eyes and glanced at his neighbor's cot, relieved to see Roman back in it. He shook his head, feeling sorry for his new friend. Seeing Roman stir, he talked softly, in case Roman had a headache. "Are you OK?

"Uh." Roman grunted as he raised himself to one elbow on the cot. His chest displayed several bruise marks in addition to the marks from the whip. "It appears they worked you over good last night," he said. "I told you to keep quiet. They have ears everywhere. You talking about escape all the time, you had it coming."

Roman attempted to sit up, but grabbed his back in wincing pain. He answered Petor, his tongue mildly thick from his hang over. "Yeah, you told me." Thinking back to his time in sergeant Rima's quarters earlier in the morning, he continued, "You would think I would keep my mouth shut."

CHAPTER 39

"OK, lock and load, you maggots!" the sergeant yelled to the eight recruits under his command. The steady rain that had begun three days ago showed no sign of letting up. Roman, Petor, and Chana stood at the rear of the eight-man assault team. Chana was the lone woman in Roman and Petor's platoon. Over the course of the last four weeks, Roman and Petor had tried to get better acquainted with her, and it seemed to have worked. Although she still did not talk, she displayed a thorough understanding of small unit tactics and unarmed combat. After the first week of training, she had stuck with Roman and Petor as much as she could. Recognizing natural team cohesion, their superiors often grouped them as a three person fire team. Today was no exception. It had helped that Roman suggested to Sergeant Rima, during one of their early morning "meetings," that putting the three of them together would be beneficial for the battalion as a whole.

Each member of the assault team was armed with a standard-issue automatic rifle, ammunition, and frag grenades. The military administrators chose not to provide more technical and powerful equipment, such as EMRs, to a penal battalion. Its members presented potential danger, and they were expendable.

Sergeant Rima walked up to the assault team leader, a large, bald man named Lon, otherwise known as 800. The other two assault teams in the company separated and marched out of sight under their own leaders. Roman noticed out of the corner of his eye the captain who initially had taken charge on the first day of training. He appeared to be keeping his distance from the recruits and made no attempt to interfere with their training; Sergeant Rima and her staff of corporals had been left in charge. Roman also noticed that all of the regular military wore pistols, and the assault ranges used for training were ringed with automated gun turrets around the perimeter, no doubt to encourage discipline and discourage escape attempts. Their obvious placement needed no explanation from the training staff. The company had spent the past week learning the ins and outs of urban combat. With the exception of the steady rainfall and mud, Roman had found the training not unpleasant and fairly well done. It appeared to him that the penal battalion was being trained to defend itself and be a truly effective force, rather than just a bunch of expendable bodies to throw at the enemy. He found more evidence for that opinion when, beginning in the third week of training, the penal companies sometimes were intermingled with conscript companies.

"This is a live fire exercise!" Sergeant Rima shouted. "Watch your line of fire and do *not* kill your teammates! There are other friendly elements in close proximity. Enemy combatants are marked by robotic sentries. They will stun you if you get in their way, so make your shots count!" The sergeant made her way to the observation tower that dominated the vast expanse of the urban training grounds, joining other trainers in the massive tower, all of them watching their corresponding troops through binoculars.

The grounds themselves consisted of several high-rise residential and commercial buildings mocked up to look like the real thing. The robotic sentries randomly placed throughout added to the reality; they had a nasty habit of shooting back. Roman had found that out the hard way yesterday. When his weapon jammed and he was unable to eliminate one, it gave him a nasty shock to simulate a shooting. Corporal Henri had been the first to chime in on the radio inside Roman's battle helmet. "Make your mistakes here, puke, because when you're downrange, you don't get a second chance!"

Roman checked his rifle once more. The digital shot counter read 45 indicating a full magazine. He turned around and checked Petor, who appeared to be OK, although his gear looked a little big on him. Roman checked Chana's equipment quickly, and she looked squared away. She tugged on a couple of Roman's ammo pouches, checking his equipment as well. She also slapped Petor on the shoulder after checking him over, both getting her seal of approval.

Roman heard Sergeant Rima's voice on his helmet radio. "OK. 800, take out your team. Search and locate target. Target is a weapons cache that may be heavily guarded. Recover the cache and get to the extraction point, where you will rendezvous with 1st and 3rd assault teams."

"Copy," he replied, audible to everyone. He turned around and, with a quick forward flick of his hand, moved the squad out. His voice crackled over the radio again. "OK, we go silent from here on, since those robots seem to locate us through our helmet transmissions as well as by sight. They got us good yesterday. Watch my hand signals."

800 led the rest of the squad, moving slowly and carefully watching the environment. Sporadic rifle fire and grenade blasts elsewhere on the training grounds indicated that other teams already had engaged. 800 moved slowly down one block, and dropped to one knee, holding his fist in the air. He turned and raised the face shield of his helmet, allowing the rain to cascade down his face. The others followed suit, raising their own face shields so that they could communicate without the radio.

"711, 769, and 777!" 800 hissed. Roman, Petor, and Chana quickly made their way to the front of the team.

"What?" Roman asked.

"I want you three to go east and conduct a sweep of those buildings," 800 said. "I'll send the rest of the team to the west. 1st and 3rd teams are clearing buildings to our west. Head east one block and clear the buildings facing that street for one block north, from there come back west to this street to regroup. We will clear out this street together, and meet with the other teams."

"What?" Roman hissed back. "Let's just clear the buildings in a straight line. We may not last long if we split up." Chana nodded her approval of Roman's plan, while Petor nervously looked ahead.

"Damn it, 769, I am in charge! Just do it!" 800 closed his visor and indicated for his portion of the team to follow him. They moved west down the street, leaving Roman silently cursing him. It wasn't that he didn't like the man and apparently he had some previous military training, but he just didn't seem to make the best decisions. The team usually lost more than half its strength when he was in charge of a mission. Only two members had survived the previous day's exercise.

"OK," Roman said his face shield still open, like those of his team members. They had anticipated that he would comment on 800's orders. "We do what he says here. Let's go. Close face shields, but turn up your external helmet amps and listen for anything out of the ordinary. Petor, watch the rooftops. Chana, you've got the rear." Roman refrained from calling his friends by their numbers when they were alone. Without waiting for a reply, Roman set off to the east, preparing to enter the first building on the left.

Hearing nothing externally except thunder and rainfall, Roman stacked his team again the wall of the building. He tested the door sensor, and it opened the door. He brought his weapon up to face level and activated the holographic sight; a red "x" now was projected forward wherever he aimed. His helmet sensors aided his aim by automatically switching to infrared and night vision. Roman panned around the darkened room, which was mocked up as a diner. Roman activated his thermal sensor. Seeing nothing on any of his sensors, he entered cautiously, followed by Petor and Chana.

Roman raised his face shield and hissed, "Chana, you take the kitchen. Petor, you watch the front door and the street. I'll check the shitters." His teammates nodded in response. Petor took cover behind an old, slashed vinyl booth and dropped to one knee. Chana worked her way to the back, with her weapon raised. Roman silently checked both the male and female washrooms, which were in serious disrepair. Nothing. Roman lowered his weapon and wondered if this training range used to be an actual city. The detail was incredible. He closed his helmet visor and continued his sweep.

His thoughts were soon interrupted by 800's panicked voice, coming over the helmet radio. "2nd team, regroup! We are under heavy attack!"

"Calm down!" Roman answered, annoyed. "You're not gonna die. What's your location?"

Chana emerged from the kitchen and shook her head. Roman walked behind Petor and peered out of the grimy window. "Anything?" he whispered to Petor over the radio. Petor shook his head no.

"Get your asses back to the main intersection!" 800 ordered. "We are taking fire from the north and the west!" The sounds of sporadic gunfire and grenade explosions came over the radio, as well as the quieter telltale sounds of the robotic sentries' stun weapons and grenades.

Roman muted his helmet mike, raised his face shield, and faced Chana. She and Petor also raised their shields. "No, that's way too quick. They usually wait awhile to attack us, and they usually hit us as a group. I think they are trying to attack our fire teams individually now. We are going to get popped if we back him up." Chana didn't react.

Petor looked over his shoulder at Roman, leaving his weapon pointed toward the street. "It's too quiet here. Perhaps we could slip out the back door?"

Roman nodded and unmuted his mike. “OK. Standby, 800. We’ll be there in a second. Don’t shoot us!”

“Copy!” 800 yelled back.

“Back door?” Roman asked, looking at Chana. Chana nodded.

“Good. You got point. Close your face shields. Watch our six, Petor. Let’s move.”

Within seconds, the trio stood in an alleyway that eerily reminded Roman of Dallas back home. The surrounding buildings looked to be constructed out of some sort of large brick, not the usual concrete and steel mix that Roman knew from most of the buildings on Hellenheim.

They moved up the alley slowly, checking each entranceway and covering each other. When they had covered about a hundred yards, Chana held up a fist, and Roman and Petor immediately hit the ground. Chana pointed to her helmet, and pointed ahead. Roman turned up his helmet amp to maximum. He kept his amp on low so he could hear the radio transmission. The rain was deafening, but he also heard the artificial noise. He turned the amp level down and he activated his thermal sensor.

The sensor indicated five to six robot sentries ahead, exiting the back door of a building and moving west, toward 800’s position. The sentries were constructed to resemble humans in their movements and their signatures on the various sensors, but not in physical appearance. Their heat signature usually was the easiest way to spot them. The thin grey “skin” over their metallic exoskeletons enabled them to blend well with their environments. They also walked with a pronounced limp but were very quick on the trigger. The team quickly learned the sentries’ programming enabled them to listen in on radio transmissions and triangulate positions of their attackers. Roman sometimes thought that the military should just build and arm more sentries and send them, rather than humans, off to battle.

Roman, with Petor close behind, made his way to Chana’s side, walking in a low crouch and keeping against the wall. He raised his face shield, slung his rifle over his shoulder, and pulled out two concussion grenades from a pouch on his tactical vest. Chana did likewise. Petor raised his face shield, still looking to the rear with his rifle at the ready.

“Petor, open fire after the grenades go off, OK?” Roman whispered. Petor quickly moved to the opposite side of the alley and took position in a doorway. Closing his face shield, he watched as Roman indicated a countdown for the grenades, raising one finger, a second and a third. On the third, Roman quickly grabbed one of his two grenades, pulled the pin, and lobbed it toward the sentries, and quickly followed it with his second grenade. Chana had done the same thing.

One of the sentries picked up the movement and spun around, but it was too late. Two massive blasts erupted in the tight confines of the alley, sending brick, mortar, and exoskeleton parts in every direction. Petor opened fire with controlled bursts through the grey cloud that appeared, taking the sentries offline for good.

"Nice work," Roman whispered to Chana. "Let's move north and hit the next street up. We'll try to link up with 800 that way." Roman followed Chana to Petor's position in front of the door to a building. They entered and found the lobby level empty of furniture, typical of the mocked up training buildings. Roman crossed the lobby and peered out of the front and saw another east-west street at the end of the block lined by nondescript buildings on both sides.

"Damn, I hate this ghost town crap," Roman whispered. He scanned through his sensors and detected no movement. "Watch the rooftops," he whispered to Petor before repeating himself a little louder so that Chana could hear clearly. "We are going to run to the intersection, and maybe we can flank them." Roman activated his helmet mike. "800? You copy?"

"Copy. We are pinned down, but I think we have them contained. What's your status?" Sounding a lot calmer, 800 continued, "We heard some explosions your way. Did you get hit?"

"Copy, we had positive contact. We are OK. We will be at your position shortly. Out."

Roman turned to face his team, and raised his face shield. "That guy is a moron. He has barely moved since we started this. And how the hell can you be pinned down, yet say you have them contained?" Roman activated the building's door, and it slid open silently. "Let's move."

Roman lowered his face shield, and the trio ran west as fast as they could while trying to watch all around them. Soon they could see the intersection of the north-south street they had veered off of earlier. The intersection, in an unusual feature, was actually dotted with trees, or what appeared to be trees. At the quick glance possible, Roman couldn't tell if they were alive. He wondered why this particular intersection had them.

"Careful," Roman said. He took over point and looked around, Chana and Petor close behind. The immediate area had nothing; the gunfire and explosions still were at a distance. Roman was about to turn south on the main street when Petor yelled at him.

"Tank!" he yelled into his helmet mike, stopping Chana and Roman cold. The hulking Mark VII main battle tank sat in a side alley a couple hundred feet in from the street they were on. It was partially hidden by some trees and a lot of weeds. Upon closer inspection through his magnified weapon sight, Roman noticed that the main gun was pointed at the ground in front of it. He detected no movement or heat in its vicinity.

"I think it's a derelict," he told the others. "Chana, be careful and go check it out. We will cover you." Chana nodded, and backtracked disappearing down the side alley, leaving Roman and Petor behind some trees, nervously pointing their pulse rifles at the tank.

"I suppose if it was alive, we would be dead," Petor reasoned.

"Shut up. You damn near blew out my ear drum screaming at us about it."

"Sorry."

They both saw Chana appear around the backside of the massive tank.

She tugged on each of the three hatches on the massive turret, but none budged. She stood on top of the hulking tank and shrugged, before nimbly dismounting and rejoining the group.

"I say its derelict," Roman said matter-of-factly. "Let's move on."

With Chana resuming point duties, the trio cautiously approached the intersection where 800 was supposed to be holed up.

"800?" Roman asked into the helmet mike. "Where are you? We are coming in."

"Copy. We are about half a klick west on the north side of the street. The sentries have bugged out."

"Next time you move, maybe let us know," Roman said acidly.

Within a couple of minutes, Roman, Chana, and Petor ran across the street and Roman halted the group, raising his closed fist in the air. He quickly took his team off the street and into an adjacent building upon seeing 800's team lined up on the street, weapons pointed down. Roman raised his face shield.

Roman took a quick glance around his surroundings and noticed the building was set up to look like a supermarket, complete with aisles and shelves filled with what appeared to be canned goods.

800 stood outside around a hundred feet down from Roman's position, consulting a holographic map displayed from his wrist communicator.

"You two wait here. Cover me." Petor and Chana nodded as he carefully made his way outside towards 800's assembled team.

Upon seeing Roman, he raised his face shield and said, "My objectives were updated, and the cache should be to the northwest, about two klicks. 3rd squad is almost on site. 1st is currently engaged, but they should be able to extract themselves."

"OK. You lose anybody?"

"No. We are good. I want you to take—"

800 never finished the sentence. A brilliant light flashed, followed by a booming concussion that blew the glass out of the surrounding buildings. Picking himself off of the ground, Roman looked around and saw several sentries lining the rooftops, raining down stun and smoke grenades. 800's team was caught out in the open, blinded by smoke and flash from the grenades. Stun rifle fire quickly picked off the ones that couldn't get away fast enough. "Idiots!" Roman yelled. "They let themselves get hit in the open."

Petor yelled back at Roman through the 2nd squad channel. "They are moving through the buildings systematically! I can see them on the rooftops and on the street!"

"Copy. I am pinned down here. You two take off and try to get to the extraction point. There is nothing you can do back here now," Roman said grimly.

"There has to be another way!" Petor's cracked voice pleaded through the helmet mike.

"No. You two take off. No sense in the whole team getting wasted."

"Copy."

Roman crawled into the nearest building and found 800 and some of his team propped up against a wall. 800 had removed his helmet and looked at the ceiling in disgust. Roman's ears still rang from the grenade blasts. Both of them were covered in orange powder from the simulated grenades. The less fortunate squad members still lay in the street, unable to move because of hits from the sentries' stun rifles.

"Damn, looks like maximum settings," Roman said in a slightly mocking manner to no one in particular as he looked over his shoulder out of the window. "They aren't playing around this week. I wonder if they'll use live ammo on us anytime soon." He turned and faced 800, looking at him eye to eye.

"OK," 800 said defensively. "If you have a problem, we can resolve it right now!" He stood up, holding his bayonet in his right hand. The other weary troopers immediately stood up, not sure what exactly was happening. "You have been riding my ass the whole time!" 800 yelled at Roman. "I didn't ask to be team leader!"

Roman slowly stood up and removed his helmet, placing it on the ground "No, you didn't," Roman replied. "But you could have stepped down once you figured out how incompetent you really were. Let's see, a few survivors today, and they may not make it out."

With a snarl, Lon lunged at Roman, who deftly sidestepped the clumsy charge and redirected 800 toward the large glass window. It shattered on impact, and 800 stumbled through it into the street, where he fell. Wearily, he got himself to a sitting position, looking around for his bayonet, only to find it underneath the boot of the one-armed captain. The captain reached down and picked up the bayonet.

"This exercise is hereby terminated." The captain's curt voice displayed no emotion as he turned the bayonet over and over in his gloved hand. He seemed lost in deep thought to the team, as if he just replayed in his mind some tragic event from his past. Corporal Henri and some other members of the training cadre began kicking some of the stunned troopers to their feet.

"Fall in!" Corporal Henri yelled.

The squad wearily formed up. The sentries by now had received the command to abort and were no longer in sight. Roman stepped through the shattered window with the remnants of the squad and got in line.

"I cannot teach you anymore," the captain addressed them, "especially since we have such limited time. Considering your level of training, some of you have performed well, and others have not." The captain paused, and looked 800 straight in his eyes. 800 averted his gaze to the ground. The captain continued, "Your element will ship out very shortly to participate in the great conquest, as directed by our supreme chancellor. There is no more training here. You are to be a reserve force, most likely performing occupation duties behind our shock troopers. Most of you will probably die, and I would bet that *all* of you would die under your current team leader." The captain walked to the second rank and stood before Roman. "I do not wish for you all to be sacrificed in vain. I have seen it too many times before. I wish you the best, and I hope that errors in command are rectified before the situation gets out of hand." The captain flipped the bayonet in the air and caught it by the blade. He threw it, and it stuck in the ground between Roman's feet. "Corporal, they are all yours," he said to Corporal Henri. The captain placed his arm behind his back and quietly walked away.

"Fall out to the hangar for dropship assignment!" Corporal Henri commanded, shouting over a thunderclap. "Let's go, double time!" Rain began to fall in a steady torrent.

The captain stood in the range observation tower with Sergeant Rima, watching the many teams moving out rapidly to the dropship hangar. The captain spoke softly, his voice barely audible over the rain pelting the metal roof of the tower.

"Sebastian's friend is actually a good soldier. I hate to think he is going to his death."

"I had assumed you were going to put him in charge of the squad," Rima said passively.

"No. Situations like this will work themselves out in the field." He turned to face Rima. "Besides, the team will follow Roman whether he is promoted or not. Perhaps they can assist him in getting back to his home. I believe that is what Sebastian had planned for him."

Rima nodded. "I already asked him to stay. I told him we could get him an alias and he could ship out with a regular army unit to a remote garrison." Rima sighed. "He wishes to be back on his planet. I envy him, in a way."

The captain smiled. "As do I. At least he has a worthy cause to pursue." The captain turned around and started toward the stairs. "Shall we go for a drink?" he asked over his shoulder.

Sergeant Rima smiled. "I would love that—but only if you are paying, of course," she replied coyly.

CHAPTER 40

Hangar Bay 95B bustled with activity. Dozens of maintenance workers wearing grey overalls loaded crates of various sizes into the numerous egg-shaped drop ships being prepped for launch. Engineers wearing blue overalls loaded fuel cells and checked the ships' onboard systems. Pilot crews checked the external surfaces of their respective pods for damage; although the engineers were careful, the pilots took special care with their own ships. The roof to the hangar bay retracted slowly, exposing the giant spacecraft to the barren grey, cloudless sky.

"Well, at least it's not raining for a change," one of the maintenance workers said to his colleague, both busy stacking green ammunition crates into the cargo hold of a drop ship.

"Quit looking at the sky and try not to drop this crate on my foot, OK?" the taller of the two said, slightly irritated. "I'd like to finish sometime today."

"Yeah, I'm sorry about that. You want to go to Bloody Blade's after shift?" the short, fat one asked. The two workers grunted in unison as they stacked another crate.

Taking a deep breath, the tall worker nodded as he reached into his breast pocket and withdrew a pack of synthetics. After pulling one out and placing it between his lips, he offered the pack to his partner, who withdrew one from the withered pack and did the same. The tall man produced a lighter, and the two workers leaned against a large crate marked "Portable Communications Array."

After a few minutes of silence, the tall worker suddenly rapped his partner on the shoulder.

"What was that for?"

The tall worker said nothing; he just pointed to a large formation of soldiers entering the far side of the hangar. The formation was at least battalion size, but it was the precision of the personnel marching into the hangar that surprised both workers.

"Who are they?" The smaller worker asked. "I've never seen a unit like that before."

The taller worker threw down his synthetic, mashed it under the toe of his boot, and craned his head to get a closer look. "I have no idea. They all looked the same." He gasped. "But look at the ends of the platoons—those robed guys. I've heard things about them."

The smaller worker, who had climbed onto a crate, nodded. "I hear they can fry your skull just by thinking about it, mystical magic or something." He jumped down, and the two ran to the opposite side of the drop ship to get a closer look. The front of the formation entered a large door leading to an adjacent building.

"Look at those troopers!" the taller one said. "Looks like those clones I heard about. They are all the same size, identical! And those helmets are supposed to be hardwired into their heads. I didn't believe it, but I think I'm seeing it!"

The heavily muscled troopers wore identical uniforms and carried their gear in exactly the same places. Their black pants had numerous pockets and a thigh holster on each leg, and each holster held a large subatomic pistol. They each also carried a plasma boot knife. They wore vests with no shirts underneath. The vests had several cables connected to a large box on their backs. Two of the cables ran from the box to the helmet, with the others attached to various parts of the vest. Numerous frag and thermite grenades hung off of the vests as well. Each trooper carried an EMR modified with a large scope, grenade launcher, and what appeared to be a slug thrower. Some of the troopers carried large rocket launchers and satchels of spare rockets slung over their shoulders.

A booming voice from behind the two workers startled them. They turned around, red-faced, like children who had just been caught with their hands in the cookie jar. A behemoth of a man almost too big for his overalls stood before them, with his arms crossed. His rolled-up sleeves exposed biceps measuring well more than twenty inches. "The supreme chancellor would appreciate it if you two would get back to work and quit wasting his time." The two workers averted their eyes and looked at the ground momentarily.

"Ah, sorry, Boss," the taller worker said. "We just saw the troopers coming in. They sure don't look like regular troopers."

The boss replied sternly, "You two didn't see anything. In fact, if you are caught again neglecting your duty, you will be arrested. Is that understood?"

Both workers replied in unison, "Understood."

The boss turned walked briskly to another nearby maintenance crew, also seemingly distracted by the procession.

The short, fat worker grabbed the handle on a crate. "What was that all about, saying we didn't see anything?"

The tall worker grabbed the other handle. He looked at his partner sternly. "Exactly what he said—we saw nothing. Now let's hurry up and finish, so we can get that drink."

The smaller worker looked slightly bewildered but said nothing further. The two quietly finished loading the crate and finished their shift in silence.

Battalion 3 marched inside a large, empty building that appeared to once have been a gymnasium, complete with a large swimming pool, which was now drained. Grime-stained windows lined the top of the walls where they were joined with the roof, allowing a grey light to permeate the dusty space, which was rapidly filling with troopers. They formed perfect ranks, and their boots rang out in a rhythmic stomping symphony. Several robed figures brought up the rear, with their hands clasped together in front. Heads bowed, these figures silently stopped, off to the side, as the troopers formed six long ranks. Their boots stomped the pavement loudly as they came to a halt and again as they executed a right face in perfect unison. Several high-ranking officers entered, with several junior officers and noncommissioned officers trailing behind.

The main body of troopers, wearing identical uniforms devoid of any name tags or unit markings, waited at attention with their battle rifles held at port arms. The noncommissioned officers, equipped with full battle gear, took up positions in front, at various intervals. In contrast to the troopers, there was nothing perfect about them, as they each wore their kitand uniforms to their liking. Each of them was accompanied by a private or junior corporal who wore a large radio pack on his back. The high-ranking officers made their way to the front and began walking across the ranks, inspecting the rigid troopers. The robed figures stayed to the side, save for one, who conversed with a colonel near the drained swimming pool at the rear of the formation partially hidden by the shadows of the building.

"The battalion will remain here," said one of the robed figures, "out of site, until the drop ships are fully prepped. I do not want any prying eyes, colonel."

The colonel turned and faced soldiers displayed before him with great satisfaction. He placed his gloved hands behind his back. "Security is tight," he said. "We will handle any problems accordingly." The colonel turned and stared into the blackness of the robed figure's hood. "The troops will be airborne soon and will rendezvous with fleet. I am more concerned that they are not fully ready of the mission they will undertake. I still have concerns about their built-in cooling units and the logistics of keeping them supplied."

The robed figure's voice came out as almost a whisper. "Do you not have faith in the program? It was you who were so enthusiastic when you were given this opportunity to build it from the ground up."

"There is no way to know if their human minders can keep them under control when in the heat of battle. Ten battalions with less than what amounts to a handful of minders may not be adequate. If they go berserk like the original did, that could be a problem for the human troopers sent to reinforce them."

The robed figure responded with the same barely audible rasp. "You have fulfilled you mission by getting them prepped and ready for war. Do not worry yourself anymore. The Shadow will take over command once we are in enemy space. If they adhere to their programming long enough for the human battalions to take over, the mission is a success. You have done well, and I sense you have a bright future ahead of you, Colonel Brenneke—perhaps as a provincial governor of X713 Delta?"

Colonel Brenneke quickly smiled as he envisioned the realm of possibilities. "Yes, I am indebted to you. There is just so much more work to be done. I fear the cloning may have been rushed, that's all."

"We did not sense that." The robed figure raised its bowed head and started walking away. "You worry too much, colonel," The robed figure said as it walked away. "Take it for what it is, a marvel of science and prophecy." The robed figure paused and turned back around. Two red orbs stared into

Colonel Brenneke's eyes. He almost gasped but held fast, transfixed. "You are serving the supreme chancellor, and that is what puts fulfillment in your life, is it not?"

After a couple of seconds, Brenneke broke out of his brief hypnosis. Stuttering, he replied, "Ye-yes. It is my greatest honor to serve the supreme chancellor."

The red orbs vanished, leaving blackness. "Good. The hour is near. Farewell, colonel." The robed figure left without saying anything else, leaving Brenneke wondering what exactly was in store for the populace of the unfortunate planet soon to be invaded.

PART THREE

CHAPTER 41

Roman let Petor in on his plan just before they entered the stasis pods for the journey to Earth, or X713 Delta, as everyone else was calling it. They had both been standing in a long line of underwear-clad penal battalion troopers awaiting a vaccination of some sort within the hold of a massive battle barge.

"You will take me with you, won't you?" Petor had hissed in a low whisper. He had taken great pains to try to remain inaudible, even though medical staff and regular army sergeants shouted orders seemingly almost every step of the way.

"Shh! I already told you I would. Now be silent before we get sent to the mines instead!"

Petor put his hand on Roman's shoulder. "Chana wishes to accompany us as well. We cannot leave her behind."

Roman's brow furrowed slightly. "How do you know that? She doesn't speak."

"I have become quite adept at communication with her now," Petor replied.

Nodding, Roman kept his eyes forward. "We all need to stay together."

"Next!" A medical orderly brought a small pistol-shaped device to Roman's shoulder. On the top of a device was a reservoir holding a lightly colored purple liquid. Roman felt a prick as a needle penetrated his skin. A loud hiss emanated from the gun, and the purple liquid vanished from its reservoir.

"Ow!" Roman's shoulder instantly felt numb. As he looked at the injection site, he could see it beginning to bruise before his eyes.

"Let's go, move out!" the technician said. "Next!"

A trooper grabbed and led him by the shoulder through a door into a vast corridor lined on both sides with stasis pods. He already felt a bit loopy and extremely tired. The trooper him to one of the cylindrical stasis pods, into which he gratefully entered. Sleep quickly overcame him as the computer took control of the pod's ambient temperature and began to monitor his vitals. Behind him, Petor and later Chana were entered their respective pods, along with dozens of others.

Dozens of massive dreadnaughts parked themselves in low Earth orbit, causing satellites and space junk to disintegrate against their outer shielding, adding to an already dense debris field. Once in position, the dreadnaughts commenced with a precise surgical bombardment, executed by an experienced battle fleet. The full force of their laser batteries and tactical missiles were loosed on the blue planet below. Power stations, suspected military bases, and other targets of infrastructure were eliminated. These attacks dropped numerous cities into perpetual darkness, from Belize and Honduras to the current front line on the Rio Grande, separating Mexico and Texas. Weapons technicians monitored hits and acquired new targets on large holomaps. Once the bombardment ceased, numerous egg shaped dropped pods carrying assault regiments and equipment descended to predetermined LZ's.

Lord Sabis advised Chuikova to separate the campaign into two distinct offensives, a southern and northern. Once the southern offensive was underway, clone units would spearhead the northern offensive. Once all resistance was crushed, occupation and subjugation could begin.

Local police stood no chance against these forces; they were too few in number, and their small-caliber pistols were ineffective. Small groups of the local populace attempted to repel the invaders, but their corpses soon littered the streets. There had been no word of a response from the White House or the Pentagon. The survivors felt alone and isolated, eventually going into hiding to wait it out. After the initial shock had worn off and the reality of what was happening had settled in, a few local National Guard units north of the Rio Grande managed to assemble a few platoons of mixed personnel, along with tanks and some artillery, but their efforts also were too little, too late. No one could get answer on who was attacking, the Russians? The Chinese? Were nuclear weapons detonated on American soil?

The northern offensive continued north at a breakneck pace until it stalled at a natural water boundary, the Rio Grande River waiting for supplies and reinforcements. After the rear area was secured just north of the Texas/Mexico border, Penal Battalion 7 touched down with its full complement of drop ships and equipment, just north of the Rio Grande near Brownsville, Texas. As his company charged down the ramp of the drop ship, Johnny Roman paused and raised his face shield. He could instantly smell the sour waters of the Rio Grande and the smog generated by the nearby maquiladoras in the Mexican city of Matamoros. A thin smile broke across his face as his company charged into the scorched-earth landscape. Fires from nearby buildings lit the evening sky like funeral pyres. "I'm home," Roman said with neither joy nor sadness. He slammed his face shield down and vanished with his company into a grey, ashen wasteland.

"I've got hostiles all over my position, where are those damn jets?"

First Lieutenant Lance Chapa of the Texas National Guard yelled hoarsely into radio handset as the dying screams of men around him threatened to drown out his transmission. The past hour had been far more intense than Chapa had ever experienced in Afghanistan. The ground all around Chapa's position was littered with the corpses of a few black armored invaders and several of those who dared to oppose them.

Chapa's handset came to life. "Calm down, lieutenant, you need to give me a proper report so I can send in those jets," the faint voice broke through the static just barely. Chapa had a sick feeling starting to rise in his gut. Radio comms shouldn't be that weak. He was only 40 miles or so from Kingsville Naval Air Station.

"This is General Shimanek, 7th Cav. Now hang on down there, son. I'm trying to get reinforcements your way. Those bastards hit us all over. We got caught with our pants down."

Chapa sat down and leaned back against the smoldering husk of a State Highway Patrol car. He stared blankly ahead, the faint silhouettes of the strange egg shaped ships still visible off in the distance. The only thing that really slowed down the black armored invaders was the Rio Grande River. They seemed confused on how to get across, almost as if they were afraid of it. Chapa thought maybe the fire mission he called wasn't such a good idea. Once the first few 155mm HE rounds hit, they scattered like angry ants and stormed across the river in rage. Within seconds of the first salvo, a half dozen or so missiles rained down from space, annihilating the battery.

"My defensive line is breached, my arty and armor is gone, how copy?" Chapa whispered into the radio handset. He was surprised he was actually holding it together. A weekend a month and two weeks in the summer hadn't prepared him or his men for a situation anything like this.

Static crackled over the radio. Chapa raised his Steiner binoculars up and couldn't count the invaders approaching his position. Time was running out quickly. Chapa tried again, "Hotel two five actual this is Phoenix 6. I need flash. Drop everything you have on my pos."

"Roger, flash on your position. Coordinates adjusted. You have jets inbound on your position. Keep your head down." Chapa detected a hint of sadness from the voice on the other end of the radio, the situation now being fully understood. The front line wasn't tenable; there just weren't enough soldiers mobilized yet. He couldn't get a word from Kingsville Naval Air Station and 7th Cav was out of Ft Hood, over 250 miles away. He could only assume the worst, that it was vaporized like most other military bases across the country.

Chapa threw down the handset and grabbed his M-4 carbine and stood up. He marveled at the black armored figures storming his position just north of the smoking remains of Brownsville Border Patrol Station. The few of his men who stood their ground were quickly cut to pieces under precise rifle fire. His soldiers were well equipped with ceramic plates and soft body armor, but the invaders weren't firing bullets. A trailing green smoke followed the rounds as they penetrated their targets with ease. After penetration, the rounds kept going, tunneling through cars, walls, and whatever else got into their baneful path.

Rifled shotgun slugs and 5.56 rounds tore into the lead invaders chest and blew of its right arm as it crested the hill. As Chapa watched, the severed arm still twitched on the ground. Even without his arm, the soldier got up and continued on. It took another magazine of 5.56 and several slugs from two County Sheriff's Deputies to drop him for good after concentrating on the helmeted head, which vaporized into a mass of high-density plastic and black mist. The body hit the ground just shy of the Chapa's feet, convulsing and leaking black ooze out of its neck. Chapa longed for a single .50 cal machine gun, but unfortunately, the Humvees that the .50 cals were mounted on had long since been destroyed. The following invaders spread out and drove on as the remaining human defenders opened up with everything they had.

Chapa inserted a fresh magazine and raised his M-4 and squeezed off controlled bursts as he lined up targets in the reticule of his Aimpoint sight. He quickly depleted his magazine, and fell back against the burned out car behind him. Within seconds Chapa heard the telltale sounds of fast movers approaching low, at treetop level, dropping ordnance from their pylons. Chapa watched with satisfaction as the cluster bomblets hit the scorched earth, bounced upward, and exploded in the air, sending lethal shrapnel everywhere.

Ground Marshal Chuikova stood in the bridge of *The Emperor's Fist* in his ceremonial battle armor, his gloved hands clasped behind his back. The bridge was busy with technicians and crew attending to their various tasks. Chuikova observed the waves of troop ships and larger supply ships being discharged from the other capital ships in the armada.

"Sir," a grey-suited technician said as he held a hand up to his headset. "We have an incoming transmission from the Battalion 3, Company 6 commander. They should be one of the leading assault units."

"Patch him through."

The technician nodded and punched a few red buttons on his console. Immediately, static and explosions could be heard.

"Go ahead with your traffic. Ground Marshal Chuikova is present."

"Understood!" After a brief pause of silence, the transmission clicked back on. "Captain Siminov reporting, Sir!" The captain yelled into his mike. Judging by the sound of gunfire around him, he probably couldn't hear himself talk.

Chuikova stared absently into the view screen, which was dominated by the blue planet. He had a feeling that he was being watched by some unseen presence, even though he could detect only his officers and the technicians around him. Neighboring dreadnaughts on either side of The Emperor's Fist occasionally let loose with a volley of blue plasma fire or tactical missiles, trailing white smoke as they exited launch tubes and streaked for the planet's surface.

"Go ahead, Captain."

"Ah. Copy. We are experiencing pocket resistance at the moment. We may have to dig in until we are reinforced. Tac strike missions will follow this transmission. Ground forces are being neutralized effectively; however, we are now under aerial attack. We are drawing casualties and may need resupply soon." The captain's voice was not panicked, but calm. Chuikova was grateful that at least he was able to review the personnel files of his troopers going into battle with the clones to ensure that experienced officers were leading. He always preferred to deal with war veterans in combat.

"What of the clones? Are they holding up?" Chuikova asked.

"Copy. They are able to withstand a lot of damage. Most are still following their programming." The transmission static clicked off as a tremendous explosion resonated throughout the bridge.

"Captain! What do you mean 'most'? Respond!"

Silence ensued. Chuikova immediately turned to the technician and yelled, "Get him back!"

The technician was already busy over his console; his hands were a blur as he punched various buttons. "The frequency is still open. He is not responding, Sir."

"Keep trying." Chuikova now felt a presence behind him, and the hair on the back of his neck stood on end. His earlier reservations were now confirmed. His robed "advisor," as he called himself, was now standing directly behind him.

"The attack is being stalled. This is unacceptable," the black-robed figure said. "I thought your bombardment erased all military opposition." The black-robed figure moved silently before the large panoramic view screen. Chuikova stood still, the view screen still capturing his gaze. From space numerous red circles of razed targets were visible.

"Resistance is to be expected, but it shouldn't take this long to pacify this planet." the black-robed figure paused, and continued, "no matter what preparations have been carried out." It was obvious to Chuikova he was being made to feel like a blundering fool.

"So far, the southern part of the continent has been pacified to a satisfactory level up to a large natural river border. North of the border, the defenders possessed better weapons than originally thought," he replied curtly. Getting no response, he continued, albeit more calm.

"Reinforcements will catch up and secure the rear areas as planned. Because you did not desire to use orbital weapons on the final push, ground forces will bear the brunt of the assault. Your wish to push the clone battalions without proper support will be costly. Unnecessary confusion is manifesting at the front. I warned you of that." He wanted to choke the figure and tell him I told you so, but he thought that probably wasn't the best idea.

The figure's face was hidden by a shadow within the depths of his black robes. The figure hissed back, "If the supreme chancellor's will is not carried out, you will answer with your life, and I will have to answer to my master. That is something I do not wish to do." The figure turned and exited the bridge, leaving Chuikova to himself with an intense look of hatred on his face, and wondering if his thoughts perhaps his mind had been read.

"I think he's back!" the technician yelled.

Chuikova again stood by himself, with a bustle of activity around him.

"Put it through."

Transmission static again came through loudly. Faint sounds of gunfire could be heard in the background, as well as a few random explosions. A faint moan drifted throughout the bridge.

"Captain, report!" Now only a faint moaning answered the marshal. The explosions and gunfire seemingly died out. The technician indicated that the communications line was still open. Chuikova heard a sickening crunch, like the one a bone makes as it breaks, shattered the static. A thick, droning voice filled the bridge.

"Destroy. Kill and destroy." The communications line went dead. The technician tried in vain to get it back up, but to no avail.

"He's not going to answer. Shut it off." Chuikova said. The clones were unstable, and if the advance units were being held up, or worse, tearing themselves apart, the offensive would be over. "What is the status of the forward units?"

"Clone battalion Four, Five and Six were committed for the northern offensive. We are unable to establish contact with any of them."

"What is the status of the reinforcements?"

"Fighter Squadron One is deploying. Three assault infantry regiments from *Mycla's Hammer* are enroute plus a penal battalion."

"Where is Matthias?"

"He is with regiment "Dreadwolves" taking part in the southern offensive,' the technician replied quickly. Chuikova frequently asked the location of his close comrades and the technicians learned quickly to keep tabs on them.

"Send a priority one message. The Dreadwolves are to redeploy to the northern offensive immediately." Chuikova turned and hurriedly exited the bridge, headed for his quarters. "It has begun," He muttered to himself. "We still may lose this thing after all."

CHAPTER 42

Roman sat between Petor and Chana as the 1st and 2nd teams bounced around in the confines of their APC. About thirty minutes ago, it had broken away solo from in a long convoy of vehicles heading north. The air was incredibly hazy, making visibility low. For a civilization that discovered or borrowed the ability to travel faster than light, Roman thought it was reasonable to have figured out a decent suspension. Once out of the drop ships, Penal Battalion 7 had been broken down into squads. After the 1st and 2nd had been stuffed into a sardine can APC and headed to who knows where. Attempts at getting any information out of Lon were futile, as he had no clue. Even if he did, Roman thought he probably wouldn't share it anyway. He was the type of person who enjoyed having power over others, no matter how insignificant it may seem. Roman assumed that the crew of the APC was regular army, as they were already in the driver's compartment when the squads boarded at the landing site.

Eventually the ride smoothed out, leading Roman to believe they might now be on a highway. The limited display in his helmet indicated only that they were headed in a northerly direction. This lack of information and equipment was just one of the limitations of being a Penal Battalion trooper. The limited ammunition and grenades, in particular, would make this a fun excursion after all. When he, Petor, and Chana did break away from Lon and the others, Roman thought that getting a regular army trooper's helmet would be beneficial.

The APC suddenly halted. For a few moments, Roman couldn't hear anything except the soft whine of the engine, soft enough that Roman suspected the interior sound amplifiers were turned off. A few minutes later, Lon's voice came over the helmet net.

"1st team will exit here and will provide cover until Cheem gets his troops off the APC. We are to rendezvous with a sizable force up ahead and assist clearing a small town." The net went silent, and within a minute the rear hatch of the APC dropped. 1st team exited and formed a small perimeter around the hatch. The squad leader, Cheem, exited and dropped to one knee, pointing to a nearby cluster of burned out automobiles. His half a dozen troops broke into a low run towards a small amount of cover presented to them. As the APC's hatch began to close, Roman caught a quick glimpse out of the rear of the APC of what appeared to be the remains of a highway that was jam packed with abandoned cars. Swirling smoke did its best to obscure the sun. Within seconds, the APC was mobile again.

"Once our team exits," Lon's voice said into the helmets of his personnel, "we will find cover and I will establish a marching order. Lock and load."

Like I needed to be told that, Roman thought. He glanced over at Petor, giving him a quick inspection. Petor lay unmoving, with his face shield down. Roman was actually impressed with the guy. He had turned out to be a good soldier, considering the circumstances. Roman glanced over at Chana and got the same impression, even if she didn't speak. Chana met his gaze. He couldn't see her eyes through the closed face shield, but somehow he knew he could trust her.

"Contact!" Lon's booming voice broke over the helmet net, waking Roman from his brief nap. He hadn't had time to collect his thoughts when he had the odd sensation that he was suddenly being tossed onto his back within his seat harness. Reality soon took over as Roman realized that the APC was indeed skidding on its side. A large hole had been blown in the side of the vehicle, obliterating two troopers that were seated there, leaving only their torsos in the seats. Roman looked out through the hole and could see grey sky as well as a shower of sparks.

The APC finally skidded to a halt. The troopers frantically releasing themselves from their harnesses. Three members of the 2nd team, including Lon, unfortunately were sitting on the side of the APC that took the hit, and they had to drop down as they were strapped in their seats on what was now the ceiling. Roman, Petor, and Chana were on their backs, and were covered with most of the bloody remains from their two former colleagues.

One of the troopers hit the manual release lever, dropping the rear ramp.

"Roman, check it out," Lon ordered.

"Check it out yourself. As far as I'm concerned, it's every man for himself." Roman put one hand on the side of the APC to steady himself and used the other to level his rifle toward Lon. "You check it out and be a hero."

Lon turned to the trooper who had opened the rear hatch of the APC. The trooper was crouched down, his rifle aimed out of the hatch.

"Lestor, you check it out. The rest of you, establish a perimeter." Lon's voice faltered. Trooper Lestor turned his head toward Lon and shook it from side to side.

"Not taking orders from you anymore. The crew is wasted." Lestor resumed his watch out of the back hatch, and continued, "We need to come up with something quick, though, before the next attack does us in."

Lon took up a position behind Lestor and brought his weapon up to bear over Lestor's shoulder. "To hell with all of you. Anybody who doesn't wish to hang can come with me." Lon stepped around Lestor and peered wearily out of the hatch. After half a minute, he turned to face the remainder of the squad in the APC, and turned again and exited the hatch solo, disappearing into the swirling black smoke outside.

"We'd better get out before this thing blows or we take another hit," Petor said. "I'll take point." Before anybody could say anything, his small frame was out of the back hatch.

The remaining troopers emerged out of the still smoldering APC wreckage and leaned against the hull. They saw no sign of Lon anywhere. Roman tactically moved to the side of the highway, between two burned out tractor trailer hulks. A twisted blue highway sign lay on the ground. Roman lifted the sign, noting with curiosity that the blue shield read "Interstate 35." Looking further north on the Interstate, Roman intensified the magnification in his helmet and noticed a large metal structure that spanned the north and southbound lanes. A bullet-ridden sign read "Sarita Checkpoint, Federal Agents." Several burned out tour buses smoldered underneath the wreckage. Further north he saw hundreds of oily black plumes of smoke snaking upward from decimated buildings. The death toll no doubt was immense unless, somehow, the buildings had been evacuated.

"What is it?" Petor called out, his helmet visor open.

"The fleet's handiwork," he said as he stared at the carnage in the distance. After a minute, he broke his trance and said, "We should get off this highway," Roman replied into his helmet mic. He was surprised when Lestor responded, "Lead the way."

Roman jumped down into the ditch ran parallel to the interstate. The rest of the squad followed suit and jumped in after him.

"Cover me," Roman said. "I'm going check the drivers."

"Let them rot," Lestor countered.

"We could use their helmets. They tap into the army grid, whereas ours don't really do much of anything." Roman emerged from the lip of the ditch and started toward the APC wreck at a run. "Keep an eye out for Lon. He's still monitoring our channel."

Roman dashed back to the APC wreck. It seemed to take longer to get there than it did to run away from it. He ran to the front and peered inside through the cracked windshield. He could see the broken body of the driver up against the glass. He stood up briefly and looked around. He saw nothing except what appeared to be tall fields of cornstalks on either side of the interstate. Glancing at the southbound lanes, he could see several large craters dotting the northbound lane. Burned out hulks and numerous parts that had been blown off the vehicles rested on the interstate, inside and on the edges of the craters, and several feet off the road. Roman still saw no sign of Lon, and he surmised it would be easy to vanish into the cornstalks.

Roman turned his attention back toward the APC and thought against trying the rear or the exposed driver's door. He kicked his foot against the cracked windshield and felt it give a little. After three more hard kicks, the windshield gave way. Roman slung his rifle over his back and reached inside, grabbing the dead driver by his collar. He was surprised when only the top half off his body came free. He yanked hard and pulled. *Coveralls and no helmet. Damn,* Roman thought to himself. Roman looked toward the back of the cramped driver's compartment and saw an armored figure crumpled in a heap by the door to the troop compartment. He too was blown in half as Roman gingerly pulled himself forward into the APC and almost leapt for joy at the body of a regular army trooper. Roman unbuckled the chinstrap to the trooper's helmet and tugged hard. The helmet came free. Roman also began to unbuckle his assault vest, which was still loaded with spare rifle magazines and grenades. A moan escaped the bloodied lips of the trooper, surprising Roman.

"Help me," the trooper cried softly. He feebly grabbed Roman's sleeve.

"Tell me where this APC was headed, and I might," Roman answered, taking what he could carry from the trooper's body. He stuffed a small caliber pistol down the back of his pants.

"Rally point," he wheezed. "Clone staging area." The trooper's head lulled to one side. "Don't let me die," he pleaded. His glazed over eyes stared at Roman.

"You're missing your lower body. You don't have much time left, I'm sorry." Roman grabbed the trooper's EMR on the floor of the cab and slowly edged himself out of the APC, breaking the weak grip the trooper had on Roman's sleeve.

Roman turned and ran back to the ditch. "How did it go?" Petor asked.

"I got a helmet and an EMR," Roman said, holding up the helmet like a trophy. "The driver said we were headed to a clone staging area. We should get moving. Petor, you take point; Lestor, get the rear." Roman put his new helmet on, tossing the old one carelessly away. The five moved quickly through the ditch paralleling the pockmarked interstate. Roman placed the new helmet over his head and activated the army net. Instantly, Roman could hear the radio traffic from other nearby companies and squads in the area. From what it sounded like, the attack had stalled for some reason, and the forces were split up everywhere, almost like the Normandy airborne drops during World War II. Numerous calls for unit commanders to report in went unanswered. As Roman scanned frequency after frequency, more and more came up only as static. Petor dropped down to one knee and gave the closed-fist signal to stop. Roman quickly made his way to the front of the formation.

"What is it?" Roman asked, his voice amplified by the helmets' internal speakers.

"You find anything out?" Petor had flipped his face shield up, and beads of sweat were streaming down his face from the humid atmosphere.

"Yeah, it sounds like we're getting our asses kicked, and it's not from the enemy." Roman looked a few seconds longer at Petor as he removed a canteen from his vest and took a long pull from it.

"Why are we stopped?" Petor asked.

"Sorry," Roman answered. "I got sidetracked. External sensors picked up something up ahead. It might be the rally point." He sighed heavily. "OK. I'll walk point with you. Let's move out"

The sun had begun its descent, and the road ahead slid into a surreal darkness. After about an hour of walking, Roman gave some new orders.

"Listen up. We may have the rally point up ahead. Activate night vision and thermo. I'm going up with Petor to check it out. You two watch our backs."

Lestor and Chana nodded in unison as Roman and Petor continued on.

CHAPTER 43

Roman and Petor moved silently through the cornfield paralleling the highway. Roman's helmet had locked onto a GPS waypoint that probably had been placed by an advanced scout party. Lestor and Chana were out of sight to the rear but were close enough to lend assistance if needed.

"Should be close in about twenty-five meters," Roman hissed over the helmet net. He pushed on, with Petor on his right, cautiously navigating the eight- foot-tall cornstalks. Nightfall was rapidly approaching as the team continued on. Sensors on their helmets started to give varying readings of concentrated heat signatures up ahead.

"It's too quiet, I don't like it," Petor said. "We should be hearing something already."

"Agreed," Roman responded in grim concurrence. "The clearing should be up ahead." Roman stopped and within a few moments Chana and Lestor made their way up to him. Petor halted as well, trying to peer up further ahead. "You guys hold here. I'm going for a look." Roman pushed the tip of his rifle through the cornstalks and stepped through.

"Well, it may have been a rally point at one time, but not anymore," Roman transmitted back to his waiting team a few minutes later. "This is definitely the place, but no one seems to be home."

"Copy," Petor replied.

Roman stepped into a large clearing created by a drop ship. Two large burn craters were visible. The touchdown seemed to have triggered a small fire, and the advance party most likely widened the cleared area. Several large crates were still stacked, as well as a radio antenna array. It seemed to Roman for a split second that whoever was here had hurriedly abandoned this position sans most of its equipment; some very useful items had been left behind. He was about to give the all clear when he saw the bodies.

He saw six bodies even in the dim light, but it was a little hard to tell. Whatever had gotten hold of them had savagely rendered them limbless and headless. A crude fire pit had two still-smoldering corpses inside it.

"I need you guys to move up. This place is torched."

The rest of the group soon entered the clearing. Lestor raised his face shield upon seeing the dismembered corpses. Petor and Chana stared blankly at the display of carnage.

"Wha-what could have c-caused this?" Petor stammered out. "It's so barbaric."

Roman knelt down and examined several of the corpses. "These were clone minders. I recognize the uniforms."

"Their heads are gone," Lestor whispered. "What did they do with their heads?"

Roman stood up. "Chana, I need you to find tracks out of here. We need to find out where they went."

Chana nodded and started checking the perimeter.

"Petor, get on that radio and see if you can raise fleet. I need to know where we are, and they need to know we are still alive.

Petor nodded and seemed grateful for not having to look at the bodies any longer.

Roman turned to Lestor. "I need you to police up what you can. Rations, grenades, ammo. Whatever you can carry."

"Understood."

Roman walked over to Petor who had uncrated the rest of the communications array. It consisted of a small table and a portable computer. The antenna itself unfolded, and once raised manually, it was about fifteen feet in height. Petor got busy on the keyboard and placed a headset on his head. He rested his helmet on the desk.

"I'll give you five minutes, and we move. I don't like sitting here."

"OK." Petor stopped typing. "The antenna should be calibrated. Let's see if it works." Petor stood and look at Roman, who had now removed his helmet.

"Fleet command, come in. Fleet command, come in. Over." Petor was about to try again when a voice responded, cutting into the static. "Unit calling, identify yourself. This is a secure high-level channel."

Roman snatched the headset off of Petor's head. "Give me that damn thing." He put on the headset and spoke into it. "Listen here, you asshole. Your advance party is history. We are cut off and need immediate extraction!"

The static resumed.

"You got that up there?" Roman handed the headset back to Petor. "They must be all nice and cozy up there. See what they say. I gotta take a piss."

"What do you have, Ensign?" The watch commander peered over the shoulder of the ensign who sat at his communications station. The ensign adjusted knobs on the console while holding a headset to his ear.

"It's a tier one encrypted transmission from Battalion 3, Company 6. It's intermittent, but I did pick this up." The ensign quickly replayed Roman's call for extraction. The bemused watch commander placed his hand on his chin.

"That is Captain Siminov's Clone Assault unit. There may be survivors." The watch commander spoke quickly, "Try to get him back. If his element is still operational, they will be the only advance clone unit in the area."

The ensign nodded and quickly resumed his manipulation of the console's knobs. "Last calling unit, identify yourself and transmit verification code."

The ensuing static quickly broke. Petor's slightly nervous voice sounded on the bridge. "Ah, yes. Hello."

The ensign turned to the watch commander with a bewildered look on his face.

Petor continued, "We are at the rally point. It looks like the advance party was wiped out. We have secured the perimeter and are awaiting extraction."

The watch commander took the headset from the ensign and covered the mic with hand. "Get the ground marshal down here at once." The ensign exited his station, leaving the watch commander alone.

"Unit calling, identify yourself," he resumed, taking his hand away.

"Ah, this is Petor. We are from the penal battalion."

The watch commander was left speechless. His brief moment of confusion was broken by the arrival of Chuikova on the bridge.

"Report."

The ground marshal's speech slurred and he rubbed his bloodshot eyes.

"We apparently have a penal unit occupying the forward rally point. It's from Captain Siminov's last known location."

"OK. Give me that." The ground marshal angrily grabbed the headset and spoke into it. "Who is in charge? Put him on, Trooper!"

Petor managed to whimper a soft "Yes, sir" before leaving the radio to static.

"What units do we have in the vicinity?" the ground marshal asked.

The watch commander quickly produced a holopad and read the latest intelligence report.

"None, sir, in close proximity. Nothing at this time since we ceased orbital strikes. The advance clone units seem to be disintegrating. No support units have been able to get through due to enemy air and missile strikes. Most are spread thinly throughout this area, just short of the large city indicated on the map here." The watch commander enhanced the outskirts of what appeared to be a sizable residential area. Numerous flashing indicators showed the current positions of the units.

"Why wasn't I informed of our lack of progress sooner?" the ground marshal asked coldly.

"Sir, you made it clear you did not wish to be disturbed." The watch commander took a step back, as if he fully expected to be struck. The marshal's demeanor quickly changed, however.

"I'm sure I did. I'll take care of this. I want a full briefing in my quarters prepared on the progress of the clone units and supporting elements. Find out why our forces are being split up. No one else will be notified of this but me. Understood?"

"Yes, sir." The watch commander did an about face and set off from the bridge, yelling orders to his junior officers.

The ground marshal gazed out of the panoramic view window at the blue planet below. His short trance was quickly broken by an incoming radio transmission. The ground marshal quickly turned off the intercom so the transmission could be heard only on his headset.

"This is John Roman. There are four of us left. As of right now, we are the rally point. The clone minders of this unit are all dead. No sign of the clones. How copy?"

"Roman, this Johann. It's good to hear your voice. When this is over, I'll buy you a drink and you can tell me how you ended up in a penal battalion." Chuikova looked around the bridge for any robed figures who might be sticking their telepathic minds where they were not welcome. He wasn't sure of the range of their mind probing, but he wasn't taking any chances. Seeing none, he continued, "Hold position and await further orders."

"You want me to stay here?" Roman's voice agitated voice asked. "Let me be the first to inform you that your clones are going cannibal. We have found some of your regular army troops. My guess is your clones are killing them, just like before when we followed that nut around my city. I hope you copied that. We will wait five minutes, and my team is moving out."

"Understood. Stand by." Chuikova turned to a nearby technician. "Patch this through to my quarters." Without waiting for a reply, he made a hasty exit off the bridge. Unbeknownst to him, a figure in black robes had blended perfectly into the shadows on the bridge. The figure quickly exited to provide information to his master.

"Roman, are you there? It's Johann." The ground marshal sat in a small room connected to a closet in his quarters, to which he had the door closed and locked. He sat in a metal chair and spoke into a handset.

"Go ahead. I hear you." Roman's voice came over the headset surprisingly clearly.

"Johnny, I am sending you new coordinates. Try to make your way there. We are reinforcing several sectors in order to contain the clones. We will attempt to get you guys out of there. You should have never been there."

"Well, we are here and will head that way. It looks like chaos down here. I haven't seen any operational regular units, just an abandoned rally point with lots of equipment, but no sign of anybody.

"Understood. We will get you out of there. In the meantime, maintain contact. Out." Chuikova put the headset down and let out a long sigh. He pushed a button on the side of the featureless wall, causing the door to open. He walked back into his quarters, sat on his bunk, and was about to pour a drink from the bottle of rotgut on the table next to the bunk when a robed figure stepped out from the shadows.

"Your attempts to hide transmissions from me are futile. You should know that," the robed figure hissed.

Chuikova slowly turned around. He made no attempt to hide the look of disgust that played across his face.

"Well, come right in."

The robed figure threw back his hood, revealing a pale, weathered face with patches of grey hair and two black eyes. What reviled Chuikova the most were several carbuncles, oozing black pus, interspersed throughout the forehead and skull. The skin looked almost rotted, as if Chuikova was staring into living corpse. Set square in the forehead was a third, pineal eye, with a purple pupil that held Chuikova paralyzed for a brief moment. He felt a brief surge of electricity surge through his body, before quickly regaining his composure.

The robed figure's dry, cracked lips formed into a thin smile upon seeing that Chuikova was unable to meet his gaze.

"There will be no extraction," the robed figure hissed. "The clone units will be reinforced once the rest of the fleet arrives from pulse space. You will continue to push your elements forward until the whole of the continent is infested with my creations."

"And what purpose would that serve? I thought we were attempting to pacify this planet in the name of the supreme chancellor. Apparently you have ulterior motives." Chuikova regained his composure and stared straight into the black eyes. His anger and contempt now overwhelmed all the anxiety and fear he had felt initially. He reached for the bottle of rotgut.

The robed figure paced the confines of the spartan quarters. He produced a jeweled staff from the depths of his robes and began to lean on it to supplement his left foot as he walked.

"You are most correct. We are not here for pacification; this is merely but a test of our new forces on an indigenous population. The home world is weary of another war, and if this experiment is successful, we will be unstoppable. Ten thousand years ago, the Auger-Lords set out to conquer the universe and nearly succeeded." The robed figure stopped for a moment, as if he was remembering events that had transpired so long ago. He continued, albeit in a quieter, soft tone, "The ways of the Auger-Lords were passed down to a select few, and over time, they were nearly forgotten. Theories and applications of the ancients' technologies are almost lost, except for the order of the Shadow. We keep the legacy alive and will continue to do so until the end of the universe. Do you now see?"

Chuikova stood up abruptly. "The only thing I see is death. I am weary from death."

The robed figure began to laugh. "It is written in the ancient texts that when a thousand years have expired, our creator will be awoken and set forth to reclaim his kingdom. Your time therefore is at an end. The prophecy must be carried out and fulfilled." With surprising quickness, he brought the staff to bear upon Chuikova. A blue light formed on the tip. Chuikova was a split second faster. He brought the heavy bottle of rotgut down hard upon the robed figure's head. The bottle shattered into several large fragments, and the rust-colored liquid began intermingling with blood. A large shard of glass embedded itself into the robed figure's third eye. The figure gasped and fell, the staff clattering uselessly onto the metallic floor. Chuikova fell upon him in an instant, sandwiching the withered head between his massive hands.

"This isn't over!" The robed figure hissed, blood pouring out of its ears. We will hunt you down wherever you try to hide!"

Renewed with vigor, Chuikova squeezed with all his might, and the skull between his hands made a loud pop. He felt the skull break in his hands and dropped the lifeless body to the floor. Just to be sure, he would eject the body into space. He immediately strode over to the wall-mounted intercom and ordered security to be on alert and to detain any and all followers of the Shadow, terminating them with extreme prejudice if they offered any resistance.

CHAPTER 44

Roman turned his team around and headed back the way they came. After about 25 meters, he dropped to one knee and held up his left arm, curling his hand into a fist. Lestor, Chana, and Petor immediately dropped to the ground, breathing heavily. Roman peered through the dried cornstalks and carefully surveyed the highway in front of him.

"OK, we are back on the interstate. You guys stay put; I'll check it out." Roman slowly emerged from cover and looked to the south along the interstate. The distinctive corrugated metal roof of the Border Inspection station could be seen about a mile away. Squinting though his helmet visor, Roman saw nothing but abandoned vehicles littering the roadway.

Petor, too curious to stay put, came up behind Roman and opened the face shield on his helmet. "I think I see someone up ahead," he said, pointing to a figure sitting behind a bullet-riddled cargo van no more than ten meters away. He couldn't see any movement.

Roman thought for a split second about yelling at Petor about moving from cover but decided against it. "I see him. I'll go check it out." Roman opened his visor, stared directly into Petor's eyes, and told him firmly, "Stay put."

Closing his visor, Roman looked left, and right. Seeing no danger, he took off from the cornfield in a full sprint. He reached the back of the van, and opened his visor. He looked at the motionless body and instantly recognized that it was Lon, or at least what was left of him. A large-caliber projectile had split his helmet and canoed his head, exposing his brains.

"It's Lon," Roman's voice boomed over the helmet radios. "The rest of you, get over here, one by one. We can try to go up the other side of the highway."

The remaining three cautiously made their way to the back side of the van. Once all three were there, Roman looked to the west across the southbound lanes of traffic. His team faced about a twenty-meter dash until they could get into the tall cornfields on the other side.

Lestor slowly peeked his head up to look through the van's rear window and further north up the highway. Suddenly, without warning, they heard a loud crack and Lestor's head snapped back. He instantly fell lifeless to the asphalt, showering Roman with bits of brain and skull.

"Get down!" Roman yelled. Two more cracks resonated, and pieces of the van were vaporized. "Snipers. Stay down." Petor and Chana needed no encouragement; they both already were hugging the ground. "We can't stay here much longer. I've gotta think of something." Two more cracks sounded, slamming into the van's engine compartment. Roman began to unbuckle his assault vest and belt. Within seconds he was out of his pants, leaving Chana and Petor staring at him with a look of bewilderment. Without any hesitation, he quickly removed his white BVDs.

"Hand me Lestor's rifle."

Petor grabbed Lestor's rifle and held it while Roman put his pants back on. Seeing that Roman was devoid of clothes on the lower part of his body, she turned away, blushing. He grabbed the rifle and affixed his BVDs to the end of the rifle barrel, securing them as best as he could.

"Let's hope this works. If they are army guys, let's hope they will take us alive." Roman slowly raised the rifle, with his underwear fluttering in the wind. He slowly emerged from the back of the van with his arms raised high.

"Well, this is weird." A heavily camouflaged sniper peered through the scope of his Barrett .50 rifle once more. The sniper spotter next to him raised a large scope to his eye and focused on the anomaly downrange.

"If I didn't know any better, Sergeant, he is attempting to surrender with his underwear. This guy has balls. Range 1,200 meters."

"Either that or we just greased our own guys. Get Duncan down there to check it out."

The spotter touched a microphone secured around his neck and spoke. "Eagle Three, this is Eagle's Nest over."

"Go ahead, Eagle's Nest," replied Duncan.

"Roger. Take your team to the highway and intercept possible hostiles. One of them is waving his underwear. How copy?"

"Good copy. Watch our asses." After a brief pause, Duncan said, "Did you say 'underwear'?"

"Ah, that's affirmative, Eagle Three."

The spotter resumed looking through the scope to see if any more viable targets would make the foolish mistake of sticking their heads up.

"You think they saw us?" Petor looked at Roman intently as he rested against the back of the van.

"Well, they stopped shooting. I just hope they get to us before the clones do." No sooner had Roman finished his sentence than he heard a firm voice coming from somewhere from the west side of the interstate.

"Place you hands in the air and slowly walk over to the sound of my voice. If you aim your weapons in this direction, you will be dead before you hit the ground."

Roman slowly stood up, motioning the others to do the same. "Follow my lead. No sudden moves. Sling your rifles." They slowly walked across the southbound lanes and entered the thicket on the other side.

"That's far enough." Four soldiers wearing ghillie suits emerged from out of nowhere, aiming their M4 carbines at the group. A big blonde headed hulk of soldier carried a Javelin anti-tank launcher at the ready; a spare missile protruded out of carrier on his back. The apparent leader stepped forward, cradling a Barrett .50 caliber sniper rifle in his arms. He eyed the group with curiosity, especially Chana. All three had removed their helmets. Her long black hair cascaded to her shoulders. Petor fished his spectacles out of one of his pockets and perched them on his nose. Roman smiled at once.

"You guys are the army, and are we ever glad to see you!"

"I am Sergeant Duncan, 21st Special Forces group. I really don't know what to say." After a slight pause, he continued, "I'll need your weapons if you don't mind."

The trio handed over their rifles to another soldier without question.

Who the hell are you people?" Duncan asked.

Roman wiped a bead of sweat off of his brow. "It's a really long story, but if you could get us out of here quickly, I'll tell you everything—the sooner the better."

Duncan needed no further explanation. He activated the throat microphone and spoke in a slightly cracked voice, "Eagle's Nest, we are coming back, with three."

"Understood," replied Eagle's Nest.

"Wait," hissed Petor. "They may treat you fine, but me and Chana are not from your world. There is no telling what they will do to us."

Roman looked at Chana and could tell she was nervous about going with the Army group. He put his hand on Petor's shoulder. "Don't worry; I won't let them do anything to you too."

Petor sighed, not fully convinced. It wasn't like he had a choice anyway. If he fled, he would most likely be shot down.

"I hope you know what you are doing," he said, sounding defeated.

The group set off north, moving quickly through a small path in the cornfield. Duncan turned and faced Roman. "Hey, I'm sorry about your vehicle and your guy there. Jeremy is a crack shot with the javelin, and well so am I. You just can't tell who is who right now ever since the nuke strikes. We also had rumors of a Spetsnaz team parachuting in here three nights ago rampaging around and we have been looking for them ever since."

"Nuke strike?" Roman repeated quizzically. "You're a little off on that one."

"Well whatever it is, our military capability got neutralized with precision. We are basically fighting a guerilla war now."

"Well, I don't think those were nukes and Spetsnaz, or whatever you call them. It's much bigger than that."

Duncan shrugged as the group continued toward the smoldering remnants of what looked like a large city.

CHAPTER 45

"Eagle One is coming in," Sergeant Duncan spoke into his throat microphone. "Don't light us up." He moved forward and motioned the others to follow. The sky was a dark grey from smoke and soot as the group entered the outskirts of a large ruined city. They walked on a main street leading east from the interstate. They found rubble strewn about haphazardly and smashed buildings that continued to spew smoke into the atmosphere. Here and there, small fires still burned.

"Is it snowing?" Petor asked quizzically to no one in particular.

One of the camouflaged soldiers replied callously, "No, its ash. This city was wiped off the face of the Earth."

Petor replied with profane sadness as he took in the environment. "I-I'm so sorry."

The group continued on without conversation until they arrived at the hollowed out remains of a police station. Several soldiers stood up from their hidden positions and looked at the group intently.

"Inside," Sergeant Duncan commanded. "Let's go." He led the way for Roman's group past half a dozen heavily armed soldiers, each carrying a belt-fed machine gun. The rest of Duncan's unit stayed outside. A few lit cigarettes and talked about nothing in particular. Roman instantly recognized the smell of real tobacco. He realized he hadn't a smoke in some time. Good a time as any to quit, he thought. A pair of F-16 fighter jets roared overhead, on their way to some unknown target.

The lobby of the police station was somewhat intact. Stacks of military crates marked as munitions, equipment, and rations were piled everywhere.

Roman noticed several men wearing distinctive green uniforms of the U.S. Border Patrol, wearing flak jackets and carrying rifles. Also armed civilians with what looked like hunting rifles walked around also. Duncan led the group downstairs into what was once the jail. Several cells lined the single hallway. Each cell had been converted into a makeshift office, complete with computers and communication equipment. Duncan stopped at the last cell on the left and ushered the group inside.

A young disheveled Hispanic man in his mid twenties stood up from behind his desk and waved them in. His uniform was covered in dirt and what looked like dried blood. He wore a thick white bandage over his left eye. Roman's group entered, followed by Sergeant Duncan. Several soldiers had followed them down the hallway and remained outside the cell, weapons at ready.

"I'm Lieutenant Chapa and I am in command here," Chapa said. "You are at the front, or what's currently holding in this sector. You had best tell me who you are and where you came from."

Roman stepped forward. Noticing the single black bar on the soldier's uniform, Roman spoke. "Lieutenant, I am John Roman. This is Petor, and this is Chana. We are unwilling combatants. Unfortunately, the story is long as to how or why we got here, and I'm not sure you would believe me if I told you anyway."

Chapa got up from behind his desk and paced back and forth, his hands clasped behind his back. "What I have seen in the last twenty-four hours defies anything I have ever encountered. I am all ears."

Roman cleared his throat, and spoke, relating the events of being forced into the penal battalion, being sent to Earth as part of a massive alien invasion, and clone soldiers going berserk. When he finished, a dead silence ensued. Finally, the lieutenant spoke up.

"Well, given what I've seen and heard lately, that no longer sounds too farfetched. The attack came without warning. The ships in space seemed to target military installations with precision and some cities as well, mainly close to Mexico. From what I have been able to piece together, the bulk of the attacks were successful, from Mexico all the way down to Rio de Janeiro. Entire cities razed." Chapa indicated a large map on the wall behind his desk, showing the state of Texas and just south of Corpus Christi, Texas. "The line is holding here somewhat all the way to San Antonio," he continued. "Ft. Hood was able to mobilize most of the 7th

Cav. I guess they didn't get hit too badly. It seems their offensive has run out of steam just a little bit."

"It seems it is a little more complicated than that," Roman interjected.

"Oh? How so?" asked the lieutenant.

"They relied on thousands of clone troopers. These guys are badass. They can take multiple hits and keep going. However, they are pretty much out of control."

This time it was Sergeant Duncan who spoke up. "Clones or not, they hit us hard last night. They only thing effective was .50 cals and concentrated fire. They seemed to get discouraged after we were able to consolidate here. Some of our forward elements weren't so lucky."

"What is the situation now?" Roman asked quizzically. Chapa looked at him and his companions for a moment trying to size them up. The group didn't fit the mold of the invaders his men had encountered earlier, and besides, he had no plans to release them anyway.

"OK. The situation is this. These ships opened up and took out key infrastructure. Our military is stretched beyond its limits, and we really don't have a whole lot here stateside. The majority is all over the Middle East: Yemen, Syria, Libya, Iran, Afghanistan ... you name it. There really wasn't a whole lot we could do."

"What about our allies?" Roman asked earnestly. "Surely, England or France is doing something?"

Chapa looked at Roman for a second, directly in the eyes. "*Our* allies?"

"Yeah, sorry about that. I used to be a cop in Dallas. Like I said, it's a real long story." Petor chuckled to himself upon hearing this.

"When you write a book," Chapa said, "I want a copy. Anyway, our coalition partners aren't helping out on this one. In fact, it's quite the opposite. I am not sure how long you have been away, but this attack came at a bad time. The US economy is in ruins. I have heard fragmented reports of Spetsnaz and Chinese Special Forces on our shores already trying to stir this mess up even more. Sergeant Duncan was actually out trying to find a team that somehow managed to land around here somewhere. Every terrorist who has a bone to pick with us are coming over, one way or another and there isn't a whole lot we can do about it. It's utter chaos. The president is gone, who knows where. A couple of generals are holding this together for now; at least we get occasional air support. The government is gone, as far as I know." Chapa sat back in his chair, the strain on his youthful face readily apparent.

Roman put both hands on the lieutenant's desk and leaned forward. "Well, I may have a solution. I just need to make contact with an old friend." Chapa looked puzzled as he looked into Roman's determined eyes. "I just hope he is still listening," Roman said softly.

An out-of-breath soldier burst into the cell. "Sir, the Desert Hawk drone is picking up a lot of movement on the east perimeter."

"Understood," Chapa said as he got up. "If you gentlemen will excuse me, we can continue this conversation later."

"What do you have?" Chapa asked, peering over the shoulder of a soldier sitting behind a laptop computer. Both men looked intently at a black-and-white aerial video feed from the drone.

"It looks like the bad guys are maneuvering into position just outside the eastern perimeter," the soldier answered. "They appear to be more careful this time, since we put Claymores everywhere."

"Who is over there now?"

"The remains of 3rd Platoon, not much more."

Chapa stood up and stroked his chin thoughtfully. "OK. Let's clear this place out and send them all the help we can get. They are going to hit a fortified position, so we have the advantage."

"Sir, we will be glad to assist you," Roman said. "Just give us our weapons back."

"OK, you got it. We need all the bodies we can muster right now."

CHAPTER 46

Heavy contact," Chapa heard through his headset. "They are holding back, hitting us with those napalm grenades again. Not sure how much longer we can hold this sector."

"Copy that," Chapa answered. "Help is on the way. Keep your heads down." Chapa replaced the hand mic on the radio receiver. "We're going to be without air support on this one. No answer from the General."

Sergeant Duncan nodded grimly in response. The Air National Guard Squadron out of Corpus Christi was the only thing keeping the line intact so far. Napalm canisters and cluster bombs seemed particularly effective. 7th Cav, with their Abrams tanks and Apache attack copters were supposed to linking up any hour now. Until then, they had to hold.

Duncan was driving the M-ATV mine-resistant vehicle, with the lieutenant riding shotgun. The M-ATV was a venerable veteran of the war in Afghanistan and served the new front line well. Roman, Petor, and Chana were stuffed in the back, with one soldier in the turret manning an M-249 machine gun. Bouncing around the cratered road closely behind were a motley assortment of soldiers, armed civilians and U.S. Border Patrol Agents riding in up-armored Humvees and a few pickup trucks with crude metal plates welded to the doors.

The small convoy soon left the outskirts of the city. Up ahead, several plumes of smoke could be seen from numerous grass fires raging out of control.

"How much longer?" Roman yelled.

"Two minutes!" Duncan yelled back.

"Roger that." Chapa picked up the radio handset. "Get ready to dismount," he said over the net.

Two minutes later, the convoy steered off the road. A few scattered buildings surrounded the remains of a gas station. Two jackknifed semi trucks blocked the east-west roadway. Several soldiers crouched down behind the still standing concrete wall of the gas station keeping a watchful eye.

Roman, Petor, and Chana followed Chapa and Sergeant Duncan southbound toward the remains of small building. A bullet-riddled sign that read "Bill's Dollar Store" hung precariously from a pole. Chapa spoke into his throat mic, but his low speech was inaudible to anyone else.

Within seconds, the group was inside the building. Several soldiers peered through cracks in the thin concrete wall. Several others lay on the round, some bandaged, and some with their ponchos covering them.

"Sir, am I glad to see you!" A soldier with a blood-soaked bandage on his thigh ran up to the group with a look of exasperated relief across his face.

"Who is in charge here?" Chapa asked.

"Corporal Delmonte was. He's wasted, sir. The bastards managed to get into the perimeter and chewed us up pretty bad, but we got the .50 cal working and drove them back. Unfortunately, they fired some kind of missile at us and wasted the .50. We are mainly holed up here, behind the semis, and a few in the Taco Bell across the street.

"How many strong? What is your best estimation, Specialist?"

"Not sure. I think the only reason they haven't attacked again was the .50 cal. I don't think they realize it's been knocked out. They were just charging in the open, firing everything they have. And they are packing some serious heat."

Roman stepped forward. "If I may interject, tell your men to concentrate on their limbs—legs and arms. The head too. Hitting them in the torso does no good; they can take multiple hits and won't feel a thing with the M4's you guys are carrying."

The specialist turned to Roman. "Yeah, we started trying to do that. The problem is that now, there are a bunch out there missing legs crawling around. We can't see them because of the tall grass in the fields. I think the head is the best bet."

"Understood," Chapa said. "You did a heck of job, Specialist. I'll take it from here."

Saluting, the specialist hobbled back off to his position, looking out across a junk-strewn field through a large hole in the wall.

"Well, it's getting dark," Roman said. "They may wait for nightfall. Their helmets should have night vision, and hand-to-hand combat would be pretty nasty with these guys."

Chapa nodded in agreement. "I'll tighten the perimeter. There are supposed to be some tanks and Apache gunships from 7th Cav on the way, but no word yet."

"Well, if these guys are cloned off the same dude I ran into, they are going to be pretty much insane, but they will know how to fight. I'll take my crew to a forward position and relieve anybody you have there. We should be able to hold our own for a while. We can draw them to us, and hopefully you guys can pick 'em off."

"Understood." Chapa put his hand on Roman's shoulder. "For what it's worth, I appreciate the help."

"No problem. Just get our back if the shit gets too thick."

I guess this place is as good as any," Roman muttered under his breath. The team set up behind two burned out Texas State Trooper cars. Petor and Chana lay prone, looking out at the highway as it exited the city. Several abandoned cars were scattered around the area, some laying on their sides or upside down, the result of the last attack, repulsed earlier in the day. Roman knew he had cover behind from well-concealed snipers and a few heavy machine guns, but that even that might not be enough. Petor had set up the portable communications array, and Roman was trying to get through to the fleet in space.

"I say again, this is John Roman. Patch me through to Chuikova."

"Sorry, sir, I cannot comply at this time. We have a situation on board."

The responding voice faded in and out over the weak link.

"Copy that. Just get a message to him that we are about to be engaged, and any help he can send down would be much appreciated. You got that?"

The reply came back even weaker, with a lot of garble. "Copy. Will relay. We have a fix on your position."

Roman replaced the handset on the receiver and folded up the foil dish. After stowing the unit back in his pack, he resumed scanning through his helmet night vision.

"I got something, to the left, heat signatures," Petor's voiced croaked on the helmet com. "I spotted them on thermal. Definitely human shapes headed their way." A moment later, he added, "I count at least twelve or thirteen."

A series of short gasps followed, coming from Chana. Roman scanned over to her sector and counted at least twenty more of the figures, bounding clumsily through an open field. The figures made no attempt to conceal themselves. Roman switched off his thermal display and switched to night vision. Much to his disdain, the figures didn't show up at all. At least on thermal they showed up as faint shadows. The soldiers probably wouldn't see them at all with their equipment.

"They have some kind of reflective coating on their gear or something," Roman instructed. "Stick to thermal."

Two detonations suddenly resonated about ten feet in front of their position, sending dirt and debris everywhere.

"Contact!" Roman yelled into the handheld radio he had gotten from Sergeant Duncan. "Multiple bad guys converging on our position."

Chana began to open up with short, controlled bursts from her rifle. Within moments, Petor joined the symphony of lead, contributing his rounds downrange. Roman watched the attackers spread out to the sides, avoiding a frontal assault. An occasional loud boom could be heard originating from his rear, no doubt Sergeant Duncan with his Barrett picking off targets of opportunity.

Roman soon realized why they were staying to the sides. The specialist had been right. The crawlers were coming up the middle, with the uninjured ones staying on the flanks. Roman could see several black shaped figures slowly crawling toward him, head on, several of which appeared to be missing legs. Every few feet, one would stop and lob a grenade or squeeze off an uncontrolled burst in his direction. The rounds easily went through the derelict cars being used for cover.

The night sky came alive for a brief moment. Parachute and handheld pen flares were fired into the air, their orange and green light lazily falling to the earth. Once the attackers were illuminated, several machine guns and M4's erupted. This had the effect of exposing their positions, and rifle grenades were launched in angry retaliation. They might be out of control animated corpse clones, but they still had some degree of tactical know-how still embedded in their brains. Once the flares went out, the firing ceased, and the attackers continued their way forward under the cover of darkness.

"There are too many of them," Petor said, "at least thirty to forty in my sector." He remained calm and let loose fire in a disciplined manner. Roman couldn't ask for a more able trooper at his side. Chana also held her own, showing no sign of letting up.

"We may need to fall back," Roman said. "If our guys run out of flares, we're done." He grimly surveyed the ever-increasing numbers of heat signatures. It didn't look good.

Without warning, a shoulder-fired rocket impacted directly between the two burned out Texas State Trooper cars, sending all three defenders hurtling backward. Roman heard a cry through his helmet, which now lay on the ground beside him, knocked clean off of his head. A large piece of shrapnel had embedded itself in its side. Roman was unable to move. He was bleeding profusely from his right leg, where a smoking metal shard had lodged itself. He thought about removing it but quickly decided against it. If his femoral artery was severed, he would be done. The embedded metal might be keeping him from bleeding to death.

"Ah damn. I'm hit," he croaked. He rolled onto his side and saw that Petor hadn't fared much better. He appeared to be unconscious, lying in a crumpled heap. The clones were upon them. One of them came into view and crashed into Chana, knocking her off balance. Roman turned over onto his other side and watched the spectacle unfold before his eyes. His rifle was gone, but he drew his hand cannon and tried to steady the weapon. Chana had regained her feet and was still firing her rifle. The clone appeared to have a large blade and attempted to slash Chana, but she parried the attack with her rifle. Her helmet crashed into the clone's chest armor with a loud crack. The clone lunged at Chana, going for her neck, but she managed to bring up her rifle and let loose a long burst under the base of its helmet, sending the clone's head fragmenting in all directions. The lifeless body crumpled to the ground. Roman breathed a sigh of relief but gasped as a flare was fired, this time showing dozens of clones, seemingly everywhere. Two legless clones began to try to drag Petor's body off, but shots from Roman's hand cannon drove them off.

The loud engine of the M-ATV roared behind the trio, and the vehicle came to a screeching halt. The machine gunner began hammering away at anything and everything that moved in his path. Several soldiers began firing their M4's into the horde. The line apparently had been breached elsewhere as well. Roman could hear faint yells emanating from the M-ATV's radio inside.

Without warning, the front of the road became instantaneously engulfed in a huge fireball, sending clone body parts in all directions. Soldiers grabbed Roman, Petor, and Chana and loaded them into the M-ATV. The driver slammed the M-ATV into reverse and drove back as another blast erupted.

"Where are those blasts coming from? The driver yelled. The gunner was busy replacing an ammunition belt on his machine gun. "Fuckin' A!," the gunner screamed at the top of his lungs as he finished reloading, slapped the top cover shut on his machine gun, and let loose another long volley of automatic weapons fire. He hadn't heard a word the driver had said.

Roman groaned as he tried to push Petor's unmoving body off of his. It was no use. Roman was out of strength and losing blood fast. Chana desperately tried to resuscitate Petor, but Roman couldn't gauge her level of success. Sleep came at him like a warm embrace, and he wasn't sure if he wanted to refuse it. His eyes began to shut of their own accord, and he was powerless to stop them.

He awoke to a hard slap across his face. Chana was shaking him, denying him solitude and tranquility. He saw that she had applied a tourniquet to his leg. The vehicle stopped, and he felt several hands drag him from the vehicle.

"Johann came … Johann …" Roman blacked out again, oblivious to the world around him.

CHAPTER 47

"There," Roman said. "You can see the ships above." He shifted his weight on the crutch he used to support himself. Daylight finally had come, and it was relatively quiet for a change. His leg was heavily bandaged, but except for some cuts and bruises, he had no other injuries. Chapa and Sergeant Duncan followed Roman's finger and were awed by a singular large ovoid shape and many smaller ones high in the sky. Several contrails high in the atmosphere head to the same position. "See those contrails? Those probably are the drop ships coming down," Roman said. "Make sure your fighters don't shoot them down." Several soldiers now peered through binoculars, awaiting the arrival of alien craft.

The next twenty minutes seemed like forever. Six drop pods, each about ten stories tall, landed with massive booms and settled several feet into earth was scarred by their exhaust. Vegetation around the landing site also caught fire, but the fires were extinguished quickly by unknown gases venting from unseen exhaust ports in the drop pods. The pods finally powered down, and large ramps began to extend from the ships toward the ground.

Chapa now had reinforcements at his disposal, albeit a little late. The thought of the extra help pleased him, but he was taking no chances. He had deployed several sniper teams and dozens of soldiers around the landing site in concealed positions, just in case these reinforcements turned out to be the enemy. A platoon of 7th CAV M1 Abrams tanks had arrived earlier in the morning, and the tank platoon leader had positioned these around the landing area as well.

Once the ramps were lowered to the ground, columns of armored troopers poured out in formation, their rifles held at port arms, helmet visors open. Their bearing and grim expressions showed clearly that they weren't a conscript or penal battalion; these were hardened battle troopers. Roman saw Ground Marshal Chuikova himself exit purposefully from one of the ships in his ceremonial regalia, including his sword. Roman nodded toward Lieutenant Chapa, and the pair walked to the waiting contingent.

"Duncan, you watch my ass," Chapa ordered.

"Roger that, sir." Duncan turned away and pulled the hood of his ghillie suit over his blond hair. He jogged over to a nearby blasted hulk of a building to rejoin his sniper team, already in position.

Roman noticed Matthias standing next to Chuikova. Each smoked a large cigar and seemed particularly at ease under the circumstances. Peering inside the drop pods, Roman noticed several armored vehicles, fully crewed and apparently on standby.

Roman and Chapa finally neared Chuikova and Matthias. The sergeant asked cheerfully, "Johnny, how are you?" He broke into a wide grin.

Chuikova nodded in recognition. "Johnny, it's good to see you again. I wish this never had to happen, but I am afraid there are more sinister forces at work than even I could have imagined."

Roman examined the two men, whom he once regarded as his friends. Many thoughts raced through his mind. Chuikova, apparently the man responsible for laying waste to a large portion of Roman's country, seemed relaxed, almost as though he was out for a Sunday stroll rather than overseeing a massive, deadly battle.

"Johann, Roger," Roman addressed each of them by name; the stepped forward and shook both of their hands.

Chapa spoke, breaking Roman's internal conflict. "I am Lieutenant Chapa of the Texas National Guard. I am in command here, and I have you surrounded. You may have superior weapons, but my weapons kill nonetheless."

Johann looked at the grey-haired lieutenant with curiosity.

"A lieutenant you say? Are you the highest ranking officer here?"

"As of now I am," Chapa replied.

Johann snapped to attention and saluted, his jeweled baton raised high. Chapa returned the salute, and both men relaxed.

"We come to offer terms for peace," Chuikova stated.

"Terms?" Chapa almost spat out the word. "I don't think you are in a position to dictate terms. You are responsible for this act of aggression and the many thousands of dead and wounded soldiers and civilians."

"Casualties are a most regrettable result of war. You must understand that our forces were controlled by another entity, which has since been eliminated. We no longer wish to pursue the destruction of cities and population, just to assure you that this action is over. I can offer the assistance of my troopers and equipment to clean up the remaining clones if that is acceptable.

Chapa stood dumbstruck, suddenly awed both by the display of alien technology before him and by the fact that the superior alien forces appeared to be human, both in appearance and in compassion, and not some monsters. His awe and surprise rendered him speechless.

Roman took over. "Sir, perhaps I could have a word with you in private?" Roman gestured with his left hand, and the ground marshal nodded and followed him. Matthias removed a cigar from his inside his armor and handed it to Chapa, who accepted it with a surprised look on his face.

"First off," Roman said, "I assume you received my transmission last night. You saved my ass."

Chuikova smiled. "Yes, I received it, and not a moment too soon, I gather. You can thank Scotts when you see him again—he personally led the assault. He is a very capable fighter pilot."

"I will definitely do that," Roman replied. "But I have to ask one question: What do you mean by "terms"? Clone units are still running wild all over the place, as far as I know, and several factions have seized upon the opportunity to exploit this situation. No less than five countries have committed acts of war in one shape or another. My own country is on the verge of collapse."

Walking with his gloved hands clasped behind his back, the ground marshal replied, "I know, Johnny. The Auger-Lords had your planet in their sights from the first day you arrived upon Hellenheim. I'm sorry if I kept you in the dark. We all were afraid of the Auger-Lords, and we still are. I really had no choice in the matter. However, a lot has changed. I am going to take the fleet into uncharted space and see if we can find an uninhabited planet to colonize, or at least one receptive to us settling down. We do not wish for war anymore. We do not wish to return to our home planet."

"That still leaves the mess you created here," Roman interjected.

The ground marshal paused before answering, his purple cape swirling behind him. "I am prepared to leave these drop pods on the planet, with full complements of men and equipment. The men have volunteered to stay behind. I only wish that they be treated with honor. They did not make the decisions that led to the destruction of your cities."

"I'm sure that would be most welcome, but the circumstances are peculiar. It's not my decision, anyway." The duo made an about-face and walked back toward Matthias and Chapa. A few other soldiers now stood around them, some of them no doubt enticed by Matthias's generosity with his cigars. Matthias was his usual jovial self.

"Terms of peace will be up to our government to decide," Chapa said. "But as of now I will authorize a cease fire against your forces. Communications are intermittent at best, so I hope you can stay for a short while as we work out details. Your sergeant here has told me a great deal about what has been going on. I would like to think we can work something out."

The ground marshal extended his gloved hand, which Chapa grasped. Matthias let out a hearty yell, "Bring out the rotgut, you sorry bastards!" The columns of troopers began to pound the butts of their rifles in a rhythmic beat upon the ground.

Chapa keyed his handheld radio and spoke. "Stand down, men. Pass the word. Stand down." He looked at the marshal. "Of course I am assuming you are in charge and have the authority to negotiate terms also.

"I am in command," he replied. "My honor is my word."

"Tell me these terms of yours and how you are going to clean up this mess." Smiling, the ground marshal replied, "Of course, but first I think a drink is due."

TWO MONTHS LATER

The ground marshal and the fleet kept their word, and the new government accepted the generous donation of men and equipment. Roman was shocked to learn how much damage his country had absorbed. Millions of people were homeless, with entire cities and communities laid waste along the southwestern border. Civil unrest took hold of much of the rest of the country, compounded by foreign agents who tried their best to exploit the instability.

Roman saw the situation as prime for a fresh start. He had made the decision to leave Earth under somewhat rushed circumstances, but without some forethought. While working with Chuikova and his crew, he wondered about the possibilities for him in a different society, given he just didn't seem to fit into his own society, which he viewed as degenerating into chaos. Maybe things could be turned around now.

Matthias related the news that Natasha was OK. Sebastian had seen to that, protecting her as best he could during the revolution that had begun on Hellenheim. The supreme chancellor was holding onto power by a thread, fighting off the military establishment and other emerging factions, and his support had dwindled to near nothing. Chuikova had informed him about the ugly situation during one of their many nights drinking and smoking his newfound favorite Cuban cigars. The ground marshal indicated that he would not be returning home, but rather venturing off into uncharted space, seeking a new world on which to settle and retire.

The remaining Auger-Seers on board the *The Emperor's Fist* had been persuaded to change their allegiance.

Although they had been cruel and manipulative, they had an intense desire for self– preservation, and they recognized that their position had degenerated into weakness.

One thing that had unsettled the ground marshal was the disappearance of Lord Sabis' body. He ordered the body blasted out of the airlock, but it was nowhere to be found. Every inch of the ship was searched to no avail. He had a gut feeling he wasn't done with him yet. It would be too easy to simply kill an Auger-Lord with his hands. He only hoped if Lord Sabis had managed to escape, he wasn't on this planet.

The rest of the Auger-Seers on board were needed to power the ship and maintain its core, creating grounds for bargaining. Not all of the crew wished to depart into the unknown, and one ship was scheduled to return to the home world of Hellenheim.

Roman sat against the trunk of a tree on a small patch of grass. He looked at the beads of sweat running down the sides of the Coke can. He took a gulp, savoring the sweet taste. He missed the simple things from home. Roman therefore faced a dilemma. He wanted to go back to Hellenheim to continue his life with Natasha there, but on the other hand, he felt he was needed here. He also was intrigued by the possibility of a venture into the unknown, possible with Chuikova and his ships. When that was finished, perhaps he could return to Hellenheim. The choices facing him were difficult, but at least they all *good* choices and he realized that making difficult choices is what makes a man. He was grateful that he had them. So many of his former friends and colleagues had stumbled their through life, just going to work and hoping they could retire after forty years or so.

Petor's unmistakable voice broke his train of thought. "I hope we are not disturbing you, Johnny." Roman focused and saw his friends Petor and Chana.

"No, of course not," Roman replied. "I'm just trying to make sense of things. Life never follows a straight path. This uncertainty is what makes people human."

"That is true Johnny. You could say the ones who dare stray from the usual path are the ones who make a difference."

Johnny stood up and stretched. The air was warm but comfortable. Even though he had spent the last couple of weeks in the Forward Operating Base surrounded by large Hesco barriers, trees provided a reminder of life that was not governed entirely by the military.

Roman, Petor, and Chana eventually had met the Air Force General who had assumed command of the country until a democratic election process could be reinstituted. Several isolated clone units remained on the loose, as well as armed gangs roaming the countryside and foreign military units whose very existence was denied by the countries that had sent them. Roman had accepted the general's generous offer to spend the last month at Fort Hood, training soldiers and leading them in clearing out sectors, one by one. Lawless areas remained, but the government was taking them back. Chuikova's troopers had proved highly reliable, and after a short time, dozens of them were interspersed with U.S. military units as advisors, training them on their weapons systems and equipment.

"I still take it you two are going to stay?" Roman asked as he looked at Petor and Chana, each wearing a set of tan military coveralls. He smiled as he noticed them holding hands. Chana was nearly a foot taller than Petor and they contrasted each other sharply, but their love could not be denied.

"Yes," Petor said. "We are going to start over here. We want to have a child. We are free here to have children, a right we did not have back home. It may not be the best timing right now, but I think it will be OK. The sky is just so *blue* here, and there's all the *green* of the plants. We haven't seen anything but grey skies and buildings our whole lives. So much color."

Petor had let his hair grow, and his bearing had changed. He was a far cry from the thin, nervous shell of a person who had pestered Roman in the Academy chow hall so long ago.

"What have they offered you two?" Roman asked.

"We will relocate to the capital city called Washington. There, we will be advisors to General Rasmussen and the new government. Perhaps when all this settles down, I can teach at one of the universities. I would really like that. A society where there is no oppression is an intoxicating concept."

"Just watch yourself," Roman warned. "I don't think there is any utopia in the works here, but I do think that you will have more freedoms than you are accustomed to. When the military wields the political power of a nation, the results aren't usually favorable for the long haul. That might not change on Hellenheim, but I think we're on the way to a good civilian government here."

Petor examined the dusty ground at his feet and began to draw a line with the toe of his boot. "I agree. The revolution at home may not turn out so well. And don't forget that Hellenheim is just one of many planets.

Those that lost in the Great War may now try to get revenge. I don't wish to be a part of that."

Roman smiled and grasped Petro's hand, a gesture that culminated in a hug. "You take care of yourself here," Roman said, "and keep a place to stay for me, will you? Who knows when I might drop in and say hi."

Petor nodded as a single tear rolled down his left cheek. "Thank you, Johnny. Thank you for everything." The two men held their embrace for a few seconds longer, and separated. Chana stepped toward Johnny, her eyes also watery. She leaned forward and kissed him on his left cheek. She opened her mouth as if to say something but instead wiped her eyes and took Petor's hand in hers.

Roman could see Matthias and Scotts waving to him in the distance beside the FOB's dining facility, each one holding a bowl of ice cream. Roman nodded in their direction and turned back to Petor and Chana.

"I will never forget you two, and I have no doubt you guys will be fine. I think I've made my own decision about the future. I want to see what's out there, you know." He fished around in the pocket of his overalls and withdrew a small, ovoid metal object. He looked at it thoughtfully, before placing it in Chana's hand, closing her fingers around it.

"I don't really have anything, but I was hoping you guys would give this to your kid, something to remember me by." Roman turned and walked toward Matthias and Scotts.

After a silent moment, Petor asked Chana, "What is it?"

Chana uncurled her hand to reveal Roman's police badge. It was a little scratched and slightly tarnished but in remarkable shape considering what it had been through with Roman. Petor read the badge's inscription out loud. "Detective, Metropolitan Police." He traced the raised lettering and continued, "Badge number 442." Petor looked up and started to call out to Roman. This memento of Roman's life was too much to accept. Roman, however, had walked away to join his friends.

"Geez, you guys aren't playing round!" Roman said, letting out a long whistle as he watched several U.S. Army soldiers loading large pallets into a solitary drop pod. Every pallet appeared to be loaded with beer.

"We're also loading up ice cream and DVD's," Scott said. "I like watching the DVD's made here. Jean Claude Van Damme is my favorite."

Scotts produced a can of Natural Light from a cargo pocket and opened it, taking a long swig.

"So when are you guys out of here?" Roman asked.

"We need to talk to you about that," Matthias replied. "We're leaving tonight as soon as they finish loading. Your government wanted us to take some people with us to study and document our journey. Johann didn't seem to mind. But obviously, you need to make a decision. Sorry to put pressure—"

Roman cut him off. "No worries. I want to go. As a matter of fact, I'm ready."

Scotts slapped him on the back. "That's great!"

Overhead, a formation of three U.S. Air Force F-15's flew in formation, followed by three of the marshal's tactical fighters.

"Maybe could you teach me to fly one of those things?" Roman pointed skyward as the fighters roared overhead.

Scotts threw back his head and laughed. "Why start small? Have you ever flown drop pod? I'll show you how to get this hunk of junk off the ground in no time."

Matthias and Scotts threw their arms around Roman, and together the trio walked inside the drop pod, the cargo doors closing behind them.

THE END

Made in the USA
Columbia, SC
16 August 2024